The Fox's
Honor

THE CHRONICLES OF
THE DRAGON AND THE FOX

*Fantasy ladies and knights come alive
in this sci-fi/adventure portrait of futuristic societies, vengeance
and betrayal, warfare and honor.*

The End of Honor
BOOK ONE

An intragalactic war threatens to tear apart
the Human Galactic Empire and the lives of
Prince John-Mark and his bride-to-be, Lyral Neuterra.

The Fox's Honor
BOOK TWO

It was a time of treachery and vengeance…
of Nobility and redemption…all because of love.
But the ultimate price could be Devon Rathenberg's life.

A Season of Honor
BOOK THREE

Baron Shawn du Locke must choose between
honor and desire…with the fragile peace of the
Human Galactic Empire hanging in the balance.

The Fox's
Honor

L. D. Alford

OakTara

WATERFORD, VIRGINIA

Grateful thanks to
Vicki Nix, Tanna Borrell, and Tammy Alford
for meticulous proofreading and terrific suggestions.

The Fox's Honor

Published in the U.S. by:
OakTara Publishers
P.O. Box 8
Waterford, VA 20197

Visit OakTara at
www.oaktara.com

Cover design by David LaPlaca/debest design co.
Cover images © iStockphoto/Ali Mazraie Shadi
Dragon and fox series logo © 2008, Tanna Borrell
Imperial star/ships logo, The Human Galactic Empire map, The Delta
diagram, © 2008 L.D. Alford
Author photo by Tim Davis Photography, © 2008 L.D. Alford

ISBN: 978-1-60290-107-0

The Fox's Honor is a work of fiction. References to real people, events,
establishments, organizations, or locales are intended only to provide a
sense of authenticity and are used fictitiously. All other characters,
incidents, and dialogue are drawn from the author's imagination.

To my master musician

and third of the name

Lowen poet

Thanks Marvin

Χάρις

23 Jan 2010

THE
HUMAN GALACTIC
EMPIRE

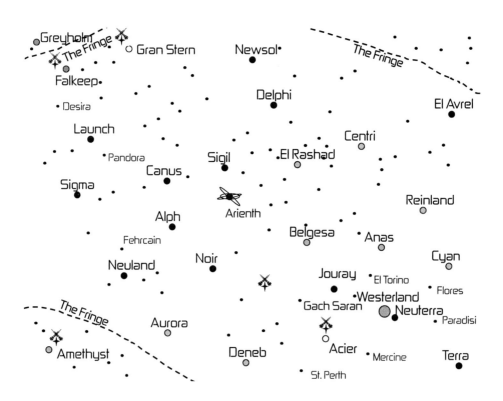

Prologue

Xares S. Neuferal
The People, Places, and Particulars of the Galactic Empire
Interstellar copyright X573 (10,573) ATA (Ancient Terran Accounting)

We now turn our attention to the Imperial Nobility of the Human Galactic Empire. No study of the Empire would be complete without considering the impact of the Nobility upon every stratum of the society. It is not enough to say these august personages were the leaders of their age; they were the veritable heroes of legend.

Today, we can see the strength of their influence in the legends of our time, such as the Fox and the Dragon, the folk tales of the Wise Lady, the fables of the Land of Crystal, and many others too numerous to mention. I don't mean to imply that the influence of the Nobility was only one of marvel and wonder. No, I simply want to point out this self-proclaimed royalty had a powerful influence on the core of society—so powerful that its exploits have trickled down to us with much of that energy intact.

Anyone with a modern knowledge of the Human Galactic Empire knows that the Nobility held their power through the direct consent of the people. Yet this concept has been long denied and debated, due to past social prejudice. Our enlightened society cannot conceive of any event that could lure us away from the democratic ideal. However, as we have matured and as the events of the past have fallen into legend, we have come to view the Empire from a different perspective.

The Nobility of the Human Galactic Empire, and in fact the entire population (including we, ourselves, as their ancestors), have the dubious distinction of being the first fully successful results of human genetic experimentation. I will not go into full detail in this chapter concerning the roots or specifics of the experimentation, but suffice it to say, for now, that the Nobility was designed for leadership. The rest of humanity wanted to follow them, because they were the best leadership humanity had to offer. Our ancestors placed themselves in fealty at the feet of these men and women, because they were worthy of that kind of honor and admiration. I say this not to try to justify their system, but to apologize for its apparent excesses. Our ancestors were not foolish men, and the initial colonization of space with its manifold dangers required the most specialized and perfected of humans. I, for one, do not regret the accident of the inevitable that solidified a colonial necessity into a social institution, for the inevitability of it made possible the human colonization of the galaxy.

So, having laid this framework, let me expound on the institutions and organization of the Imperial Nobility. The leadership of the Human Galactic Empire was one that originated from the bottom up. It was organized upon feudal lines and based on the control of land. There were Thirty Kingdoms represented roughly by our thirty sectors (another holdover from the ancients). These kingdoms were each ruled by a Duke, who was granted the consent to reign from and held fealty to 20 to 100 major planetary holders. These holders were generally titled Counts, although some were Barons, and they each oversaw an entire planet.

Under the planetary holders were Barons and some lesser Counts. These men controlled cities and vast expanses of land and sea. They too held fealty—from lesser Barons and Knights. These men provided the main leadership of the people. These titles and lands passed from father to son, based on the strict Codes of the Noble Accords. These rules guaranteed the genetic purity, and therefore the leadership ability, of the nobles. They also caused an insidious inbreeding that ultimately led to the end of the Human Galactic Empire.

The sovereign over the Thirty Kingdoms was titled the Emperor.

He reigned from the small kingdom today called the Arienth Sector. In fact, the planet Arienth was once the Imperial Capital. The power of the Emperor was far from absolute. It was based to a large extent on tradition and the consent of those he ruled. But his power was also real. He could inject into it both the teeth of the Accords and the strength of his military arm.

Although the rulers of the Human Galactic Empire were certified by the Codes to be outstanding leaders, they were not all good in a moral or ethical sense. You will be wise to remember that there are many types of leadership, not all of which are necessarily founded on beneficence or the trust of others. Even though such rogue, autocratic leaders tended to be diluted through breeding, the horrible environmental conditions of many planets in the early Empire made their ruler's harsh leadership skills irreplaceable. A firm hand was a necessity, and the people gladly bowed to this type of survival leadership.

So, the leadership qualities of the Nobility ran the gamut from beneficence to the autocratic, and each noble had a place and each tended to fill the position required of him. There is some debate today as to whether these nobles were more molded by the requirements of their environment or molded the environment to themselves.

One more explanation must preface my analysis. To understand the Nobility, and indeed the people of the Human Galactic Empire, you must appreciate that they were a society polarized by gender. We see the traditional expression of this polarization in our own society. Even so, we can only grasp futilely to comprehend the depth of it in theirs.

I will not discuss this concept further, except to say the men and women of the Human Galactic Empire had reached an understanding of gender that affirmed the full capability of both the male and female but also fully acknowledged their differences. The evidence of this is recorded in the history of their educational system, where they optimized teaching for males and females. Men and women used different vocabularies to describe certain political, social, and economic events. They spoke of these events in word-concepts that could be understood by one sex but were completely alien and incomprehensible to the other.

Now, with this background into the fundamentals of the nobles of the Human Galactic Empire, let us go on to describe their society....

One

All the young maids, and the old ones as well, discreetly watched the young men announced to the ballroom. The same was true of Duke Falkeep's three daughters. The two oldest, though already wed, spent a delightful evening weighing the rank, title, and characteristics of each nobleman who entered the ballroom. They justified their occupation in the interest of their youngest and unwed sister, Tamar. Tamar didn't necessarily agree with their assessments.

Of particular, disdainful interest were the less choice of the young gentlemen—those who, through valor and accomplishment, attained noble standing, yet whose manner pointed irrevocably to their previous unpolished beginnings. One such gentleman aroused even the looks of the Duke, and a quaint unsettled quiver of his eyebrows left no doubt of his thoughts.

This young man was arrayed in colloquial finery. An officer's uniform, yes, but the style and the natural materials left little doubt that it and its owner obviously came from a culturally deprived planet. The gentleman's boots were real leather; they creaked. His pants bloused over his boot tops, and as he walked they swaggered like a Cossack dance.

The seneschal announced the young officer: "Sir Devon de Tieg, Knight of the Red Cross." A small number of the Duke's less cautious guests let loose a traveling titter that lost its momentum in a few muffled guffaws.

The knight said nothing. Those who recognized the order of

Knight of the Red Cross instantly sobered, and the Duke made a second appraisal of the man.

The knight's eye glinted with his bold smile, and he strode across the broad floor of the ballroom. His ceremonial dagger clinked against his left leg, balanced by an oddly shaped cylinder on his right, and his knight's spurs jingled with each step. He stopped with a flourish and a low bow before the Duke. "My lord Falkeep, will you grant me the privilege of a dance with your daughter, the Lady Tamar?"

Strange knights did not dance with a duke's daughter; it just wasn't done.

The Duke raised his eyebrow, and a smile tripped across his lips. "You may, young knight. That is, if she will dance with you."

"My lord." Sir Devon bowed again and turned toward the ladies. In a few solid steps, he stood directly before the Lady Tamar.

Tamar Falkeep was a beautiful young woman. Her face was formed in the most classic shape of an Imperial Princess. Her eyes, shaded by long, dark lashes were large, a smoky gray that could display fire or ice. Her nose was slight, curved gracefully from her eyebrows, and matched the gentle oval of her face. Her heart-shaped lips were full and seemingly touched by a permanent knowing smile. Her silky, blond hair billowed over her bare shoulders and shined like satin as she tilted her head.

Tamar's figure reflected the perfection of her features: a dancer's frame, graceful and yet full. In her stance, however, was the firm hauteur of a true princess. Not the simple pose of pride or icy frigidity, but a glance of power and purity that stopped most men cold. Her femininity beckoned; the princess spurned. It was unfortunate she was only a lesser duke's daughter and not a true princess.

"My lady, would you give me the honor of this dance?" Sir Devon's eyes glimmered with humor.

The women beside Tamar, including her sisters, turned their faces from the knight and flipped their noses upward. With their faces primly averted from Devon, Tamar's sisters chattered their advice in both her ears. Tamar looked to either side, then stared piercingly at the knight. Her flaxen curls laughed at him. Her gray eyes flashed with rebuke.

The knight's smile lost its flavor. Under her hard appraisal, the shine stole from his eyes. The princess that embodied the spirit of Tamar Falkeep daunted even this knight.

I could disgrace him now, Tamar thought. *He's a fool to try a trick like this, but he has a style. He risks his honor to dance with me, and he is not hard to look at.* In fact, Sir Devon was very handsome—in a military sort of way. His burnt blond hair was clipped short on the sides but left slightly long on top and parted across his forehead. His jaw was firm, yet his lips turned up humorously, and slight crinkles showed that was their normal position. He was not tall, but Tamar had to look up to meet his gray eyes. Her smile softened, and she held out her hand to him. "Yes, sir knight, I will dance with you."

Gently for all his bravado, he took her hand and placed his arm around her waist. With a flourish of noble gown and leather shirt, he swung Tamar into the dance.

Tamar stepped with a practiced grace cultured by the best dancing instructors of the finest young lady's finishing schools on the Imperial planet Arienth, yet the knight matched her with a strength and surety that led her into steps she never knew before.

After they made a couple of circuits about the dance floor, Tamar cocked her head, smirked, and coquettishly remarked, "You know, I promised this dance to Peter Vigin, the son of Count Vigin."

Concern crossed the knight's features. "He is not particularly a man of honor, my lady. Pardon my forwardness, but I believe you should seek a more honorable companion. I, on the other hand, promised this dance specifically for the Lady Tamar, and your honor is renowned."

Her retort stuck in her throat. She could only blush and agree with his reply.

A twirl brought them close to Count Vigin's party.

"You know, my lady, I confess I came to your father's ball for two reasons."

"I know you didn't come to impress the Nobility with your wardrobe," she returned.

With a light step, the knight gracefully twirled her, sent her reeling, and brought her breathless back into his arms. His laugh covered her frown, and the mischief in his eyes made Tamar again swallow her angry retort.

"I would like to claim that I came all the way from Arienth just to dance with you, but, alas, that isn't exactly true. I also have business with one of your father's holders. The man and I could not meet respectably by any other means."

"Did this person know you were coming?"

"As much as you did, my lady." His tone was ominous. "But, for now, please believe I came for only one reason—to dance with you."

After a few moments, Tamar started, "I am curious, Sir..."

"Sir Devon."

"Yes, I am curious, Sir Devon. Is your family's estate on Arienth?"

"No. I hail from Greyholm."

Tamar's face fell a little. She didn't expect the knight to come from a Duchy, yet she hadn't expected the fringe either.

Devon evidently noted her look. "And how do I rank?"

"I didn't say that."

"Your pardon, I believe you thought it."

Tamar blushed again.

He continued, "I am simply the son of a good family who was in the right place at the wrong time."

She looked at him inquiringly.

"You see, where I was, the beams and bullets weren't, and so I am here now. Many men are more worthy than I to wear these knight's spurs, but most of them are dead. Don't feel badly for me. Many more are truly unworthy of the nobles' crown they wear."

Tamar really didn't want to, but she discovered herself in agreement with this saucy knight. Until she caught herself, her head even bobbed an affirmative. She enjoyed the banter with the knight. *Here is a real man,* she thought. He spoke his mind and didn't care who heard. He was so unlike the common gentlemen of her acquaintance— so unlike Peter Vigin. Peter was preoccupied with events within the Empire but had no effect on them.

"Have you ever been wounded?" she asked.

"Many times." His smile drooped. "Yes many times, but none permanently affected me." He smiled again.

"You are a Captain in the attack forces?"

"I, my lady, am a Field Major in His Majesty's Huscarls."

Tamar was impressed, and she tried not to let it show.

Sir Devon was an animated and intelligent speaker. As they stepped in dance after dance, before she knew it, Tamar became engrossed in his conversation. This oddly dressed knight intrigued her. In the middle of a step, as they were talking about the upcoming wedding of the Imperial Prince John-Mark and the Lady Lyral, she asked, "Did you dress this way just so you would have an opportunity to dance with me?"

"My lady, I already told you, the reason I came to Falkeep was to dance with you. You were right when you said I didn't dress this way to win a fashion contest."

They both laughed.

"You just came from Arienth. Have you met the Prince John-Mark?" asked Tamar.

Sir Devon's face took on a guarded look, then he smiled. "Yes, I have seen His Royal Highness. After all, he is the Marshall of the Huscarls."

His answer left a lot unsaid, and when he didn't continue, Tamar prodded him. "So, what is he like? I know Lyral. She is so sweet, a beautiful person, and my best friend. Don't you think John-Mark would make a great Emperor?" She breathed the last quietly and conspiratorially.

He looked intensely at her. So intensely, she blanched under his stare. "I'm sorry, my Lady." He gazed more gently at her. "Such thoughts are seriously contemplated, but out of diffidence to His Royal Majesty Perod-Mark, the rightful firstborn son of the Emperor Maricus, and especially considering the current security of the Empire, I believe such thoughts are best left unsaid."

Sir Devon pronounced this so gravely that Tamar thought for a moment she'd insulted him. But he continued, "John-Mark is indeed a favorite with the people and the Nobility, and I fear for his safety from his brother's jealousy. But we speak of things too serious for your father's ball. Falkeep is beautiful this time of year, don't you think?"

In quiet conversation and graceful dance, the hours passed like moments. Tamar, a brilliant woman, discovered a challenge to her knowledge and thinking few men ever delved. She described her life to the knight. She talked about her experiences in school on Arienth, the beautiful estate of her father, Duke Falkeep, the society on Arienth, and in every subject, she found kinship and agreement with this man.

They danced toward the garden and then out on the terrace. Here the music was muted. The night was cold and dark, only partially illuminated by Falkeep's small moon. The night was still and the garden deserted. Led by this pleasant knight, Tamar's steps were sure. She felt as if her feet barely touched the flagstones. She found herself looking intently into his face. His features seemed almost familiar, but she realized how foolish that thought could be. When they neared the edge of the terrace, the knight stopped suddenly and caught her in his arms. In a passionate kiss, his lips pressed against hers. The kiss caught Tamar unawares, but she instantly realized this was just what she wanted. She returned his intimacy and gently melted in his arms.

The kiss lasted a long time. Then Sir Devon lifted his face and stepped back. His movements were unusually stiff. He nervously cleared his throat and looked away from her into the garden. Then his lips took on their accustomed smile, and he almost seemed as if he were about to turn and leave.

Tamar caught his arm. "Wait, don't go."

"I'm sorry, my lady, but my business requires it."

Her hand stole to her lips. "You kissed me."

"Yes, I couldn't resist, and if I had more time and no responsibility, I would have taken more of you."

Tamar punched him straight across his jaw. The blow hurt her hand, but he didn't move at all. Tamar stood, on the verge of tears, and nursed her hand. She wasn't going to give him the opportunity to know how much he'd wounded her.

"I'm sorry," he apologized, "I deserved that." He smiled disconcertingly. "But I meant it, and this is the time for honesty. You are beautiful—so beautiful—and from the first moment I saw you, I loved you. I'm afraid I will never see you again, nor you me." With that, he turned and walked back into the ballroom.

Shaken and confused, Tamar stood alone on the cold terrace. Tears of anger and remorse filled her eyes. No man ever kissed her like that. She was a reserved person. She spent most of her school years at Lady Pembrook's finishing school on Arienth, and she was to return there at the end of Falkeep's summer to complete her last year. At Lady Pembrook's, she was generally secluded from the society of men. And though she was twenty years old, as the third daughter of the least of the Imperial Duchies, she had few suitors. The Lady Lyral was her best friend at school, and Lyral always said Tamar acted too much like a Princess. That characteristic, according to Lyral, scared off the gentlemen. Perhaps Lyral was right, but no man Tamar met was like this young knight. Not one of the true gentlemen she knew would dare to make such a claim on her body and her love. And she knew, if he asked, she would have given herself to him. Was she in love? She hardly knew this man, yet she thought she might love him. Tamar trembled at that revelation and thought fearfully what his loss suddenly meant to her.

She wanted to chase him into the ballroom and demand why they would never see each other again, but she shuddered, afraid to let herself be drawn to him, afraid to recognize the unexpected power he held over her. She did rush to the French doors, to peer through them. Sir Devon was not in sight.

Shaking with emotion, Tamar reentered the ballroom. The room was huge. Her father, the Duke of Falkeep entertained often. His formals were the main social events of each season. Every noble in this sector was represented. Even His Majesty, the Emperor Maricus, sent his emissary, Duke Rathenberg. Tamar caught her sisters' eyes as they waved at her. She avoided the sight of Sir Peter Vigin and walked toward them. She didn't care to dance again tonight—not with anyone else…maybe never again.

When Tamar reached her sisters, they kidded her about the amount of time she spent with the unknown knight, and she dutifully accepted their thinly veiled criticism in silence. While they spoke, her eyes scanned the crowd. She fearfully sought the answer to her heart's question in a single face. Inside her turbulent thoughts, Tamar tried to understand what magic transpired there or to determine if anything, outside her imagination, had really happened at all.

Two

Sir Devon slipped through the French doors and into the crowded ballroom. *There,* he thought, *I accomplished my first goal for the evening.* He speculated sadly, for a moment, on the circumstances that would not allow him to see the Lady Tamar again. Then, with a sigh, he headed into the throng of people.

Now, thought Devon, *to find that traitor Count Yedric, and keep out of sight of the few who might recognize me.*

Yedric was not difficult to locate. He and his retainers skulked around the vicinity of Duke Falkeep. Yedric patently tried to drum up support for his views among the Duke's distinguished guests. However, Yedric was not a popular man among these people. The chief strike against him was he did not support the current dynasty. He claimed the more ancient Rathenberg family belonged on the Imperial throne. That thought reminded Devon to keep out of sight of Duke Rathenberg.

Devon should know: five generations displaced the House Rathenberg from the direct line of Imperial descent, and as a House, Rathenberg did not claim the throne. Count Yedric, however, used this dispute as an excuse to confront and conflict with the Haupenberg Emperor, Maricus.

Duke Rathenberg was the chancellor of the Empire. He held the traditional position of steward for Emperor Maricus and was himself the master of only a small estate on the Imperial planet Arienth. His cousin, the Count Frederic Rathenberg, was a close relation to the Emperor. He controlled a wealthy system in the Kingdom of Nior, and with Yedric's support, Count Frederic Rathenberg claimed to be the rightful head of the Empire.

So far, no actions backed the claims of the Counts, Yedric and Rathenberg, and they had little support in the Landsritters, the official parliament of the Nobility. But the military might these men were massing concerned the Emperor. Right now, the Empire had enough problems keeping the frontier under control; it could not cope with a powerful internal rebellion at the same time. That was why Devon was here. His mission was to start a premature rebellion.

Count Yedric held fealty in this sector. He wanted to maintain good relations with his lord, Duke Falkeep, and he wanted to reassure the other nobles of his honorable intentions. He was doing an outstanding job. Few, other than Devon's Imperial Intelligence, realized the extraordinary growth of Yedric's ground and space forces. In fact, Yedric already laid the keels of at least five Capital class starships—a privilege reserved only for Ducal rank. But Count Yedric wasn't quite ready to strike. He needed another three to five years to consolidate his gains and develop his political power. This was the time for the Emperor to force the count's hand.

Devon determined a sequence of two events that would pressure Yedric into action: first, a direct and undisputed line of ascendancy for Count Frederic Rathenberg to the Empire's Iron Throne, and second, undeniable proof of Yedric's treason against the Emperor. Devon hoped to achieve both these events tonight—both in one fell swoop.

With practiced insolence, Devon swaggered toward the party of Nobility around Yedric. Contemptuously, Devon shouldered a baron to one side and stood directly before the Count. The baron stumbled forward and dropped his drink. His glass clattered noisily to the floor. When the man regained his balance, he turned angrily toward Devon and was about to issue a challenge, but Yedric, his eyes registering shock and surprise for only a moment, cut the baron off with a gesture. Even in his frontier garb, Count Yedric recognized Devon.

Devon smiled haughtily at the Count.

Count Yedric was no small man. He stood a full ten centimeters above Devon. He was thin and wiry, built like a greyhound, with a musculature developed on the weapon practice floor. Yedric's eyes blazed out of deeply recessed eye sockets. The skin, parchment tight, stretched bare and pallid from the broad dome of his forehead to the solid point of his chin. A grim and wrinkled smile split his face, while a gentle salting of pockmarks accentuated the eggshell appearance of his white, partly bald head.

Devon, intimidated, tried not to show it. The Duke cut an awesome figure, fully calculated to bring fear to the peasantry and demand the respect of his peers. He was a man of nearly indecipherable expression that fronted a brain of genius proportions.

The Count coolly returned Devon's smile. "Good evening, my lord. I scarcely recognized you in that colloquial costume."

"I, on the other hand, my dear Count Yedric, recognized your traitorous murmuring the instant I entered my lord Duke Falkeep's ball."

Yedric's views on the Emperor's legitimacy were well known but patiently ignored by most of the Nobility. A quiet descended on the men and women within earshot. The Count simply smiled more broadly and nodded slightly.

"I am interested, for the Emperor's sake, in what conspiratorial devilry you have been up to lately," continued Devon.

"You are premature in your accusations. Let's not quarrel on the eve of Duke Falkeep's party." Yedric gestured toward the Duke, who was well out of hearing.

"I know exactly what you want, Count Yedric. I can propose how you think you will achieve your goals. But, I warn you; all true nobles of my House serve the Empire and the Emperor. We will gladly lay our lives down in the service of our sovereign." With that remark, Devon inclined his head, snapped about, and walked quickly away.

"You may be given that opportunity, my friend. Indeed, you will," whispered Count Yedric under his breath.

Most of the crowd didn't recognize Devon, but they knew his name. That's why he gave the seneschal a false one. He was the commander of the Imperial Intelligence Service; so, although a noble, he was not often seen in the company of nobles. He was a fighter, a soldier, and an officer, not yet ready to give that up for politics and flattery. Candidly, he speculated, he wasn't destined to live long enough to give it up, either.

Devon wandered to a dark, tapestried corner of the room. Along the way he gathered sweet meats and pastries. Though Duke Falkeep was well known for his cellars, Devon didn't touch the wine; he needed a clear head tonight. The knight hadn't eaten before he arrived at the ball, so he might as well stock up now. *A sort of last meal,* he reflected. Anyway, he had over an hour to wait.

Devon knew, tonight, Count Yedric planned to meet clandestinely with a few unscrupulous nobles. They were influential men and sympathetic to Yedric's cause. Yedric desired for them to join his rebellion. Tonight Devon would push them over the brink. He hoped to embroil them in a conspiracy that would weld them together in guilt. He would force them to insurrection, to become the heralds of Yedric's treachery...God help their souls.

As Devon silently watched the events of the evening unfold, one of Yedric's knights approached him. Devon recognized the knight and realized he should know the man's name, but couldn't remember it.

"My lord," the knight began with a slight bow, "Count Yedric sends his regards." He paused to discern Devon's response. When Devon said nothing, he continued, "Count Yedric requests a truce—that, tonight, you desist your attempts to discredit him." Encouraged by Devon's silence, he went on, "The Count prays you would recognize your responsibility toward the Crown as he recognizes his..."

"And that I join him," finished Devon for him.

"Yes, and that you join him."

"I will do nothing to discredit my Emperor," Devon stated. He smiled inwardly, for here was the real reason for this visit—the bait.

"This evening, my lord, Count Yedric will speak with certain supporters of his viewpoint. He cordially requests you join him..."

"And listen to him spout his traitorous remarks?" Devon finished blandly.

"My lord, he begs you to consider your responsibility to the

Empire as a whole."

"Where will he present his imprudent theory?" Devon continued in the same tone.

"In the far garden at midnight."

"The witching hour. That is appropriate."

"Simply consider the invitation, my lord."

"That I will," and Devon reinforced the answer in his thoughts. *That I certainly will.*

With a bow, the knight turned and walked away.

Good, thought Devon. *My agents correctly ascertained all the pertinent details.*

So far, Devon's planning was perfect. Now, if everything else worked out correctly, he would give Yedric the surprise of his life.

Devon sighed as he considered the events of the night and the Lady Tamar's sweet kiss. The girl almost caught him off guard with the crack about Prince John-Mark making a better Emperor, and that was another cause of tension in the court. He almost laughed; if the Prince John-Mark succeeded, much of the Empire would soon be under his control.

But the Crown Prince Perod-Mark was a man to be reckoned with. He craved power without responsibility. Devon wished the betrothed John-Mark and Lady Lyral well. He thought with regret of the circumstance that would not allow him the same happiness with the Lady Tamar.

As time for the illicit meeting drew near, Devon worked his way through the thinning crowd to the terrace side of the ballroom. He walked along the French doors until he reached the last pair, then slipped through them onto the terrace and into the garden.

All evening, Tamar faced her sisters' questions and ribbing. Who was that young knight? Why did she dance so long with him? What did he say? She answered them carefully and didn't give a full account. She told them only enough to stifle their curiosity.

Tamar asked herself precisely the same questions. She didn't know exactly who he was. She couldn't be sure what he said that so affected her, only that she felt a strong attraction to him. She felt comfortable with him, and as much as she could, she discretely tried to find him again. Sir Devon didn't leave the party: she had inquired of the seneschal.

Why had he said he would never see her again? She wanted him to explain everything to her. Where had he first seen her to fall in love with her? How did he know she was here now? She was supposed to be at school on Arienth for another month. Tamar was confused and a little frightened, and although she knew nothing about such things, she was curious and intrigued with the very thought of his unsolicited love.

Tamar almost gave up her search, when at half past eleven, she noticed Sir Devon steal through the last set of French doors. He disappeared onto the terrace. Tamar took a close look around to see if anyone else noticed the knight's departure, then made some excuse and followed Sir Devon through the doors.

Because the weather was still cool, no one stood on the terrace, but Tamar caught the glimpse of a shadow that cut into the garden along one of the walkways. She followed the shadowy figure. Now she was not as interested in catching up with the knight as she was in finding out where he was going. Tamar almost called her father's guard, but decided quickly that the gardens were not forbidden to the guests. Her precaution would only look foolish.

She wouldn't dare let herself think Devon's words on the terrace meant nothing to him. She wouldn't let herself believe he stole off to a rendezvous with someone else. Tamar tried to convince herself the feelings of her heart were nothing, and whatever was going on couldn't involve the knight romantically. Again, she almost called the guard but stopped. She convinced herself once more her suspicions were the product of her overwrought imagination. What accusation could she make against the knight? That he took a late-night walk in the gardens?

The moment her feet touched the path, the garden seemed to rise up around her. With the night, the garden engulfed her and filled her senses with thick, heady fragrance. Even the breath of the still air on her cheek felt heavy, laden with moisture, pregnant with the early spring of the garden. Tamar turned slightly to catch a last glimpse of the brightly lit ballroom as it slid in flashes behind the foliage. Almost as quickly, the lighted windows of the house disappeared and left her straining ahead to see the path.

Tamar wondered where the knight was bound. At first, she thought, he headed toward the house. All around the building the garden turned into private alcoves and smaller partially surrounded nooks. These alcoves furnished the individual suites with private retreats and made perfect sites for a secret meeting. But he turned away from the house.

More than a thousand square kilometers of gardens and forest bordered the manor, and deeper in the garden lay guesthouses and private pavilions. He headed into the depths of the garden. Perhaps one of these was his destination.

Tamar kept the dark figure just at the edge of her vision and tailed him as quietly as she could. Her slippers barely made a sound, but neither did the flitting ghost she followed. Like a hunt or the wild and frenzied dreams clasped deliciously at the edge of sleep, the chase exhilarated her. Oddly, she didn't fear for herself. The security of the gardens and her own inexperience gave her a false sense of invulnerability.

Tamar had walked quite far into the huge garden when she suddenly lost sight of the knight. She was certain he disappeared into the foliage, and she ran silently to the last spot she saw him. In the thick darkness, she paced up and down the path and strained to see him among the trees.

Just ahead lay one of the larger pavilions. It was probably still sealed for the winter. She focused her eyes further down the trail and glimpsed lights through the trees. Now Tamar was really curious. She wondered if her father knew about this private party in his garden.

Tamar decided the pavilion must be the goal of her mischievous friend, Sir Devon. Incautiously, she walked up the path toward the lights. Tamar began to hear voices. Just as she was about to step within sight of the pavilion, someone grasped her around the waist, and before she could scream, a hand clasped roughly over her mouth.

The intruder dragged Tamar into the thick undergrowth. Whipping branches stung her arms and legs. Her assailant stopped in a crouch and held her tightly and as easily as a child. She felt a sigh beside her ear, then a loud whisper. "You little fool. You shouldn't have followed me." There was a pause. "If I let you go, do you promise, on your life, not to make a sound?"

Tamar was frightened. The voice sounded like Sir Devon's. She nodded.

"Very good," the whisper continued, and though the pressure slowly released from her face, the hand still hovered about an inch before her lips. Tamar tried to turn her head to look at him, but he grasped her jaw and held her face firmly forward.

The voice whispered menacingly, "You don't know why those men are meeting over there, do you?"

Tamar licked her lips and was about to respond, but he must have felt her breath change on his hand because he cut her off. "No, just nod."

Tamar vigorously shook her head. She suddenly became very frightened, and her lips started to quiver. He must have perceived this movement because he whispered, "Not a sound. Unless you have something to do with those men, you have nothing to fear from me. Tell me, you didn't know they were meeting here? Tonight? Did you?"

She again shook her head in the negative.

"Good. Now listen to me very carefully. I can't take any chance of your being seen. If you value your life, you will sit here quietly. No matter what you see or hear, don't make a sound, and don't let yourself be seen. What I do, I must do for the Empire and the Emperor. I don't ask you to believe just my words." His hand left her line of sight and returned with a plain gold ring. Its only decoration was the Imperial seal: crossed needle-shaped ships below a star. She stared wide-eyed at this rare token from the Emperor's hand.

"Do you recognize this?" he whispered.

She gave a vigorous nod.

"Good." He placed the ring in her hand and curled her fingers around it. "You must hold it for me. Don't give it to anyone. Don't let anyone know you've seen it. I would have left it here, lost in this garden, but you will be a better surety."

Tamar knew the importance of such a ring. It was an Imperial seal. The Emperor only entrusted his closest advisors with it—only three or four nobles in the entire Empire. Tamar knew that the ring must not fall into the wrong hands, and she wondered anew who this knight could be.

"Don't move until you no longer see lights or hear voices. If you do, I guarantee it will be your death. Do you understand?"

Holding back tears, Tamar nodded.

"Do you swear?"

She nodded again.

The arms encircling her suddenly took on a different quality. They held her gently, and she thought, almost lovingly. Then they fell from her, and she watched Devon steal silently to the edge of the trees and disappear into the brush.

Three

After he left the Lady Tamar, Devon stopped in a dark clump of shrub at the edge of the trees. Out on Duke Falkeep's summer pavilion, a group of nobles surrounded Count Yedric. Devon could hear them across the lawn but wasn't close enough to make out their words. As Devon watched, the tone of their conversation changed from the good-natured greetings he heard when he first arrived to quiet and serious discussion. They must be getting to the matter at hand.

Yedric attracted a good turnout of about ten lesser holders. Devon recognized two or three Counts, but the rest were Barons. These nobles represented newly terraformed planets and developed moons; they agreed with Yedric's ideas, or they wouldn't be here. They believed Yedric's rebellion an opportunity to increase themselves and their Houses in ways that would normally take hundreds of years. Second-generation heirs who lived through the great gains of their fathers, they didn't have the motivation or the capability to match their sires.

Yedric's retainers and knights completed the balance of the company and brought the number up to about twenty.

Devon wished Tamar hadn't followed him. He hoped she didn't do anything foolish. He looked back to where he'd left her; she was invisible in the trees. Good.

He again surveyed the clearing. On the whole, the pavilion was open, and the group of men stood near its elegant front facade. The pavilion was still closed for the winter: its lights were covered, the doors to the side buildings were shuttered, and gaping holes along the walls and columns indicated where the more delicate ornaments should go. Darkness cloaked most of the pavilion, but Yedric's knights surrounded the Nobility and illuminated them with portable lamps.

Devon waited for the right time. Before Yedric finished the balance of his appeal, Devon quietly climbed to the floor of the pavilion. Hidden in the deep shadows, he crept toward the group. He timed his entrance, and at the moment the noblemen nodded their agreement with Yedric's plans, Devon stepped without warning from the darkness into the direct light of the lamps.

The astonished men started, and Devon kept them off balance by calling out to Yedric, "Greetings from the Emperor, traitors."

No one said a word. The men moved away from Devon and formed a solid half circle facing him. While the nobles stood shifting guiltily from foot to foot, Devon strode right up to Count Yedric. Devon slapped Yedric with his glove and shouted, "In the name of the Emperor, I claim grievance."

Count Yedric stepped back in surprise. He did not anticipate Devon's action, and the slap was not gentle. Yedric's cruel squint repudiated the crooked smile that immediately jumped to his lips. "Sire," he protested.

"Do not use that title with me, false noble," Devon seethed. "My family does not claim the Iron Throne."

Cut to the quick, his smile slipped, and with a dangerous evenness in his tone Count Yedric replied, "One of your family does indeed claim the Imperial Throne, my lord, Devon Rathenberg."

"That worm Frederic, you mean. I would take his ears if the Emperor allowed it, but now, I am to have yours. By your leave, my lords." From its belt loop, Devon released his plasmasword and flicked it on. As the blade coursed in a meter-long, centimeter-thick cylinder, the plasma bathed him in a fiery light. "Before your renegade Count Rathenberg can claim any right to the Iron Throne, you have to kill me."

"That is true indeed, my lord Rathenberg." Yedric signaled one of his knights, who tossed him a plasmafoil. With a sneer, Yedric activated the energy sword. "Your life is exactly what keeps my ambitions in check." He bent his head toward the surrounding nobles. "Your word, gentlemen, Prince Devon Rathenberg challenged me."

"Unnecessary, false noble. You will not live to face the Landsritters on this account."

Count Yedric crouched in the stance of a practiced fencer and advanced toward Devon. Devon matched his position. With a slight turn, they touched blades. The edges of the swords blazed and crackled, and Devon backed to keep a sword's length between the blade tips. In spite of the danger, Devon realized that, to be most effective, he must keep the Count engaged. He must make Count Yedric and these men realize the accomplished sword skill of Sir Devon Rathenberg. Devon knew he could kill Yedric here, and he must make all of them realize that. In the minds of these men, he must demonstrate the strength of the Emperor's desire to eliminate the Count and accentuate the regard with which the Emperor held the danger of Yedric's rebellion.

Devon must show them his skill; then he must allow Count Yedric to kill him.

He must be careful about it. He must let Yedric have his life, but his death must be dearly won. He must make the outcome look like Yedric was able to overcome him with cunning and maturely guided skill. Devon had planned this duel for months: the exact effort, the perfect positioning, and the perfect timing of the end.

Warily Yedric followed Devon. His blade tip made tiny circles in the still air. He used small taps to test Devon's guard and explore his skill.

In a quick lunge, Devon engaged, disengaged, and came over the top of Yedric's blade. At the last moment, Devon slowed his attack. Yedric rolled his hand up, and Devon's blade deflected upwards and off the top of the blade. Devon came immediately back to guard, and Yedric could not take advantage of the parry to return Devon's attack. But Yedric moved forward to profit from Devon's extension in the lunge. Yedric beat Devon's blade to the side, and a cascade of bright energy lit the dark. The Count's blade moved forward toward Devon's chest, but in a gentle arc, Devon turned the blade downward and deflected it away.

The two continued to trade lunge and riposte. Each time, at the last moment, Yedric deflected Devon's close attack. In this way, Devon cultivated the idea he had a weakness fighting in close.

Devon's sword work drew the admiration of the men. The nobles knew excellent swordplay, but they couldn't know Devon intentionally slowed his attacks. They would have to see the action in slow motion to perceive that the Count achieved each of his sensational parries only through Devon's gentle manipulation. The conclusion of the duel must appear as though Yedric discerned a fault in Devon's technique and turned an exceptional attack against him. The nobles must be convinced that Yedric bested him through superior strategy.

Devon crossed Yedric's blade again. He led with a combination of disengages that left harsh bright images on his vision. Yedric was hard-pressed to parry the attack. The Count's riposte was slow, but Devon intentionally countered the attack late and fell back a little more than was necessary. Now was the time for Devon to make his final move. The Count appeared to have him off balance, but instead of falling back again, Devon commenced his final lunge. With a slight overextension, Devon deliberately wavered forward further out of balance. He had never let his guard down like this before, and never with the full knowledge that the man before him would kill him! Devon called on all his will to continue the doomed attack.

Yedric caught Devon's blade against the lower third of his own, but the Count was backing, and as the blade deflected Devon's sword, the tip of the bright, hard plasma stream flipped up. *Too high,* thought Devon. Then the blade came down. The Count stood exactly where Devon wanted him, inside his guard, within easy striking distance of his chest. The kill would be clean, Devon thought, and he steeled himself for the shock.

In a glide, Yedric's blade slid along Devon's sword. Nothing stood between them but Devon's leather shirt. Devon intently watched the blade tip dive toward his chest. But Yedric parried Devon's lunge too close and not enough clearance separated the blades! In the last instant Devon thought he had left to live, he watched Count Yedric's blade tip bury itself in the handgrip of his plasmasword. The tip cut like butter through the unshielded plasteel. It forced itself into the atomic core of the sword, and in the resulting explosion of leather and plasteel, Devon lost consciousness.

Four

Tamar shuddered in the cold gloom of the forest. This turn of events astounded and confused her. She waited for the faint rustle that indicated Devon moved out of the brush. She listened for his quiet steps as he crossed the short lawn, and perceived his cat-like leap up onto the platform of the pavilion. When Tamar heard Devon address the men in the pavilion, her curiosity grew, but she couldn't understand what he said.

With a gentle nudge of guilt, Tamar crawled forward to the point she last saw Devon at the edge of the wood. She settled in a bowl-shaped depression surrounded on all sides by scrub. It was a perfect site to observe the events on the pavilion without being seen.

As Tamar quietly positioned herself, out of the corner of her eye, she caught sight of an abrupt movement on the platform. Sir Devon stepped up to Count Yedric and slapped the count across the face with his gloves! Tamar gasped. Devon challenged Count Yedric to a duel.

Count Yedric and Sir Devon squared off with blazing plasmaswords, and Tamar breathed faster. The excitement of the men on the pavilion touched Tamar, and she caught herself leaning forward. Suddenly, an embarrassed blush crept up her face; she realized with revulsion a man would die tonight—with plasmaswords, neither party would give quarter, and no one would call a halt at first-blood. She reached up and felt her flushed cheeks. They were warm against her cold fingers, and now she trembled with fear.

The sound of the swords as they struck one another made crisp explosions in the night. The splattered light of their collisions outlined the strained faces of the men encircling Devon and the Count.

Tamar couldn't believe this was happening. In this age of enlightenment, she knew of duels, but she never imagined they really occurred. As the fighters moved from side to side on the pavilion, she watched in horrified amazement. With the burning atomic blades, each barely missed the other, and every attack could result in maiming or death.

Tamar couldn't tell who was winning or losing. She had no idea whom she should pray to win. Count Yedric was a sovereign noble in her father's sector. He was a great ally of her father's, but Sir Devon, who was he? A direct representative of the Emperor, a knight in the service of the Empire, a man who said he loved her. In an instant, she realized the desire of her heart and prayed with all her soul that fate would leave the count's body lifeless and not the knight's.

All at once, Tamar realized the reason for Sir Devon's actions. He gave her his royal signet. He assured her she would never see him again. He told her of his love, and left without knowing if she returned his love. Tamar's thoughts were unmerciful—the knight was inhumanly cruel to lift up her heart when he meant to intentionally end his life. A rain of tears surprised her, and she wished fervently that Devon would not die.

In the pavilion, the fight continued.

A flash of intuition brought Tamar's full attention back to the two figures on the pavilion. The count pressed Sir Devon to the edge of the platform. Devon parried the Count's blade, and in an instant, Sir Devon lunged. To Tamar, the Count's blade arced straight up and came straight down toward Sir Devon. In the resultant clash of blades, the flash of energy almost blinded her. At the same moment, an explosion split the night.

The blast knocked Count Yedric to the floor of the pavilion, and with surreal slowness, it lifted Sir Devon off his feet and threw him into the grass. He sprawled face downward on the lawn a full two meters from the edge of the open building.

Without thinking, Tamar leapt up and ran a couple of steps from her hiding place toward the pavilion. When the men began to stagger to their feet, she realized her danger and dove back into the covering darkness of the woods. Her new location was not as concealed as before, but now she could plainly hear their conversation.

The noblemen recovered quickly. The main force of the blast was a powerful shock wave loosed when the Count's blade pierced the atomic core of Devon's sword. The atomic containment in Devon's sword suppressed the energy and localized the explosion to the area close to him.

Count Yedric struggled shakily to his feet. The blast tore the sword out of his hands and tossed it out onto the lawn. The count stood pale and bloodied; he staggered dazedly as he called to the men around him, "Gentlemen, we must move from this spot. If we are discovered, I don't believe Duke Falkeep will approve of our meeting or a duel in his garden."

One of the other nobles had stepped off the platform and gone to his knees beside Sir Devon. He called up from the ground, "Yedric, this man is dead."

Count Yedric smiled cruelly. A semblance of his old self returned to his features. He stared at the noble, amusement on his blood-streaked face. "Then we have the answer to our dilemma. Now nothing and no one can supersede the ascendancy of Count Frederic Rathenberg to the throne of the Empire. Gentlemen, the Emperor fears us. He sent his best to destroy me. Prince Devon Rathenberg, the Emperor's Fox, is dead. Gentlemen, now is the time to act!"

A shared murmur of excitement ran through the men. Yedric signaled to them, and without another sound, they departed. At once, the men ran away from the pavilion. They each followed different forest paths that would return them back to Falkeep's main ballroom.

After the last man left the clearing, Tamar waited only a heartbeat before she ran to the prone body of Devon Rathenberg. With strength induced by her fear, she rolled him over. Only moments had elapsed since the blast had thrown him to the ground. The explosion had burned his shirtfront away to the skin. His face was lacerated by bits of plasteel, yet was not bleeding. And he was not breathing!

Tamar didn't pause an instant. She tilted his head back and placed her lips on his. She forced a breath into his lungs—then another. She placed her full body weight behind the balls of her hands and compressed his sternum. "Don't die!" she prayed under her breath, "...2, 3, 4, 5, 6, 7, 8, 9, 10, 11, 12." She expanded his lungs twice again. "Breathe!"

Suddenly, Devon's back arched. He gave a strained gasp and started to breathe.

Tamar froze. She stopped compressing his battered chest. As she watched the tortuous rise and fall of his chest, she held her breath and trembled violently. Then, as if she could breathe for him, she matched each ragged gasp.

For a few seconds, Devon fought for air, then his breathing smoothed.

Tamar felt for his pulse; it was strong and regular. "Thank you, God," she cried. "Thank you, God." She knelt and stared at him, afraid to touch him, terrified his breathing would stop again.

Slowly, Tamar's thoughts caught up with her, and a sudden fear overtook her. She scanned the entrances to the clearing. Surely, when her father's guards investigated the explosion, they would discover them. The Duke of Falkeep would not take kindly to dueling in his gardens. He definitely would not approve of his daughter sneaking about in the woods in search of nobles, knights, or whatever. He also would not have a lot of good to say about a knight who challenged one of the chief holders in his sector—particularly one who lost on purpose!

Tamar grasped Devon's arms to pull him into the brush, but his right arm bent back at an odd angle. It had a rubbery feel. Though unconscious, Devon moaned and the muscles of his arm convulsed abruptly and ineffectually. Tamar was almost sick. The arm was broken—likely shattered. She laid it across his chest and, fumbling, fixed his arm by the hand under his belt. After a fierce struggle, she dragged him by his feet into the woods.

By the time she hid Devon in the trees, Tamar was exhausted. She plopped down beside him and rested her head in her hands. The cool night was turning icy, and in thick, white wisps, her breath curled around her face and hair. After her heart slowed a little, Tamar looked at Devon. She marked his labored breaths, and his shrapnel wounds had started to bleed. In the pale, partial light of Falkeep's moon, long streaks of black ran down his face, arms, and chest. His lips were blue, and his skin as pale as the almost invisible moonlet. Tamar knew he was in shock, and she felt as though she was going into shock herself. To survive, the knight needed warmth, and his wounds required treatment.

Who was this man who said he loved her? Count Yedric called him Prince Devon Rathenberg. Tamar covered her mouth with her hand. She stared down at his bruised face. Could this really be the Emperor's Fox? Could this be the Chief of Imperial Intelligence, Emperor Maricus' wisest advisor? If this was Prince Devon Rathenberg, he was one of the most important men in human space. And...Tamar gave a choked cry...if he were Devon Rathenberg, he could not love her. She was not an Imperial Princess. She was only a minor Duke's third daughter. Devon Rathenberg could not marry her; the Landsritters would forbid the match. Now she realized the full degree of his twofold mission. He came to announce his illicit love, and he came to die. He didn't care how much pain those two events caused. Tamar raised her hand to strike him. Devon lay quiet and unmoving; Tamar breathed deeply and lowered her fist. In spite of how he hurt her, he needed help.

Tamar knew she couldn't ask her father for assistance. The political intuition she learned from Lady Pembrook's School told her she had become embroiled in a situation that required secrecy and high diplomacy. Not only did the life of the prince stand in the balance, but she guessed, the Empire and her father's Duchy were somehow threatened. She knew enough of the art of this high diplomacy to understand she must let Devon's actions take their course. Unenlightened tinkering might result in cataclysm.

She stared down at Devon. He was supposed to die. What would it mean for him to live? Devon had achieved what she assumed was his goal: Yedric and his accomplices thought Prince Devon Rathenberg was dead. Now, except to her, what did it matter whether he lived or died? Tamar promised herself she would not let him die, but how could she save him? He needed professional medical help, but she had no idea how she could deliver it to him. She didn't think she could get him off the estate by herself. If he could walk, she might chance it. And she couldn't imagine sneaking anyone on the estate to take care of him, much less keeping her actions secret afterwards.

She pursed her lips and pictured the layout of the gardens. The pavilion was located to the south and east of the main house. "Ah, there," she whispered. A guesthouse lay just south of the pavilion. She could hide the knight there. Like many of the garden houses, it was designed to integrate with the surrounding environment, and it was self-sufficient. Guests occasionally used this garden apartment in the summer, but it was too far from the main house and too isolated from the normal events of the spring and winter to be in use now. Indeed, it was isolated enough to be seldom used at any time in the year.

Tamar was especially fond of the guesthouses. When she was a child, they had been her favorite hiding places. This house would provide perfect concealment for the injured knight. But how could she move him there? She was afraid to leave him—afraid he might die while she was away. Wait. She remembered that each of the garden house storage sheds held a heavy baggage transporter.

Tamar placed her hand gently on Devon's chest and held her ear next to his lips. He breathed regularly and his heartbeat was strong, but his skin was still clammy and pale. As she stood up, Tamar caressed his face. Then she quickly stumbled through the woods toward the guesthouse.

As she scrambled through the foliage, Tamar tripped wearily over exposed roots and ran against low branches. In a few minutes she found the garden house. It was just as she remembered it: low, encased in a hillock, and with only a few of its features revealed. With shivering fingers, Tamar entered the door lock code. It took three tries, but finally the dark portal opened and the lights blazed on. Inside the doorway, the exterior house controls allowed her to open the storage area, and with a mechanical whine, a segmented door rolled open near the base of the hill. A few moments later, Tamar wrestled the baggage transporter out of the hillside. The controls were simple but activating them in the cramped confines of the storage closet was another matter. And when she finally got the gravplatform out, because the motion switch only worked while she walked beside it, she couldn't ride back to the pavilion. So, Tamar stumbled all the way back while the platform obediently floated behind her on humming gravrepulsors. She cursed it the whole way.

Sir Devon was in the same condition she had left him. No better, but at least he seemed no worse. She lowered the platform and worked him onto it.

After Devon lay securely on the platform, in exhaustion Tamar sat down beside the wounded knight. She wearily let the frosty evening air waft over her face. The sweat dried quickly, and she was suddenly very cold. Without consent, Tamar's head nodded forward, and for a long moment, she didn't care about anything; she almost fell asleep. A pricking in her subconscious jerked her head up straight, and she glanced over her shoulder at the bleeding knight. Tamar struggled to her feet and started the platform. Dutifully, the transporter lifted and followed her halting steps into the dark woods.

Tamar wrestled the loaded baggage platform into the house, and the door whisked shut behind them. She let out a sigh of relief; the temperature of the house was already well above that outside. Unable to move farther, Tamar staggered to her knees, and before the heavy platform stopped, she felt it hit her lower back. The push forced her forward, and as her body lay full length on the floor, she felt blessed sleep take her.

Five

The sound of driving rain awoke Tamar. Though the walls of the garden house were set halfway in the ground, they could not entirely muffle the force of the storm.

Tamar's body was stiff, and her mind confused. She didn't know where she was. She shook her head a few times and used the wall to pull herself to her feet. Tamar leaned wearily against the side of the corridor, and her head drooped. She almost closed her eyes again when a ragged intake of breath startled her. Drugged with weariness, Tamar turned around slowly. At the sight of the wounded knight, Tamar shrank against the wall. Fright overwhelmed her until her lethargic thoughts could recognize the figure lying on the baggage cart. With a relieved sigh, her eyes blank and her lips slack, Tamar slid down to sit on the floor and remembered the events of the evening. They were so unbelievable that, for a moment, unable to compose her thoughts, she could only stare stupidly.

On the baggage transporter lay the man she remembered to be Sir Devon de Tieg of Greyholm...No, not de Tieg. She could hear Yedric's exultant shout: "Prince Devon Rathenberg, the Fox!"

The Emperor's Chief of Intelligence, she remembered anew. Tamar gazed, dumbstruck, at the unconscious man. He was not recognizable as the dashing gentleman of the night before. His face was caked with dried dirt and blood. It was swollen, bruised, and outlined in blue-purple, tiny shrapnel wounds that made a random pattern of ugly gashes. The knight's shirt was all but torn away. A red encrusted area covered his chest, and a large bruise over his heart showed through the burn. The lower part of his right arm contracted slightly. It was so swollen the remnants of his sleeves cut deeply into the flesh. He breathed raggedly, and though unconscious, quiet groans escaped his lips.

Tamar turned away her head. She fully remembered how he came to look this way and recognized the bruise she caused on his chest. She stumbled to him and put her head delicately to the damaged skin.

He said he loved me. The thought seemed improbable—that this man, high in the Imperial Court, who so callously offered his life for the Emperor, loved her. Tamar found the thought inconceivable. Yet a tear squeezed from her eye and ran along a lash. She shook her head to clear her thoughts.

The knight seemed to be out of danger now. His skin, though bruised and cut, looked less pallid than Tamar remembered the night before, and his pulse beat strong and steady under her fingertips.

Tamar gently stroked his face. She backed, grasped the controls of the gravplatform, and led it to the bedroom. She carefully undressed him, gently cutting the shirt from his broken arm.

In her innocence, Tamar marveled at his naked form. At the sight of him, her breath caught in her throat, and a deep flush covered her face. As she slid him onto the bed and covered him, a strong desire filled her and caused her to tremble. His skin was rougher than hers. Where she was soft, his muscles were firm and hard.

Tamar tenderly cleaned his wounds and face. She immobilized his arm with bandages she made from strips of bedding and with a splint of his dagger sheath. She made Devon comfortable, then went to the bathroom and undressed. Tamar showered and washed off the dirt and blood of the previous evening.

While Tamar stood under the warm water, a thought wrenched at her mind. Devon had known he was going to die when he'd told her he loved her: perhaps he only said he loved her because he knew he would die. Surely, he could not have expected her to love him. The fact he had not died changed everything.

No! No! It's worse, she thought. Tamar suddenly realized Devon had no right to love her—he could not marry her. He was the Prince of the Rathenberg family, the first son of the highest Duke in the Landsritters. She was the least daughter of one of the least of the Ducal holders. He must have observed her presented to the court on Arient. Tamar had not noticed him; her eyes marked only the Emperor and not the spectators and counselors in the hall. Her anger grew. This silly Duke's son took a fancy to a schoolgirl, one well below him in noble rank.

Now Tamar understood his decision to arrive secretly in the garb of a simple knight. He knew he was about to offer up his life, so he offered her his love. But he knew his love was worthless. He could love her, and she him, but they would never be allowed that love. They could never marry. The Duke Rathenberg, the Landsritters, and the Emperor, would all forbid their love. And when Devon said he loved her, he knew he would soon die. What kind of love was that?

But Devon Rathenberg was alive. What would that mean to him? Could he still love her? Tamar could not believe he would be so unkind to ignore his profession last night. Because of his rank, he could not love her in full honor; he could not marry her, and she would not be kept as any man's mistress—or would she?

Tamar stepped unwillingly from the warm shower and toweled her hair. She laughed a little hysterically. How foolish to think such things when the man might still die. She realized her lack of experience clouded her thoughts. Before this young knight, no man had told her he loved her. Many had brought her suit. Her father entertained many nobles' propositions for her hand, but none offered her his love.

No, Tamar sighed. She must allow him to withdraw his confession. Her feelings meant little to the Nobility of the Empire, and this man was a ruling Prince. He was heir to millions of stars in human space. She was a fool to believe he could love her. Tamar almost caught herself wishing he were dead. Her life would be much easier if he had died; to ignorantly accept his profession would have been nobler. Now all she could look forward to was the time when, because of her rank, he would have to reject her.

Tamar dressed in her bedraggled ball gown and walked back into the bedroom. As she stared at him, her thoughts were bitter. When he looked as he did, she thought she could easily reject and hate him. But her heart betrayed her. As she remembered his gentle voice and his lips on hers, Tamar's eyes filled with tears. *Fool,* Tamar thought, *fool.* She hardened her heart and went to the front room for some paper. She wrote him a note on it and placed it on his pillow.

Tamar touched his cheek with her hand, a gentle caress, then rearranged the sheets. Oh, how his love was infecting her mind and heart. She prayed under her breath. Could she ever return his love?

Tamar hunched herself away from the cold rain. Because she didn't dare call for a ride, she trudged all the way back to the main house in her gown and slippers. She hoped the ball wasn't over yet, and that she had not been missed. Under the insufficient light of Falkeep's moon, she examined her ruined evening dress. She couldn't appear like this...or could she? If worse came to worse and the knight were discovered, though her father would have a fit, she could plead the foolishness of lovers. Her brothers would probably overreact too. Maybe confession wasn't such a great idea. Tamar decided to enter by a side entrance and sneak to her room. Stealing past her maids and the matron would be difficult, but as a child, she did it routinely, so she could probably pull it off now.

The rain had soaked her to the skin. Tamar was shivering when she reached the house. At an alcove door, she quietly inserted her crystal laser key in the lock. Coded to the household, it didn't register who of the family opened the door, only that one of the Duke's family unlocked it. With equal care, Tamar pushed open the door and peered down the hallway. A tremor shook her; the corridor was clear. She stepped through the door and slipped down the hall. Tamar crept past servant's positions, behind arras, along hidden walkways, and back staircases to the private section of the house. She saw no one. Dirty, cold, wet, and dispirited, she quickly locked herself in her own room.

Tamar ripped the ruined ball dress from her body and hastily shoved it into the trash. She raked the jewelry from her and left it all in a heap on the floor. Enclosed by the warmth of the shower again, she finally began to feel herself. No, not totally herself. Tamar perceived that in the last few hours she had changed, taken on new and incredible responsibilities. At once, in her hands, she held the politics of the Empire and the life of one of its most powerful men. The problems of the Nobility that once slid so easily from the shoulders of her innocent youth now became irrevocably yoked to her.

Tamar had no idea how she would get medical care to Sir Devon. His heart had stopped, he was in shock, his arm was broken, and God only knew if he had internal injuries. Tamar shuddered at the thought of him alone and hurt in the summer house. She must think. She must find a way to preserve his life, to protect him, his mission, and his identity. *At Lady Pembrook's School for Young Ladies, they never taught me these things,* Tamar sighed to herself.

Though Falkeep's sun was just showing in the east, Tamar dressed for bed. *There,* she thought. *If they missed me, I was here all morning; the party bored me, and I went to bed.* With the lights out, she lay down. The repulsors of her bed lent a slight bluish glow to the sheets. Their low gentle hum lulled her to close her eyes. She finally felt warm. It was good to be warm and safe, though thoughts of the night drifted in her subconscious and made her wince once or twice in her sleep.

Tamar sat up suddenly. The bedclothes fell damply from her body. Her eyes were wide, and she was not truly awake. The sounds of explosions—no, simply someone pounding on her door.

"Lady Tamar, Lady Tamar."

Shaking her head and swinging her feet to the floor, Tamar answered, "Please stop, Dulcia. I'm just getting up now."

The crono read 1000 local time, and the sun was high but invisible under a low ceiling. Tamar felt feverish and dizzy, and sitting up didn't help matters any. As if its owner didn't expect to find the Lady Tamar in her own room, the voice stopped suddenly. Not sure why she felt so weak, Tamar stood up carefully. She stepped uneasily across the room. Tamar leaned against the doorframe while she unlocked and levered open the door. "Dulcia," she winced, "whatever is the matter?"

"Beg pardon m'lady, but everyone's been looking for you since early this morning. Your sisters worried about where you'd gone," explained Dulcia.

Dulcia was Tamar's maid. A slight girl, she was the daughter of one of Falkeep's knights. Dulcia was not yet sixteen and small for her age. Her pretty face was marked with a serious look for one so young. Dulcia bobbed once or twice in a curtsy, "M'lady, you...are you well?"

Tamar held to the door like a lifeline. She caught a glimpse of herself in the mirror. A white and haggard face stared back at her. *I do look ill,* she thought. No, she couldn't be sick. She had too much else to worry about. When she swayed on her feet, Dulcia caught her hands and helped her back into the bed.

Just as Tamar lay back down, the Matron Maria looked in through her door. At the sight of Tamar, her face relaxed, "Oh, thank goodness we found you, my lady." Then her features tensed again. She walked up to the bed and put her cool hand against Tamar's burning forehead. "My lady, are you ill?"

Tamar's mind wasn't thinking as quickly as she liked, but she had the presence of mind to answer, "Yes, Maria, I felt ill at the ball and came to bed early."

"You should have summoned us, my lady. Your bed wasn't even prepared," returned Maria, but she was visibly relieved she had solved the mystery of the evening so easily.

Tamar almost smiled, but she felt more like being sick. To think that most of the household turned out to look for her in what her father and her sisters, or maybe just her sisters thought, were the arms of the colloquial knight. What a dramatic thought...she almost wished it was true.

Maria went to get the household doctor and to inform the other searchers she'd found Tamar.

Well, thought Tamar, *this illness solves a problem I didn't know existed.*

Dulcia tried to make Tamar comfortable. She puttered about and fluffed up the pillows, then had to stop and help Tamar make a sudden rush to the bathroom.

Six

Her unanticipated illness frustrated Tamar. In her fever, she imagined all kinds of harm to Devon Rathenberg. Tamar knew Sir Devon could be crippled in his right arm unless she located professional medical attention for him soon. At this moment, he could be dead from internal bleeding. Tamar recognized the need for haste, yet she knew she must work under some secrecy. Devon Rathenberg had been willing and expecting to give his life in Duke Falkeep's garden. If Devon's miraculous recovery became known, the information would waste Devon's sacrifice and ruin the Emperor's plans.

The doctor tapped once on the door, and Dulcia let him in. Maria had sent Duke Falkeep's household doctor. Tamar stared up at him. The Doctor, tall and spare, was a man you could trust. Laugh lines crossed his face, and his smile filled the room with gentle warmth. Tamar also knew he reported directly to her Father.

When Tamar was younger, the doctor wore a gray and black uniform. He was a colonel, and in retirement, he was an advisor to her father's medical corps. No, Tamar couldn't trust him with the treatment of Devon Rathenberg. He would excellently heal the knight, but he would take the information directly to Duke Falkeep.

That would be something. If her father and brothers found out that during the spring ball, Devon Rathenberg and Count Yedric fought a duel on the Falkeep estate.... Worse, if they found out Devon Rathenberg started the duel and intentionally lost it.... Tamar doubted they would demand no less than the life of the young Rathenberg; the Nobel Accords required it. From Tamar's training at Lady Pembrook's, she evaluated that the repercussions of their actions would be disastrous for Falkeep. The revelation of Devon Rathenberg's mission would either put her father in the camp with Count Yedric, a dangerous and uncomfortable place for as loyal a vassal as her father, or would result in Falkeep becoming a neutral alliance. Unwanted by the Emperor, and unwilling to join with the rebellious Yedric, Falkeep would be crushed between the two.

There was also the problem of her brothers. If they knew Devon Rathenberg so brazenly demanded her love, then given the circumstances of the Empire and the rules of the Code, they might challenge him. They would certainly want his life. Devon asked for a woman, who because of his noble rank, he could only have illicitly and indecently. It didn't matter if Tamar would accept that love from him. If that was all Devon Rathenberg offered her; she might gladly accept it. But her brothers would kill him.

Tamar felt the great load of responsibility toward both Sir Devon and her family. Adding to her confusion was the growing knowledge that she was falling in love with Devon Rathenberg. Whether her love was infatuation, the product of her imagination and illness, or a mature decision, Tamar could not tell. She only knew that, right now, her heart, mind, and soul went out to him. She could not say what in time and under better scrutiny, her feelings would become. She only knew she loved him now.

The doctor kidded and joked with Tamar, but her mind was crowded with all these thoughts, so she wasn't a good audience. The Doctor shook his head as he looked in her throat and placed a diagnostic near her chest. He sighed when she didn't appear to be listening to him, and he asked her for the fourth time to breathe deeply. Tamar took a deep breath but continued her musing.

How to sit and walk, and read and write, and how to curtsy to King or Queen were not the only things taught at Lady Pembrook's Finishing School for Young Ladies. Highly placed ladies also learned the fundamentals of political and Imperial theory. The purpose of this training was to prepare those women who would be married to men of rank and position to guide their future husbands in proper interpretation, management, and manipulation of political events. The final seminar allowed the Ladies, in a controlled environment, to work within the political system. Though the third daughter of a lesser Duke, the Lady Tamar had been trained, at her father's insistence, in these political specialties. She was naturally proficient in them and considered brilliant by her teachers.

The doctor finally finished. He held Tamar's hand, and with his other hand, caught her by the ear and looked in her eyes. "I think you will live, but if you don't stop thinking so intensely, you are going to wear out your brain."

Tamar looked back at him and almost smiled, then did smile. She saw an opportunity for help. Almost apologetically she asked, "Where do the people of Falkeep go for medical attention?"

Taken aback, the doctor paused before answering. "Well, my Lady, many go to hospitals or have private doctors, but the poorest go to a Medical Clinic for all but the most serious problems."

Tamar saw the question in his eyes and answered it, "I just wondered where they received medical treatment. I didn't think they all had their own private doctors."

When the doctor finally left, Tamar sent Dulcia away with instructions to let her sleep. But instead of sleeping, Tamar opened her bedside computer and keyed up the nearest medical facility. The closest was a hospital in the city of Falkeep. Tamar didn't want a hospital. She knew from movies that hospitals only accepted immediate emergencies and referrals. They also required money and identification. She expanded her search and found an Emergency Medical Clinic not much further away than the hospital. The clinic was at a greater distance from the city center and in a less-traveled area. It would lend her the anonymity she needed for her plan to work.

The difficulty was that she must get Sir Devon to medical treatment as soon as possible. His survival might depend on how quickly and secretly she could get him off the Falkeep estate.

Near dusk, Tamar locked the door to her room and dressed in some of her most common clothing. She wore something of the prevailing fashion, very simple and unisex: baggy clothing with a cloak to disguise her face and figure.

A major highway traversed the estate about a mile past the furthest gardens. Tamar calculated the time she needed to dress Sir Devon, maneuver him onto the baggage sled, and travel to the main road. Then she called a taxi to pick her up on this highway near the back of the estate.

When Tamar was a child, the best way to sneak out of the house was to climb down the trellis and vines just outside her bedroom window. She opened the window and looked out. Cool and green in the gathering dusk, the garden stretched out below her. After the rain the night before, the air was clear and smooth. The muted sounds of insects and birds cheered Tamar on. This close to dusk no one should be near the gardens.

Tamar sat on the sill and swung her legs out. She closed the window behind her, shimmied down the ironwork, and slipped between the trees. She made it to the summer guesthouse in fifteen minutes.

Tamar carefully inspected the area around the house before she ventured to the door. Everything was quiet and undisturbed. She opened the door as quietly as the mechanics allowed and was astonished to see Devon Rathenberg sitting at the bungalow's tiny table.

"Hello, Lady Tamar," he croaked. Then he cleared his voice and quietly breathed, "I guess I owe my life to you, but you really should have let me die."

Her heart beating very fast, Tamar turned around and slid the door shut. Head bowed and facing the door, she stood, unmoving, where he couldn't see her. Hot tears rolled uncontrollably down her cheeks. She took a moment to regain her self-control.

"I'm sorry," he grimaced. "I know you think I should be thanking you. Well, thank you. You only prolonged my death. In fact, I chose to fight the Count with an energy sword, so I would die quickly." Devon sighed audibly. "You did a great job with the bandages, and I guess you were the one who punched me in the chest. Yes. Thanks." He took another drink from the bottle on the table and turned his face toward the wall.

The lights weren't on, and the remaining daylight rushed quickly out of the small room. Finally, Tamar lifted her head. She gave a muffled sob and fiercely wiped the tears from her face with the flat of her hand. She turned stiffly around. Her face was set. The anger in her heart lighted her eyes. If Devon looked at her, he would have seen nothing but her burning anger in the darkness.

"Why? Why!" She moaned. "Why did you even speak to me last night?" In the dark, she rushed forward and slammed her hands flat on the small table. She spoke less than a decimeter from his face. "Did you truthfully mean anything you told me yesterday?" Her voice was hard and angry.

He winced and the silence grew. Then he answered uncomfortably, "Yes."

"Then if I felt anything at all for you, why do you think I could leave you to die? If you love me, how do you think I could let anything take you from me? Do you hold my love in such contempt?"

He was silent.

"You thought the love you offered me," she spat out his name, "*Prince Devon Rathenberg,* was below me. You were wrong. And you are wrong to wring it out of me this way. How could I not love you? You are the man cast out of my dreams. How could I not cherish your existence?" In exhaustion, Tamar fell to her knees. "I am worth much more than that."

He winced again and looked directly at her. His eyes were filled with astonishment and a dark fierceness. "You know who I am?"

"Yes," she exclaimed triumphantly.

"And you would still love me?"

"Yes. Yes! I love you as I have never loved any man before."

Devon laughed suddenly. A pain-filled moan cut off the laugh, and he reached for his chest. But Tamar still felt his mirth. The silent laughter stopped, and he wearily wheezed, "You might not believe me, but I was willing to leave my position behind for you. Now it makes no difference. I have no position left. I had no hope then, I have no hope now, but I do still love you, Lady Tamar Falkeep."

Devon reached out his good arm, grasped Tamar by the shoulder, and drew her toward him.

Tamar struggled back and pushed him away. Devon weakly let her go. She gasped between sobs, "I love you, but I may never forgive you. You planned to die, yet you tempted me to fall in love with you. I may never forgive you, Devon Rathenberg. So put on your clothes, I have to get you to a doctor."

Devon didn't move from his seat. "I must not be discovered or identified."

"Look, Prince, don't worry. I know that, and I've taken care of it. You know I am a student at Lady Pembrook's, where you saw me on Arienth? I am not ignorant of these things."

Tamar couldn't tell if his look of astonishment came from her knowledge of where he saw her or from her familiarity with Imperial intrigues. Her guess that he had first noticed her on Arienth was probably right. It was written on his face.

Devon stood up and turned away from her in one movement: his motion was slow and painful. At first, Tamar looked away, embarrassed, but she put away her modesty and helped him to the bedroom and into his ragged clothes. She placed her cloak around his shoulders. He muttered thanks to her and stood steadily. Close beside him, Tamar could feel the effort he expended just to stand, and she couldn't help but notice that his body was hot with fever.

Devon tired quickly, and Tamar had to lend her strength to help him to the baggage sled. At first, he protested lying down on it, but she pressed him down, and he was unable to resist that slight pressure. After that, he had no energy to resist at all and lay quietly.

Pulling the sled through the dark garden, Tamar headed for the highway. She hadn't expected an argument with him, but those wasted minutes offset the time she thought it would take to clothe him by herself. At least, in that he was able to help her.

After they trudged through the trees a few minutes, Devon asked weakly, "Where are we going, and what story will you give them?"

"I'm taking you to an Emergency Medical Clinic in the city of Falkeep. I'll tell them that you had an accident while we were camping. A stove blew up in your face or something." Devon fell silent after that.

The trip seemed endless. Tamar was still ill, and she tired quickly. She tried not to show it, but Devon was in no condition to notice anything. He lay motionless on the sled. To monitor his condition,

Tamar turned around at intervals, but his eyes were closed. Each time she checked, he breathed regularly.

Until she picked up the faint noise of traffic far ahead, Tamar was afraid she was lost in the forest. Soon vehicle lights came into sight.

Just before they reached the edge of the woods, Tamar stopped the sled. Devon's condition appeared much worse than at the guesthouse. She tried to wake him fully by lightly tapping his cheeks, but he was feverish and unresponsive. Through great effort, she helped Devon off the transporter and onto his feet. She had to carry a good deal of his weight, and he mumbled incoherently. His body was sweaty and hot against her, and under her hands, she could feel the sticky dampness of his blood-saturated bandages. Tamar laid him on the grass at the edge of the roadway, and he collapsed to the ground. His bandaged arm hit the earth as she eased him down, and he groaned weakly.

"Do you have some water?" he asked.

Tamar sat down beside him and held her hand against his cheek. "No, you must wait."

She brushed the sweat away from his eyes, then checked her watch. *Just thirty minutes more.*

Earlier than she had planned, a small gravvehicle pulled off the side of the road about a half mile down from where they waited. Tamar jumped up and waved to it. In a moment, it was parked beside her. The front window came down and the driver asked, "You call for a taxi?"

"Yes." Relieved, she leaned her hands on the window ledge. "My friend hurt himself while we were hiking, and I need to get him to a clinic."

The driver looked at her disheveled condition, then squinted at the place Tamar pointed to on the ground. He looked around warily. "I don't know, lady."

"Please, you must help me. He is badly injured." Tamar's voice shook. Fear overwhelmed her that the transportation she wholly counted on might suddenly go away and leave them far from any help.

"All right," the cabbie answered, cautiously. "Don't worry. I'll wait. Just bring him to the door and let me see him. Then I'll decide whether I'll drive you."

Her fears only partly relieved, Tamar went to Devon and started to pull him up from the ground. By then he was almost entirely unconscious. He flopped over like a rag doll. Tamar tried to get her shoulder under him, but it was no use. She was about to just sit down and give up when she felt his body raised from her. The cabby stood with his arms around Sir Devon's chest, and he easily dragged the unconscious man to the taxi and laid him on the back seat. Tamar got in beside Devon and sat down. She placed Devon's head on her lap and listened for each breath. "Thanks," she told the driver huskily.

The driver got in and turned the gravvehicle around. "Hey lady, you sure you don't want to take him to a hospital?"

"No. Please take us to the clinic on Greenham Drive." A bit of hysteria tinged her voice.

Tamar had never been into this part of the city of Falkeep, even though she'd traveled to the city center countless times. She shopped the malls and the streets of the main square, but she did not know Falkeep. *How embarrassing,* she thought, *not to know the premier city of your own planet.* Not to know how to get around the city that was the center of government for the sector her father ruled. As Tamar held Devon gently and stroked his hair, she felt foolish and small—like a nobody.

In the city lights, the driver looked back and could see more of his passengers. The further he drove, the greater he felt that they should be headed toward a hospital. "Look, lady, are you sure you don't want me to take you to a hospital?"

Tamar shook her head numbly. Then, realizing he probably couldn't see her, she answered, "N-n-no."

"What is it? You kids don't have much money, that it?"

Money? Tamar had forgotten about money for the clinic. She didn't carry money. She used it, but she always went out with her maid or with her driver. They carried her money.

The cabby took her silence for agreement. "Bet you don't have any insurance, either. Look, lady, maybe the people at the hospital can work something out for you."

"N-n-no," answered a shivering Tamar. How stupid she was to forget something so simple. She was such a great planner that she had nothing to pay for the taxi. Then she thought of Devon. He was sure to have a wallet. She searched in his pockets and was relieved to find a pocketbook with about 100 cash credits in it.

The cab drove up to the door of the clinic and the driver helped Tamar drag Devon out. By this time, she shivered continuously.

"Are you OK, lady?" the driver asked.

Between clenched teeth she answered, "Y-y-yes."

Tamar could barely walk as the driver half carried, half dragged Devon into the clinic.

When they passed through the doors, Tamar was hardly aware of anything. She saw the receptionist get up quickly and call loudly behind her. While two nurses rushed forward to get Devon she pressed a handful of bills into the driver's hand.

"That's way too much, lady." The bills were forced back into her hands.

"Please, take what's fair," she stammered.

"Lady, I won't take anything. Here, you need to sit down." He pushed her into a chair. Tamar still held stupidly onto a handful of bills.

Far away, Tamar heard the driver repeat the same story she'd told him. He explained that he picked them up at the edge of the woods and he thought she was hurt too. She meant to stand up and tell them it wasn't so. She needed to get back to the house, but as she stood, everything went dark, and she slumped back into the chair. Tamar's fingers relaxed, and the bills scattered from one side of the room to the other.

Seven

Duke James Falkeep was generally a patient and cautious man. He carefully planned every political venture to maintain solid neutrality. His mechanizations neither threatened his enemies nor ostracized his friends; they simply aided him and his holdings. The events of the last few weeks, however, placed him in a position of extreme discomfort. *If only communications weren't so slow through this Empire,* he thought. *But,* he acknowledged ruefully, *then the Empire itself would not be possible.*

Well, the die was cast, and now it was up to the Landsritters to again patch the unwinding threads.

Duke Falkeep reread the immediate transcript he'd received this evening. He rubbed his eyes with thumb and forefinger and held them closed. *God help us now.* The message was short but ominous. The Beneficent Emperor Maricus was dead, apparently of natural causes.

Natural causes could be a knife in the back, thought Falkeep.

The Empire was in the hands of Perod-Mark, now the Emperor Perodus, the elder son of Maricus. For aiding his brother, John-Mark, in traitorous conduct and unspecified actions in opposition to the Code, the new Emperor declared the Landsritters disbanded for a period of six months. In addition, the Empire was under the direct legislation of the new Emperor and his appointed representatives.

As if Perodus by himself could control his own small planet, chuckled Duke Falkeep.

The new Emperor called for the unanimous acknowledgment of

himself as the sole ruler of known space and the renewal by all noble vassals of their fealty. He further banned his brother, John-Mark, the Duke Neuterra, the Duke Rathenberg, the Count Acier, plus the nobles of another eight Duchies—in all, fully ten of the Thirty Kingdoms, plus an assortment of smaller holders.

He granted a boon to Count Yedric that gave him status as a Duke of the Realm and ceded to him all the territories once controlled by Duke Neuterra. He also granted a boon to Count Frederic Rathenberg of the office of Chancellor once held by his cousin, the banned Duke Rathenberg.

Ominous, thought Falkeep. The other papers in the packet expanded on the official message. His sources—quite simply, spies on the Imperial planet Arienth—reported that the Emperor Maricus had died suddenly and that the body was hidden away without access to anyone but the Imperial family. According to Duke Falkeep's spies, Prince John-Mark's absence from the planet had precipitated Perodus' actions. Such a thing would not occur with the strong hand of John-Mark nearby.

The murder of the Emperor, as Falkeep classified it in his mind, had taken place on the eve of the nuptial ceremonies for the upcoming marriage of Prince John-Mark and the daughter of Duke Neuterra, the Lady Lyral Neuterra. The King's elite guard, the Imperial Huscarls whom Prince John-Mark commanded, were undermanned at the palace. Because of sporadic fighting on the planets near the Fringe, the Huscarls were busy with the events off Arienth. And, of course, Prince John-Mark was with his men fighting for the Emperor. The palace servants further rumored that some of the Huscarl guards were also missing.

Well, thought Duke Falkeep, the Landsritters, were so divided by petty rivalries and hindered by the Code that they might never learn the truth of the Emperor's death.

Duke Falkeep's notes went on to say that Perodus apparently discovered Prince John-Mark's true reasons for marrying the Lady Lyral Neuterra. Perodus learned of his brother's plans from Count Yedric, one of Falkeep's holders.

Prince John-Mark was not a man content with the figurehead

status of the second son of an Emperor. He was a born leader and fighter whose prowess in war was officially recognized by his command of the Emperor's Huscarls. Numerous times he successfully led the Emperor's forces into war.

The Codes allowed the Emperor only one army, the Imperial Huscarls, and historically, an officer from a leading family of the Landsritters led them. The Huscarls were a small but powerful strike-force that incorporated aerospace, land, sea, and space assets.

However, the Codes gave the Emperor other sources of power. In fact, the origin of the Emperor's power was intertwined in the Code. It required that all major events of the Noblesse, such as marriages, christenings, investitures, alliances, and trials take place on the planet Arienth. In theory, this gave the Emperor the power of suggestion and arbitration, since his approval, though desired, was not required. In actuality, the Code gave the Emperor the power of hostage and death. The benevolent and intelligent Emperor ran the Empire through political manipulation and loyalty to the Code; the foolish and incapable controlled through fear and assassination. Typically, the latter's reign didn't last long, since violence begat violence, particularly when applied against a disenchanted majority in the Landsritters.

Prince John-Mark wanted to unite the Empire such as it had never been before. He sought to bring together two of the largest, most powerful, and most industrious houses of the Empire: the House Neuterra and the House Arienth. Duke Neuterra produced no male heir. Because of Prince John-Mark's popularity in the Landsritters, when he married Lyral Neuterra, he would have been invested as the sovereign of Neuterran space. That, plus the inheritance of the Second son of the Emperor, would have given him a voting and military power unmatched by any Noble House. He would have been, in effect, a new Emperor, and his father, the late Emperor Maricus, had supported John-Mark's plans.

All these arrangements had been smashed when Perodus, John-Mark's brother, executed the Lady Lyral. Duke Falkeep's sources reported her head was displayed in the Hall of the Landsritters. The whereabouts of Prince John-Mark were unknown, and the banned Houses were gathering a coalition to challenge the Empire.

This was Duke Falkeep's dilemma: should he join the banned houses and be banned himself? That might be dangerous because of the situation in his own sector. Yedric was a vassal under him, and for years, the Duke knew Yedric stockpiled munitions and alliances. Obviously Yedric acted illegally, but so did every other House. Further, if he joined the banned houses, many of Falkeep's own holders might not support him. In the ensuing political and military turmoil, to be banned and lose meant the destruction of his House. On the other hand, to join the Emperor Perodus would legitimatize Yedric's actions and even encourage them. Duke Falkeep's own vassals might react with rebellion, and that would tear asunder his kingdom, the Duchy of Falkeep. Yet to remain neutral was to either court the wrath of both sides—or perhaps, to escape any notice. The issues were much more complicated than this. He was simplifying. The Duke would give the entire situation to his experts, and then he would make a decision. God help him if he were wrong.

Eight

Tamar awoke suddenly. She could not identify her surroundings. The air smelled dry and sharp, scented with something like cleaning fluid. She restlessly moved her arms under the sheet. The bedclothes felt rough and thin, and a slight pressure tugged against her wrist. A wash of sunlight fell brightly across her eyes, and she had to squint and turn her head to see clearly. Tamar tried to sit up, but she had no strength. For a moment she was afraid, then it all came back to her, and she realized where she must be.

Tamar lay in a hospital bed. A long clear tube stretched from her wrist to a half empty bag near the headboard. Tamar looked curiously at it and decided that she should probably leave it in. She pulled the sheet down a little. She was dressed in a pastel gown. It opened immodestly in the back, she noticed with distaste.

Now what? Before she could answer that question, a nurse briskly entered the room.

"Good morning." The woman smiled. Tamar could see her nametag: *Joanne.* "How are you feeling now?" Joanne shut the blinds slightly to get the sun out of Tamar's eyes, then sat next to her on the bed.

Tamar tried to speak, but her voice was so dry she could say nothing at first. The nurse handed Tamar a small cup filled with water, and Tamar sipped gratefully at it. "I'm all right," whispered Tamar, hopefully.

"I'm sure you are. The doctor will be along in a little while to check on you. Until then, if you need me, just push the red button, and I'll come."

The nurse started to get up, but Tamar grasped her arm. "I can't stay here. I must leave."

"But you can't leave yet," Joanne explained as if she spoke to a child. "The doctor must say you're well."

Tamar had tried to sit up, but the nurse pressed her back and fluffed the pillows behind her.

"Wait." Tamar forestalled the nurse's departure again. "At least tell me where I am."

"You're in the hospital at Falkeep's spaceport," answered the nurse abruptly.

Tamar wanted to ask more questions, but the nurse was out the door.

This was bad. By now she would be missed. But, at least, Tamar thought, no one could track Sir Devon. It would mean nothing if anyone found him here injured. He could make up any story, and she could corroborate anything. He was no longer on the house grounds. He was a nondescript knight again. No one but she cared what had happened to him, and he would get the medical treatment he needed.

Ages seemed to pass before a doctor finally came in to see her. Before he got around her bed, she asked, "What happened to the man who was with me?"

The doctor frowned so balefully that Tamar was startled.

"Did you bandage him?" the doctor returned her question.

"Yes," answered Tamar.

"You did an excellent job. How did he get burned that way?"

"A tank of fuel exploded while he was fixing the stove."

The doctor whistled. "He's lucky to be alive."

Thank God, thought Tamar. *At least, he is alive.*

"You haven't been extremely kind to yourself either," chided the doctor, "You have a good case of pneumonia, but rest and the antibiotics will take care of that."

"I can't stay here."

"I don't think you will be able to leave." Her look of astonishment almost made him laugh. "Well first," he explained, "you probably aren't strong enough to walk out of here on your own. Second, you are on the starport. The retinal scanner identified you as a transient, so we brought you here. Until you can get any more documents, I think the customs and Falkeep's boarder police will not let you planetside. And third, the Empire is under martial law, so, for now, you will not be allowed to leave this planet or go planetside. I'm sorry, but it will benefit you to stay here until you are well, or, at least, your credentials are secured." The doctor stood and took his leave, while Tamar mused on everything he said.

As soon as the doctor left, the nurse, Joanne returned with breakfast and a paper. As Tamar hungrily ate the bland food, she learned from the paper incredible news. The information was almost a week and a half old, but it was reported directly from a consulate ship just in from Arienth. The Emperor Maricus was dead! His son Perod-Mark had taken the throne and was now the Emperor Perodus. Prince John-Mark was declared a traitor, and his affianced, Lyral Neuterra, was dead, executed by Imperial order before the entire body of the Landsritters.

Tamar's throat tightened. Large tears rolled from her eyes along her cheeks and nose and onto the reader. *How can this be?* Her best friend from school, the Lady Lyral Neuterra, was dead. Tamar's sorrow was so great, she could barely continue reading. Prince John-Mark, the beloved son of the Empire, the most popular warrior and diplomat in human space, was marked traitor, his beloved murdered. The events heaped on one another, crushing Tamar's heart with their horror. In disgust, she almost threw down the viewer, but instead forced herself to continue reading. The article listed other nobles declared traitor along with those honored in Perodus' takeover of the Empire. She was astounded to read of Count Yedric's advancement to Duke.

Her mind scrambled to make sense of the events of more than a full week ago. Then, along with the happenings at her father's ball, the situation suddenly became clear to her. Count Yedric and Count Rathenberg conspired against the Emperor Maricus as a front to weaken the Empire and lure away some of the Emperor's protection and advisors. Perod-Mark must have been scheming for years to completely develop his plans because the timing of his attack was perfect. Duke Rathenberg, Prince John-Mark, and Prince Devon

Rathenberg were all off Arienth. Tamar knew the Huscarls themselves offered military advice and protection to the Emperor's holders and were deployed over many systems and the Fringe. Maricus' beneficence destroyed him. His own son, Perod-Mark, most likely had killed him. Not everything was clear in her mind, and she couldn't prove half of what she believed, but Tamar knew—her intuition and special training guided the logic of her thoughts.

Now, what of her knight? She must speak with him, and she must get out of this place.

She knew it was already too late for herself. She could picture Matron Maria and Dulcia, frantically searching for her. She could imagine her father's concern, fear, and anger. Well, at least Devon Rathenberg was safe for now. A contented grin suffused her features, and Tamar closed her eyes. *He is safe, and I love him. I may even forgive him.* She felt herself slipping into unwanted sleep. Her last thought was that his life rested thrice in her palm. She'd held the power of life or death over him and had chosen life for him and life for herself.

When Tamar woke again, Sir Devon Rathenberg sat directly across from her. His eyes were locked on hers. Tamar thought she was still enveloped in a dream, but the growing light in the room and the unconscious pain from the IV in her arm, along with the hungry growl from her stomach, brought her quickly to full wakefulness.

Devon didn't say a word. He looked away for just a moment and signaled someone at the door, then resumed his contemplation of her.

Tamar wiped the sleep out of her eyes and ran her fingers through her hair. His stare made her suddenly conscious of her appearance. She probably looked like an ogre. She licked her lips nervously, then turned her head to the side. Devon reached out his hand and gently caressed her cheek. He touched her lips and chin before gently turning her face back toward his. Tamar looked at him again. His face was raw but healing; he held himself tensely, like few positions were comfortable and that even now something pained him. A plastic cast encased his arm and was suspended by a sling from the front of his robe.

Devon smiled slowly, painfully. She couldn't help smiling back at him. Then in a clear and even voice, the knight pronounced, "I love you, Tamar. Will you forgive me?"

Tamar could feel the blood hot in her neck and face—a nervous and revealing flush. She continued to smile. "In spite of everything, I have foolishly proposed to forgive you." She sniffed, then laughed gently.

Devon understood her and quietly laughed with her. They continued to grin at one another until the nurse, Joanne, brought in two trays of breakfast. Without another word they both began to eat ravenously.

After a few minutes, Devon closed the door to the room. He sat back and cradled a still steaming cup of coffee while he asked, "Have you heard the news concerning the Emperor?"

Tamar nodded.

"Things have taken an entirely different course than I expected. Some spy and advisor I am. I should have seen the events evolving. Now, my Lady, it is I who am far below you. My family has lost its place in the Empire."

"That's foolish," Tamar interrupted. "The Landsritters will not let the Emperor strip your House of its honor."

"I'm afraid they may have no choice. We...no, *I* missed so many things transpiring in the Imperial Family that I have no idea who or what may support the new Emperor. Perodus would never make so bold a move unless he knew he had the backing of the Landsritters. Or, at least that he had a certain control over the Landsritters. My predicament is even worse." He shook his head. "I am a nonentity. My Emperor ordered me to give my life for his House. I could not complete what he set for me to do. In that, I am a traitor."

"No! You had no control of the events that let you live. And anyway," Tamar continued furiously, "the man who sent you on this mission is himself dead. I doubt anyone else knew about it."

"But in my heart, I know I failed my Emperor. He had my word of honor, and I failed."

"So your word is worth nothing now," she teased him cruelly.

His eyes narrowed, then he smiled. "You're right. I have no position. I am stripped of my nobility."

"Perhaps I'll keep you with me." Tamar sniffed haughtily. "Who are you, after all, to question my wishes?"

Devon smiled even broader at that.

"Don't be foolish," she quipped. "The men who oppose the unjust actions of this new...*Emperor*...need you. To them, you are still Sir Devon Rathenberg, Knight of the Red Cross, Major in the Imperial Huscarls. Don't give yourself a eulogy when none is due."

Devon looked about nervously. He shushed her and moved his chair closer to her. "You are right." He sat very straight, very close to her. "You're right. But in my soul, in my heart as a warrior, I know I stained my honor." His voice became husky and his face drawn. "Forgive me for not believing what I know in my mind is true. I will fight again for the Empire, but for now my strength is taken—my potency is sapped."

He was close enough that she could feel his breath as he spoke. She put her arms around his neck and drew him to her lips. She kissed him slowly and gently. Then she pressed his face tenderly against her breast and kissed his hair. "I forgive you. You have me. Am I not enough to encourage your warrior's prowess? Am I not enough for you to live to return for? I am yours. What else can anyone offer you?"

Devon put his good arm around her and held her. She gasped at his strength. After releasing her, he sat straight again in the chair and smiled broadly. "I accept your offer. I offer you, in the name of my family, upon my honor and oath, by the rules of the Code, by the power invested me by my household, the Ladyship of my House. I, Sir Devon Rathenberg, Knight of the Red Cross, Officer of his Majesty's Huscarls, do swear this by my honor and by the honor of my House." He scribbled this on a cloth napkin from the breakfast tray. Removing his House ring, he wrapped it in the napkin and handed it to her.

Tamar remained deathly silent. She took the small bundle from his hands and turned extremely pale as she read the words and signature written on it. "Are you sure? Do you realize what you offer me?"

"Lady, I loved you from the first moment I saw you. I heard you speak when you were presented to the Emperor. He was himself charmed by you. You didn't know that." He grinned. "You disregarded your own safety more than once to protect me, and you saved my life not once but three times—that only makes me love and cherish you more. Without any promise from me, you, the daughter of a Duke, offer yourself to me. You shame me with your honor and your loyalty. Because I love you, I offer you the greatest thing I can possibly give you—the Ladyship of my House."

Her eyes glazed and fixed on his as she recited, "I accept your offer, in the name of my family, upon my honor and oath, by the rules of the Code, by the power invested me by my household, the Ladyship of your House. I, Lady Tamar Falkeep, daughter of Duke Falkeep, do swear this by my honor and the honor of my House. I accept your House into my stewardship, as I accept your presence into mine, your honor is mine, your life is mine, your peace is mine, your children are mine." Tamar wrote this below his signature on the napkin and signed it herself. She then took the signet from around her neck and held it out to him. Devon put his head forward and let her place it around his neck.

"My father must sign this to make it fully legal." Tamar sighed deeply. "And I don't think he will do that."

"We must also present ourselves on the planet Arienth before it is fully accepted, but we have until a child is born to do so. Your father cannot offer you to anyone else so long as this agreement stands. I must either die or he must seek the dissolution of the pledge through the Landsritters. The match is completely legal, and I am empowered by my father to make decisions concerning my House."

Tamar stared at him. "Your father must trust you utterly."

"He entrusted to me the full stewardship of our House."

Tamar looked at him even more amazed. "I have never heard of such a thing."

Devon chuckled. "When he finds out what I have done, I expect that will change."

And she laughed with him.

Devon continued in a more serious and quiet tone, "My father granted me this honor at the request of the Emperor. My mother is the Imperial Princess Catherine Haupenburg, the sister of Emperor Maricus. My father is the principal of the family Rathenberg, the oldest

Imperial line in the Noblesse. However, by blood and tradition, as long as I am the principal of House Rathenberg, I am, or would be, the third in line for the Imperial Throne. My father granted me the stewardship of our House, so the Emperor Maricus could have a third heir. Under these conditions, the Landsritters were delighted to grant it to me if only to further ensure the proper investiture of the crown."

Tamar looked at him in disbelief. "You are an heir to the Iron Throne?"

"Third…well, perhaps second now." He looked down. "The possibility of me rising to that position is incredibly low, especially since my family and I are banned. And further, I no longer exist. I am the casualty of a duel."

"No casualty, my lord, unless you decide to be." She slipped her hand in his, and as if by mutual consent, they turned their conversation to happier thoughts.

The visiting hours long expired before their nurses' frowns forced Devon to take his leave. Tamar still held his hand in hers, and their parting kiss was long and impassioned. After their lips parted, he touched her hair. "We must leave here soon. I must return you to your family, and I must go where I can help support the banned Houses." Before Tamar could protest his words, Devon was gone.

Another day and a night passed. Devon visited Tamar from the morning to the evening. She felt and looked better and stronger. Under the advanced treatments he received, his wounds healed rapidly. That night, they put into practice the plans they discussed for the last two days. First, they dressed and stole out of their wards. Sir Devon paid for their medical treatment and, using his identification, signed for both of them. "They will follow you to the end of the universe to get their bill," he commented with a grin. They left the hospital and entered the spaceport mall proper.

The spaceport of both the planet and city of Falkeep was a class A facility. It was a small city itself that supported and supplied the five other Imperial space facilities on the planet. It was the mainstay of the entire sector that Duke Falkeep and his holders administered. Imperial spaceports, like Falkeep spaceport, were technically under the administration of the Empire. Imperial rules and laws took precedence over all planetary jurisdiction. In reality, so long as the Empire's laws were upheld, the planetary holder, in this case, Duke Falkeep, kept direct control of the facility. To guide the Duke in his rule, Baron Herstet represented the Empire on the spaceport. Herstet could revoke Duke Falkeep's privileges and authority over the port and leave the Duke with only his military space facilities. In the case of a planet like Falkeep, this would almost certainly wipe out its interplanetary trade and destroy its economy. Duke Falkeep would be forced to either take over the spaceport and challenge the might of the Empire or negotiate and acquiesce to the Emperor's wishes.

Devon was sure they could lose themselves in the spaceport forever if necessary. Space vehicles, mostly shuttles from orbiting FTL, Faster Than Light, ships arrived and departed night and day. The main portion of the port stayed open all hours. Their first stop was a couple of clothing shops not more than a kilometer from the hospital. Devon and Tamar exchanged their clothing for new smart gear appropriate for nobles of lesser prestige. Devon carried an almost unlimited supply of electronic credits, and they had no reason to scrimp.

Devon replaced his weapons and bought luggage to fit their disguise as travelers. He acquired false papers for both of them through the computers at the port headquarters. The prerogative of being a clandestine bureaucrat, he told her. Then under his name, they checked into the main hotel.

As soon as they entered their room, they started their clandestine honeymoon, and consequently, achieved very little sleep during the entire day-night period.

Refreshed, they checked out of the hotel, and oblivious to the people around them, walked hand-in-hand to customs. At Falkeep Customs, Devon presented their false papers, and Tamar was surprised at how quickly the guards passed them through. They took transportation to the hotel he had stayed in prior to the ball, and though the day was young, they spent the rest of the time locked in the room and each other's arms, then later in quiet conversation in the restaurant.

That night, in bed, lying face-to-face, surrounded by the warm glow of their lovemaking, she traced the edges of his cast and the solid warmth of his lean body. She giggled. "It tickles afterwards." Her voice became serious with a note of sadness about it, "This has got to end, you know. No matter how long we postpone it. I've got to go home to my family, and you must go to your duty...I can feel the need in you now."

"You understand the situation precisely. I need to go." He smiled. "But, right now, I need you more." He gathered her more tightly in his arms.

She ignored his overture. "After you leave, what are you going to do?"

"I—yes, what am I going to do?" His eyes closed. His features tensed, then in a moment, he relaxed.

"What are you thinking?" She snuggled closer to him.

"I remember the only time I was not true to my honor. It was for my Emperor and Prince, but now, I will right that wrong." He smiled. "You read the paper?"

"Yes." She traced his face with her fingertips.

"What do you think was Yedric's part in this whole escapade?"

She thought a moment. "He diverted the attention of the Emperor away from Prince Perod-Mark and the internal events on Arienth."

"Excellent!" He beamed at her as though she was the most intelligent being in the world. "That's why I love you. You see, I figured it all wrong. You know, I was the Emperor's Chief of intelligence."

She propped herself up on her elbow. "That's what Yedric said. You are the Emperor's Young Fox."

"For two years, I have been watching over these affairs. Prince John-Mark played a dangerous game. I knew about it from almost the beginning. He is like a brother to me. We are the best of friends. I kept the information secret from the Emperor and from Prince Perod-Mark. Not that I feared any disagreement from them if the full story were known, for I knew the Emperor Maricus would support John-Mark, and I knew Prince Perod-Mark would fear to act by himself. I thought he would get the Landsritters to halt his brother's plans. I counted on the fact that no major House would support Perod-Mark. I was wrong. Under the pretense of rebellion against the current Imperial line, Yedric, with my cousin, Count Rathenberg, along with a few other Houses actually bound themselves to Prince Perod-Mark. Further, I know Yedric engineered the whole scheme of the Emperor's assassination and the betrayal of John-Mark. I know it because he chose to move when the Emperor did. He knew the Emperor was going to force a confrontation. I don't think he knew what form the attack would take, but as I made my way toward Falkeep's sector and Yedric's holdings, Yedric's trap fell shut on the Emperor, on Prince John-Mark, on the Landsritters, on Lyral." His voice choked off.

She settled back next to him and held his face against hers. Her voice was a whisper, full of tears. "Lyral was my best friend. I cannot believe she is dead." After a moment she asked with a sigh, "But what did Prince John-Mark have to gain? I thought he was going to wed the Lady Lyral for love."

Quietly, "Yes, he loved her. He loved her as I love you. But, by wedding her, he would have put in action a series of alliances and relationships that would produce a new dynasty. Neuterra would become the seat of Imperial power. The Landsritters would have been united in a single man and kingdom. The reign of beneficence and strength started by his father, the Emperor Maricus would have continued. That is no longer possible."

He paused. "You know? I have nothing now to offer you, and in the Empire of Perodus, I stand to inherit nothing. By now, my holdings are void; they all reside on Arienth."

She kissed him. "You can give me yourself." She paused in thought. "But you never said: what you are going to do? What is so important that it will take you away from me?"

"Like I should have in the first place, I will kill Yedric. Then I'm going to fight for the censured Houses. I know I will never get back my inheritance, but for you, perhaps I can earn another."

She sighed, dreading her own words, regretting them as she announced, "You may go, my lord, but you must promise to come back to me." Tears again tinged her voice. Then she cried roughly, shaking off her sadness, "Enough talk, my lord, love me!"

Nine

The next evening, Devon took Tamar back to the Falkeep estate. From his previous planning, Devon knew the security of the house and grounds. With Tamar's reassurance that she had long ago disconnected the alarm on her window, they stole through the gardens to the alcove just below it. The night was moonless and cold. They waited only a moment before climbing the trellis and vines to the locked opening. Devon applied a few tools out of the kit he retrieved from the hotel, and in a minute, they were across the sill and in Tamar's room.

Duke Falkeep and his forces searched long and hard for the Lady Tamar. His daughter's disappearance was a mystery to everyone. The house was in an uproar; in the history of the House Falkeep, nothing like this had ever happened.

She had either been kidnapped or run away on her own, but the clues pointed to neither possibility. Perhaps she was off alone in the garden: the gardens were still being searched. She might be spending time in one of the garden summerhouses. Someone recently occupied one of them. The computer records showed someone had unlocked the house and activated it, but the automatic housecleaning systems destroyed any other evidence. The Duke's men were still trying to find the baggage sled. Those stupid gravsleds left no tracks and most of the garden trails were paved.

If Tamar had been kidnapped, where was the ransom note? Where was the evidence of a struggle? To all appearances, she left of her own free will and then disappeared—but where?

Duke Falkeep put his hands over his face. His youngest daughter was the joy of his life, the child of his old age. Since his wife's death fifteen years ago, Tamar had been the bright joy of his existence. He recognized her native brilliance and sent her to the finest school for young noble women in the Empire. He looked forward to each school holiday because she would bring her smile and cheer into his tedious days. He was ashamed to say she was the center of all his parties and balls, and his other daughters recognized this. But, to his credit, they acknowledged his captivation and encouraged it: they all made good matches, they loved their husbands, but their father only had his little Tamar. And they, too, welcomed Tamar's help and advice because of her intuition and political training.

Perhaps he had protected her too much. Tamar was a shy girl, and he safeguarded that trait. His two sons, the elder married to the daughter of a Duke, the younger, unmarried, an Imperial officer, usually escorted and looked after her. She was the apple of their eye as well as his. She was the little one, the quiet one, the smart and loving one. She was their little sister, who had no mother and on whom they bestowed extravagant love.

But neither of his sons had been able to attend this ball. Tamar had danced the night away with some colloquial knight. She had left the party early. She...*Oh*, thought the Duke with anger. He pounded his temples, unable to halt his grief. At least his sons were here now. In the Capital, they led the search from street to street. Even now he requested the permission of Baron Herstet to search the spaceport. Since the day of Tamar's disappearance, his troops had reviewed all the port's passenger manifests. The Duke would leave no stone unturned. He would overlook no clue. He would find his beloved child...and only death would stop him.

But the Duke felt like he was beating his head against the wall. He blamed himself for her loss. Where was she?...Where was she?...Where was she? The epitaph whirled around inside his skull.

These thoughts distracted him while Duke Falkeep turned along the corridor between the family's private suites and his study. Hesitantly, he paused beside Tamar's door. His little Tamar. Twice, he reached for the doorknob, each time without touching it. He remembered when she was a child, how he looked in on her every night. He remembered her smiling, cherub face pressed against the pillow, serene and innocent, framed by her blond hair. He grasped the doorknob. His heart pounded as he remembered the joy she brought to his old soul. The Duke turned the knob and silently opened the door.

The curtains were open. From the rising moon, a hazy light shown into the room. The bed was turned back. The Duke's heart beat faster with the possibility of finding Tamar miraculously where she belonged. Then it beat with fear. "Tamar?" his voice wavered with emotion.

He saw the covers gently stir and took a step into the room.

"Tamar!" slightly louder.

The sheets rustled with movement.

"Father?" The voice was filled with dismay, an emotion the Duke never knew in his daughter. So unusual were the circumstances, so strange the voice that he stood frozen, silent, listening. It took a moment before his mind truly convinced him that he indeed heard the voice of his daughter. "Father?"

In the half-light, the Duke perceived that the bed held more than one human form, and his heart mercilessly filled with anger. The rage overwhelmed his spirit. His voice took on an edge that only those who fought in battle with him ever heard.

"Daughter," he spat out, "you...What have you...? You have defiled yourself..." Then, louder, "You have defiled our family." His hand reached for the snub pistol holstered at his waist. A loud click sounded as he drew and armed it.

The other figure reacted immediately. Like a cat, like a being whose nerves, muscles, and sinew are trained for instant action, a man's naked body rolled off the bed. The man touched the floor for an instant, then with a somersault, slammed through the windowpane. A heavy crash, followed by splintering glass and the loud creaking of metal succeeded the figure's exit.

The Duke leveled his pistol late. By the time it pointed at the disappearing figure, Tamar had interposed her naked body between them. With a growl, Duke Falkeep cuffed his daughter out of the way and rushed to the window. Tamar gave a strangled cry as she fell heavily against the bed.

Duke Falkeep fired at the running shadow. The shots lit up the darkness and filled the night with small explosions.

"No!" screamed Tamar, "No, Father, I love him. Stop!" She grabbed at his pistol arm. The hot gun touched her naked forearm, and she cried out. The Duke shrugged her off and emptied his clip into the garden. In a final great exertion, Tamar captured his wrist, and with a flick of the pistol the Duke caught her across the face. The hot pistol burned her cheek and slashed her lips. Tamar fell to the floor on her face.

The Duke looked out over the garden for a moment. His security men and the servants converged from all parts of the house. Duke Falkeep yelled and motioned them in the direction the man had taken through the trees, then turned back into the room. He heard an anguished sob.

His daughter lay in a pool of her own blood; he saw it glisten in the moonlight. He wrinkled his nose. The room was still filled with the scent of their passion. Frightened maids and nervous guards stood in the doorway. Moonlight bathed the room, but he saw their undisguised astonishment. He stepped over Tamar and signaled Dulcia and Maria. He waved away the others and walked quickly to his study.

The pistol was empty. Duke Falkeep searched through the drawers for a single bullet. He pulled down the contents of shelves. He emptied boxes and drawers. Sense left him. Finally, he found the box and loaded a single, high-explosive snub round. Duke Falkeep placed the pistol's barrel in his mouth. The metal was still hot against his lips. He put his thumbs on the trigger and tried to pull it. He couldn't do it. He tried to use one thumb to lever the other. In disgust, he threw the gun away and put his head in his hands.

After a long time he looked up. He picked up his favorite picture of his child, his daughter, his Tamar. She was ten, a stringy girl carrying books and a portable computer out into the garden. She was exploring. He was about to crush it in his hands, but he grasped it suddenly to his bosom. His eyes, unaccustomed to tears, overflowed. With great sobs, he mourned the loss of the little girl, his daughter. He mourned the loss of her innocence. He was overwhelmed by remorse for his actions. How could he have treated his own child like that? She was still his child, no matter what she did. In his mind, he saw over and over her fear, fear of him, her pain, caused by him, her blood, flowing black and copious at his feet.

Until the first light of the sun finally entered the room and filled it, Duke Falkeep stayed behind the locked door and yearned for the past.

The knock the Duke expected came. He slowly rose to his feet. Groggily, the events of the evening came back to the Duke.

His eldest son, George, called through the thick portal, "Father. Father! Are you all right?"

"Yes. Yes," wearily. The Duke opened the door. He shouldered his astonished son out of the way and returned to his rooms to shower and change.

After Duke James Falkeep dressed, he walked down to the large dining room. His sons were waiting for him. At his appearance, they stared at one another, confused and concerned.

"Father, what's going on?"

Were they so stupid that they knew nothing of the evening's confrontation? He waved them to silence and took his position at the head of the table. Together, the three of them looked like a judicial tribunal. Duke Falkeep cleared the thought from his mind. He composed himself. He was at war internally. He knew his duty, and his love of honor and Nobility compelled him to act. His responsibility was to face this embarrassment, to weed it out, to punish it, and to be finished with it. But his love of family and his love for Tamar also compelled him to mercy. His heart broke as he said, "Send for Matron Maria, immediately." His voice did not betray his feelings. It was as strong and certain as ever.

His sons again registered confusion. A servant relayed the message, and soon Maria stood before them.

"Tell the Lady Tamar Falkeep that I will grant her a boon. Within the next thirty minutes, I am prepared to give her a private audience." *Any excuse*, he thought. *I grasp for any reason not to continue.* His mind was in anguish, while his body felt like a block of ice.

"Begging your pardon, my lord," stuttered Matron Maria, "I don't think she is well enough to appear before you."

He cut off Maria's gentle defiance. "Make her well enough then," barked the Duke.

"Yes, my lord."

Oh dear Lord, the thought rushed into the Duke's mind, *that was my excuse.*

"Father," started his elder son, George. With a commanding motion of his hand, the Duke cut off his son's protests again.

Falkeep kept his head and eyes level. His sons sat rock still; they had never seen their father like this. He was well beyond anger or rage. He was filled with a deadly resignation.

Within fifteen minutes, the Lady Tamar appeared at the top of the wide stairs. On either side, Maria and Dulcia steadied her steps. Tamar limped, and as she stepped closer to them, her brothers saw her face was slashed and bruised. She wore a long-sleeved dress of brilliant silk, but the sleeves could not entirely cover the burn on her arm. Her wounds still bled, and random splatters flawed the dress. She was deadly pale and obviously in pain. Her beautiful face was so swollen and colored that, from a distance, the Duke would not have immediately recognized her.

Her brothers knew who had marked her. They knew the general events of the evening. His heart sinking, the younger turned his face from her. He feared for his little sister. They were embarrassed for their father, embarrassed for their family, and not sure they felt anything but loyalty for their sister. As she entered the room, the two of them stood.

Tamar stepped boldly to the table. She faced them across the length of it. Duke Falkeep waved away the serving women, and that left Tamar standing alone.

"May I please sit down, Father?" She looked as if in the next moment she would collapse. After a brief hesitation, George, her elder brother, walked around the table, pulled out a chair, and seated her. She gazed gratefully up at him. The Duke glared at his son. Then the brothers seated themselves.

No one spoke or moved for a long time. Then the Duke began.

"You know why you have earned the disfavor of this House, Lady Tamar. You know the concern you caused us. After you ran away, we searched the entire city for three days to find you. In our concern, we even applied to the Empire for the right to search the spaceport for you. Because of that, the Empire knows House Falkeep cannot keep track of its own children. You betrayed our trust; you gave away to lust the honor of our House. It did not belong to you, Lady Tamar. It was not yours to give away."

Tamar sat solidly in her chair. Her brothers saw, though she didn't make a sound or move, that she trembled, and her eyes blinked bright tears that ran across the light swell of her cheeks.

The Duke did not appear to notice any of this. He paused, as if to let the meaning of his rebuke sink in, then continued, "I felt such anxiety at your loss last night. I so wanted to open your door and see you there, like a child once again. The moonlight bedazzled my eyes, but I saw you there. You were safe. You returned. My heart, at first, overflowed with joy; the next moment it filled with foreboding. Your seducer lay with you in your bed, in this very house."

He stopped, his voice choked with rage. "I would have wrested our honor back to us. The event could be explained as rape or coercion. For you, I, your subjects would believe instantly that was the truth. I would have returned your honor by killing the man who'd taken you, but you—you protected him," he spat. "Even in the shame of your exposure, you leapt to stop me from harming the villain. You stood unashamed and naked to the whole world while you cried out your love for this less than noble."

A slight sob shook Tamar, and she bit her lip.

"Do you know how to return the honor to our House?" His eyes locked on hers. "Can you undo the damage you wrought in our hearts and to our integrity?" He stood up. "You cannot. You selfishly betrayed our Nobility."

Tamar sat stoically, and for Tamar, unusually quiet.

She is unashamed, thought her younger brother, Roger. He fidgeted with a speck on the table. *And she is taking this better than we are.* Roger looked nervously at her, and in her eyes saw the explanation. She hid something. Tamar was always the best with secrets, but what would she conceal with her whole honor? In her actions she revealed to the world the greatest shame to the honor of any noble woman— something was not right, something was left unsaid. In Roger's mind, Tamar's eyes begged him for understanding. Roger felt a righteous pride in his sister, an extension of integrity that clashed with the unjust way their father had attacked her. She took this sour medicine without complaint. Why?

"Father," Roger butted in lamely, "Father." He ignored the glare and signal. "Let Tamar speak. Let her tell her side."

"No!" cried Tamar. The eyes of all three stared with unbelief at her. "Never." She trembled, then stated more loudly, "There is nothing to explain. I have nothing to say."

Dumbfounded, the brothers looked at one another. *If that is so,* they thought together, *this is the first time.* She looked like a tragic character. Slight already, she seemed to shrink before them and become small and helpless. Her face was filled with misery. In her features they saw pain overlaid with more pain and a bereavement they knew had nothing to do with her virginity.

"Father, this is enough," continued Roger.

"It is enough for you, Sir Roger Falkeep. You may leave." The Duke turned back to his daughter.

"Father, stop this, please." Roger Falkeep stood.

Coldly, the Duke answered him, "That is quite enough. You are dismissed already. Don't risk my further displeasure, or I will have you removed."

About to protest again, he caught his brother's warning look; Roger bowed and began to back from the room. As he straightened, something caught his eye. His sister rarely wore jewelry, yet on Tamar's hand, or was it clutched in her hand, she held a ring. Roger caught another glimpse of it as he backed from the table. It looked too large for a woman's ring.

George noted Roger's stare. Tamar nervously placed that hand on the table, and George saw the ring too. She grasped the facing in her palm, but the band was large enough that it looked incongruous on her slim hand.

Tamar glanced fearfully at them both and put the hand back under the table. Roger continued to back through the door. As he closed it, he heard his father start in again.

Perplexed, Roger stood in front of the ornate door. What was going on here? Tamar was hiding something. For some reason, she quietly accepted everything their father could hurt her with. Was she protecting someone they knew? Was she really a tramp all this time? In his heart, he knew that wasn't so. Why did she sit there and let the Duke continue emotionally the injury he started physically six hours ago?

As Roger stood lost in thought, he noticed not five meters from him Dulcia and the Matron Maria.

Dulcia cried softly over and over, "My poor mistress. My mistress."

Maria seemed in a different state. She wrung her hands so intensely they were blue and scalded red at the same time. An extreme indecision filled her face as she stared at Roger. Then, as if making up her mind about something, Maria came over to him. She sighed, as if relieved, but didn't say anything.

"Go ahead, Maria," he prompted her.

"Sir Roger," she began, "I have something that might be important to the Lady Tamar..."

When she didn't continue, Roger continued for her, "You found something she might not want others to see, but you think could help her with the Duke?" He said this slowly and watched her nod agreement to his words.

"I wouldn't want it to hurt her further, sir," she stammered.

"Let me see it." He opened his hand. "I'll make sure it will only help her."

"I found this folded up in her jewelry box. I think she meant to hide it." Maria removed a stained cloth napkin and a signet ring from her pocket and ceremoniously placed it in Roger's hands.

Roger delicately opened the cloth, and what he read instantly amazed and beguiled him. "That sly wench." He grinned under his breath. "That crazy child. That woman. Tamar, you are unbelievable. If I ever father a child of half your wit..."

Roger burst through the dining room door. He held the cloth like a holy symbol before him. The three at the table turned to look at him.

66

His brother, George, frowned with a "well, now you've done it" look. His father's scowl threatened that Roger would be next. Tamar showed a different aspect altogether.

"No!" Tamar screamed, "No, don't." She lunged at the fluttering napkin and almost fell on her face, but Roger caught her by the arm. Tamar writhed in his grasp and almost threw herself to the floor. "Give it to me. It's mine." For the first time since she came into the room, she burst into forlorn tears. "Please, Roger, as you love me, don't—don't let the words be known." She saw her entreaty was hopeless. Tamar folded her head in her arms and sobbed as he had never seen her cry.

"I'm sorry, Tamar, but I can't let you be hurt like this. I know you hid these for a reason, but your secret cannot match the humiliation we are putting our family and House through."

"Please," she pleaded.

"What are you doing, Roger?" yelled the Duke.

"Father, I am righting a terrible wrong."

"What reason can you give that would change anything that has happened? What honor can be found in her defilement? What logic will justify the end?"

"A pledge of love," she answered his statement, quietly.

Duke Falkeep was taken aback. Unconvinced, he started in again, "No, you mean lust. She dishonored our House. She blatantly paraded her dishonor before our House. Lady Tamar, are you not shamed?"

She answered him in the same quiet voice as before. "No, Father. No, I am not. I am proud."

Roger placed the cloth reverently on the table. "Father, she is not dishonored; she sits before us in great honor. She is pledged!"

The Duke looked at him, astonished. Roger's eyes filled with triumph. Tamar took off the ring and with a light clink laid it on the table before her father. Roger placed the other signet ring beside it.

The Duke stared at Tamar. "This is the sigil of the House Rathenberg, and beside it lays the Emperor's signet ring." An anguished fear replaced his rage. "What does this mean?" He glanced at his youngest son again.

Roger pointed at the stained napkin on the table. Duke Falkeep glanced down and read the simple contract on the cloth. He bowed his head lower and lower toward the table as he read the pledge. "Why? Why? Why didn't you tell me, my child?" His voice was full of regret, filled with sorrow.

She caught her breath. "I didn't think you would approve. He has no inheritance. He is nothing in the Empire."

"Tamar," he pleaded, "Prince Devon Rathenberg is a bulwark of our beliefs, of our strength. I would love him as I love you."

"I thought you would never acknowledge him. You have yet to decide which or any faction to join—the Emperor Perodus or the banned Houses. I know on which side he fights. I feared you would choose another."

After a prolonged silence, Duke Falkeep spoke. "My child Tamar, I am no longer worthy to be called your father. I know you can never forgive me for the way I treated you." His words were full of sorrow, the depths of a hard and troubled heart drifted from the tearful confession.

Tamar stood. Her brothers came around the table to help her. She limped to her father's side and put her arms around him. She held him tightly. "Father, I love you, and I forgive you. Please don't blame yourself. You reacted as a father should. Please stop. I will be healed with time. My husband escaped into safety. You have not permanently hurt me or our family."

"My child, I can never make amends. I thank you. I thank you from the depths of my old and foolish heart." He raised his head to stare at her in amazement. He kissed her forehead. "I can do little to reconcile, but I can give you this." He took a pen from his pocket and signed his name below hers on the pledge. "On Arienth, I will stand for you and this man. I will do more. Today I join with the banned Houses. I will live or die for your noble Sir Rathenberg. I know the man. I know his family. You could not pledge yourself or our House to a more noble family."

He looked at his oldest son. "Prepare our forces to attack Count Yedric's holdings. He is no longer any vassal of mine." He looked at his younger son. "Take one of our ships. Proceed immediately to find Sir Devon Rathenberg, and inform him that he is one of our family. Find him and with your life protect him so that he will someday return to my Tamar's smile."

"Thank you, Father, thank you," Tamar could only cry.

James, the Duke of Falkeep stood up slowly, and lifting up his daughter, held her in his arms. Speaking softly as he could with a voice worn through care, he gently took her to her room and saw her to her bed. His eyes promised what his lips could barely speak. He kissed her forehead again, and as the Lady Tamar Falkeep Rathenberg fell into exhausted sleep, her last memory was her father's gentle caress across her cheek.

Ten

As he ran naked from the mansion, Sir Devon Rathenberg thought he was extremely lucky he left his luggage in the gravcar. Brush whipped against him as he cut directly through the gardens. When he fell from the window, he slammed his freshly healed arm against the ground, and he was in excruciating pain. Without thinking, Devon used that side of his shoulder to cushion his fall. He also bled from a cut on his shoulder but not seriously.

Devon had hidden the gravvehicle in the brush next to the front drive, and in his haste, he ran past it. He scrambled back along the drive and plunged into the brush again. He heaved an inadvertent sigh of pain and relief when he finally scraped his knees against the body of the car. With every expectation that in an attempt to capture him, the Duke would deploy his household guards, Devon took only the time to put on a pair of pants. Then he quickly started the car, backed it out of the woods, and headed back toward the city. He applied every ruse and shortcut he knew to throw off immediate pursuit and was rewarded by easily making the port city.

As Devon drove through the city, he noticed the Duke's forces along many streets. Until just moments ago, they concentrated on the search for Tamar. With his military trained experience, Devon could see they were being alerted to look for him. He could imagine their instructions: stop a man of unknown quality and unknown appearance, and that order came after they were on the alert for Tamar the last three days. Predictably, they were in utter confusion.

Near the spaceport, in the cramped confines of the gravvehicle, Devon threw on the rest of his clothing. Fully dressed, he abandoned the car and processed with his baggage through the port authority as Sir Devon de Tieg. He counted himself lucky to slip through without arousing any suspicions.

For the moment, Devon felt safe in the port. If Duke Falkeep ordered his troops to enter the spaceport without proper approval, that would be the equivalent of a declaration of war against the Emperor. Approval would take the Duke at least two days of gentle negotiation. Devon estimated he had a full twenty-four hours.

Devon took less than half that time to get his arm checked at the port hospital and sign himself on a military space available flight to Arienth. He presented himself under the forged identity of Sir Devon de Tieg from Greyholm. Devon was certain the deception would gain him the priority he needed to get to the Imperial Capital, Arienth, without arousing the suspicions of the Emperor's forces or revealing himself to Duke Falkeep.

As Sir Devon boarded the military orbital shuttle, his mind was entirely on Tamar; he had no idea what was happening to her. He hated leaving her like this, but he was absolutely sure of her security; she would be safe with her family. She would possibly face some rejection from them, but his life and his self-imposed mission for their newly declared alliance meant as much to her as it did to him.

He missed her as he missed no one in his life. He loved her. She was a breath of fresh air to him. In all the universe Devon could not imagine another woman he desired to entrust with his love. Devon thought of his father's reaction when he learned of their marriage, and he smiled a rueful grin. When Devon was safely seated aboard the shuttle, he closed his eyes, and half thinking, half asleep; he remained in that position until the shuttle docked with the courier ship that would take him to the Imperial planet.

Because of his rank, the skipper allotted Devon a cabin of his own on the small ship. The ship had a few stops to make before it reached orbit around Arienth, but Devon was not in a hurry. Give Yedric time to get comfortable in the retinue of the Emperor. Devon was sure that the House Neuterra would contest hotly and militarily its deposement to Yedric. It would be a long time before the traitorous Count felt Neuterra under his feet—if ever.

The courier ship, *Saint Anne,* was small, but Devon was used to space travel and found many ways to occupy his time. The skipper was an excellent swordsman, and they practiced fiercely whenever they had time. The first officer had a bent toward shooting, and using laser-targeting pistols, he and Devon competed heatedly simulating all types of armament. Devon also worked with his own weapons: he reequipped himself with a plasmasword and snub pistol, and adjusted them to his exacting requirements.

In spite of his activity, the intersystem travel still took a long time. New thoughts and emotions dogged him that he had never felt before. Devon knew the loss of Tamar like a physical pain. Each day and night he felt the desire to hold her in his arms. His mind, unbidden, recalled vividly their gentle days of loving together. He could not forget their parting, yet he was absolutely sure no harm befell her. Devon couldn't imagine that Duke Falkeep would hurt Tamar in any way. Still his heart beat fiercely for her, and it was only with physical and mental exercise that he could control his anguish and desire.

Devon almost thought his resolve to avenge himself on the Count had diminished; the urge to return immediately to Falkeep took its place. He constrained himself with the knowledge that grave harm would befall both House Rathenberg and Falkeep if he didn't achieve his mission. In any case, he planned everything carefully: he knew exactly how he would kill Count Yedric. The only problem was that to survive, he needed some help.

The *Saint Anne* stopped at Desira and was diverted on a priority courier run. Since no other ship was at Desira, Devon continued with the craft, hoping it would soon set course for Arienth.

They were again diverted when they reached Pandora, this time to Fehrcain. At Fehrcain, Devon was relieved that the crew received high enough priority messages to require an immediate departure for Arienth.

During this leg of the voyage, Devon made use of the excellent relationship he cultivated with the skipper and first officer to discover the contents of the messages the ship was carrying. If they realized

Devon's intentions, the men were honest enough officers that they would never have approved of Devon's spying. Devon's gentlemanliness and rank deceived them; after all, that was why he was the Emperor's Chief of Intelligence. If they understood their guest was Devon Rathenberg, they might have taken bolder precautions.

Devon used his equipment to break into the ship's safes. In his own computer he stored a majority of the Imperial security codes, so with ease, he opened the safes, removed the chips and laser discs that contained the documents, and broke the codes on the seals. He recorded the messages on his own equipment and decoded a sample to see what secrets they held. The content was militarily critical and contained the Emperor's battle plans, rendezvous points, and formations. As soon as his own mission was complete, he must find a way to pass on these secrets to his alliance.

Many of the texts listed the actual alliances of a large number of the Houses in the Empire along with an enumeration of their assets and possessions. This would be enlightening from both a military and a propaganda standpoint; the documents could point out the lack of strength of their enemies, as well as evidence the power of their own forces. And, it would give the banned Houses the names of the rest of the families in the Landsritters willing to support their rebellion. This was critically important information, mused Devon.

He carefully rearranged the messages so that the Houses named for and against the Emperor were listed randomly from the original information. He further changed the inventories of House possessions so they showed more power in the hands of those aligned with the Empire. Devon resealed the messages and undetected, returned them all to the ship's safe. No blame would fall on the crew; who could ever guess that the man who originally approved these very security codes would have traveled via this ship. He laughed at the thought and chuckled at the consternation the eventual discovery of the falsification of the messages would cause.

Finally, at the edge of the Arienth system, the ship came out of null space, and the crew activated the main drives to propel them to the planet Arienth. Within a day, the planet, surrounded by its triple rings and three moons came into visible range of the ship's scanners. It was beautiful. *Like coming home,* thought Devon. He realized suddenly, though, that Arienth was no longer his home. He sighed and wished again that Tamar were with him.

The ship fell into a breaking orbit, and tiptoed through the battery of sign and countersign that electronically identified the vehicle as an ally. Devon wondered whether the Emperor's forces had thought to change these codes. If not, he could, in theory, lead an attack tomorrow on the Emperor's own palace.

They entered the atmosphere and rapidly approached the city of Arienth, Capital of the Human Empire. Already from his vantage-point on the bridge, Devon could distinguish the tower of the Hall of Accords. Slowly, the massive shape of the Galactic Library came into sight, and dwarfed by the size of the other two, at the apex of the triangle of Library and Hall, the Imperial Palace came into view.

The courier ship made a long turn around Arienth, and at the edge of the enormous city of Arienth, the spaceport filled the viewscreen. The lack of activity at the port astounded Devon. Devon had not noticed any of the sleek destroyers or battleships at the orbital port either. The system was stripped of protection. The Emperor must be using the fleet for some purpose other than his own defense. Devon must get this information to the alliance of banned Houses. If they could make a single attack on the Capital and take the Emperor that would immediately avert the oncoming war. He must get his business done and bring a report to Neuterra's forces as soon as possible. But what if the fleet should return while he was gone? Could he possibly revise his plans and take the Emperor himself?

Security would be intense and provided by Huscarls, the Emperor's traditional guard. There were difficulties surrounding such plans, but Devon had been the Chief of Emperor Maricus' Intelligence. He could succeed, assuming the new Emperor was planetside. The Emperor might be with the fleet, though Devon didn't think the cowardly Perodus would leave the protection of his Capital.

Where Perodus was, Yedric would be also. Devon smiled cruelly; if the Count, now Duke Yedric, were not on the Planet, Devon would simply wait for him. The fleet and the Emperor would have to return eventually. That is, if the Emperor were able to return. His smile broadened at the thought.

The ship set down gently on the runway and Sir Devon Rathenberg went to his cabin to prepare to deplane. His thoughts were solemn; he solidified his plans with the intensity that originally made the young knight a man of reckoning in the Empire. The Emperor's Young Fox was ready for action.

Eleven

Roger Falkeep quickly mobilized his father's forces to find the errant knight Devon Rathenberg. However, the young Falkeep's search was unsuccessful. With the assistance of Falkeep's security forces, he traced the path of the knight after he arrived at the spaceport and discovered he used the name Sir Devon de Tieg. Because Roger didn't want to give away the true name of the knight or let the port's Imperial personnel know Duke Falkeep's plans, his inquiries were discreet. Even so, it only took him a few hours to determine Sir Devon left on an Imperial courier ship. Discouraged, Roger reported to his father. The time for geniality was over.

Sir Roger made a personal visit to Baron Herstet, the Emperor's spaceport administrator. Three of Falkeep's combat soldiers accompanied Roger. Baron Herstet was a large man of a stern disposition. When Roger entered the Baron's office, Herstet simply waved the younger Falkeep to a seat and continued his viewphone conversation. After five minutes, Roger received an encoded signal on his communicator from his elder brother. That indicated the spaceport was entirely cut off and their fleet had taken the orbital port. Baron Herstet's viewer suddenly went blank.

"Hey, vat's dat," snarled the Baron. He yelled at his secretary, "Get me repair, right now." When she didn't respond, he stared at Roger and seemed to notice him for the first time, "Vell, vat are you smiling about, young Roger?"

"I'm sorry, my lord Baron, but repair won't do you any good. My brother George cut off your communications."

"Vell it's about time. I'd hoped you'd been here yesterday." The Baron stood up and proffered his large paw-like hand toward Roger. "I'm a retainer of Duke Rathenberg. I am at your service. Tell your vater dat I vill gladly swear my fealty to him. And dat he doesn't have to pay de land'n fees anymore if he gives me back my communications in de next ten minutes."

With a broad smile, Roger took the offered hand and clasped it. The Baron gave back a wide smile, and with a firm shake released Roger's hand and turned again to the viewer.

Roger called up his brother on his communicator. In a few moments, with a crackle of static, Baron Herstet's viewer snapped on.

"Dat's better," beamed the Baron. "I don't dink dis cost us even a single credit in lost time, but I'll tell you later ven I can figure the numbers out myself." The Baron turned a rueful eye toward Roger. "Go on. You've done vat you needed to do. It's possibly cost us some money, but vat's done is done."

"Baron, we have another problem I think you can help us solve. This must be kept in utmost secrecy."

The Baron nodded impatiently and was about to speak, but Roger cut him off, "Sir Devon Rathenberg was on this planet for almost a week. I was trying to intercept him just before he left on an Imperial courier. It's possible he is in terrible danger."

The Baron's face showed a great deal more affinity. "De Duke's very son. De young Lord Rathenberg here, und his vater never knew about dat. He spoke to me himself."

"Baron, I need a fast ship prepared immediately for a trip to Arienth."

"Yah, you certainly can't go in a Falkeep Navel ship. Dat vould give you avay fur sure." He turned to the viewer and typed in a query and some instructions. "Dere. De fastest ship right now on the port is dis Imperial corvette dat ve ver put'n back togeder. I dink you could get the codes and such from de computers und..."

"Baron, I can't go to Arienth in a Falkeep Navel ship or in an Imperial corvette. Do you have a fast civilian yacht in port?"

"Yah, your right der, young Falkeep, but you can't go tak'n da ship from de civilians. Dat's just not good business."

"Baron, we are talking about the life of Sir Devon Rathenberg."

"Yah, Yah. Okay, you've convinced me. I dink you might even be able to smood dings out mit a little bit of compensation fur der owner."

"My father will be agreeable to any suggestion you make that will provide for the undisturbed operation of the spaceport; however, let me warn you, Baron, we are currently at war with the Emperor. Your responsibility, along with seeing to the operations of the spaceport will be to actively prosecute this war. You are authorized to act as the representative of Duke Falkeep as necessity demands. He will judge your actions in relation to his own policy, not to any other policy."

"Okay, Okay. You make yourself quite clear. I understand very vell. De ship, *Silent Dawn*, a fast yacht, vill be ready for your boarding tonight. I vill take care of de owner myself. You can be assured, my young Falkeep."

Roger stood and bowed to the Baron, then he signaled his men and left. Before they were out of the door the Baron had already turned his attention back to his viewscreen.

Sir Roger Falkeep maintained no foolish ideas about rushing to Devon Rathenberg's rescue. He only wanted to make contact with the knight and tell him that his father accepted his suit. His father also placed on Roger the responsibility of reaching Duke Neuterra with the news that Falkeep cast its lot with the banned Houses. After that, by his father's orders, he was to provide his expertise in any way Duke Neuterra required in support of the rebellion. His father also imposed on him the requirement of fealty to Devon Rathenberg. The Duke ordered Roger in the capacity of a brother and retainer to the knight to provide any help he could. Roger was only too glad to have that responsibility; although he believed the knight would never remember him, he had worked with Devon Rathenberg before.

They attended the Royal academy together. Devon was an upperclassman and Roger fell under his authority in the Ruby Battalion.

Devon's leadership and wisdom saved many of the cadets from academic and military grief. But, in addition, Devon protected the young Falkeep from dismissal after he started a fight in defense of his sister Tamar's honor.

Due to uprisings on planets close to the Fringe, during that time, just as today, tensions ran high in the Landsritters. Neuterra and Acier promoted united action against the uprisings rather than the Emperor's use of the Imperial Huscarls. Because of their advice, they were unpopular with a large contingent of the more conservative Houses. The Lady Lyral Neuterra, as the highest-ranking permanent representative of House Neuterra on Arienth, along with her friends, became the brunt of unkind rumor started by the junior members of those conservative Houses. Most of the comments came from the unthinking lips of sons and daughters attending schools on Arienth. Because of the power of Duke Neuterra, however, none of them were about to attack the Lady Lyral directly. The Lady Tamar, unfortunately as Lyral's best friend, became the victim of much of this gossip. It was also unfortunate that Tamar and Lyral were both unnaturally gifted in the art of political manipulation, for by way of sabotage and revenge, they were well able to take care of any rumor, gossip, or comment.

Together, through subterfuge, they were highly capable of applying whatever force was required to embarrass and have banished from Arienth whoever insulted them. So successful were they that their abilities had even come to the attention of Emperor Maricus. He was especially interested when he found out the son of a major holder was banished for something he could not have done. The Emperor looked into the matter further and found that in a gigantic push to rid the planet of this holder's son, someone manipulated events and records up to the Imperial level. When his investigators sifted through all the evidence, he found the only crime this young man committed was that at an Autumn dance, he made numerous unkind and derogatory remarks concerning the Lady Tamar and Lyral. The young man displayed a habit of obnoxious behavior, but the Emperor recalled him to the academy, and that is where Maricus made a mistake he later regretted.

The holder's son, in revenge for the wrong he attributed, quite correctly to the Lady Tamar and Lyral, tried to physically accost the Lady Tamar. Before he laid a hand on the lady, however, Cadet Roger Falkeep, her brother, came to Tamar's rescue. The fight that ensued was not pretty and numerous cadets on one side or the other joined into the brawl. The Emperor was forced to send the holder's son home again. Roger Falkeep came up before a disciplinary board, but Roger's cadet commander, Devon Rathenberg, ridiculed the charges against him, and by his testimony the young Falkeep received probation.

What none of them realized was the Emperor's interest in the events. Through his intelligence corps, the late Emperor Maricus put a close watch on the Lady Lyral and Tamar. He enjoyed the reports almost as much as he liked the theater. He was convinced that "those girls," as he habitually called them, would end up controlling the Empire one day.

So, though Devon might not recognize Roger, Roger recognized Devon as his chief benefactor.

Roger accepted his current assignment with delight. He felt a burden of responsibility toward Devon that he'd never discharged. On commission from his father, with the intention of taking off alone for Arienth, Roger commandeered the *Silent Dawn*. The "alone" part required extensive discussion with Duke Falkeep. Roger's father finally allowed logic to overcome his natural inclinations and let Roger go by himself.

The ship was perfect for his requirements. It was a rakish yacht and very powerful for a civilian ship. It had comfortable accommodations and was operable by a single crewmember. At the academy and in his father's forces, Roger had trained as an intersystem naval pilot. His commanders considered him an excellent small vessel skipper, and he dreamed of someday commanding a large Imperial Navy ship.

The *Silent Dawn* was built like a modern military escort vessel. The basic form of the ship was common to most small craft of the time. The vessel was cigar-shaped. Its long nose protruded from a large ventral scoop. At the scoop, the body expanded into the main volume of the ship and curved back to the fusion engines and primary gravgrids.

The nose of the ship contained the cockpit crew stations, forward sensors, emergency reaction thrusters, and small maneuvering gravgrids. The main portion of the *Silent Dawn*'s fuselage contained four staterooms, a combination common room and recreation center, and the cargo bay. The ship's ventral scoop supplied two important functions: first, it allowed the vessel to refuel by skimming the atmosphere of a gas giant, and second, for atmospheric maneuvering, it provided the pneumatic source for the vortex generators.

The ship was designed for gravitational as well as unassisted letdown, so in addition to the large gravgrids under the scoop, it was vortex-streamlined. To aid atmospheric reentry, electropneumatic vortex generators protected the ship. These stuck out at varying lengths of a decimeter to a meter from the fuselage and covered the primary reentry surfaces of the ship. Unlike earlier ships that depended on insulation and aerodynamic streamlining, the *Silent Dawn* used the vortex generators to dissipate heat and develop an insulating boundary-layer. The fins of the generators did both; they were made of superconducting composites to dissipate the heat and shaped to a precise aerodynamic design. Further, the computer-directed air flow on and around the fins increased the aerodynamic efficiency of the surfaces they covered nearly a thousandfold. So, in addition to protecting the ship from the forces of atmospheric reentry, the generators produced an amazing amount of lift. The pilot could maneuver the *Silent Dawn* for landing automatically, using the main gravgrids, or manually, using vortex-generated lift. In the unlikely instance the ship reentered without electrical power, the mechanical vortex generators would protect the vessel until an emergency venturi turbine produced enough power to run the electropneumatic systems.

Manual landing using vortex lift was once considered only an emergency or military procedure. Now, to save fuel and gravgrid life, it was quickly becoming a common practice with civilian ships. Manual landing required an approach similar to that used by ancient Terran fixed wing shuttles. The vessel fell through the atmosphere until the vortex generators had enough air pressure to operate; after that the pilot maneuvered the ship with vortex flow. As long as the ship remained above stall speed, the vortex generators provided sufficient lift and the ship could accomplish extensive maneuvering. If the pilot let the ship get near a stall, the computer would automatically activate the gravgrids to provide necessary maneuvering and lift. The common landing pattern for populated planets was a high-speed aerodynamic approach to a gravgrid set down. The military and occasionally civilian pilots would take the approach down to a full aerodynamic landing on a shuttle landing strip, but this was considered an act of daring.

Most planet-fall-capable military vessels were equipped like the *Silent Dawn*, and they were shaped similarly but on a much larger scale. The Empire designated these ships escort class and below.

The next larger class of ships was labeled the Capital class. By definition, Capital ships were never intended for planetary landing and their exteriors were designed primarily for crew protection and battle functionality. They sported immense armor and power-producing structures all put together for the sole purpose of acceleration and extended battle.

The smallest class of Capital ship was the destroyer. It was designed for planetary attack and to battle other Capital ships. Unlike larger Capital ships, it could enter an atmosphere to bombard the planet or to refuel by skimming, but it was not designed to touch down on the planet's surface.

Like its larger sisters, the problem with the destroyer was size. The structure of all the Capital ships was so large that while under acceleration stresses, only exact computer control of their gravity dampers could prevent them from coming apart. Destroyers, because of their planetary attack role had another problem: when in an atmosphere, their structures, required internal pressure to compensate for the pressure of the atmosphere. Normally, all spacecraft entered combat depressurized with the crew in vacuum suits. In the vacuum of space, a large enough hole in a pressurized ship could cause the failure of the entire exostructure, but when a ship is in an atmosphere the opposite is true, internal pressure provides support and limits the effect of rapid decompression. Destroyers remained pressurized while making a planetary assault, and if it was ambushed in the atmosphere, it could easily be destroyed.

In orbit, the Capital ships were attended by their own escorts, intrasystem shuttles, and orbital ports, the special component of most modern spaceports.

Roger let the *Silent Dawn* run through her prelaunch sequence: tests, diagnostic and mechanical, were made of the entire control and operating systems. The entire sequence required 24 hours and during that time, Roger convinced his father to let him go alone, packed his clothing and essential equipment on the ship, and rebuffed Tamar's poignant appeal to accompany him.

Amid preparations for his brother, George's assault on Yedric's planet, Gran Stern, the available family came to see him off. With an admonition to propriety and wisdom, his father kissed him with more emotion than Roger ever remembered.

Tamar tendered him with a stony glance that Roger knew concealed her fear and disappointment, but she finally broke down and held him for a moment. Her smile, further disarranged by the bruises on her face was askew in an unsuccessful attempt to mask her tears. She wished him a throaty farewell, which he responded to with a gentle kiss. "I promise you, Tamar: I will find your suitor and lord, Devon Rathenberg. Don't fear."

Tamar pressed the Imperial Signet ring into Roger's palm and closed his fingers around it. "My lord may need this."

Roger tendered her a wry smile. "I will hand it to him myself."

Tamar nodded, and Roger turned to walk over the damp permacrete to his glistening ship.

As he stepped aboard the *Silent Dawn* and sealed her, Roger felt a rush of freedom and excitement like none he'd known before. He walked boldly across the Velcro carpeted deck through the pressure doors into the cockpit. On most military ships the cockpit or bridge, was placed either deep inside the fuselage or at the thick juncture of the nose and the scoop. The nose normally held passive sensor equipment that needed to be isolated from the rest of the ship and the forward weapons systems. On this ship, the nose was the bridge. As an embellishment and to save on the cost of electronics, like the windshields of simple atmospheric craft, the front top of the bridge was clear ceriplast.

Filled with elation, Roger sat at the left-hand controls. He felt strange not to have an astrogator at the right-hand controls and an engineer behind him. This ship contained positions for the extra crewmembers, but they were not required. He spent part of the 24 hours before the ship was ready, studying the ship's operations manuals, and though this ship was not much different than those he was used to, he still felt excitement born of unfamiliarity and anticipation.

Roger touched the instrument panel, and the ship awoke into instant activity. Screens displayed the systems' status: those systems operating normally, those under self-repair, and those requiring port maintenance. Though a few systems, all unnecessary for normal operations were down, the ship was ready for an extended intersystem flight. He started the activation of the ship's basic systems and checked to see they reported back normally. The ship already ran through all this in its prelaunch tests, but Roger was a cautious pilot, and he wanted to reassure himself the ship was ready. He ran the fusion reactors up to their full capacity then requested departure clearance. The controller released him and gave him a system escape orbit, then cleared him to takeoff.

Roger activated the gravgrids and vortex generators. With a growling whine, the pneumatic system kicked in, and he felt the controls come alive. With a gentle pull on the control stick on his right armrest and a push forward on the power lever on his left, the ship began to slowly rise. Roger adjusted the thrust vector with the power lever and sent the ship skimming out and up from the port. The gravgrids cut out immediately, and Roger could hear and feel the rumbling strength of the vortex generators lifting him and the Silent Dawn into orbit. At the legal acceleration altitude, he increased the thrust to full power, and for one moment, he slammed the ship into full vortex lift. As the atmosphere became thinner and then nonexistent, he cut in full gravgrid lift. As he cleft the ionosphere, Falkeep fell away from him, and the naked stars seemed to burn all the brighter as he sped in his departure path toward them.

Twelve

"Duke Yedric of the Duchy of Neuterra," announced the Emperor's seneschal, Count Rathenberg.

"Greetings, my lord Duke." The Emperor Perodus emphasized the title as the erstwhile Count approached his throne.

"Your Majesty, for your generous boon, I thank you from the bottom of my heart." Yedric bowed.

"It was my pleasure." The Emperor nodded. "Secure the throne room Rathenberg. I want to speak in privacy with my new counselor."

"Yes, your Majesty." Rathenberg directed the Imperial Marines around the magnificent chamber to secure the doors, check for uninvited electronic surveillance, and post the guards. The room took a while to secure, but the Emperor felt himself overborne by Yedric during their previous discussions. Now that Perodus had been confirmed, he did not want Yedric to take his Imperial power too lightly. The throne room with its trophies and Imperial magnificence, along with Perodus in his majestic robes should counter the threat of Yedric's arrogance and defiance. Sealing the room would further prevent any rumor of his confrontation with the Duke, should the environment not prove to be awe-inspiring enough.

While they waited for Count Rathenberg's report of the room's security, Perodus offered wine and sweetmeats to the new Duke.

Yedric was not so dim that he did not understand the posturing of the new Emperor. He would be very careful with Perodus.

"Sire, the room is secure."

"Thank you, chancellor."

The Count bowed.

"Now, my Lord Yedric, what news do you bring of our preparations?"

"First, your majesty, the Imperial Navy is outfitted and ready for orders. Second, my holders and forces are enroute to the arranged rendezvous point. They left my County, Gran Stern, little more than a week after I did. Third, our support in the Landsritters grows by the day. Already, of the Thirty Kingdoms, eleven stand under our banner, although five of those have not committed their forces. Eleven kingdoms should easily counter the ten that were banned. Finally, Prince Devon Rathenberg is dead."

The Emperor's eyes widened. "The Young Fox is dead?"

"Yes," continued Yedric with a feral grin. "The son of Duke Rathenberg is dead."

The Emperor smiled. "I hope you saw him dead yourself; the Fox was not my father's Chief of Intelligence for nothing."

"Devon Rathenberg challenged me to a duel. I killed him in single combat. I saw him lying, unbreathing and lifeless, before me."

"My Lord Yedric, you have indeed brought welcome news to me. With the young Rathenberg dead and John-Mark separated from the Huscarls, my two greatest thorns are removed. Within the House Imperial, we will be largely unopposed. By this single stroke, the banned Houses lost nearly a quarter of their leadership. This news must be relayed across the realm. Count Rathenberg, send out diplomatic couriers immediately. Rathenberg, Neuterra, Acier, all the banned Houses must know." The Emperor was giddy with delight.

"It is done, your Majesty." Count Rathenberg tapped on his portable computer console.

"Now, Sire, comes the difficult question," drawled Yedric. "We must decide where to strike. The time is now. The logical force is the full power of the loyal Empire. We need to destroy the combined strength of the banned Houses."

"That is all very well, Yedric, but how do you propose to know where their forces are?"

"Your Majesty, we need not destroy their forces. We need to

destroy their capability to fight and supply themselves. Where is their best army? Where are their resources to build fleets and repair ships? Where is their major support and defiance?"

"Acier! Of course," boomed the Emperor. He thought of the defiance of Count Ian Acier in the Landsritters. Ian who, with his deep bass voice had called Perodus a false noble before the entire council. *Murderer,* the Count had roared as he'd torn down the executioner's pike and thrown the head of the Lady Lyral at Perodus. Yes, the conquest of Acier would be a sweet revenge. Already, with the execution of the Lady Lyral, he rewarded his brother and Duke Neuterra's treachery. They felt his sting. Count Acier would be next; the banned Houses would lose their chief benefactor and supporter. Perodus' eyes glinted harshly.

With only a small tug at his fears did Perodus perceive that Duke Yedric manipulated him. He didn't care. It was what he would have commanded himself—if he had thought of it. He beamed at the new Duke, liking him more and more. He felt as though a kinship existed between them, a kinship of vengeance and hatred.

"Your Majesty, such a move will leave the Capital unprotected," stated the hesitating Count Rathenberg.

"That is true." Yedric's tone was contemptuous. "But the forces we oppose are yet dispersed. They do not have a central commander or command. If anywhere, their forces will be centered on Neuterra. We must strike them before they can gather and plan how to strike us themselves. This would be the most crippling blow we can make against them."

Count Rathenberg nodded lamely.

"I find no fault with Lord Yedric's plan," pronounced Perodus. "Deliver these orders to my commanders. You work by my leave, Lord Yedric. After you are successful, you may use the fleet to take possession of your new fief, Neuterra."

Yedric bowed deeply.

"Are we agreed?" The Emperor scowled darkly.

"Yes, your majesty," the Count responded in deference.

"Good. Let us drink to the health of the new Empire and to a resolution of our current problems."

Thirteen

Sir Devon Rathenberg stepped out of the Imperial Courier Ship *Saint Anne* onto the surface of the Imperial Capital, Arienth. This was his homeworld. At least, it had once been his homeworld.

Devon breathed deeply. To his ship-tainted senses, the air was brilliantly fresh…heady and blazingly hot. The atmosphere was filled with the heavy fragrance of jungle forest mixed with the acrid stench of reaction fuel. Scents wafted across the hot permacrete of the spaceport and brought back fleeting pictures almost older than Devon intelligibly remembered. Yet, his earliest memory was this very smell: he could see his father at the head of the Emperor's victorious fleet arriving home, kissing his mother, and placing his son triumphantly on his shoulders. The son was himself, and they greeted the Emperor in this family procession. Devon's father never ceased to tell the story of the Rathenberg Prince who sat before the Emperor—upon his father's shoulders. His father might never learn the later boons Emperor Maricus bestowed on him. If Duke Rathenberg only knew how much autonomy and responsibility Devon had been privileged to during the reign of Emperor Maricus, he would have been truly proud.

Any joy in his homecoming suddenly left Devon; the Emperor Maricus, his friend and benefactor, was dead. In his place, Perodus, a weak but ambitious man yanked against the fetters of the Code of honor that bound the Noble Houses to the House Imperial. Perodus would quickly find what weak bonds those were; the harder he pulled, the greater the number of Houses that would slip their traditional yoke.

Eventually, the peace of the entire human galaxy would be sundered into aristocratic savagery. Soon, if Devon could alter nothing, the death knell would sound on all he, his father, and his ally, Prince John-Mark, had done to quell the interfamily conflicts and stabilize the Empire.

A month ago, none of them could have guessed at the twisted plans of Perodus, Yedric, and Count Rathenberg. If Devon even had the slightest inkling of Perodus' intentions, he would never have left the Emperor's side. Only, three weeks ago, Devon left Arienth on a mission for the Emperor. The purpose was unknown even to the Chancellor of the Empire, his father, and the Marshall of the Imperial Huscarls, Prince John-Mark. As the Chief of Imperial Intelligence, Devon worked with both men, but for reasons of necessity, Devon himself would not let them know the plans he and Emperor Maricus developed.

Devon realized, nearly a year ago, the logical conclusion of the treachery of Count Yedric and his cousin, Count Rathenberg. If, along with their successful appeals to the younger Houses, they were allowed to continue their military build-up, they would soon have the power to blackmail the Landsritters and the Emperor. The solution became academic. The Emperor could not actively confront the Counts Yedric and Rathenberg—that would be an admission of less-than-honorable conduct and place suspicion on all the intelligence activities of the Emperor's forces. To distrust your nobles was an indication of a lack of fealty, and the revelation of the efficiency of the Emperor's intelligence gathering might drive many older Houses into Yedric's ranks. Nor could the Emperor continue to let the Counts build up strength until they were capable of actively confronting his forces, which would certainly place the Empire into turmoil. It would destroy the trust placed in his office and lead to the sundering of the Empire's Thirty Kingdoms like so much chaff.

The idea to try to force Count Yedric to an early military action was Devon's. It was fundamentally a decision of pure logic, and the Emperor was finally convinced to accept the inevitability of it.

Devon had developed the plan by degrees. Through study of the personality of Count Yedric and the stated goals of the Count's coalition, the solution became deadly simple. Sir Devon Rathenberg must die, and he must die by the hands of Count Dominic Yedric. The

Emperor opposed the plan. He opposed the solution, but the logic was indisputable. The solution was like a puzzle piece. The plan was a masterwork. And the man to carry it out was proven the most trustworthy of any in the Emperor's service.

The only problem was the primary; the man condemned to death was like a son to the Emperor. Devon was the only son of an Imperial Princess, the Emperor's youngest sister. He was Prince John-Mark's greatest friend. He was the bulwark of the Emperor's Intelligence Corps. The Emperor argued that he couldn't lose such an important man. Their private disagreement, as the Emperor called it, went on secretly for months. The Emperor even declared that Devon should kill Yedric in the duel and forget the plan, but Devon gently pointed out to him, that would only stir up greater insurrection. The death of Yedric would create a martyr, and in anger, many Houses would flock to the side of Count Rathenberg. The Houses already in the confidence of Yedric would continue their quiet rebellion.

Eventually, the power of the Counts Yedric and Rathenberg could not be ignored. After they goaded the Imperial Territories in the Fringe into insurrection and clandestinely supported them against the Empire, the Emperor was finally convinced.

The Emperor's and Devon's leave-taking was emotional and secret. Only they knew the plan; despite its necessity, Devon's father or John-Mark would not have approved it. In the entire universe, no one but Maricus would properly mourn the death of Prince Devon Rathenberg, Knight of the Red Cross, Field Major in His Majesty's Huscarls, the Emperor's Fox.

But Devon was alive. And he had every reason to continue living: the Lady—his Lady Tamar—awaited him on Falkeep. Better that this business be completed…and as quickly as possible.

As meticulously as he planned the original confrontation with Count Yedric, Devon developed a strategy to consummate his revenge. He knew he required help. The most successful scheme he devised, so far, needed the assistance of at least one other person. That individual would be the deciding factor. Otherwise, again, the prospect of death stared him in the face. For Tamar's sake, he must return to Falkeep. For his family's sake, for his honor's sake, for the Empire's sake, he must succeed in destroying Yedric.

The harsh roar of a landing ship finally broke Devon's concentration. Almost absently, he looked out across the ramp. The heat of the hard permacrete made the brilliant whiteness of the operations building a desirable refuge. Devon picked up his bag, and the waves of heat radiating from the raw permacrete drove him relentlessly toward the air-conditioned building.

Devon sighed in relief as he entered the cool interior. The operations building was almost empty. In the early afternoon, a skeleton crew relieved the main duty squad; the reduction of afternoon traffic caused by the movement of the Imperial fleet made a full crew unnecessary. Devon guessed the decrease in personnel could also be attributed to the fleet's draw on the Imperial Navy's human resources.

Apart from a few Navy personnel, Devon only noticed one other person, a young nobleman who waited in the VIP lounge that overlooked the operations ramp. He could see little of the man's face but was assured by what he saw that the man was unfamiliar to him.

Devon stepped by a marine who guarded the flightline entrance. As he passed, the trooper came to attention. Devon ignored him and continued to the other side of the building, where he could call a base taxi. As he stepped into the cool corridor that ran the length of the building, behind him he again heard the guard come to attention, but put that out of his mind and continued to the phone lounge.

Devon picked up his luggage at the main terminal and a military taxi conveyed him to the billeting office. He tried to play the role of an insignificant noble to the hilt. If anyone of consequence identified him, his plans and, most likely, his life would be forfeit. Devon dressed in clothing less colloquial than those he'd worn on Falkeep, but his garments still identified him as an outer system knight. On his uniform he bore the rank of an obscure Imperial office—one that would grant him flexibility of movement in the Empire's lower government offices but not arouse in-depth research into his background.

Devon had let his beard grow into a goatee, and he sported a balancing mustache that connected to the goatee at the edges of his upper lip. Using a cosmetic growth extenuator, he grew his hair so it fell about his shoulders in an antique style. These precautions should prevent immediate recognition, yet because the style was still popular among the older Nobility, it should protect him from undue attention. He toyed with the idea of making up his face and hair to look more consistent in age with his assumed style, but put the idea away when he thought of the continual effort he would need to play the part properly. He planned to confine himself to undercover operations, and he hoped to avoid any social or coincidental encounters.

Billeting assigned him a room precisely in the area Devon wanted. He feigned that the noise of aircraft and spaceship operations disturbed him and asked for quarters furthest away from the port landing ramp. His room was in a building for junior officers not more than a half mile from the boundary of the base. Usually two officers shared the same quarters, but in deference to his rank, the billeting staff gave Devon an entire suite. The room was on the ground floor, also as he desired. Devon didn't have to ask for the ground floor; base billeting was so empty, there weren't enough officers to fill the lower floors.

Devon went directly to his room and changed clothing. Instead of putting on dinner wear or leisure attire, he donned a pair of gray fatigues. With an eye toward detail, he unpacked and checked his equipment. He placed most of it, along with a suit of dark evening clothes, in a small black bag.

Devon waited impatiently until the sun fully set, then completed his costume by donning a dark gray skintight mask and a pair of Light Amplification Goggles. With the LAGs supplementing his vision, his eyes could easily penetrate the darkness of the room.

Devon carefully checked the approaches to the window that faced the fence at the base's perimeter. He pushed the window full open and lowered his black bag to the ground. As he was about to follow the bag through the window, 100 meters to his left, a figure came unexpectedly into sight. Certain the intruder wouldn't be able to distinguish him in the gloom, Devon froze in the darkened opening. As the figure came closer, the building's front light illuminated him. With the aid of the LAGs, Devon recognized the young nobleman from the operations building. The man paused at the building's entrance to read the building number. Assured this was the right building, the man entered the doorway and passed out of Devon's sight.

Devon slipped silently out of the window and climbed to the ground. He lay quietly in the grass, stuck his arms through the straps of the bag, and slung it onto his back like a pack. Devon rechecked his path to the base fence. The way was clear, and with an easy rolling motion, he rose to a crouch. Devon raced the moon and ringlight that threatened to rise over the eastern sky and leave him silhouetted against the open heavens. Within five minutes, he reached the stand of scrub and low trees that discretely hid the security perimeter from the rest of the base.

Devon decreased the speed of his hunched run and picked his way through the irregular ground and low scrub. In minutes, the fence came into sight. It stood four meters high, with razor and microfilament wire strung across the top—very nasty to climb. Ten meters on each side of the fence line the brush was cleared away. Devon continued through the scrub, and paralleled the fence. He looked for a particular sign. When the ground dipped suddenly, he knew he found the right place. With his soft soled boots, he searched in the brush for a moment—ah, there. The ground was very firm, yet rocked beneath his foot. Devon swept the branches and ground cover to one side, and there, under his searching fingers, lay a permacrete plug.

In a line with the plug, the fence crossed a shallow depression that once was a creek bed. To reduce and control the drainage of the spaceport, the creek had long ago been diverted into a conduit. Now the underground creek became an austere and clandestine way off the base. Should his efforts against Yedric prove successful, Devon's billet at the port was a perfect alibi. He would sneak back to his quarters the same way, with no one the wiser. This was the simplest part of his plan.

Using his intelligence forces, Devon scouted out many bolt-holes in Imperial holdings with such operations in mind. Most of these back entrances were unknown to anyone but his intelligence troops, and nearly all of those troops were Acierians, who now fought against Emperor Perodus on the side of their proper Lord, Count Acier. They would not betray him.

Devon wrenched the permacrete plug from the hole and gingerly lowered himself into the conduit. The languidly flowing creek filled the stone pipe, and the water rose to his chest. That left him barely two feet of breathing room at the top. He carefully pulled the plug after him, and lowered it back into the concealing hole.

When he seated the plug, the wet tunnel went completely dark. Tiny UV auxiliary lights clicked on the LAGs, but inside the tunnel, in the humidity and inadequate illumination, everything blurred and the LAGs were worthless. Devon pulled them off his eyes and let them dangle loosely around his neck, then turned on a plasmalight. Bent nearly double, Devon followed the pipe under the fence.

The walls of the tunnel were foul with moss and small insects. They grappled at his head and shoulders. His light drew the crawling pests so Devon almost turned it off and continued in the dark. He was fortunate that he didn't. Under the water, a soft baglike object bumped against his shins. He reached for it, but in the sluggish flow, it moved away from his touch. The object was nearly neutrally buoyant. It bumped against him again. This time, he grabbed quickly and brought up the upper torso of a human being.

With an irrepressible shiver, Devon dropped the grizzly carcass, but controlled his disgust and retrieved it again. The top of the skull was missing, as was one arm, most of another, and everything below the sternum. The face was bloated and seethed with water scavengers. Devon forced himself to clinically examine the remains; the cuts were clean. No energy weapon did that. Devon held the body out before him, and stepped gingerly ahead. He watched carefully for the trap that had caught this man.

The torso had stayed near this side of the perimeter fence, though the weak current drove the water in the same direction he was moving. Devon believed the man was one of his intelligence troops who tried to escape the new Emperor's purge, too late. Something touched the body part he held in front of him. A slight resistance ahead caused the part to twitch. Then, as Devon released the bust, it stopped and stuck. He played his light ahead at the walls and ceiling of the pipe. Ah ha! Just visible ahead were glistening filaments set in a crossing pattern. Microfilament! A single crystal structure wire less than three or four molecules thick, but as strong as steel. The unfortunate escapee ran up the culvert and hit the microfilament full on. The wires easily cut his body to pieces. It passed through him like a laser through plastic. Devon was grateful the man left evidence of his flight; otherwise the same fate would have befallen him.

Ordinary tools could not be used to break or cut the wire. Devon took out a pocket laser. The filaments were at least a few months old. They showed the molecular tarnish that eventually coated microfilament and made it less effective. Devon wondered who ordered a beef-up of the base's security. He didn't think it had been done specifically to catch his people, but Devon had enemies in the Landsritters and the Imperial forces.

Devon stopped himself before he cut any of the filaments. He didn't think they were alarmed, since that was a very expensive option to apply with microfilament. If they knew the trap had been sprung, Devon reasoned, they would have taken the body away—at least to identify the man. Devon took out an electronic sensor. Because the filaments were almost invisible, as close as safety allowed, he checked for electronic devices. Nothing indicated on his scanner, so with the laser, he sliced the molecular-thin wires.

The ceiling wires cut easily, and the upper crosswire came loose without a problem, but Devon had to take the laser underwater to get at the other filaments. He couldn't see through the water, so he cut straight down the left wall then down the right. He hoped the filaments would be caught in the current and washed away from him. But before he could make a second cut down the walls, the laser winked out.

With an angry exclamation, Devon stepped involuntarily back from the trap. He carried nothing else with him that would cut the filaments. His plasmasword was too long and produced too much energy for the cramped space in the pipe. For a moment, Devon thought about sneaking back through the conduit and to his billet. But the idea of failure so early in his plans was a harsh thought. With an impatient shake of his head, Devon discarded the idea. The planet's rings and moons would be full up, and that made a simple return impossible. In addition, he had no idea who might be monitoring this trap. Just because his sensor didn't pick up any activity didn't mean the wires were cold. Devon had to move quickly now; otherwise he could be trapped in the pipe. Capture and identification meant as certain a death as having his legs cut off in this conduit. The cold water was affecting him too. The growing lack of feeling in his limbs meant he might miss other traps further down.

Steeling himself, Devon walked carefully ahead. The remains of the other traveler, he noticed, already moved along downstream. That was a good sign. At least he had cut the filaments holding it. Devon moved through the unseen barrier at exactly midstream. If the microfilaments were still attached to one wall, at a touch, they would slice his skin open. A filament wrapped around his arm could slice it off. The hairs at the back of his neck tingled, and he stepped with exaggerated care. Finally past the obstacle, Devon moved with renewed vigor toward the opposite escape hole.

Moss covered the plug, so it was almost indistinguishable from the rest of the ceiling. He nearly passed it. Devon turned off the plasmalight, reseated the LAGs over his eyes, and using his shoulder as a lever, gently pushed the permacrete out of its seat.

Devon peered through the widening crack between the plug and the ground but saw no one. The manhole opened into an area still covered with forest and thick brush. Whoever installed the trap in the conduit obviously meant the way to be used; otherwise they would have cleared the brush around the entry and exit. Devon felt like he was under observation. Reasonably, anyone who knew about the bolt-hole would want to see who used it. Then he reconsidered, whoever set up the grizzly trap had done it for no other reason than to prevent ingress to the base. Otherwise, the trap would have been designed to maim and not kill, and the remains of the dead man would have been removed long ago. With a heave, Devon set the plug on edge and crawled out of the hole.

As Devon resealed the entrance to the conduit, he noticed he had not escaped the trap without injury: a long, spiraling cut dripped dark blood down his arm. Devon shuddered when he thought how close he'd come to losing his limb. He consoled himself that the wound would heal quickly; microfilament lacerations usually did.

Devon lay on the ground and adjusted his LAGs. Through the trees, he scanned the base. He could see nothing in the IR, UV, or visible spectrum within his line of sight. He saw no indication that anyone detected his clandestine departure.

With considerable relief, Devon headed away from the spaceport and made his way toward the city center of Arienth. He stayed in the forest and approached the main city thoroughfare unseen. At the edge of the brush, Devon hid in a thicket and took off the outer dark gray fatigues, LAGs, and mask. He packed these in his bag and dressed the wounds on his arm. When he stepped out of the woods, he wore his dark evening suit.

In the distance, one of Arienth's brightly lit, outlying malls was in sight. This was the spot Devon aimed for. A 30-minute walk should take him to the mall, and from there, he could enter the city via a taxi—every step unremarkable.

Devon crossed the main road and was transiting a block of large warehouses when he encountered another small problem. As he rounded the side of one of the buildings and entered an alleyway, a faint sound alerted him. Devon continued forward without an indication he'd heard anything. Again, he heard a sound behind him. This time he could tell it was closer and on his left. The noise was a stealthy shuffle. Devon knew an amateur shadowed him. Another distinct shuffle sounded from his right, behind him. Expecting the worse, he changed course a little. Another sound, a muffled whisper, broke the quiet night just ahead of him. Three, no four, he counted in his thoughts. Not too many to handle hand-to-hand, but he could be in trouble if they carried slug throwers. They knew the terrain better than he, but they were not as well trained as he. He looked down at his dress clothing. *Should have left on the camo,* Devon thought wearily.

In splotches, the bright light of Arienth's rings and companion moons lit the lanes between the buildings. Devon was trapped in one of the long alleyways with no place to go. He couldn't go up the sides of the buildings; the sides were too slick and high. Two stalkers waited before him and another two followed behind him. *In teams of two,* Devon thought, *good technique.* He hoped they weren't very proficient at their business. No shots yet. So far so good.

Devon put on the LAGs. Yes, there they were. Ahead of him, at the juncture of the warehouses, he saw two crudely dressed young men. The other two behind him were not in sight. Time to launch a surprise. Devon stole into the shadows at the edge of the wall. With a quiet dash,

Devon overtook the two men he spotted ahead of him. They lounged at the end of the alleyway and didn't look as if they expected him for a while. Devon congratulated himself at his close approach when one of the youths turned toward him, and Devon saw he wore night-vision goggles! Not as good as his LAGs, but they revealed Devon in the building's shadows.

"There he is," hissed the man with the goggles. "Get 'em."

That really disclosed their intentions. Devon brought out his plasmalight and flipped the switch to high intensity. With a long vibrablade outstretched and buzzing in his hand, the goggle-wearing youth leapt toward Devon. Devon covered his own goggles and turned on the plasmalight, full power, at the blade wielder's eyes. With a surprised bellow, the man clawed at the debilitating goggles and fell at Devon's feet. In a burst of righteous anger, Devon jumped over the groaning man and ground his heel into the assailant's blade hand. Devon felt bones crunch beneath his foot, and the man added a second cry of agony to the first.

Devon stepped around the corner of the building just in time to get out of the way of the other man's chainblade. The weapon was a microfilament-edged knife mounted on the end of a long sprocket chain. The blade slashed toward Devon and missed him. It struck the corner of the plasteel warehouse and with a metallic clatter pierced and stuck in the wall. Devon grabbed the chain, yanked the man toward him, and brought his knee up and across. The kick caught the unsuspecting attacker solidly in the groin. The man gave a hurt grunt, bent double, and waddled backwards. Before he could escape, Devon rammed the gasping man, head first, against the corner of the building. A dull crack announced the collision and the man fell to the ground.

Untrained, thought Devon.

The two men that followed Devon now came running toward the end of the building. When they beheld their fallen compatriots, they slowed. They hadn't contemplated this turn of events. Their usual prey curled up on the pavement without a fight. The men stopped suddenly, and intense wariness replaced their initial, feral smirks. They crouched and glanced from side to side as if they expected an attack to come from all around them. When they noticed Devon was unarmed, they smiled eagerly again. The thug closest to the building turned on his vibrablade. It buzzed and hissed like a disturbed bee hive, and he swung it menacingly once or twice toward Devon.

I could use my snub pistol or plasmasword, thought Devon, *but that would leave evidence of military type weapons. The explosions and concentrated plasmalight would probably bring the local police.*

Devon had loaded the snub pistol with high explosive projectiles instead of gas. He did have some gas grenades in his pack, but they weren't very accessible. He didn't think these men would wait for him to remove a couple.

Devon listened for the approach of anyone else—wouldn't be good to be surprised from behind. The other man, as if reading Devon's mind, started to move stealthily around him. The two displayed more intelligence than Devon initially gave them credit for. The blade wielder tried to hold his attention while the other man crept behind him. Devon noticed a microfilament garrote in the stalker's hands. The garrote was almost two feet of molecular fiber embedded in ceriplast handles. Devon put his back to the building corner and kept the men in sight. He blocked their view of the chainblade imbedded in the corner. As the man with the garrote came closer and closer, a malicious smile betrayed his intentions.

Devon assumed a look of indifference. The men glanced knowingly from one to the other, then the garrotter made a rush at Devon. The predictability of the attack amused Devon. He grasped the free end of the chainblade and yanked it from the wall of the building. The recoil of the chain added to Devon's strength as the chainblade sprang loose from the metal corner. Devon swung the blade into his attacker's face and stepped out of the way. The chain crashed with a very satisfying thunk into the mugger's nose, and the man almost followed the first two into unconsciousness. Unfortunately, as he fell, the microfilament garrote bit into his abdomen. With a scream, the man released one of the garrote handles and arched over. He insanely clasped his belly and the other handle of the garrote. He vainly pointed the handle toward Devon as if that alone could protect him.

Meanwhile, just after the garrotter, the blade wielder started his attack. At the sight of his almost disemboweled comrade, he stopped cold and made a half-hearted swing. Devon nimbly evaded the attack, and before the man could lunge again, Devon grabbed the loose handle of the garrote. With the eviscerated man still holding onto the other end, Devon brought the microfilament up and through the arm holding the vibrablade. The man stared at Devon in horror. As the now disconnected hand let loose its grasp, the buzz of the vibrablade went dead. A great gout of blood surged from the stump, and the man fell to the permacrete.

Devon leaned against the warehouse and caught his breath. He didn't know which of the four men was dead or alive, and he didn't care. If anyone came to look for them, then let the coroner sort them out. In his activities, though they were clandestine, he, at least knew he always acted for the good of the Empire. He proved over and over that he would give himself for those wholesome principles of honor and morality encapsulated in the Code. He proved it by his willingness to die for it—yet he was brought back to life. That miracle didn't increase his respect for the life of this scum of humanity; rather, it increased his belief in the power of honor and Nobility.

The men lying broken in the shadows chose to attack me, Devon thought, *and I chose to give them the honor of dying by my hand. For my benefit, others have killed more worthy men than they.*

The cooling night slowly quenched the battle fury that had gripped Devon. He wearily averted his eyes from the carnage and, with greater stealth, headed again toward the mall.

Devon climbed a few link fences to eventually arrive at his destination. He stopped at the outskirts of the mall's lighted parking area. The exploits of the evening had not damaged his clothing too badly, but he felt it was a good idea to stay out of the bright illumination of the mall. He called a taxi, and when it arrived, he climbed in quickly.

"Take me to the hotel Marquise de Seine. It's near the city center."

As Devon paid the cabby in front of the hotel, he could just discern the tower of the Hall of Accords almost three kilometers away along the avenue Seine. The Emperor and Yedric were so close, he thought. Soon he would be free of that responsibility, and his honor would be redeemed.

Fourteen

Devon watched the sidewalk from his hotel room with increasing agitation. Yes—yes! There he was again. Out in front of the building Devon recognized the same young nobleman he'd seen in the spaceport's operations lounge. He was certain it was the same person...the same man who also entered the billeting building just as Devon left through the window. And that same man not only stood directly beneath Devon's hotel window, he gazed with expectation directly toward the window as if he discerned by telepathy alone where Devon was. The man could have the decency to take his stakeout to the building across the street or, at least, view the window by its reflection in the glass of the building opposite the hotel. That, in fact, was how Devon watched his unwelcome and unprofessional tagalong.

How did he find me? mused Devon. He was certainly not an agent of the Emperor—unless the Emperor's intelligence program declined well below the level at which Devon left it. *To have found me, the young nobleman would have to know exactly who I was and what I was planning.* Devon's eyes widened at the speculation. That meant his mission was ended before he even stepped a foot into the Royal palace. With an angry shake of his head, Devon refused to think about the possibility and instead continued his preparations.

Devon engaged an outside room in the hotel Marquise de Seine. He slept the rest of the preceding night and through most of the next day. He had used the previous day and night to finalize his plans and then, again, slept through the day. The long twilight of his third night on Arienth approached, and Devon prepared himself for action.

Already, Devon despaired of finding anyone to help him. Using the computer terminal in his room, he searched every source available to discover a friend or compatriot on the planet. He might have friends on Arienth even now, but what he didn't have was the time or resources to physically search out the resistance groups on the planet or discover an ally. Most likely, at the suggestion of Count Yedric, the new Emperor had made sweeping changes in the governmental structure and purged the people of the old order out. Luckily, they had not changed all the old computer passwords and access codes. With these codes, Devon could get all the information he needed. He knew both Yedric and the Emperor were still on the planet. He knew, in fact, just where Yedric was housed in the Imperial Palace, and he copied enough data from the computers to keep the rebel Houses' intelligence organizations busy for a year.

Devon's equipment was ready. He was ready. The time had come to undertake the full recovery of his honor, but, stalking back and forth in front of the hotel, this unquestionably tenacious shadow dogged him. Devon did not have much time to delay.

Candidly, his options were three. First, Devon could give the man the slip again. That would solve the current problem, but if the nobleman were the representative of some other agent on the planet, Devon was discovered. If, before the deed was done, Devon became the object of a planet-wide search, he would not be able to complete his mission or escape. Moreover, if this persistent amateur happened to trace him to the palace, the entire plan would have to be scrapped. Second, Devon could kill the man outright. But that went against his basic code of honor. So far Devon had nothing but circumstantial evidence that the man knew Devon existed. Yes, such a fatal confrontation was the most thorough conclusion, but Devon had a third option. He could capture the noble and discover exactly what he was up to. That was the most difficult solution, and during the capture or to protect himself afterwards, Devon might still end up having to slay the nobleman. All three of the choices tempted him. Perhaps Devon should start on number one and see what chance brought.

Devon velcroed the dark fatigues over his street clothing and rechecked his equipment. He fully charged his laser cutter, plasmalight, plasmasword, scanner pack, and computer decoder-scrambler—these hung in pouches around his belt. Also, on his person, Devon had concealed a graphite blade, a snub pistol loaded with high explosive and gas rounds, the Light Amplification Goggles, and four gas grenades. He carried his bag, filled with extra clothing, additional rounds, and grenades. Devon prepared for a battle, but other than with Yedric, he hoped the affair would not escalate into open fighting between himself and anyone else. That would undeniably lessen his chance of survival.

Devon walked quietly to his room door and listened beyond. He heard nothing in the corridor. With an electronic tool connected to the computer decoder, he opened the security sealed master panel next to the door. After only three tries, the small access panel popped open, and Devon reprogrammed the system: now, after he left, it would register him still in the room. The program Devon wrote was kind of sketchy. It had him awake for a set number of hours, reported him asleep, and repeated the cycle continuously. Good enough to keep out the cleaning robots, and leave the room registered under his name.

Devon pushed the unlocked door panel open and slipped into the open hallway. The door shut with a solid click, and Devon smiled.

He moved about 20 meters down the hallway to a low robot access port. The port was almost hidden by the wall decor and comlocked with no physical access on this side. Devon stooped quickly and let the decoder cipher the lock for a moment. When it hit the right frequency and code, with a click, the lock snapped open. Devon pulled open the heavy door and crept inside.

Inside the accessway, he had just enough room to sit hunched against all six walls. From the inside, Devon relocked the panel, and put on his LAGs. The goggles turned on their tiny ultraviolet auxiliary lights and adjusted to the totally dark area. After a moment, Devon could dimly discern the walls. He plugged his decoder into the master computer connections along the wall and, in seconds, logged into the hotel computer.

From the coded information he reviewed at his room terminal, Devon already knew the route he wanted to take through the hotel.

The computer confirmed this data, and Devon shut off the intruder alarms and non-robot sensors along his chosen path. Behind him, the wall opened suddenly, and again with a smile, Devon disconnected his equipment and pushed his way into the cramped elevator.

After Devon signaled the door to shut, the elevator dropped at a sickening velocity and took him down to the lowest level of the complex. It stopped with a back-breaking lurch, and Devon signaled the door open and gratefully pried himself out of the uncomfortable transportation. After he was clear of the door, he could stand to almost his full height.

Except for his goggles, the darkness was unrelieved. He stood in a large and echoing room filled with soft squeaks, metal bumps, and the soft thump of plastic tread on permacrete. Outside the range of Devon's dim ultraviolet eyes, wheeled things traveled unerring in the dark.

When they weren't required in the hotel, the hotel robots were stored in this room. Here, out of sight, out of mind, and ready at an electronic summons to ply their duties far above, they were repaired and maintained.

The air was oppressive and hot: robots didn't feel or think about their conditions. The place was pitch dark: robots didn't need visible light to see. After a moment, Devon set off, stepping carefully through the maze. The jaunt required more time than he expected. His route took him straight across the basement, but the varying walls and small robots made walking in a direct path difficult. He had to take a circuitous route through the place and eventually reached the other side.

Here, just below the ceiling, a conduit stretched from this building to a garage across the street. Devon jumped up to the opening and climbed into the square crawlway. The accessway was meant for robots and difficult for a person to navigate. Devon ended up on his back, pulling himself along using the pipes that ran along the roof. After 15 meters, the crawlway suddenly opened up into the automatic garage. The garage was also totally dark, and from one end to the other gravvehicles lined it in spotty rows.

Because Devon hadn't been able to connect with the garage computer yet, its intruder systems and alarms would be fully operational. Devon knew he must be extremely careful. When he set a foot on the floor, he got a practical example: a tiny laser beam, invisible in the darkness but outlined by his goggles, burned a hole in his ankle. "Blast it—varmint system." He winced as he grasped a pipe and chinned himself back up off the floor. He wasn't fast enough. Before he could get above the sensors, he received a second blast. Devon couldn't hang like this forever. He pushed off and stepped onto the nearest vehicle. He hoped the garage pursued an aggressive policy of cleaning the exterior of the gravvehicles; otherwise his footprints would mark out his exact path across the closely spaced vehicles. In spite of hopping from car to car, he made better time than in the robot storage.

When he reached the center of the complex with its patch terminals and connections, Devon tied into the computer, turned off the alarms, and called the elevator. Within minutes, he stood in the window of the garage offices opposite the hotel Marquis de Seine.

The young nobleman still stalked back and forth along the sidewalk. As Devon watched, the man glanced at his wristwatch and entered the hotel. Shaking his head, he came out in a moment and paced even more nervously than before.

Devon laughed out loud. The man must have tried to contact him! However, the computer sequence Devon programmed wouldn't let anyone disturb his room. No matter what the young man did or how long he waited, the computer in that room would never answer the prompter.

Now Devon was safely away from the hotel. He was registered, probably photographed going in, but no one had witnessed his departure. Now was the time to force a confrontation on his terms.

Devon took off his fatigues and stored them in the bag. He slipped out of the automatic parking garage, walked about 100 meters down the street, and crossed it. The young nobleman didn't seem to notice him.

Devon walked slowly along the sidewalk toward the man. He was less than three meters away before the man saw him. Devon didn't pause, but out of the corner of his eye, he glimpsed the surprised, then amazed expression his appearance evoked in the man's face. In confusion, the man turned toward the hotel; then, throwing caution to the winds, he started warily after Devon. Devon continued at a slow pace down the sidewalk. He intentionally varied his stroll to see what his shadow would do. *Clearly the man has no training,* thought Devon. Devon went into shops. He looked in windows. His tail, perhaps not completely convinced he followed the right man, kept pace and tried to conceal himself at each stop.

Devon determined one very important thing during the time he led this bumbling spy around. The man was alone. Unless his partner or tags were much better than any shadow Devon ever worked with, as he followed Devon away from the city center, no one crept after the nobleman.

As they progressed, the streets became less well lighted and more barren. They entered the residential area of the Capital. According to Arienth time, it was nearly 2100. Fewer people roamed the streets.

Time to strike.

Just before an alley, Devon knelt and, as if he picked up something, he bent toward the ground. As soon as he had knelt, he saw his tail rush into a recessed doorway, Devon slipped into the deep shadows in the alley. This was almost too simple. The man hurried past the meter wide lane, where Devon hid. He paused only when he reached the next corner. The man wasn't stupid. After discerning his quarry hadn't continued as far as the corner, he searched the doorways and openings back along the way he'd come. *Perfect,* thought Devon.

The young noble eventually reached the alleyway and apprehensively peered down it. Devon waited almost two meters above the man. Devon had climbed the permacrete walls like a chimney. Held by the tension against his hands and feet, he now perched in the shadows above the nobleman.

The noble made a cautious foray into the alley, and Devon dropped to land silently behind him. Though Devon's motion generated almost no sound, something, perhaps the wind of his passage, caused the noble to stand suddenly straight. He began to turn, but before his body could twitch in response to the thought, Devon wrapped his arm around the man's neck. He kicked the young noble's legs to either side, drew his blade from its boot scabbard, and pricked the man's throat as a warning to silence.

Devon carried the man, still on his feet, deeper into the shadows.

Finally entrenched in the darkness, with the open end of the alley still in sight, Devon left off a little of the pressure. As Devon clutched the helpless spy in his grip, Devon felt the nobleman's pulse tremble in agitation.

The noble strained between clenched teeth. "Sir Devon Rathenberg?"

With a tremor of absolute surprise, Devon almost severed the man's life. He halted the involuntary motion of his hand, but as it was, the blade fell with a startling clamor to the ground. The noble gasped as Devon's grip became even tighter.

"Are you alone?" Devon hissed in the man's ear. "Not a word. Nod, if you are here by yourself."

The man nodded.

"You were seeking Sir Devon Rathenberg?" he pronounced this at an almost inaudible level.

Again, the man nodded.

"You have placed yourself so close to death, it is an offense to the grave. We cannot converse for long in this place and under these circumstances. I know you are a nobleman. Do you surrender to hostage?"

The man nodded again, and Devon released him. The nobleman stumbled forward a pace. When he'd gained his balance, he turned around and ruefully rubbed his neck. Devon retrieved his knife and replaced it in his boot.

"May I speak?" asked the noble.

"Wait a moment," Devon took out the scanner and checked for surveillance. "In the Emperor's domains, you cannot be too careful." Only the street lights registered on the tiny display, and that satisfied Devon. He moved to the opening of the alley where he could view the street but remain in the shadows. Devon motioned for the man to follow and stood him on the opposite side of the alley.

"Speak," remarked Devon quietly. "You have already delayed me immeasurably."

The nobleman conquered his anger with difficulty. "Sir Devon Rathenberg..."

"Don't use that name," hissed Devon. "I am Sir Devon de Tieg from the County of Greyholm."

The noble exclaimed, "And I am Sir Roger Falkeep from the Duchy of Falkeep, your brother-in-law, Sir Devon."

Devon gazed at the man in unbridled amazement. The silence stretched between them. Finally, Devon found his tongue. "Tamar!"

"Yes, Tamar is my sister." Sir Roger stepped toward Devon. "You abandoned her in a precarious position."

Devon looked away. When he turned toward Roger again, his face was a painting of alarm and anguish. "She—she's all right, isn't she?"

"Nothing time will not heal."

"Unless you are here to kill me, Roger Falkeep, Duke Falkeep honored our agreement?"

"You do not know Tamar well enough. She attempted to conceal you and your agreement from the Duke. The Duke is a man of honor. Because of you, he was ready to disown my sister! When we discovered the whole story, the Duke gladly affirmed your alliance. He sent me here to...to protect you, but instead, I believe I need protection from you." He rubbed his neck meaningfully.

Devon stood silent for a long time, then spoke with emotion, "Sir Roger, I crave pardon for my treatment of your sister and your family. I love the Lady Tamar, and if I were so privileged, I would gladly exchange my life for hers. She gave me back my own life, and when I had the greatest need, she gave her love freely." Devon quickly outlined his reasons for visiting Falkeep, the duel, and his current resolve. "...the only satisfaction for my House and honor is the death of Yedric. He must die under my hand. You may choose to support me or oppose me. My quarrel is not yours; rather, I unintentionally find myself the source of a quarrel with your family. I also freely accept this."

During Devon's explanation, Roger's countenance mirrored surprise, anger, and amazement, but at the last, his face took on a serious look of resolve. "In your name, my father declared our House in rebellion to the Emperor."

Devon looked quizzically at the man.

"My father cherished you through me. You defended my sister and me before the Emperor's board and the Academy board. Since then, I worshipped you as my highest example of Nobility and honor."

The light of recognition came into Devon's eyes. "I remember you, Roger Falkeep. You defended the honor of the Ladies Tamar and Lyral. I remember the incident. I loved her then, and I could only agree with anyone who would protect my Lady. I pray, Sir Roger, that you will overlook my rudeness at our meeting. I am glad I didn't inadvertently kill you. I hope you will pardon me when I explain, if discovered, I am in grave danger, and already, during this mission, I faced death twice." He put out his hand to Roger.

With an easy smile, Roger clasped Devon's hand. "Now as to the purpose of my mission, first, Tamar returns this to you with her love." Roger handed the Imperial Signet to the knight.

Devon reverently accepted the ring and kissed it. "This may aid me immeasurably in my task."

"Second, can I help you, Devon?"

Devon smiled crookedly in return. "As a mater of fact, you can. Do you have a ship?"

"Yes."

"Can you pilot it?"

"Tolerably well," Roger responded with candor.

"Do you have a gravvehicle?"

"A sport model in the garage across from the Hotel Marquise de Seine."

"Good." Devon explained his plan and outlined Roger's part in it.

"But why just kill Yedric?" queried Roger. "Why not the others, the false Emperor Perodus, Count Rathenberg?"

"That would violate the Codes and is anarchy. The Landsritters would have no choice but to condemn me, and the end might be worse than it is at the present. I have a right to Yedric's blood. My right is embodied in the Codes. In any case, he is the brains of the Emperor's campaigns. Without the support of Yedric's coalition, the Emperor will be forced to concede to the will of the Landsritters."

Roger nodded. With a warrior's clasp, they parted. Both headed back toward the city center by different routes.

THE DELTA

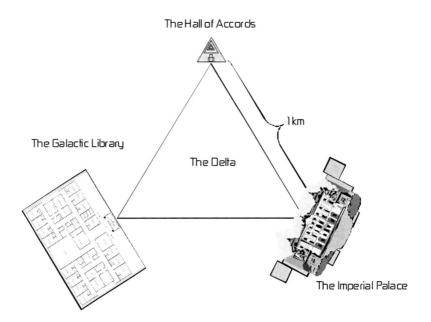

The Hall of Accords

The Galactic Library

The Delta

1 km

The Imperial Palace

Fifteen

Less than an hour passed before Roger drove his gravvehicle along the street he and Devon had agreed on. Roger had returned to the port and activated the yacht *Silent Dawn.* By way of its computer-controlled preflight, within a few hours, the ship would be fully ready for a quick departure.

Roger turned the corner and stopped the vehicle for only an instant while Devon flitted from the shadows and slipped into the gravvehicle.

"The ship ready?" Devon gasped breathless.

"Yes, activated and sequencing."

"I tied into the Imperial security system—don't know how long the breach will go undetected. The time is now or never."

"Where to?"

"Continue straight ahead to the Galactic Library. We can't enter the Palace directly; the external security is too extensive." They had a few kilometers to drive. "Roger, how long had you been looking for me on Arienth?"

"More than two weeks. I left the same day as you, but I traveled directly to Arienth on the swiftest ship in the port. I watched for you on each ship that came to rest at the port. Unfortunately, I couldn't recognize you when you disembarked from the *Saint Anne:* your disguise was excellent. A moment later, when I checked the manifests, I realized I missed you. To wheedle your building and room number from the billeting orderly took a while, but after I had the information,

I came immediately to talk with you. I pounded on your door for ten minutes, then waited most of the night outside your room for your return. When you didn't come back to the room, I checked to see if you'd left the base. According to the base records, you were still in your room. A physical search of the base didn't yield any results, so I acted on the off-chance you'd slipped into the city. I ran a check on the hotel records for the evening before, and voilá, there you were. By the time I secured the information, it was late in the afternoon. I still wasn't sure I'd traced the right person, but I went to the hotel anyway.

"I was indecisive about barging in on you at the hotel. Afraid I might disturb your plans or, by my interference, reveal you were on the planet, especially if I tracked the wrong man. When I finally made up my mind, your room indicated it was occupied, but would not allow inquiry. When you came strolling by, you gave me the shock of my life. I thought there might be three of you! You know the rest."

For a while, they rode in silence. Devon thought in what ways he could best use this unexpected resource, and Roger wondered exactly what his part was in Devon's plans.

Before either finished his musings, they entered the Galactic Library complex. Devon directed Roger past the automatic parking garage, and when they reached the periphery of the roadway, he stepped out of the vehicle.

Devon, on foot, led the gravvehicle through the darkened gardens, around the buildings, and finally directed Roger to stop in a copse of brushy vegetation on the side closest to the Imperial Palace. They hid the vehicle with large fronds from the bushes.

From this vantage, Devon estimated the distance to the brightly lit Palace at a quarter of a kilometer. Directly in front of them lay the permacrete expanse of the Delta. The Delta was the huge triangular court that separated the Hall of Accords, the Imperial Palace, and the Galactic Library. Across the low expanse of the Library, the Hall of Accords lifted itself almost a kilometer into the sky.

"Come on," called Devon softly.

They circumnavigated the immense building of the Galactic Library again and entered it. The Library was busy even at this time of night. Devon led Roger directly to the elevator. As soon as the door shut behind them, Devon opened the master panel and, using his decoder, infiltrated the security system. The programming changes he'd made were still in place. He commanded the elevator to descend to its lowest level, much further below the main gallery than normally permitted. In minutes, they stood in the dimly lit expanse of the Library's vaults.

Devon led through the darkened maze. He moved quickly and with little hesitation. The vaults were loosely arranged, sealed, metal rooms. They connected throughout the structure with the main Library above. These metal vaults stored the compendium of human memory. Each room contained thousands of silver laser disks, and each disk held billions and billions of words and pictures. Except when their internal mechanisms failed, the vaults were never opened, and they seldom failed. Some of the vaults had not been opened since the day they were first interned. For ease of data access, the vaults were arranged in precise patterns; in their seemingly random positions, the weak emanations of their operating fields technically canceled each other and allowed the super-conductive circuits to work without interference. This was true most of the time; however, rumors circulated for almost a century about a certain professor, whose estimated five-second search lasted a decade. This unexpected event completely tied up the man's computer access, and thereby his research, for ten years. The neutrinoelectronic computer engineers said the chance of that event occurring again was extremely unlikely, but they warned, the uncertainty principle governed subatomic neutrinoelectronic systems. And the user should beware.

Devon and Roger traveled deeper and deeper into the vaults until they reached the outer wall of the level. At the edge of the basement, Devon led Roger into a cramped hallway. After the vaults were lost to sight, the corridor continued for almost 100 meters, and at its end, a steel door blocked their way.

The door was uncommonly simple. It mounted neither electronic nor advanced mechanical locks. A chain that appeared to be as old as the door and a mechanical key lock held it shut.

"This is as old as the building," mumbled Devon. He took out his laser cutter and sliced through one loop of the lock. The thin cut was almost invisible. He rotated the loop so that the chain released and cautiously pulled the door open. They slipped through the door. Through the space between the door and the jamb, Devon replaced the lock and chain.

They stood on the landing of a staircase that descended deeper under the Library. Here there were no lights, and with the door closed, they turned on their plasmalights. When Roger visited his ship, as Devon had instructed him, he brought back fatigues, an extra pair of LAGs, and a couple of UV torches. They pulled the dark gray fatigues over their clothing, turned out the plasmalights, and put on the LAGs. With the UV torches on low power, they allowed their eyes to adjust and could just make out their surroundings. Devon explained they needed to use the poorer UV source because any light in the visible spectrum might give away their movements, and infrared would mask an attack in the dark. However, the UV, through the goggles, lit everything in an eerie and surrealistic radiance, making objects glow dimly out of the only partially relieved darkness.

The staircase was permacrete, and in dusty seclusion it descended as far as Roger could see. In spite of the permanence of the material, the stairway showed signs of age. He saw no wear from use, but in places, the stairs and walls were cracked and discolored. The dust was thick and almost uniformly covered the floor, but small footprints didn't escape Roger's notice. He looked slyly at Devon. "You were here when you were a child."

Devon, noticing the direction of Roger's stare, didn't show any surprise. "Yes, this is one of my secrets—one of the many secrets with which I tantalized my cousins, the Princes John-Mark and Perod-Mark. Perod tormented me to tell him these ways, but only John sought them out with me. John is my best friend. John and I were always together. He kept our secrets, and even when we were children, we realized they would eventually serve us well."

They descended down into the darkness. The stone-like material of the stairs evenly absorbed the UV radiation, and only cracks and stains on the old permacrete relieved the solid uniformity.

At one point the walls burst in from either side and almost came together, but, after moving some of the larger stones, they squeezed by.

Eventually, they arrived at a landing with a corridor that ran into the distance as far as they could see. The stairs continued downward.

"We follow this way now," remarked Devon, "The stairs go further, but this leads into the Imperial Palace."

As they started out on this straight hallway Roger asked aloud, "Why do these sunken ways exist at all? What could be their purpose?"

"In the days when the Palace was built, almost 1000 standard years ago, Atomics and plasma weapons could decimate a planet. The Emperor built these subterranean galleries to provide for the safety of his family if war should ever wipe the surface clean. Although few realize the fact today, the halls below are a perfect duplicate of the Palace above. Even the furniture is the same. During that Emperor's reign, we perfected the nuclear damper and the stasis field. In less than a generation, 1000 years ago, this whole underground city became functionless. My mother told me ghosts dwell in these echoing halls, and you can hear the horrors and joys of the Palace above repeated through the ages in these mirror rooms. Nuptial joys, death screams, a lover's murmur, a moan of terror—as a child I imagined I heard all these sounds here, and perhaps I did hear them.

"This dungeon contains rooms in which no man has placed his foot in perhaps 1000 years. Who knows what dwells in the magically repeated memory of a house that old, with so many parts of it hidden skillfully away? I know of more than one legend of young Princesses of the House whose anger at the Emperor's choice for their betrothed drove them into the solitude of these chambers. Yet in the ancient stories, none returned. When I was a boy, I sought out those pale, red-lipped apparitions. I wanted to find a mummy heap and create a new legend. With that knowledge I could scare the petulant Perod to, at least, near death. But I was never so lucky, and many portions of this underground palace were impervious to my childish, persistent prying.

"No, we won't see any of those mummified young women, so don't get your hopes up, Roger." Devon laughed.

The corridor ran as straight as an arrow from the stairway to the mock palace. The place was a ruined splendor. A thousand years aged it significantly. Wooden furniture was as fragile as the dust that covered it. Rugs and tapestries showed little decay, but age muddled their colors into a nondescript murky brown. Some tapestries showed as clear as the day they were first woven, but the persistent dust coated them and hid their beauty with a gray frost.

"Because of this place, I discovered the secret passageways in the upper Palace," declared Devon. "One day I tried to hide from Perod. A tapestry seemed the best solution to my problem. As I stood in the solid dark, my finger chanced on a thumb-shaped depression in the back wall. Intrigued, I pressed against the spot. Almost a meter of the wall moved aside and I walked impetuously forward into what I thought was a hidden closet. The door closed firmly after I entered, and dim lights came on at the bottom of the wall. I stood in a passageway between the walls. The way was as old as the original above, but it may never have been used. I investigated this unusual place and gave Perod the slip. Luckily, the exits are marked much more clearly than the entrances. When Perod left, I came out of the passageways.

"In youthful vigor, for months, I explored these ways. After a while, I started thinking, if this underground place were an exact replica of the palace, could hidden passageways also crisscross the palace above? I tested my theory by looking for the same hidden catches I found in the subterranean palace. The secret doors are uniquely difficult to discover, and I believe, diffusion fields protect some so locks are invisible to all but tactile investigation. My search was rewarded on the first try. I found my original conjecture was right, from one end to the other; passageways secretly interconnect all the chambers of the Imperial Palace. To this day, I don't believe any other soul knows of these ways. I am sure Perodus is ignorant of them, and I shared my knowledge with no one, except you today. You are privileged." In the solemn stillness, Devon's words fell flat. As if he were suddenly oppressed by the environment, he quit his dialog almost as quickly as he started it.

Treading as quietly as they could through the empty corridors, they walked on in silence. Devon led with Roger just behind him.

Around the sides of the goggles, Roger was aware of the infinite darkness. It pressed over him, and he hunched his shoulders against it. He almost believed he could feel the cold touch of those ladies. Their streaming hair seemed to reach out to stroke his defenseless back. The feeling was foolish and he tried to shrug it off, but every now and then, when his imagination got the better of him, he looked back and was relieved to see the empty corridor illuminated in his goggles. *To tread these places as a child, Devon must have nerves of steel,* he thought. His nerves were already on edge, and they had been underground for barely two hours.

Roger turned around from one of his cautious rearward glances to find Devon no longer ahead of him. For a moment, he was panic-stricken, but he glanced back and noticed a cross corridor. He hurried back to the intersection and was relieved to see his leader's gray fatigues retreating through the darkness. He quickly caught up and made certain he kept a closer march. He almost tread on Devon's heels once or twice when they changed direction.

Finally they reached a set of narrow stairs that led upwards. Devon motioned toward them. "These will bring us to the wine cellars."

They climbed carefully. The stairs were so small that two men could not walk side by side. All along the way, meter square conduits and grilled openings alternately blew on or sucked at them. The sound from them rose like a deep moan from the subterranean palace.

Obviously the Library's elevator took them a long way down, thought Roger. He wondered if this was how the young Devon got to the underground palace and was about to ask, but before he could say a word, Devon answered his question.

"These stairs are part of the maintenance breezeway. They were never intended for access up or down. Five elevators communicate with the surface, but those are monitored and connect with the main traffic areas in the palace. If we tried to use them, we would be detected immediately. When we get to the cellars, we will be able to enter the secret passageways. Once in the passageways, we must do our utmost to avoid detection. I coded all the intruder sensors to pass us and set them to turn off completely in about four hours. At that time, unless I deactivate the programming, the palace emergency computer functions will go crazy. We must leave the Palace at or near that time."

Again they climbed in silence. Roger almost had time to let the feelings of the underground palace catch up with him again. Though they moved quickly, the oppressive darkness below seemed to climb with him. The moaning of the ventilation system only confirmed his fears, and he was relieved they would not use this route for their escape. At each switchback on the steep permacrete stairs, he straightened his shoulders and shook off his unreasonable imaginings.

The stairs ended abruptly at a plasteel grill. Devon stopped and put his ear to the semimetal. After he was certain the area above was clear, he applied his laser torch to the lock, through the grill. Again, he cut it in an almost undetectable line. This lock was more stubborn than the one at the Library stairs, but with Roger's help, they turned it in the block, removed it, and entered the cellar. Devon carefully reset the grill and replaced the lock so it looked untouched. He used saliva and dirt from his boot to mask the thin laser line on the bolt of the lock.

With hurried steps, Devon led Roger down the wide stone cellar. On either side, they passed huge wine casks—most unused and cracking. Finally, near the center of the cellar, Devon walked between two casks and dropped to his hands and knees. He reached under a cask into the dust at its foot and pressed an unseen mark. The bottom four bricks swung into the wall like a door and made a half meter square opening. Devon dove for the opening and disappeared. Roger followed quickly on his heels. When Roger was fully inside, Devon turned a switch, and the bricks swung back out and sealed the entrance in the wall.

They stood in a meter-and-a-half-square room whose only visible exit was a ladder that led up through the ceiling. Roger followed Devon closely as they proceeded up the ladder. They passed a couple of stone openings and climbed almost 20 meters before Devon said a word.

"Goggles!" came to Roger in an intense whisper. Before he could react, light blazed around him. The goggles corrected adequately or he would have been blinded, but, in any case, the light wasn't very bright. After spending nearly three hours in complete darkness, it was just extremely intense. The light gratified Roger. He pulled off the goggles with relief. The wispy shapes the goggles displayed strained his eyes, and without them, he could see colors once again.

Above Roger, Devon held up a dark curtain that covered the hole at the top of the ladder. The light came from this aperture. When Roger stepped through the opening, he saw they stood behind a lattice overlooking one of the grand ballrooms of the Palace. The light came from the great chandeliers, on the same level as they, that illuminated the room as brightly as daylight. Down below, a robot and human crew cleaned the remains of a state dinner.

Devon paused to whisper, "That is our escape route. You see the open double doors on the side?" He pointed to the right and down.

"Yes."

"Through those doors and straight ahead is our hidden getaway car. On the other side of the doors is a corridor, and at the end of the corridor is a large window. The window is not alarmed. You can unlock it by hand or break it. If we get separated, go for the window and escape. Do not come back, or I guarantee, you will be killed. If the Huscarls don't waste you, brother, I will for disobeying my orders. To reach the floor of the ballroom, unlock and pull on the lattice, here." Devon demonstrated, and the lattice moved outward a millimeter. "Hang from the lip of the balcony and drop. The distance is not great." He gave the rest of these instructions as he continued down the passageway. Roger followed closely behind.

"It would be a shame to find Yedric in a drunken stupor," commented Devon. "I would be much more pleased to kill him while he is in possession of his full facilities. We are now entering the area of the private suites and family quarters. To get back to the ballroom, follow the main corridors and head down the stairs. You could also try to escape through any of the outer windows in the living complex, but they are all blast-resistant and some are shielded. You could open them with my snub or your gauss pistol, but be careful of the recoil."

After only a few turnings they came to a dead end. Devon stepped up to the wall and lifted a flap. He put his eye to the hole. Roger watched him tense. Devon turned about and with exaggerated care whispered, "The man is there. He is working at his desk." Devon glanced at his watch. "For the timing of the computers to be correct, we must wait an hour." Then, with his back to the wall, he sat on the floor.

The lighting from soft plasmalights near the floor of the passageway supplied plenty of illumination. Devon mapped out the room, explained the mechanism of the secret door, and reviewed their attack plan.

"We will enter by way of the bedchamber. You station yourself at the entrance to the suites. Yedric will alert the guard with a silent alarm. Keep the guard off my back until the business is done."

"I don't much like the idea of killing Huscarls," stated Roger.

"Either you kill them or they will kill you. The choice seems simple to me. You have your gauss pistol?"

Roger showed him his pistol loaded and ready.

"Take my advice: shoot to disable. The miserable racket of a wounded man is a much greater deterrent than a dead one. This is a very serious business, Roger. You have play-acted war and death a long time. Now you will encounter the real thing. It is one thing to think about combat and quite another to experience it."

"I won't let you down." Roger took a deep breath. He felt the inexperience Devon communicated, and in spite of the fact Devon was no more than five years his elder, he accepted the man of action's advice with gratitude.

"Your duty, Roger...." Devon seemed about to say something different. He started again. "Your duty is to keep the guard away until I am finished with Yedric." His voice became almost inaudible. "Your other duty is to bring word to Tamar of my success. If the battle looks hopeless, you must escape." He appeared shaken for a moment but quickly regained his outward show of calm. "Take my Imperial Signet with you. It will open doors that are shut to all others. It cannot fall into the wrong hands." Devon placed the ring in Roger's palm.

Roger swallowed hard and stowed the ring in his pocket.

Every five minutes, Devon checked on Count Yedric. Finally, before the full hour was over, he came away from the peephole, poked Roger, and winked. "The Count is heading for bed; now is the time to spring the trap."

They moved around the corner of the passageway. With a quick and silent motion, Devon opened a hidden door panel. Through the open portal, Roger saw a dark bedroom filled with elegant furnishings. No one was in the chamber, and he copied Devon's stealthy entry. Devon sealed the secret door and pointed out the hidden latch.

Devon ran to the bedroom's main door. He put his ear to the portal for a moment and, without another word, unlatched and swung the groaning door back on its hinges.

Sixteen

Prince Devon Rathenberg slammed the heavy bedroom door open to its full width; the hinges groaned audibly in protest to the mistreatment.

Triumph written on his face, Devon stepped into the room. In spite of fatigue, worry, and responsibility, his body was filled with the wine of vengeance. He felt it flow like fire through his veins. The smell of combat was in his nostrils. He tasted blood on his tongue. In a single graceful motion, he ignited his plasmasword and it responded with a heavy thump of cascading energy. Devon was dressed in dark gray, and in the shadows of the doorway he appeared like an apparition in a funeral shroud. He stood with feral eyes examining the trembling Yedric.

Count Yedric, in the process of locking away his personal computer, turned at the violent noise from the doorway. The Count gave a startled gasp, and the blood went out of his face. "Devon Rathenberg?"

Devon didn't say a word.

The Count took an involuntary step backward. "This cannot be. Devon Rathenberg is dead. I saw him die. I killed the man myself. I saw Prince Devon Rathenberg lying dead on the lawn of Duke Falkeep's summer pavilion." Yedric pulled in a ragged breath and clutched at his heart, not in pain but in terror.

Roger stepped behind Devon and ran to the chamber's main entrance. He had to cross the study that contained Yedric and the parlor office. From this station, he was fully in the view of Devon and Yedric.

Yedric was still shaken, but the motion of Sir Roger across his line of sight brought him back to reality. He stepped back toward his desk and let out a false laugh. "Whoever you are, the destroyer does not bring henchmen; he works on his own."

"Count Dominic Yedric," intoned Devon, "I am Sir Devon Rathenberg, Knight of the Red Cross, Major in His Majesty's Huscarls, and a Prince of the House Imperial. We have not yet completed our duel."

"It cannot be." The Count's face fell and his lips moved soundlessly—seeking succor, his eyes darted from one side of the room to the other.

"You are a traitor to our Lord, Emperor Maricus. You betrayed the Prince John-Mark. You are responsible for the death of the Lady Lyral of Neuterra. You left a noble to die on the field of battle and never offered him the surety of the blade. I am your death, Yedric. Unleash your blade; I call you out."

The Count slowly regained his appearance of self-control. The shock had befuddled his mind. Yedric inhaled sharply and muttered under his breath, "A ghost doesn't mask his face with a beard and mustache. Its hair cannot be longer." Yedric abruptly recognized that this was indeed the young Rathenberg before him and realized his own danger. He reached for his personal alarm—odds and ends scattered from the desk before Devon's sword sliced the panel in twain. In spite of this, Yedric managed to press the button on the communications panel.

Devon hissed, "Unsheathe your blade, traitor, or I will instantly make your life more painful than you ever made mine." He called to Roger, "Yedric alerted the Imperial Guards; keep a close watch!"

Roger put his eye to the door's peephole to observe the hallway approaching the Count's rooms.

Count Yedric swallowed dryly. "So," he croaked, then cleared his throat, "So, you are alive."

"Don't attempt to put me off, Yedric. I did not come to talk with you." Devon swung his energy sword in a graceful arch and sliced off a solid chunk of the Count's cheek. The skin vaporized instantly and left a large raw burn on Yedric's face. "You feel my sting. Take up your sword," Devon thundered.

Count Yedric made haste to unclip his plasmasword from the belt that hung over his chair.

"Hurry, traitor!"

Before Devon struck the small electronic device with his sword, Yedric managed to signal an emergency again on his portable communicator attached to the belt. The box exploded in fragments, but Devon did not touch the Count's hand.

"You must be able to face me, false Count." He brandished his sword menacingly. "Roger." He signaled again. "Keep watch!"

"Surely, Prince Rathenberg—" the Count backed farther behind the large desk—"you don't believe you can hold off the entire complement of the Emperor's guard?"

Devon stepped forward and launched a cut at Yedric's beaked nose. The slash split Yedric's nose, and he bent over in pain. "I warned you before, Yedric. I did not come here to talk. I came to kill you. Your choice is simple: defend yourself and die quickly, or die slowly as befits a traitor."

Count Yedric stood straight. His eyes took on their old look—the same look that filled them on the night of that fated duel. Like a beacon, his plasmasword came on. Its crackle was startling in the room.

"I beat you once, Rathenberg; I can beat you again," boasted Yedric. Without any other warning, Count Yedric flung himself at Devon. His sword flew out, trying to encase itself in the knight's vitals.

Devon moved aside and carefully placed his blade in a lingering touch on the Count's chest.

The Count screamed in pain. He retreated and stood with one hand to his chest, his guard down.

"You see Count Yedric, the Emperor ordered me to lose that duel to you," spat Devon. "You could never stand against me. You shall know what it means to be betrayed. You are betrayed; my blade shall exact from your flesh every ounce of the sorrow you gave. That was for John-Mark, to whose heart you caused such great agony." Devon pressed around the desk toward Yedric.

Yedric's sword came up. Devon swung at him, and Yedric parried the heavy attack awkwardly. The Count ducked and ran through the door to Devon's left.

Devon cautiously followed. He came upon the Count using his blade to cut through the wall to the chamber on the other side. Devon swung low at the man, and Yedric's blade moved quickly to intercept the attack. But when Yedric's energy sword arrived there, Devon's was not. The sword slashed upward and cut precisely; Yedric's right ear became a stinking mist. He gave a throaty croak and, without warning, crashed through the three quarters-finished hole he had cut in the wall.

From Roger's direction, Devon heard gauss pistol shots. He peered out into the suite. Roger was firing through the open door of the office and appeared to be in control of the situation. The bloodlust was on Devon. He turned and deliberately followed Yedric into the next room.

Darkness cloaked the room. The only light came from Yedric's sword, brightly visible in the opposite corner of the chamber.

"That was for Lyral, Count Yedric. She was my friend, and because of you, she is dead."

Not far from Yedric's shadowy form, a woman screamed. The noise suddenly cut off, and Yedric's plasmablade came up to the level of his chest. Yedric fumbled for a moment on the side of the wall, and the lights blazed on.

"Look, you." Yedric's voice was strained; it rasped almost hysterically. "Look, Rathenberg." He laughed wildly. "I also possess the power of death." In his grasp he held a young woman. One of his arms locked around her neck, and the plasmablade almost touched her cheek. Her face was filled with terror. She rolled her eyes beseechingly between Yedric and Devon. Yedric held her almost off the floor; the folds of her nightgown, caught at her neck, barely covered her thighs.

"I will kill her," screamed Yedric.

"I cannot allow that." Devon bowed his head.

"Drop your sword, Rathenberg, so I might end your life like it should have been ended long ago."

Devon dropped his sword. With a sputter, the blade went out as soon as he released it. Unbelieving, Yedric followed its fall to the ground. The sword hit with a slight ring. Out of the corner of his eye,

Count Yedric warily stared at Devon. The Rathenberg Prince barely moved. As Yedric released the girl's neck and propelled her to the floor, he looked up. Devon's eyes gazed powerfully into the Count's, and Yedric didn't notice the movement of Devon's left hand. A tiny red dot lighted the Count's left ear, and a loud thump reverberated from Devon Rathenberg's left side. Precisely where Devon aimed the dot, a high explosive snub round touched the Count's ear and went off. The Count's head shattered like a soft melon.

The girl was easily clear of the blast. Even if the Count still held her, Devon planned his shot so she would not be harmed. Brains, skull fragments, and blood spattered the room. The girl screamed hysterically, and Count Dominic Yedric's headless body crumpled to the floor.

"That was for Emperor Maricus," stated Devon unemotionally.

Devon picked up his sword, then checked the girl on the floor. She cried out when he touched her, but she wasn't injured. Devon stood up. The sounds of battle in the late Count's parlor were increasing.

As he ran back to the study, Devon heard the solid hissing thud of gauss cartridges and the cries of wounded men. He smiled. Roger had heeded his advice. Devon stopped at the Count's desk, took the disks out of the small computer, and stuffed them into his belt pouch. Then he continued to the office door.

The whiz of accelerator rifles and Roger's gauss pistol cut through the night. Devon heard the soft pings and ricochets that announced the strike of the small accelerator pellets. Imperial Huscarls didn't use accelerator weapons; by choice and policy, they used gauss weapons. Devon was confused until he gazed down the corridor. They were not Imperial Huscarls—they were Naval Marines. That was, at least, a blessing. If he had to kill his own men, he would feel as felonious as Sir Roger. Devon sent a couple of snub rounds into the hallway and heard a cry of pain follow the explosions. Out of sight of the doorway, he grasped Roger by the arm and propelled him toward the dead Count's bedroom. "Leave by the passageway. Make your getaway. Don't wait for me. The Count is dead. Tell Tamar I love her."

Sir Roger bled from several slight accelerator projectile wounds. He stumbled to a halt. "I want to see this through!"

"To see it through means both our deaths. Go now! That's an order."

Roger stared angrily at Devon, but the other man was already firing with good result down the hallway. "I can't just leave you."

"You can and must," insisted Devon. "If I can fight my way out of this, we might both survive, but not if you don't open our escape route. Go, before it's too late. Go!"

Roger turned and ran to the secret panel. He fumbled with the latch and was relieved when the doorway in the wall finally slid to the side. He carefully closed the panel and retraced his steps toward the ballroom. The passageways took him in a roundabout manner, and it was some minutes before he dropped to the floor of the ballroom.

As his feet touched the ground, he unexpectedly heard the sounds of gunfire approaching, and unmistakably, most of the shots came from Devon's exploding snub pistol rounds. Roger heard a gas grenade go off. If Devon was already so close, Roger thought, then he better get to their gravvehicle.

Roger dashed out of the ballroom doors toward the window Devon had indicated previously. Just before he reached it, a group of Marines rushed toward him from the crossing corridor. Roger threw himself at the window. It shattered agreeably and he exited in a sprawl. Roger lay for only a moment on the lawn of the Imperial Palace. Then he leapt up and ran three meters into the shrubs around the perimeter of the building. He lay hidden in the brush and gazed across the Delta at the Galactic Library, where the gravvehicle was hidden. He would never be able to get to the vehicle; if he tried to cross the open ground, the Marines would cut him to pieces.

The sounds of battle still came from inside the Palace. Roger ran around the nearest corner of the building and was pleased to see Marine and police gravvehicles. They were not completely abandoned; a couple of Imperial Policemen anxiously gaped toward the building and waited for orders. Callously, Roger picked them off with his gauss pistol; they both fell without a sound.

Roger jumped to the controls of the most substantial-looking vehicle—a Marine armored carrier. Roger had driven one like this in training but had to think for a moment before he got it moving. He backed 50 meters from the Palace doors and poured on full power. The heavy vehicle gained speed quickly. With a loud crash, it hit the doors and literally blew them off their hinges. The foyer of the Palace was enormous. Aiming for the snub explosions and dodging anything inordinately solid, Roger headed into the bowels of the building.

Near the further end of the foyer, a group of frantically retreating Marines scurried into defensive positions at the bottom of a huge staircase that led into main portion of the Palace. A snub round exploded at the top of the stairs. The fury of battle made him reckless, and Roger slammed the armored vehicle sideways into the unsuspecting Marines. The men who weren't crushed instantly dropped their weapons and ran frantically to either side. In the doorway at the top of the staircase, Devon staggered into sight. He fired back in the direction from which he came. While Roger watched Devon struggle through the doorway, accelerator rifle fire struck the man twice. Devon's legs buckled under him and he fell to the floor.

Roger jumped out of the gravvehicle; it would never be able to get near enough to Devon for Roger to pick him up where he lay. Roger fired at anything around the stairs that moved. He took them in a rush.

Devon struggled to crawl. The Rathenberg Prince lay on his stomach firing intently down the corridor. Devon's legs were cut and bleeding from a dozen wounds. His forearms looked like chopped meat; Roger wondered how he could hold the gun at all.

"Devon, it's me. Hold on." Filled with the strength of fear, Roger heaved Devon over his shoulder. Devon was almost his size, maybe a little smaller, but he felt as light as a feather. As Roger lifted his burden, a siren started to scream, the lights in the foyer flashed, and in a deluge, fire suppressant gas and water rained from overhead sprinklers.

When Roger hesitated, he heard a hoarse whisper near his ear, "Go! It's the computers. It's my programming..."

Roger almost ran down the steps. He threw Devon into the back of the armored gravvehicle and gunned it toward the door.

As they soared out of the Palace into the sunshine, Roger breathed a sigh of relief.

"It's not over yet," he heard weakly from just behind him. "Get lower!" ordered Devon.

"At this speed, the thing won't go any lower."

Devon reached over Roger's shoulder and under the high dash. He ripped at the wires; connections sparked, and a flash of blue flame came out from under the panel. Devon leaned back, leaving blood tracks on the seat and dashboard. "Try it now," he groaned

There was no need to say anything. The moment Devon pulled the wires, the vehicle accelerated and Roger put it right down on the deck.

"Now what?" quipped Roger.

"Head for the port. They may be expecting us, but I don't think we'll be able to escape them while planet-bound."

"I don't see any sign of pursuit..."

"They're biding their time. They don't think we can go anywhere they can't find us..." Devon's voice became more and more hushed and then was suddenly silent.

"Don't go and die on me," whispered Roger.

An idea came to Roger as they approached the base entrance. Huscarls stood guard. He slowed slightly and at their signals, came to a stop. With a ferocious look, he snarled at the men, "Get out of the way! Can't you see Major Rathenberg is seriously injured? I've got to get him to the base hospital fast. Clear the way ahead for me." Without waiting to see if his words had their desired effect, he put the gravvehicle into full power again and drove through the gates. As he sped out of sight, they didn't shoot. Roger thought that was a good sign.

As they reached the field, the security was provided by Imperial Marines. When they crossed the marked flightline, the Marine guards fired on them with accelerator rifles, but the effect against the armored vehicle was like rain on a tin roof. Roger maneuvered the armored car in zigzag switchbacks to make them a harder target in case they had something more powerful.

The *Silent Dawn* stood ready. Roger only hoped the preflight sequencing had not blown with any errors, otherwise they might never get the ship off the ground. As they neared the ship, he turned off the gravity repulsors and let the vehicle skid to a screeching halt. He hauled the unconscious Prince out of the seat with difficulty, but Roger managed to drag him to the lock. Roger took two tries to code the door open, but finally it slid to the side, and he dropped Devon in the outer lock and sealed the exterior door.

In a flash, Roger jumped in the pilot's seat. He coded immediate lift off and, unfettered, the ship leapt into the sky. As soon as the atmosphere dropped below them, he started the ship's computers, calculating a coincidence for Neuterra, then went to see if Devon was still alive.

When Roger reached him, the Knight of the Red Cross was pale and barely breathing. Roger picked him up and carried him over his shoulders to the cargo compartment. He gently placed the dying knight into an emergency hibernation berth. Roger hoped he wasn't too late. He sealed the berth and turned on the cold sleep system. Maybe, when they reached Neuterra in a few days, the doctors could patch Devon back together. Not only did Roger himself feel a great affinity for this man, but, if Devon Rathenberg died, Roger dreaded the thought of having to break the news to his sister. If Devon Rathenberg died, Roger knew, the information would destroy her.

Seventeen

The *Silent Dawn* was an extremely fast ship; in less than a day, it achieved the safe distance and proper position to allow operations in null space. By the time Roger activated the *Silent Dawn*'s FTL drive, the Imperial Navy had not made even a cursory attempt at interception. With a gentle vibration, the ship completed the phase shift and passed into null space, headed for Neuterra.

FTL stood for faster than light. Although no ship could travel at speeds approaching light, much less at a speed above the constant, an FTL ship could move from place to place in space without regard for that limitation. The FTL drive worked through the principles of gravitation, and its operation was very similar to the gravity repulsors and dampers found throughout the Empire.

The trick of moving between stars was not as easy as pushing against a gravity well until you gained enough velocity to coast the rest of the way. You could only go so fast, then relativity got a hold on you and the limit was the speed of light. The trick of the FTL drive was in taking advantage of the unique folds gravity placed in the universe. Because of gravity, space is folded in the continuum of time. This means light, which was dependent on time, travels in a straight line relative to everything else. Gravity, however, is instantaneous: it is a force, independent of time and unfettered by Euclid. Taken all together, if you wanted to get somewhere fast in space, you didn't go the long way around—following in the wake of light. You sought the shorter way by slipping through the folds created by gravity. Indeed, at light speed, the trip from Arienth to Neuterra would have taken thirty years, but by FTL that same trip generally took less than three weeks. However, the length of a null space voyage was only partially dependent on the interstellar distance. In spite of the unfortunate occasions where ships took too long to reach their destinations, got lost in null space, or came out in the wrong place, the advantages of FTL travel were obvious. And, for quick escapes, null space provided a unique degree of autonomy and security.

Even if the Imperial Navy had traced the *Silent Dawn* into space and marked the exact position it winked outside the normal universe, the computations necessary to determine the exact destination of the ship would have required nearly a day for the Galactic Library's computer to solve. Even then, the answer to the null space problem for the *Silent Dawn*'s probable destination would have a billion galactic solutions. If you excluded nonstellar nodes, which were many, you might be left with only a million possibilities. If you allowed for only habitable systems, you could reduce the number into the thousands. If you placed a limit on the range and applied some reasonable deduction, you might willow down the list to only a hundred. Once the investigation got to this level, the searcher would be best advised to visit each system and comb its average 320 trillion square kilometers for a ship, which at its greatest section, was around 300 square meters. That is, if you restricted your search to the plane of the ecliptic, otherwise, you might as well give up now. To put this in human terms, finding a ship like the *Silent Dawn* in a solar system would be like looking for a single needle hidden somewhere on the surface of Terra—very difficult.

The best resolution to the problem was to send a ship with a detection range of around a million miles, into null space behind the fleeing vessel. As the ship pounded along the folds of the galaxy, the emanations of the FTL drive were easy to follow. The only danger was if the ship you followed had no particular destination in mind, and in that case you could be carried forever behind a vessel that chose a null space solution without any nodes. An ancient strategist used this technique with great success. His automaton decoy fleet drew an entire Navy to this fate. Crewmen still whisper of these ghostly ships, still in trail, searching for a node that might never exist. Some claim they have seen this fleet as it streams eternally through null space.

In any case, thought Roger, the Emperor Perodus should have ordered his remaining vessels to give chase to the *Silent Dawn* and, at least, save face by attempting to intercept it. Roger was almost disappointed the possibility didn't manifest itself, especially after all the attention the Imperial Navy showed Devon and him at the Palace.

Roger learned later that no interceptor was sent because none were available: the entire Navy was preparing for a massive surprise attack and therefore was nowhere near Arienth. The Emperor would have been well advised to make some sort of last-ditch effort to stop the *Silent Dawn,* because Devon Rathenberg held, in the computer data he took from the Imperial intelligence system, Count Yedric, and the *Saint Anne*, all of the Emperor's plans. Luckily, for Roger, no attack came, and now with the ship safely in null space, none was possible.

Three weeks alone in null space is still a long time. This was nearly twice the length of the trip Roger made from Falkeep to Arienth. In his youthful mind, it was an eternally long trip, and he was angry that Devon would not be sharing it with him. As simple as he thought this mission would be when he left Falkeep, it had turned out to be incredibly complex. He wanted more facts about how Devon met Tamar, the duel during the ball, the origins of Devon's mission for the Emperor Maricus, and the implications of it in the current Empire. He desired to discuss the information Devon gathered on Arienth, and he was particularly interested in the general and specific opinions of Devon Rathenberg, whom he knew was an accepted expert on Imperial intelligence. Beyond that, the accomplishments of Devon's advice and leadership overawed him. Roger felt his short brush of experience under Devon's guidance changed him; he had matured and grown as a man. With foreboding, he hoped his father would approve.

The selection of Duke Falkeep's son-in-law was not fully the Duke's own. And, though the Duke gladly accepted Tamar's choice of Prince Rathenberg, Roger wasn't sure his father knew what that choice completely entailed.

Duke Falkeep was a man of careful neutrality and political genius. He liked the status quo because it was generous to rule and profitable to enterprise. The son of Rathenberg was a rogue spirit, undeniably honorable, unquestionably skilled in politics and war, but incredibly predictable in his fervor. Rathenberg would overturn the galaxy for the cause of right, and Roger was uncertain that his father was familiar with the cause of right. This is not to say the elder Falkeep would not uphold the most honorable course of action or that he would accept anything but the most upright position. Duke Falkeep was a man of lofty principle, unwavering honor, and unmitigated justice. The difference between Devon Rathenberg and him, however, was that the Prince would not accept anything less than his own principles in anyone else. Devon's desire was to bring the greatest good to others and let them feast. Those who thwarted good were not worthy of consideration. They were to be expunged from the universe.

Duke Falkeep expected his lofty principles to be reflected in his House, but he did not expect any other House to reflect them. They were unworthy of that consideration. Perhaps another House's honor and deportment might affect its trade or political relationship with Falkeep, and then it became an issue to the Duke, but not before. For Duke Falkeep, the evidence was in the results. For Sir Devon, the result was the evidence.

Roger smiled. Perhaps the friction generated between the two would prove entertaining as well as enlightening. He could not imagine the outspoken Rathenberg cowed by the Iron Duke, yet he couldn't picture his father resigning himself in the name of general or specific principle.

Now that Perodus was Emperor, a further difficulty presented itself: Devon Rathenberg was the second in line to the Iron Throne of the Empire. When Maricus was alive, the line of succession descended through Perod-Mark to John-Mark, then Devon Rathenberg. Perodus and John-Mark had no male children, and Devon was the son of Catherine Haupenburg, Emperor Maricus' sister and the first son of the House Rathenberg. From the generation of Maricus on, there were no other male children in the line. The possibility of Imperial succession might itself generate problems for his father, the neutral Iron Duke.

But, in spite of the difficulties, Roger suspected the Duke would have with his new son-in-law, there was still hope; Tamar was the Duke's favorite child. How the most difficult child in their family became the Duke's most prized progeny was beyond Roger's conception. Roger did not begrudge his father his affection. He himself was never mistreated or ignored because of it. He never received less love from his father. Duke Falkeep was a close man, but affected by extremes of emotion. His love for his children was never cold or formal, but his example in deportment and timeliness was precise. They learned to show appropriate emotion at appropriate times, which is the best goal in any human upbringing. The only one who showed a glint of difference was Tamar.

That is not to say, the Duke's other children were not exceptional in their own right; it was just that Tamar was unique. Her spirit was undaunted by anything. To her, a goal was always something to be exceeded. She provided her own motivation. Her love of others and love of life shown like a blazing fire in a field of cold and bitter darkness. After Roger's mother died, the Duke warmed himself with this fire. Tamar provided a motivation of love to the Duke. Her essential difference was his reason for life.

Roger laughed. He wasn't sure if the motivation was a result of the Duke's attempt to tone to a respectable level the young Tamar's powerful drive or his endeavor to keep up with it. In any case, Tamar developed like a star going nova. The years found her more and more shaped by noble principles and political aptitude. These studies rounded her personality and expanded her already delicious depth of humanity to a level incomprehensible to those who didn't know her. In the very words of the Emperor Maricus to Duke Falkeep, "The Lady Tamar Falkeep is the most politically sensitive and personally empathetic member of the Noblesse to be born in the last 500 years. She was the epitome of an Imperial Princess."

Unfortunately, in comparison, she was the least understood person who walked the thousand planets. Because she looked, acted, spoke, thought, and in general was the precise, definitive model of a princess in the Empire, she was perhaps the loneliest individual in the galaxy. In Roger's knowledge, only two people outside Tamar's family became her close friends: the Lady Lyral Neuterra and the Lady Elizabeth Acier. Tamar was everyone's friend and no one's friend. Her abilities placed her on a high pedestal she seemed exactly suited to fill. She was the most popular person in Imperial society, but in that society, she was treated as an archetype and not as a person in her own right. Though Tamar complemented the court and the Noblesse so well, her friends amazingly were not capable of integrating her perfection into their lives. For example, the now-deceased Lady Lyral had been so unlike the true princess she was. She did not have the personality or aura of a princess, yet she was incredibly personable. With Tamar, she had shared the ability of political mastermind, yet Lyral had balanced that ability with the application to individuals as well as the court where Tamar couldn't.

And so, Lord Falkeep's daughter, so little understood by others, little understood others. She was crippled by her own capability, a princess among normal humans, or at least normal, noble humans. She was as ignorant of an impassioned kiss as the youngest child. She was naive of human interaction by lack of interaction, a child unspoiled by the world. Yet, she was as perfect as the Empire thought her. She was as innocent, wise, and accomplished as she seemed.

That the Prince, Sir Devon, son of Duke Rathenberg, a person of solitary habit yet universal acknowledgment, found the Lady Tamar so tempting he would give up his rank and position in his House to have her was astonishing. His honor would never permit him to take her in any way except through marriage, but by position, his honor would dictate that he could never marry her. The knight's only hope of happiness, his only hope of honor came when the Lady Tamar reprieved his irrevocable decision to die. *Without that,* thought Roger, *my sister, Tamar, would yet never know another's romantic love.* She would not have changed, and Devon would have spent his life pining after a woman, a kindred spirit, he could not rightfully have.

When they reached Neuterra, Roger hoped someone could put Devon back together. The kindred spirit of Devon Rathenberg had to return to his sister. Her happiness was worth more to the soul of his father and peace of his family than Roger cared to admit.

Roger predicted the trip would be boring, and he was right; it was.

With an easy precision, the *Silent Dawn* shook off the confines of null space and reentered the normal universe. Roger was gratified that his calculations resulted in a close terminus with the Neuterran system. So close, in fact, that within moments of the phase shift to normal space, a coded signal interrogated the *Silent Dawn*'s antennas for the proper electronic signs and countersigns. The ship, programmed for commercial travel, ignored the indecipherable requests of the transmissions and instead sent out its normal port call information. Within nanoseconds, the ship's computers generated and beamed the registry, serial number, name, destination, crew, and cargo log to the waiting outer system stations. With clearance from system traffic control, Roger engaged the gravdrive and headed at high velocity toward the heavenly body that was the political center of the Dukedom of Neuterra.

Because a system, its primary star, and its primary planet were generally named after one another, a discussion of the events of the Empire with individuals not familiar with the traditional naming conventions sometimes became difficult. This was especially true of a system like Neuterra. Neuterra was not a primary planet in the system of the Duchy of Neuterra; it was the moon of a gas giant that fortunately had its own name, Asa-Thor.

The Neuterran system was unusual, in that the gas giant Asa-Thor's orbit was very close to the system's star. This was very good because Neuterra's star was a small white that barely put out a tenth of Sol's energy. The climate of Neuterra, unlike most inhabited gas giant's moons was very hospitable. Between the even heating of the white star and Asa-Thor's thermal activity, Neuterra's summers were gentle, and its winters comfortable. The extremes of Neuterran climate were so even, many environmentalists considered the planet a single biome.

Anything would grow on Neuterra. The planet provided the most pleasing environment for any crop needed by modern man. In fact, some plants grew with more vigor in the climate of Neuterra than on their native globes. Crops, however, were not the business of Neuterra. For millennia, Neuterra developed exact duplicates of natural products. On the planet, billions of plant types became the blueprints for organic synthesis. In orbit, thousands of laboratory factories output the biological needs and luxuries of the Empire. The inhabitants of Neuterra were, by trade, biochemists, biologists, biosynthesists, druggists, geneticists, and bioengineers. Neuterra provided the seasonings for Imperial palates, the pharmaceuticals for Imperial medicine, the drugs for illicit Imperial recreation, the organic electronics for advanced Imperial computers. The list of products was almost endless, the applications untold.

At first glance, that Neuterra of all the planets was the most influential in the Landsritters seemed an enigma. That it was a Duchy of only moderate rank in the Thirty Kingdoms did not reflect its actual influence. And indeed, that the leader of a biological factory planet held so much strength in Imperial circles seemed strange. The enemies of the House Neuterra quietly said the Neuterrans developed drugs that improved the capabilities of its inhabitants. That is an assertion open to much debate, but the House and indeed the entire populace of Neuterra showed a disposition to extremely long life and incredibly capable offspring. Whether this was a direct result of their own experimentation or the pleasant climate of the planet, the Neuterrans kept their knowledge a patent secret. The actuality was far simpler and more along the lines of the historical establishment of the Empire. The scientists of Neuterra were biological engineers. They developed the strains of humans they preferred. Natural selection was permitted, but, in the Empire, genetic manipulation provided the impetus for human development. The people of Neuterra were carefully designed to be prosperous, happy, pleasant, beautiful, capable, and specialized to the extent that the work of the planet was always obscenely profitable.

The leaders of the planet were not excluded from this development. The people of Neuterra wanted a powerful voice in the Empire, so they engineered one. The House Neuterra was known for its gregarious and popular rulers. No House could boast as personable or invigorating a line of Nobility. Within the framework of the Code, these leaders became the bastion of the Landsritters. Part of this ability derived from the efforts of the bioengineers, but more interesting, the House was experienced through its knowledge and latent abilities in the realm of biological leadership. To understand what controlled another's tastes and mental activities was the key in designing and selling the products of Neuterra; the noble Neuterrans were well versed in human needs and desires. And they controlled others with a delicacy of voice, personality, and business. The Landsritters bowed to their control without an inkling of the basis for it.

Perhaps, it could be conjectured that the Imperial seat should have sprung from the House Neuterra. That was a development the original geneticists could not have foreseen. And yet, men who looked and acted like Emperors always ruled the House Imperial. They were given to few extremes, dauntless in their self-control, subtle in their negotiations, regal in their character, whether for good or bad. The Imperial strain perhaps could have improved, and indeed did improve through its occasional unions with House Neuterra. But this assertion of innate superiority could be argued using the examples of the Lady Lyral, who had exemplified the epitome of the personality of the House Neuterra, and the Lady Tamar, who, though from Falkeep was a perfect archetype of the House Imperial. Lyral had been an open personality, whose leadership was by association, while Tamar was a recognized figurehead whose leadership bounded from her perfect deportment. Lyral had to impress individuals to lead them; Tamar led by the force of her existence, no personal interaction was required. The geneticists who put together the models for their leaders three thousand years ago would have been happy with either genetic consequence.

The House Neuterra was historically a productive House. In line for ascendancy to the honor of Duke of Neuterra, it usually boasted at least three boy children. For some reason, not released into general knowledge, the Duke Paris Neuterra and his Lady Nieva, after the birth of Lyral, could not produce another child. Fortunately, that was not a particular problem; the House Neuterra was a large one and qualified relations abounded. The Duke could make his choice of the most capable and stalwart of these to take his place. This was true especially now that the Emperor Perodus had executed the Lady Lyral.

Roger thought harshly of the new Emperor's judgment: the Lady Lyral had been a bright spot of humanity among the cruelty of rule. Duke Neuterra had allied himself with the Imperial Prince, John-Mark and had promised the Lady Lyral to the Prince as his bride. With their marriage, John-Mark would become the next in line to the Duchy of

Neuterra. Roger himself was not privy to the particular agreements of Neuterra and Prince John-Mark, but he knew the Prince's older brother, the new Emperor Perodus, radically opposed them.

So strongly had the Houses under Neuterra and aligned with John-Mark been opposed by the Emperor that he had banned them. They were thereby no longer governed by the Codes; now any agreement, marriage, birth, inheritance, or alliance in these Houses could not be recognized legally by the Emperor or Empire. These Houses had no option other than rebellion. Their hope was in the alignment of the other Houses in the Landsritters to their cause. Roger bitterly reminded himself that his own House, now in alliance with the other rebelling nobles, was also banned. He gathered strength in the realization that he and Sir Devon struck perhaps the first telling blow against the Empire. He felt pride that his own rebellion against the Emperor supported the honor of the Empire.

The huge mass of Asa-Thor grew in the forward viewers. Its swirling colors radiated a brilliant flow of shapes and shadows and initially hid the moon, Neuterra, from Roger's inspection. System control passed him to orbital traffic control and assigned him a high orbit to await customs inspection. The naval traffic in orbit around Neuterra was notably scarce. The system was not as bare as Arienth, but the intersystem ships were missing from their usual posts around the planet.

Roger didn't have long to wait for customs to approach the *Silent Dawn.* In less than 30 minutes, he noticed an electronic emission on his screens that signified the patrol corvette that would receive his vessel. He had cautiously announced himself as a delegation from Falkeep; that way, whatever was going on in Neuterran space, he should be able to back out with honor. The corvette matched orbit with him, and after scanning the *Silent Dawn* for a few minutes, the skipper requested boarding.

When the vessels were connected, a young lieutenant and a grizzled chief came on board the ship. The Lieutenant was very thorough: he went carefully through the ship's papers and Roger's credentials. After he discovered Roger's rank, he became very differential. The Chief kept quiet and let his officer conduct the inspection with proper decorum. Roger was sure if the Lieutenant made an important mistake, the chief would gently and almost silently correct him. He remembered his first days in training as skipper of an intrasystem corvette and thought ruefully that he himself wasn't much older than the lieutenant across from him.

It didn't take long for the pair to go over the ship's papers. After checking everything off on his list, the Lieutenant asked, "Sir, about this person in the hibernation berth, would it be possible for us to check the bioreadings, and could you give us a little more information about the individual inside?"

Roger answered, "Yes, certainly, Lieutenant." Roger wasn't sure he wanted to disclose the identity of the contents or the status of Sir Devon without knowing just where Neuterra stood against the Emperor. "Lieutenant," he began as they walked toward the cargo bay, "how does Neuterra stand in relation to the Emperor Perodus?"

The Lieutenant stopped short. "Sir, you have not heard of the ban of the Emperor?"

"Yes, I know of the ban. I want to know what Duke Neuterra is doing about it and whether, in his domains; I will be safe from Imperial interference."

The Lieutenant looked at his chief. They conferred quietly. Then the Lieutenant lowered his electronic clipboard. "Sir, I don't know what has been said away from Neuterra, but the Duke, though he is on Neuterra now, sent a majority of our forces to support the other banned Houses against the Emperor. As far as I can tell you, Neuterra is engaged in active warfare against the Emperor Perodus."

This convinced Roger. He held back the sigh of relief that threatened to escape his lips. No use letting these men know how critical that information was to him. They continued on to the cargo bay and the cold sleep berth.

When they stood in front of the coffin-shaped object, the Lieutenant waved his chief to the controls. The Chief made a careful sweep of them and reported each of his findings. "The berth contains a male human in stable hibernation." He checked the activation history. "The man was critically wounded before he was entered into the berth. Low blood and fluid level. Intense shock. Heart rate regular. Breathing ragged. Injuries are listed by the machine as shrapnel and lacerations, arms, legs, and lower torso." He glanced expectantly at Roger.

"How can you explain this, sir?" queried the visibly shaken Lieutenant.

Roger could barely contain a smile. The Lieutenant obviously believed he had discovered a case of criminal activity. He answered solemnly, "The man is Sir Devon Rathenberg, Knight of the Red Cross, son of Duke Rathenberg." Both the Chief's and Lieutenant's eyes grew wide as Roger spoke. "We escaped from Arienth on business for the banned Houses. The knight needs immediate medical attention."

"Ye-e-s sir," stammered the Lieutenant, as he immediately brought his communicator to his lips. "If you will be so kind as to activate your ship's systems and follow us, I will personally lead you to the surface."

The Chief made an elaborate hand signal.

"Right, Chief," returned the Lieutenant. "My Chief will remain on board with you to help you guide your ship into the port. I will signal Duke Neuterra that you will be coming in. And," he added, "alert our medical emergency team."

"Thank you, Lieutenant," Roger responded.

"My pleasure, sir," returned the Lieutenant with a bow.

While the Lieutenant cycled through the lock to his own ship, Roger led the Chief back to the *Silent Dawn*'s cockpit.

When in the trail of the customs ship, they settled in an approach orbit, and the chief spoke seriously to Roger, "Do you really have Prince Rathenberg in that hibernation berth?"

The Chief did not sound to Roger as if he were questioning the truth of Roger's assertion, only reassuring himself that he'd heard properly.

"Yes it is the Prince Devon Rathenberg. He was injured fighting his way out of the Imperial Palace."

"We heard that the young Rathenberg was dead." The Chief's voice became surprisingly gentle. "It was said that if the son of Rathenberg died, the honor of the Empire died with him."

Roger was suddenly curious. "What was Devon Rathenberg to, to...?"

"What was he to me? Sir Roger Falkeep, two men in the Empire are known throughout the ranks. They are the men who never fail. One is the Prince John-Mark, the Dragon. The other is the Lord Devon Rathenberg, the Fox. There is not a man in the forces of Neuterra who would not die for either of those two men."

Roger was intrigued. He heard his own men speak of the Dragon and the Fox, but he never understood the terms. "Why the Dragon, and why the Fox?"

As if quoting a code of honor, the Chief replied, "The Dragon consumes his enemies, yet he is not without wisdom. The Fox is a crafty creature born of wisdom, yet is also strong. You know yourself of the campaigns of the Dragon and the Fox. Together they are unconquerable."

Roger did know much about the campaigns of these two men. Although the Prince John-Mark was less than 25 years old, the Landsritters and his father Maricus had elected him to be the Marshall of the Huscarls. The battles John-Mark fought were studied in the Imperial Military Institute. And Devon Rathenberg, though less than 30, two years ago was appointed the Chief of the Emperor's Intelligence and Security. He became a Knight of the Red Cross for gallantry in action. He was the late Emperor Maricus' most valued advisor. A popular saying had even sprung up about him. The people said it when a lawbreaker temporarily escaped justice: nothing escapes the notice of the Fox. Roger never realized just what the Fox was until now. The proverb was not a threat; it was a promise.

The Emperor's Fox was considered the highest example of Imperial honor. Roger remembered a story he'd heard about Devon Rathenberg as a lieutenant. The knight ordered his men not to injure the populace or despoil the countryside. When he caught some of his troops needlessly destroying a farmhouse, he shot the guilty soldiers himself. Then, working alongside his men, they built back the destroyed house and grounds. The official record said the actions of Sir Devon Rathenberg rallied the populace of the entire planet against the rebels, and the victory was directly attributed to him, to his honor. In the minds of many men, the Fox had become the honor of the Empire.

The Chief was silent the rest of the journey, and in less than an hour, they touched down in a courier spot on the port parking area.

A medical team met the *Silent Dawn* when it landed. They approached the ship before Roger shut the engines down. With reverence, the Chief himself helped load the cold sleep berth into the hospital gravvehicle, and with a precise salute, saw the knight off across the field. He gave a final bleak look as he saluted Sir Roger and returned to his own ship.

In hopes he wouldn't need to make a quick escape from Neuterra, Roger sealed the *Silent Dawn*. Then he walked to the operations building, where a delegation from the Duke of Neuterra himself met him. Concern and curiosity evident in their every word, they bundled him off to the Duke's mansion. Roger held his tongue and was soon situated in a small suite, where he awaited the pleasure of the Duke.

Eighteen

The Emperor, Perodus Haupenberg the First, sat brooding in his study. The events of the day were a blur to him. Since time immemorial, nothing like them had ever touched the face of Arienth. True, Emperors lived and died, and some were assassinated. He smiled humorlessly. But for an attack to come so openly, directly under the nose of the Navy, Marines, Secret Police, and Huscarls was unforgivable.

Count Rathenberg, his new chancellor now that the Duke Rathenberg was banned, entered hesitantly into the office.

"Your majesty." He bowed.

"Count Yedric?" Perodus instantly berated himself. Couldn't he remember he raised Yedric to the Status of Duke?

The Count's eyes shifted. Then he spoke quickly. "Duke Yedric is dead, your majesty."

Perodus' eyes bulged. His mind thought frantically. Without Yedric's support, his power was reduced threefold. "You are absolutely positive it was him?"

Again that hesitation. "Yes, your majesty. The Lady Charis Myridon provided identification...and a description of the events that led to Yedric's death."

"And that description?"

"The lady was very distraught by the incident..."

"What does that mean, Rathenberg? Go on."

"I merely point out, your Majesty, that because of her unbalanced state of mind during the moments of the attack; the lady's testimony is in question. She rests comfortably at the hospital now."

"I don't care to be protected from the facts. Tell me the lady's testimony, and I will judge its accuracy for myself." His voice rose in anger.

"Yes, your Majesty." Rathenberg blanched. "The lady told us that in the early hours of the morning, the sounds of rough words and a scuffle near the back wall of her apartment awakened her. The lady thought it was but a simple quarrel and went back to sleep. The next thing she remembered was a harsh grating sound, and in the darkness, from where the sound originated, she saw a beam of plasmalight cutting through the wall. From the indications in the room, it is safe to conclude a plasmasword was used to cut into her chamber—evidently it was Duke Yedric's plasmasword."

"I take your meaning that Yedric was involved in some sort of argument and at some point he attempted to escape from his suite," summarized Perodus. "Did the Cou... Duke ever summon help?"

Rathenberg looked toward the ground. "Yes, your majesty. The Duke twice signaled an alarm to the Palace Marines."

"And, where were my Marines?"

"Gauss pistol fire kept them away from the entrance to Yedric's quarters. We think two men accosted the Duke."

"Continue with the lady's story, I don't care to hear your conjecture about the excuses of our Palace Marines."

"The lady said she was too confused and befuddled by sleep to try to escape. She was frozen with fear when Duke Yedric, waving a plasmasword, crashed into her bedroom. As soon as he entered the room, the Duke noticed her by the light of his sword. In a moment he grasped her about the throat and held the sword blade not less than an inch from her face. The lady did have indications on her body that she was mishandled; her neck was bruised and a plasma-scald marked her from chin to forehead.

"The lady said that although she was nearly blinded by the Duke's plasmablade, she both saw and heard another man follow the Duke into her chamber. She could mark him also by the glow of his plasmasword. The Duke turned on the lights, and then she identified the second intruder. Yedric addressed the gentleman and threatened to kill the Lady Charis. In response, the other man dropped his sword. Apparently, in an attempt to rush forward and kill the now-unarmed individual, Yedric threw the lady to the ground. The next thing she heard was an explosion, and she was drenched with blood. While the Lady Charis lay on the floor afraid to move, the second man picked up his sword, checked her breathing and pulse, and retreated back through the hole in the wall. We found the lady hysterical with fear, still on her bedroom floor."

"What killed Yedric?"

"The Duke's body bore the brunt of a master swordsman: a plasmablade score deeply branded his chest, and although difficult to discover, his left ear was burned off and his nose split."

"Very well, but how did he die?"

"A carefully placed snub round blew off his head."

"How do you know that?"

"The medical pathologist indicated the round hit Yedric's right ear and exploded. My conjecture is that the man fired to kill Yedric and protect the lady."

The Emperor stared at his seneschal. The Count wore an almost smug look. A sudden thought struck Perodus. "Count Rathenberg, you know who invaded my Palace, who fired that shot, and who killed my noble." The Emperor's face grew darker with each assertion.

"Sire, the lady was hysterical. She babbled about ghosts and specters. Her evidence of anything but the most certain facts is doubtful."

With insight the Emperor asserted, "Yet she recognized the murderer."

"Sire, she thought she recognized the murderer. She was overcome by the terror of her experiences."

"Who was it, Rathenberg?"

"Sire there is no proof. Someone tampered with the computer system. We have no visual or verbal record of the man or men who invaded the Palace."

"Rathenberg! I don't need you to tell me why it can't be a certain person. Who did the lady say the killer was?" The Emperor had never seen such stubborn defiance in his seneschal before.

"The man is dead, your majesty," asserted the Count with equal force and obvious fluster.

"Who was he?"

Count Rathenberg hesitated. He was unwilling to reveal the name, not sure whether the Emperor's continued displeasure would be better than his certain wrath. He made his decision and quietly stammered, "The lady said it was the Prince Devon Rathenberg."

Perodus blanched. "She must have been mistaken. Yedric himself said he killed the man."

"Sire, we checked her assertions with a mental scan. The Lady Charis Myridon believes the intruder was the son of my cousin, Duke Rathenberg. In fact, she said Yedric himself identified the attacker as Devon Rathenberg."

Perodus sat back in his chair.

"Sire, all the indications point to Devon Rathenberg: the sabotaged computers, the swordsmanship, the honor shown the lady, the accuracy of the killing shot. But how could he be alive? Yedric, for all his other faults, was neither a liar nor a man given to flights of fancy. I am myself convinced that my young cousin is dead."

"And I am also, Count Rathenberg," intoned the Emperor. "After reviewing the papers of my late father, I now believe Sir Devon's attack on Yedric was ordered by Maricus, and the knight was commanded to die in the ensuing duel."

The Count almost took a step backwards. "He ordered Devon Rathenberg to die?"

"To die, Count Rathenberg. There is reason to believe that our deception completely fooled the Emperor and his Chief of Intelligence."

Not so much a deception as a change of plans, thought Count Rathenberg.

Rathenberg contemplated the possibilities Perodus' information invoked. The Count became very alarmed at how much of his and Yedric's plans the late Imperial personage knew. If they had not taken the opportunity to join with Perodus, the careful manipulations of Maricus would have extinguished them. Even now, Count Rathenberg felt a surge of fear. Yedric's and his plans to control Perodus, and thereby the Empire, were fast dissolving. The Count realized he was too weak by himself to persuade and manipulate the impetuous Perodus. Yedric despaired of it, though he achieved a modicum of success. The forces of the banned Houses now opposing them were dedicated, and they had reason for their anger. In retrospect, Prince John-Mark's plans were much less perilous to the peace of the Empire than anything Perodus accomplished or proposed.

But Count Rathenberg had cast his lot, and he had to eat the stale bread of the Emperor Perodus' dynasty. Against the Dragon and the Fox, he believed, they had little chance of success. The Count prayed that the attack against Yedric was indeed the work of a ghost. Of the two men, Prince John-Mark or Devon Rathenberg, he preferred the straight-forward Dragon to the vindictive Fox. He sighed. Life could be short either way.

"...now Rathenberg."

The Count tuned back into the Emperor's words.

"I received dispatches that our fleet is on its way to Acier. Soon we will hear of the capture of the County, and that will seal the destruction of the banned Houses."

Rathenberg didn't think victory would be so quickly forthcoming. The plan was Yedric's and on paper, an excellent one. They ordered the entire Imperial Navy to Acier to attack and take the system. That should be a step unforeseen by the banned Houses: Acier was only a County, yet it was the most important ground in the Galaxy. Acier's production of heavy metals and radioactives meant unlimited military resources for the Emperor, and its capture would deny those same critical resources to the banned Houses. In addition, the Emperor would take into his hands the greatest plum in human space, the most valuable jewel among all the planets.

Duke Yedric and Count Rathenberg predicted the banned Houses would gather at Neuterra. There they would bicker over the issues of allegiance and rule and would divide their forces to uniformly protect the ten rebelling Duchies. That seemed a reasonable course of action for the banned Houses, and based on that conjecture, they convinced the Emperor to commit their forces against Acier.

Perodus folded his hands over his chest. "Count Rathenberg,

ensure my Secret Police do their utmost to discover the full identity of the man who killed Yedric. You must accomplish everything in your power to squelch any rumor that Devon Rathenberg is alive. He must be dead; lay his memory to rest. Execute all the Marine officers of the Palace Guard who were on duty during the attack."

"...but Sire," interrupted the Count.

"I want such incompetence rewarded with death." The Emperor was adamant. "And instruct the young Lady Charis that if she speaks a word to anyone concerning the identity of the attacker, her head will end up like Lyral's, before the Landsritters."

"Should I bring the Huscarls back from rotation to reinforce your personal guard?"

"No!" The Emperor's eyes slitted. "You know they are tainted by my brother's leadership. I would trust my person to the ghost of Devon Rathenberg before I would trust Marcus' Huscarls."

"You cannot continue to exclude them, Sire. They hold fealty to the Emperor alone, and the Codes do not allow you any other ground arm."

"Do you presume to teach me the Codes, Rathenberg?"

"No, Sire," gulped the Count.

"I know very well what the Codes allow and don't allow. I must protect myself. Increase the size of my police and intelligence forces."

"Very well, your majesty. The Landsritters may not sit quietly if you continue to disregard the Codes."

The Emperor answered in a bored tone. "The Landsritters need not know. They do not dictate policy to me; I dictate policy to them. Thank you, Lord Rathenberg. I do not need your services any more at this time." Perodus turned back to the terminal on his desk.

Count Rathenberg, the Emperor thought, *you tread very closely the line between advisor and director. I will watch you carefully, and if you fail me by a single step, I will immediately end your miserable life.*

Count Rathenberg stood opening and closing his mouth for a moment. Then, thinking better of offering any further comment, he bowed and backed hurriedly out of the room.

Nineteen

Roger nervously entered Duke Neuterra's private study. He wasn't given any time to worry about confronting the domineering nobleman. The Duke paced in front of a window at the right of his huge and ornate desk. The desk was covered with printouts and old documents. A heavy office chair, sofa, and stuffed leather chair rounded out the furnishings. These were placed in the center of the windowed end of the long room. The uncovered windows brightly lit the chamber. It was walled with ancient books and floored with real wood. At random intervals, more to suit their display than by any definite design, brilliant rugs covered the polished flooring. The room smelled of fresh earth and paper mold, but Roger could not tell if the former was simply the scent of the planet that stole through the open window lattices.

Each object in the study had a used look, not shabby but as if time matured them to a richness of comfort and utility. The Duke seemed to reflect the same presence as his room, but in the Duke's stance, Roger identified a somberness not shared by the things around him.

Roger's study of the room so absorbed him, he barely noticed the Duke's agitated turn toward him.

"Sir Devon Rathenberg is dead!" boomed the Duke.

Roger was speechless. He felt the blood draw from his face. Devon, dead. In anguish, he stepped toward the Duke.

The Duke raised his hand. "Come no closer, sir." Roger stopped suddenly. "Prince Devon Rathenberg is dead!" repeated Duke Neuterra,

"So, whom did you bring to my planet bearing his name?"

Roger was dumbfounded. He mouthed soundlessly as he fought to refute Duke Neuterra's assertion. "My Lord Duke," Roger began, "the man I brought with me from Arienth is Prince Devon Rathenberg. There can be no mistake."

"What do you take me for, Sir Roger Falkeep? What would it profit the Emperor to announce a falsehood so easily proved wrong? Not a fortnight ago, an Imperial courier delivered the news. At the hand of the new Duke of Neuterra, in a duel, Dominic Yedric," spat the Duke, "killed Sir Devon Rathenberg with a plasmablade. A dozen other nobles witnessed his death. The son of Rathenberg." His voice became quieter. "The Emperor's Fox is dead."

"He is not dead, my lord. And, if he still lives, you can question him yourself. Check his genetic record. Check his brain scan. That man is Prince Devon Rathenberg!"

"Young man," faltered the Duke, "Roger Falkeep, do you realize what a blow it would be, if I let it be known that this man was Devon Rathenberg, and he was not? If I announced Devon Rathenberg is alive and the man died, or worse, if he lived and wasn't really the Fox?

"I resigned myself to his death, much as I resigned myself to the death of my daughter. His father, Duke Rathenberg, accepted the news already. Do you know what a blow it would be to Duke Rathenberg to have his hopes raised by your rumor, then find his son was truly dead? I know, young Falkeep. How well, I know." The Duke bowed his head.

"Examine him yourself, my lord. Surely, you can identify the man."

"There you are wrong, young knight. By the Emperor's command, the Fox did not display himself often before the Landsritters. Aye, his own people and the hangers-on in the Imperial Palace know him well enough. But his face is as little known to me as it was to you before you met him.

"Now, that won't make any difference. I already saw him. I hoped to glimpse some trait that would alert my mind. I looked at him. He is so battered and bruised, his own mother, the Princess Catherine could not identify him. No. No! You, Sir Roger, you must convince me this man is the Prince, Devon Rathenberg. If you succeed, I will watch with you to see if the young Prince survives. But only then will I pray with you in earnest. If he is not the Fox, better that he died now and the question never came up again. Otherwise, the news may destroy our resolve by dashing our hope. Do you understand this, young Falkeep?"

Roger nodded. He took a deep breath.

"Do not speak until you are certain of what words you will say," cautioned the Duke.

"What other man," started Roger slowly, "would in the same evening, announce his love to my sister, the Lady Tamar Falkeep Rathenberg…" The Duke's eyebrows rose. "…and that same night, in a duel, obey the command of his Emperor to die?" Roger's speech quickened. "And who else could be snatched from death's door by a maiden's breath, the woman of his dreams, whom only through giving up his Ducal rank he could make his own?"

Roger turned toward the Duke and with his hands emphasized his statements. "What other man, to avenge his honor, would travel alone to Arienth and, with only a single other soul enter the Imperial Palace and expect to succeed? Who but the Fox, in the chambers of the Imperial Palace could duel and kill Count Yedric and then fight his way out alive to return to your aid? Who but Devon Rathenberg? Could any other man achieve this?" Roger's last appeal rang defiantly in the muted chamber.

The Duke stood silent for a long time. In deep thought, he bent his head, then turned and walked to the garden window. For a moment he absently scanned the sill. "Could this be so?" he whispered to himself.

In the quiet room, Roger made out the Duke's whisper. Roger pulled a ring from his pocket and strode toward Duke Neuterra. "This ring belongs to Prince Devon Rathenberg—it was given to me by the man in the hibernation berth. Who else could he be? I would have forfeit my life for him."

"No, no other man." The Duke shook his head. "I know of no other." He grasped the ring Roger proffered and examined it. "Roger Falkeep, this is an Imperial Signet. I have only seen its like once before—on the hand of the Emperor Maricus. This ring belongs to that man?" The Duke's voice was filled with astonishment. "What other marvels can you divulge to me?"

"What of my sister, the Lady Tamar? Whether you accept him as Devon Rathenberg or not, my sister, the Lady Tamar, loves him. Without the pretense of Noblesse, she would accept him for the man he is. If you must choose, choose life for the man and death for the noble."

"The Lady Tamar loves him so well? I know the Lady."

"She already accepted him once without rank. Indeed, with your decision, her future hangs in the balance."

As if thinking of another woman bereft of love, the Duke smiled sadly. "I will beseech God with you for the life of our friend. You have convinced me, young Falkeep." Duke Neuterra sat heavily at his desk. "Leave me now. I need time to think about what we will do."

Infinitely relieved, Roger silently let himself out of the study and wearily returned to his rooms.

Twenty

Sir Devon recovered remarkably quickly under the best treatment Neuterra offered. Roger visited him daily in the hospital, and they spoke of their experiences on Arienth and the unique events that brought them together.

The solemn Duke of Neuterra made frequent visits. During these calls, Devon and Roger shared with him in full the occurrences on Falkeep, along with the details of their attack on the Imperial Palace. They did not reveal the paths they took into and through the Palace.

The Duke managed a smile every now and then in response to the account of their adventures, and as a result of their conversations, the two younger men sensed the Duke's spirits revive. Perhaps, where before the death of the Duke's daughter completely reft the joy from him, now he celebrated the atmosphere of Devon's unexpected resurrection.

Soon Devon pined to be let up from his hospital bed, and as Devon fought to renew the strength in his arms and legs, Roger found himself caretaker to the struggling knight. Devon's muscles and tendons were severely damaged, but through tissue restoration, the doctors rebuilt the torn ligaments and crushed musculature. The process was very painful and caused Devon to remark more than once, "I don't know which is worse: being wounded or being healed?"

Within a week, with gravsupports strapped under his arms, Devon was hopping around the Duke's gardens. In another three days, the doctors released him to the care of the Duke. The chief surgeon laughingly explained they could no longer stand listening to the knight's loud campaign songs and complaints. But Devon actually made many good friends among the Duke's subjects, and the hospital personnel were unhappy to see the charismatic and gracious knight leave.

At Devon's insistence, he and Roger shared the same suite. This gave Roger the opportunity he craved ever since he had known of Devon as a Cadet. With a like mind, they discussed battles and leadership, rule and military intelligence. Every day, Roger became more impressed with his brother-in-law. The man had a greater perception of politics and military affairs than he ever thought possible. In these discussions, they not only reviewed the theoretical, they also considered the factual data taken from Count Yedric and the Palace computers on Arienth.

"John-Mark rallied the banned Houses to Acier," stated Devon as they walked alone through the Duke's garden.

"How do you know?" asked Roger.

"Notice the Neuterran fleet is missing. This is the place the banned Houses would have first met to conclude their differences and agree on leadership. They are not here; therefore John-Mark took the decision from them. He commanded their assembly at Acier. That is the only target worthy of the full power of the Imperial Navy. You noticed yourself, the Imperial Navy left Arienth en masse. I suspect the other Houses supporting the Emperor will rendezvous with them and from there converge on the County of Acier. This is a step in line with the Emperor's basic nature and the style of Yedric's military planning. Yedric's computer information doesn't lay all this out precisely because it contained no current data, only future plans, but it does support my conjecture."

"How would the Prince John-Mark know of the Emperor's attack?"

"He would guess, like I did, that Perodus, who so keenly desired the wealth of Acier, would attempt an initial move against it. The Emperor could not understand how well organized are the forces under John-Mark's command. Perodus is blinded by the belief that John's authority extends only as far as the Imperial Huscarls."

Deeply engrossed in conversation, they approached the main

house.

When Duke Neuterra stepped out into the cool, darkening garden, Devon noticed the stalwart Duke's approach and called, "Good evening, my lord."

"Good evening." Without any other conventionalities, the Duke came directly to his business. "I understand you intend to leave soon, Lord Rathenberg."

"That is correct, my lord. Tomorrow, Sir Roger and I hope to be on our way to join the fleet at Acier. With your permission, of course," he added congenially.

"That request is, of course, granted, my friend. Never let it be said that I kept a Rathenberg from his business. But how did you know our fleet is at Acier? That is a secret from all but the highest placed leadership."

"Conjecture alone; John-Mark and I think much alike."

"You should have been here when Prince John-Mark took control of the assembly. He and Count Acier, that old scoundrel, walked out with the entire Nobility of ten kingdoms in their train." Duke Neuterra stared off into the distance. "Do you think the Empire will attack?"

"Yes."

"I'm only sorry that I couldn't go myself or send a son to bear the honor."

"Ah, my lord Duke, you will have a son in that battle; whether recognized officially or not, Prince John-Mark is your son."

The hard face of the Duke softened, and he almost beamed with pride. "Indeed I accept him as such. He is my son; he even said it himself. Young Rathenberg, you were ever one to discern a man's thoughts before he spoke his mind."

Devon bowed at the compliment. "I have information, my lord Duke, that I must deliver to John-Mark at all cost. It may mean the difference between our Houses' eventual victory and defeat."

"I am only sorry, my Lord Rathenberg," continued the Duke, "that your stay could not have been more comfortable."

"I don't understand your meaning, my lord. You extended every comfort to us."

"I would like you both to eat with my family tonight. I want to introduce you to the House Neuterra and to the other families of the banned Houses here. Many have gathered to Neuterra as a safe haven. The spirits of our families needs to be lifted by the knowledge of your victory; then the Emperor will not seem so formidable an opponent. Because your success is a blessing to our people, some of your adventures would make welcomed conversation. I want them all to see you, so that the significance of Devon Rathenberg, the Fox, will grow within the banned Houses."

"My lord, you give me too much credit. I am only an officer in the service of the Empire. I seek nothing except the honor of service. Sir Roger and I will be proud to eat at your table. Do not count it against your House that we could not seek your board before now." The ancient formula spoken, both men nodded to one another.

That night, the Duke's table was set in a far corner of the garden. Devon and Roger wore borrowed eveningwear fitted to them that day. The time it took to prepare the *Silent Dawn* for tomorrow's takeoff delayed them, and because of their tardiness, Devon's tailor balked at fitting his formal military dress over the gravsupporters under his arms. So, with the knowledge he could wear the formal uniform after he fully recovered, Devon shrugged to the inevitability of showing off his disability. In the interest of rounding out the adventurers' meager wardrobes, the Duke gave them these items along with many others.

So Devon presented his more common appearance. He also had his hair cut to its more accustomed length and shaved his mustache and beard. After Roger and he inspected each other's uniforms for precise military appearance, they were ready to sit at the Duke's table.

With the Duke's chief steward as their guide, Roger and Devon found their way to the evening's dining location. They traveled through the complex elevator and subway system that crisscrossed the gardens, house, and grounds. After traversing multiple intersections and making two or three shuttle changes, they finally reached the outdoor pavilion. They both agreed they would have had little hope of finding it themselves.

The platform sat on the top of the garden's tall escarpment. Next to it, a river cascaded in a thousand misty sheets down the side of the cliff.

In spite of their delay at the *Silent Dawn* and the rush to prepare for dinner, Devon and Roger found they were slightly early: the society of Neuterra developed a custom of dalliance in regards to certain events, and dinner was the chief offender. The Duke had not appeared yet. So they watched the other guests arrive to the traditional "co'tell" time and stood quietly conversing about the people they recognized.

Most of the guests were women and older children: the wives and children of the banned Houses.

Until the Duke arrived, Devon and Roger drew little attention. The Duchess Nieva Neuterra accompanied the Duke. She looked worn and leaned heavily on the Duke's arm, but defiance filled her eyes and her face still held a faded beauty.

"She," Devon whispered to Roger, "is perhaps the most astute political advisor in the Galaxy. She is a beautiful woman, but beware, Sir Roger. Women are all capable of incredible feats of perception and intuition. If you have a secret you don't want to share, use caution around the Lady Nieva."

"Gentlemen, this is my wife, the Lady Nieva Neuterra. Nieva, this is Sir Devon Rathenberg and Sir Roger Falkeep." The Lady Nieva lifted her brow and curtsied with a smile to Roger, then Devon. But her eyes lingered on Devon a long moment. "Sir Rathenberg, I pray you are nearly recovered from your injuries—both those from Falkeep and Arienth."

"Due to the kind and capable treatment of your subjects, I am healing quite well," responded Devon, gesturing to the gravsupporters under his arms.

"My Lord Neuterra has not informed me fully concerning your business here." She glanced sidelong at the Duke. Then she turned her piercing gaze toward Roger. "Sir Roger, pardon my forwardness, but you are a long way from Falkeep."

"My father," started Roger, unprepared for the implied question, "my father decided to support the banned Houses. I am his delegation."

The lady gazed intently at him. "My curiosity is still not relieved. I heard a portion of the events you and Sir Devon played a part in, but knowing the mind of Duke Falkeep, I would have thought to find you hunting the young Rathenberg rather than allied with him."

Roger turned red to the roots of his hair.

Devon smiled at the Lady Neuterra. "My lady, I allied myself with the Family Falkeep. Duke Falkeep allows his son to accompany me due to the concern borne of his affection."

The Lady Nieva's brows rose. "How is it you are allied with Falkeep? Particularly in light of present and past Imperial associations, and specifically since you have no authority to ally with any House."

"I pledged the Lady Tamar Falkeep." Devon forced a smile.

Roger stepped forward. "The Lady Tamar Falkeep is betrothed to Devon. My father approved both the alliance and the obligation. Duke Falkeep sent me along to look after his new son-in-law, Sir Devon Rathenberg. My sister, Tamar, is the Lady Tamar Falkeep Rathenberg."

Lady Nieva started and turned a reproachful look to the Duke. Duke Neuterra grinned foolishly. He shrugged. "I thought you would have heard already, my dear." The response earned a second stern look.

"This is a surprise indeed." The Lady Nieva lifted her face. "Sir Devon, I don't need to tell you the priceless commodity you have won. Yet, by the match, you reduce your rank among the Noblesse; I'm surprised your father signed the agreement."

"He has not signed the agreement, my lady. In the first place, my father bestowed on me the control of House affairs, and in the second, I have no rank; for the moment the Emperor banned my House." His eyes twinkled.

The Lady Nieva's eyes became slits. "You will no longer have control in your House when your father finds out, young man."

"You do me ill," Devon responded lightly. "You know the Lady Tamar is the most capable, available woman of rank in the Court. I feel she will have some strength in the political affairs of the Empire. Indeed, I can imagine a time when her name will be applied toward the study of Imperial issues, just as another certain noblewoman is known."

The Lady Nieva pursed her lips and stared at Devon in a most disconcerting manner. "Enough of this equivocation, Sir Devon. What is the real reason you lowered your family name and honor to contract with the Lady Tamar?"

Sir Devon's neck flushed slightly as he pronounced with quiet intensity, "I love the Lady Tamar as I love life. I would give up anything for her."

The Lady Nieva stepped forward unexpectedly. She grasped Devon in her thin arms and held him tightly. She lifted her face and kissed his cheek. When she stepped back, her face was wet with tears. They did not reflect in her voice. "Young Lord Rathenberg, you made a marvelous choice indeed. May your House prosper and grow." She smiled.

Noticing his wife's discomfiture, the Duke gently matched her smile. "My dear, if you would corral the ladies, I could introduce these gentlemen better." With a curtsey she turned and moved off into the gathering people.

As Duke Neuterra introduced them to the nobles of the banned Houses, Roger could tell Devon memorized the name, rank, and appearance of each person, but Roger himself could barely retain the names of a quarter of the people they met. He reminded himself to ask Devon how he kept everything straight.

Just before they were seated at dinner, the Duke introduced them to the family Acier.

"This," gestured the Duke, "is Elizabeth Acier, lady of Ian Acier and her daughter, Elina." Roger and Devon bowed deeply. "Ladies, this is Sir Devon Rathenberg and Sir Roger Falkeep." The ladies curtsied.

"Oh," Elina Acier exclaimed in amazement, "you must be the Emperor's Fox."

Her mother tried to shush her, but Devon bowed again to the girl. "Yes, my lady, I am the so-called Fox."

Elina Acier was dark haired and slight, only twelve or thirteen years old. She had beautiful, large gray eyes that drew Devon's gaze. Those eyes seemed to engulf him, almost as if they gazed into his thoughts: so like the Aciers. She was the only child of Ian and Elizabeth and looked amazingly like the Lady Lyral Neuterra, God rest her soul. He wondered what kind of Empire she would grow in, and who would claim her, that is, if she lived. The man who was given the Lady Elina's hand would control the most valuable system in the galaxy, the County Acier.

Devon shook off his musings with difficulty.

In her quiet voice, Elina continued, "My father says that you are the greatest intelligence officer in the Empire? Is that so?"

"If Ian Acier says it is so, then it is so. For Acier is the greatest trainer of military intelligence and strategy in the Galaxy. But, I warn you, my lady, do not depend on the reputation of an individual; an individual can fail you. Entrust yourself to your subjects. There is more power in the trust of your subjects than in all the strength of your forces."

Elina thought for a moment. "Then the Emperor made a grievous mistake."

"We must all guard against the same mistake."

Elina's features took on a sly cast. "That is why we must trust in the individuals who have earned it. Their failure would become our failure. My father trusts you, so I will also."

Roger stared open-mouthed at the young lady. The Duke wore a smile that threatened to turn into a laugh. The Lady Elizabeth frowned slightly, unsure how the heir to a Duchy would accept her daughter's gentle rebuke.

"You speak wisely, Lady Elina." Devon smiled. He unclipped a golden pip from his uniform coat. It was a noble sigil formed in the shape of his house coat of arms, a fox savant. He handed the pin to the girl. "To recall the time you outwitted the Fox, take this. But remember, my lady, test those you've been taught to trust, and seek the trust of those whom you would command." He held her hand loosely and covered the fist that held the pin.

"Thank you, my lord. May I ask you another boon?" She ducked her head shyly. Devon nodded. "You are going to see my father soon?"

"Yes." Devon's eyes registered surprise.

"Would you tell my father that his daughter loves him, and she patiently awaits her recall from the planet Neuterra back to her proper position of responsibility in the defense of the House Acier?" The Lady Elina sighed to mask the tear that slid across her cheek. "I miss my father, Lord Rathenberg."

Devon bowed over the small hand and pressed it to his lips. "My lady, I love your father. He is a stalwart friend. I will deliver your message to him from my heart, and if he does not recall you to Acier and the work is within my capabilities, I will take over your responsibilities until I am no longer needed, or until you can return to them."

"Thank you again, my lord. I have tested the trust and find that trust returned. Excuse me, please; my heart is full and my eyes are weary." She bowed her head and was about to turn.

"My lady," spoke Devon softly as he knelt to put his face level with hers.

Elina lifted her tear-filled eyes.

"My lady—" he handed her his handkerchief—"I believe I understand your feelings more than you know; I will protect your father. No harm will come to him that doesn't come to me." Devon crushed the child in his arms and held her until she stopped shaking.

The Duke turned away, his features flooded with emotion.

The Lady Elizabeth touched her daughter's shoulder. "Thank you, Devon Rathenberg," she rebuked him softly. "But you made two promises you should not keep. I release you from them both."

"Nay, my lady. They were made with my full understanding. I shall keep them because they are honorable and fully within my power." Devon touched Elina's cheek. "Dry your tears, Elina. On Falkeep, a maiden cries for me, and her tears, though hot with fear and love, will not turn the universe any faster nor bring me home any quicker. Save your tears for the moment you see your father again. They will explain your love to him much better than your lips will ever tell him."

"Yes, my lord." Elina's voice still shook.

Turning carefully controlled features to Devon, the Lady Elizabeth nodded. "Thank you again, Lord Rathenberg. In a single instant you have done more to quell our fears and relieve our sorrow than any time since we have left Acier." She bit her lip, "My husband has the greatest respect for you. I understand why now." The lady took her daughter by the hand and they turned to go.

"Lady Elizabeth," called Devon. The lady only turned slightly. "Do not keep yourself or the child from dinner. Your sadness will pass more quickly if you let your friends cheer you."

She nodded, then looked at the Duke. Forcing a smile, the Duke nodded to Elizabeth. Then she and Elina left to sit in their assigned places.

The Duke wiped his face with his handkerchief. "Hot night. Come, let's take our places; I'm sure dinner is ready by now."

Neuterra's white star rose across the horizon of Asa-Thor and added its light to the moon's morning.

"I don't know if I'll ever get used to this planet's crazy diurnal cycle," laughed Roger.

"You won't have to think about it anymore," returned Devon good-naturedly, "not if you finish getting this thing ready for lift off."

"All right, all right. Keep your harness on. Another ten minutes will do the trick."

During the early morning hours, Duke Neuterra accompanied Roger and Devon from his manor house. In near silence, they traveled through the still quiet streets of Neukoln to the spaceport. The *Silent Dawn* was serviced at the Duke's expense, and the Duke had replaced all of Roger's and Devon's immediate clothing and personal equipment, most of which they left unceremoniously on Arienth. To facilitate their acceptance on Acier, the Duke supplied them with code generators, decryption circuitry, and the codes now used by the banned Houses. He briefed them on the more technical aspects of the defense of Acier as he understood them, and then clasping them each around the shoulders, the Duke wished them, "Godspeed."

The Duke turned to Devon Rathenberg. "My lord, Sir Roger gave me your ring as a surety." He handed the Imperial Signet to Devon. "I return it to your hands. If Maricus thought you worthy to carry his ring—I cannot be the one to gainstay his desire." The sad Duke's smile seemed heartfelt when he left them at the space port.

Finally, without a warning from Roger, the *Silent Dawn* rose abruptly into the sky. To comply with Neuterran noise abatement restrictions, they lifted at a velocity just under the speed of sound, but as they rose, their speed increased dramatically with altitude until they exited the atmosphere entirely, and then Roger accelerated the ship at full speed. Inside, during the acceleration maneuvering, the gravdampers easily compensated for the forces that would have turned unprotected flesh and bone into bloody puddles.

Devon and Roger watched the moon, Neuterra, and its giant primary Asa-Thor, quickly shrink behind them.

"Roger, I wish you could have met the Duke's daughter, Lyral. She was a woman of uncommon distinction. Her heart was as blithe as the day of Neuterra is calm. She was a brilliant star in the Empire, a beautiful jewel in the human universe. The Emperor Perodus' greatest crime may be that he destroyed the Lady Lyral. But of even greater concern to me now is my friend, Prince John-Mark. I wonder how her death affected him. I'll tell you a secret, since you are privy to so many of mine already. The Prince John-Mark loved Lyral as much as a man can love a woman. He would have forfeited his throne for her. If his brother Perodus had only asked, John-Mark would have turned over all the rights of the marriage to the next in line and accepted a lesser title."

Devon sighed. "I wonder how life stands with my friend now?"

Twenty-one

The *Silent Dawn* reentered normal space at the edge of the Acier system. Acier was a County under the Duchy of Neuterra. It was close enough to Neuterra that the *Silent Dawn* made the journey from Neuterra to Acier in less than a week. That was plenty of time for Roger and Devon to discuss their suppositions on the Emperor's possible actions and work out military strategies to counter him.

Devon healed slowly, and though he still walked with a slight limp, after half the journey he discarded the gravsupporters. While Roger and he practiced with swords and target pistols, Devon forced his sore limbs to respond. When Roger and Devon could forget the reasons for making this voyage, the trip was pleasant, and the time did not drag as it had when Roger was by himself.

When Acier's large white primary became visible in the viewscreen, hailing codes and flight directions immediately bombarded the *Silent Dawn*. Roger and Devon anxiously waited while the ship's computers worked out the complicated identification signals.

Acier's military control recognized the codes as those of Duke Neuterra, and the lights on the *Silent Dawn*'s identification console turned green. Roger and Devon breathed a sigh of relief, and Roger deactivated the FTL drive. If the signals proved to be Imperial, they would have slipped the ship back into null space and headed back to Neuterra with the information.

After the cipher circuitry and computer codes relayed the ship's identity, Roger activated the gravdrive and put the ship dutifully through the maneuvers directed by Intersystem Traffic Control. Interestingly, military control did not ask them to identify the passengers, cargo, or crew. When Roger informed Devon of this apparent inconsistency, Devon merely leaned back. "At this distance, an enemy's spy drones might be able to pick up the personnel codes or identity signals, and contingent on the importance of the cargo or passengers, they might be programmed to attack. When we get in closer, they will insist on the usual coded manifest; then we will be scanned and perhaps boarded."

As they drove through the system, numerous large and small ships appeared on the *Silent Dawn*'s sensors. Intrasystem Traffic Control kept their ship at normal separation distance from the other vessels, but Roger could not discern any communications between those ships and the controllers. The lack of communications with the systems controllers was unusual, especially in a commerce ingress lane. It was also unusual that most of the ships moved at orbital velocity or even less than system terminal velocity.

Devon bent over the main scope repeater and diligently fine-tuned the controls. On his scopes, Roger noticed Devon focused on the unusual system traffic.

"Look at this," Devon finally reported and turned Roger's repeater gain full up. Just at the edge of the detector's visual magnification range, one of the larger, nearly stationary ships rotated irregularly. As they came closer, the viewer automatically homed on the vessel. The ship was gutted. Around it hung a bright patch of vapor and more solid debris. The scars of plasma and nuclear fire covered the hulk.

"Here's another," whispered Devon. In an eccentric orbit, a frigate wobbled end over end and spewed a track of vapor in its path. Near it, a large tender tried to match orbit. "That one is not too badly breached, possibly repairable."

Devon manipulated the viewer onto another frigate; they watched spellbound as, without any evident cause, the ship disappeared in a silent flash of gas and whirling particles. As the *Silent Dawn* moved closer to the system center, many more ships entered into scanner range. Most of these were battered and gutted. Some were rudely marked with a bright red cross. Many more showed the Imperial seal:

crossed ships below a star. It became apparent to Roger and Devon that the Empire and the banned Houses waged a terrible battle here. As they neared the planet Acier, they perceived that the major portion of the battle was engaged there. Clumps of three and four ships rotated in a ballet of death. At this range, they viewed the unmoving bodies of vacsuited crewmen as they swirled in the wake of the dead ships. Yet everywhere they looked, the ships bore the Emperor's sigil.

Devon's eyes grew bright. "He exacted a terrible revenge. And he accomplished it under the cross of the Huscarls. What an embarrassment that will be to Perodus. Roger, my brother, you must meet my cousin John-Mark."

When the ship came close enough to Acier, Orbital Traffic Control directed them into a high orbit. Military control electronically requested their manifest, and the *Silent Dawn* automatically delivered it. In less than ten minutes, two corvettes approached the *Silent Dawn*. The hulls of both of the nearing vessels showed dark plasma scars and the signs of minor internal and external explosions.

Devon and Roger waited breathlessly while the battle tested ships scanned and detector rayed them.

"I never explained the difficulty I had convincing Duke Neuterra you were actually Devon Rathenberg. He believed you were irrevocably dead."

Devon frowned at Roger. "That is something I did not take into consideration. You should have told me earlier. The Emperor used that information to its best effect against our forces. In any case—" he laughed to take the sting out of his rebuke—"I hope they don't shoot first and identify the bodies afterwards."

At Devon's insistence, they both put on the dress uniforms made for them on Neuterra. When they landed, he reasoned, if military control did not initially accept their identities, the uniforms might enhance their credibility.

After a tense 15 minutes and a confused burst of radio traffic, a third ship, a frigate that was not as damaged as the corvettes, drove up through the planet's atmosphere and matched orbit with the *Silent Dawn*. After a few more minutes, without the customary airlock connection, a frowning Marine captain and two armed Marines dressed in vacsuit battle gear forced their way through the lock.

The Marines were surprised to find two knights in full dress uniform, but with no hesitation, they pointed their weapons at the men and motioned them to the center of the yacht's small cabin. Devon and Roger complied immediately with the silent orders.

"Is there anyone else on this ship?" The Marine Captain barked the question. Reassured by Roger and Devon's nods and his own electronic sensor scan, he turned back to the lock and cycled it again. A fourth suited figure clumsily negotiated the lock. The man obviously found it difficult to maintain his ordinary regal bearing in the confines of the vacsuit. He physically turned the Marines' weapons away from Devon and Roger. Then, with an audible sigh of relief, he unlatched and shrugged off his helmet. "Thank God that's off." He nodded slightly to Devon, and stiffly or rather emotively, depending on how well you knew the man, he stated, "Devon, my son, I thought you were dead."

Devon stared in disbelief for a moment, then stepped directly to Duke Rathenberg. "Father." He knelt, grasped the Duke's hand, and touched it to his lips for a moment.

The Duke lifted Devon up and clasped him tightly. "My son, my son, I despaired that I would never convey your body to rest under our hall. But now you bring life back to an old man and youth back to a dead House."

Many who knew the Duke would have been surprised to see a damp glint in his eye. Devon, though he never mentioned the event to his father again, remembered that token for the rest of his life. In the long stern lineage of the House Rathenberg, like no other occurrence, it signaled a release from Imperial subjection. With the strength of undisguised joy, the old Duke clung to the son of his old age, his only son, his reborn son. When they separated, the Duke still could not take his eyes off the man. His face radiated a smile that had not been seen in public for almost a decade.

"Father," gestured Devon, "this is Sir Roger Falkeep, son of Duke Falkeep. We have much to speak about, my lord—much that concerns the House Imperial and the alliance of banned Houses. Shall we continue to Acier's headquarters, where we can discuss these things in common with the other Houses?"

"By all means, my son. Captain," the Duke addressed the Marine officer, "request our landing clearance at Acier's port and alert my ground car. Send the message ahead: Prince Devon Rathenberg is indeed alive and will be presented before the Houses." Devon thought it odd his father emphasized the title.

"M'lord," responded the captain as he and the guards quickly and gracefully cleared the lock.

Roger received clearance for an approach into the spaceport and sent the *Silent Dawn* out of orbit on an intercept course with the instrument approach path.

In the main cabin, Devon and Duke Rathenberg sat across from one another. "Where is Mother?" asked Devon.

"Your mother is on her way to Neuterra. You just came from there, did you not? She will be relieved to find that you are safe and alive. But, I grant you, her heart will be empty until she has held you again. Devon, when we heard that you were dead, I thought her heart would break. I must say, I—I feared myself for the future of our House." He paused, then continued briskly. "I know about the mission. I know the Emperor sent you to die." He held up his hand to halt Devon's reply. "I also realize you advised the Emperor to that course of action. How did I find out? The Emperor sent me an apology on the day of your alleged death. He explained the circumstances and the reasoning behind his command. He wrote the most gracious eulogy I have ever seen. In fact, I never realized you played a part in many of the incidents he mentioned. Your life, I came to realize, has been a series of successes unknown before in our very successful family. I am very proud of you, son. Did you realize the Emperor, in your honor, granted our family the boon of the County of Gran Stern? Little good it will do us while Yedric controls the system. Until official sources confirmed your death, I didn't tell your mother of the events. How you got out of that one— convinced Yedric and his nobles of your death—is probably the best story ever told, but..." The Duke stopped suddenly, as if noticing his son's faraway look.

In the silence that wrapped uncomfortably around them, Devon finally found the words to speak. "Father, I chose to fight the Count with plasmaswords because I was afraid of death. Once I was resolved to die, I wanted my death to come quickly. I did not engineer a plan to escape the reaper; my survival was both an accident and the result of a more courageous and honorable person than I." He sighed and licked his lips. "Father," his voice became almost a whisper, "Father, I committed our House in a way you may not be able to approve, but I cannot go back on my promise, nor do I wish to. I pray you will try to understand my motivation and reasoning, because they are not products of the training of my House. You raised me to be a Prince, a bastion of the honor of the House Imperial. I am a Prince. After John-Mark, I am the Emperor. But father, I have chosen and indeed contracted a bride without your permission."

"Would I disapprove of the lady?" commented the Duke stiffly.

"No, she is a woman whom you would accept in any other status with honor."

"Then where is the difficulty, Sir Devon?" The Duke raised his eyebrows.

"The question is one of rank, Father. The question is one of acceptance, for I would rather start a new House with this woman than for our House to exclude her because of her rank. And, Father, you will never be able to exclude her. She is no unknown damsel." Devon grasped his father's hand. "I loved this woman before I started on the Emperor's mission. One of the reasons I accepted it so gladly was that, at once, I could resolve the conflict between my love and family honor. Although I presented myself to this woman in disguise and raised a false hope in her, she willingly saved me from death. She raised me back to life and gave me a reason to live. Because she loved me enough, even though she knew my rank would not let me marry her, without shame she would have accepted me. Before the new Emperor divested us of our position, I resolved to give her House alliance and marriage. In the capacity of your reigning heir, I made this contract, and in my mind, the agreement is irrevocable."

The Duke trembled with suppressed emotion. His cheeks burned red beneath glowering brows. "So who is the next Lady of House Rathenberg?"

Devon stared defiantly at the Duke. "Lady Tamar Falkeep Rathenberg."

The Duke's lips worked for a moment. He looked to the side and gritted his teeth. His fist touched the table twice. He kept his face turned away from Devon. "You ask me to make a choice. Accept you back to the living with your bride, or leave you in your grave and let my House die." Devon was surprised the words were not filled with bitterness. Instead, his father seemed tired.

He returned Devon's gaze. For a moment, the Duke seemed to see a mirror. In it, he viewed a reflection of himself 40 years ago. The face in the mirror, he noticed, was his son's. *So alike,* he thought. A smile actually crept across his features. He loved his son. Love, he realized, was a concept one seldom learned more about when one was 65 years old. "The Lady Tamar, is she not the lady who shamed Maricus' own daughters with her grace and deportment? Is she not the one whom the Lady Lyral Neuterra said was created to be a princess, although not born one? Did not Nieva Neuterra state that child would someday build an Empire, and didn't the Emperor once grant her an audience though she was only 18? The toast of Lady Pembrook's School. The most sought-after and run-from lady in the Empire. The woman whom no noble's son could cause to lower her gaze? You have taken her into your House and bed?"

The Duke laughed. "I grant you, the match is improper and will lessen the rank of our House. Aye, I'll not hide that. But, son, you've grabbed the most tempting jewel in the Empire to be your lady. I may have difficulty convincing the Landsritters of that fact, and your Mother may debate the value of the match. But I cannot fault your thinking. Although," he held up a finger and smiled broadly again, "you confuse the issue with ideas of love and gratitude. Don't fear. I will support your claim to this girl, in our House, in the Landsritters, and to your mother."

"Thank you, Father." Devon could not join in his father's mirth.

The *Silent Dawn* touched down softly on Acier's spaceport. Roger, Devon, and Duke Rathenberg stepped off the ship into blowing sand and grit. The hot wind was filled with the fierceness of the bleak planet. They didn't wait long before a gravvehicle moved alongside the ship. The powerful wind whipped the three as they dashed to the vehicle and entered it. In their hasty rush from the ship to the car,

Devon limped slightly and stumbled twice. The Duke, noticing his son's affliction, gently grasped his arm to steady him.

When, at last, they were out of the wind and in the car, the Duke stared pointedly at Devon's legs. "Is there anything else I need to know?"

"Duke Yedric is dead." Devon brushed the blown sand off his sleeves.

"How was he killed?" asked Duke Rathenberg suspiciously.

"I challenged him to another duel," replied Devon.

"One he could not refuse, I'll wager."

"He confronted a ghost from his past."

"How is it the Emperor allowed this duel?"

"Although the challenge took place in the Imperial Palace, the Emperor Perodus was not invited." The Duke's face registered surprise, and Devon continued, "Sir Roger helped me and we escaped from the Palace with nearly the Emperor's full plans for military operations."

"Devon, the people rightly call you the Fox. I would not have bet any amount that such a thing was possible. My days have been filled with pain and conflict too long. Your return is a great joy to me, son. Like nothing I experienced in years."

"Father, what of the battle for Acier? I perceive the Emperor was defeated, or we would never have found one another, but at what cost to the banned Houses?"

The Duke scowled. "Prince John-Mark is like a madman. He predicted the Emperor's mind exactly. He and Count Acier drove the other Houses here—convinced them through sheer force of will. At the Prince's command, we deployed our forces in hiding throughout the system and awaited the coming of the Imperial fleet. To the Imperial Navy, Acier appeared unprotected, and with the bait of the planet, John-Mark drew them in. When the Imperial forces, still unsuspecting, reached the inner range of Acier's defenses—why, some of their ships entered the planet's atmosphere before John gave the signal. John called for the attack. He led the battle himself, and the Imperials were decimated. They attempted to disengage immediately, but John foresaw that, and a squadron of frigates and corvettes harried, then drove the escaping vessels into carefully deployed stationary defenses. Finally, the

Imperial Navy retreated in a rout. Perhaps a third of their ships escaped, maybe less, and not one of those was undamaged. We were not unscathed. We lost a quarter of our own ships, but at the beginning, we were outnumbered three to one! The stationary defenses and Acier's powerful planetary defense made up the difference."

"Why do you say a madman? What is wrong with John?"

"Since the Emperor executed Lyral, he has not been the same man. He is fighting this war as though it were a personal battle. I believe he has a death wish." Conspiratorially, the Duke continued, "Among the Houses, the Prince lost much honor; they only begrudgingly accept the rule of a man who put them in this position in the first place."

The gravvehicle came to a stop before Count Acier's walled fortress, and in spite of the wind, the Count's men received them with full honor.

While they proceeded down the long foyer, Duke Rathenberg whispered to Devon, "You were wise to wear your ceremonial uniform; the Houses will be impressed." Duke Rathenberg and Roger caught Devon as he stumbled again. The Duke counterfeited exasperation. "Before we stand before the banned Houses, what else do I need to know, Devon?"

Devon smiled blandly. "Nothing of note. I am slightly damaged from the Imperial Marine's treatment in the Palace, but I assure you, they quickly regretted their lack of proper deportment. And my stay on Neuterra brought me a long way toward full recovery."

John-Mark and Count Acier himself met them in the anteroom to the audience chamber. If Devon had not personally known the Crown Prince John-Mark, he would never have guessed the man standing before him orchestrated the massacre of the Imperial fleet. John was dark-haired and nearly average height. He was noticeably slight with a wiriness and energy that caused you to overlook his easy muscled strength. His face was not remarkable, but John cultivated his expressions to be striking, and a rakish beard and mustache accentuated his features even more. His hair was short, cut in the style of the Huscarls, to whom he was the Marshall, but the most evident aspect of his person, were his eyes. Light gray, like smoke, they changed with the Prince's emotions from iron hardness to near blue warmth; they stared into your depths and discarded pretense and falsehood.

Almost in direct contrast to the Prince, Count Ian Acier was a massive man. He was imposing physically and intellectually. The Count's good-natured face was permanently lined with worry, and to Devon he looked as if he'd aged ten years since the last time they met. He was a fierce man among forceful people to govern a severe planet, thought Devon.

The three men bowed to the Prince John-Mark. Then, like schoolboys, John and Devon clasped hands and pounded each other on the back. John showed a face unlike the one he wore for the last month: he displayed no smile, but his mouth was no longer paralyzed in a grim frown.

"Devon, I was convinced you were dead." John shook him. "Let me welcome you back to the living and to our victory. Your father told you?"

"Yes. My prince, I also have information that may increase our victory. I just returned from Arienth. There Sir Roger Falkeep and I acquired the Emperor's campaign plans."

John's eyes turned as hard and cold as ice. "That's exactly what I want, Devon." Then only audible to Devon, "Perodus must and will pay dearly."

"Count Acier," Devon addressed the Count, "Sir Roger holds memory chips that contain not only the computer information we took from the Emperor, but our own opinions, derived from direct observations of the Emperor's Capital and forces."

Ian gratefully took the packet Roger proffered and in his broadly accented brogue stated, "Gentlemen, you could not come at a better time; we must soon choose our next course of action. We can strike while our fleet holds together, but we need a target."

"I think you will find one there," returned Devon quietly.

"Come, Devon." Prince John-Mark took his arm. "We must introduce you to the leadership of the Houses in our rebellion."

John led them through the large doors into the Count's audience chamber. The entire assembly turned to watch their entrance. The number of nobles present and their scrutiny surprised Devon. The leaders of ten banned Duchies, the lords of eight Kingdoms, sat around

Count Acier's table. Behind them, the nobles of the lesser Houses under the Duchies perched uncomfortably on hard wooden chairs. Yet, in the crowded greatroom, a visible space separated these men from the nobles of each of the other Duchies.

Duke Neuterra was represented by his cousin, a Count whom Devon only vaguely recognized, but in every other place, Devon saw the key nobles of the Empire, almost a full third of the Landsritters' Thirty Kingdoms. After the addition of the Houses Falkeep and Rathenberg, they lacked only the Emperor himself to complete the inner circle of the oldest Houses of the Empire.

Devon recognized the approval in these men. They accomplished a great victory, and the flush of their achievement flooded their features. Devon saw they welcomed the opportunity to challenge the dishonorable actions of the Emperor Perodus, yet he knew they desired reunification with the Empire. And he discerned that they would only accept the Emperor's authority again on their own terms.

But in the powerful aura of victory, Devon sensed a keen disharmony. He entered a room divided, a group united solely by victory. The Houses glowered in their sprawling groups, as separate in spirit as they were physically. The entrance of the procession of Prince John-Mark, Duke Rathenberg, Count Acier, Sir Roger, and Devon seemed to further split the groupings of nobles. Where tentative conversations once reached out at the periphery of the eight great Houses, now there remained only an intense silence.

The group's sudden attention and careful inspection caught Devon off guard. As he slowly limped behind John-Mark, the nobles' eyes turned unmistakably toward him, and from the entranceway to the head of Acier's council table, a whirlwind of indistinguishable whispers rose in the room.

Devon gazed out over the nobles. He realized part of his father and John's purpose in presenting him to them. After John-Mark, he was the heir to the Emperor's throne. Until Perodus or John-Mark produced a male child, Devon stood next in line for the Iron Throne. His return came on the sprigs of an incredible victory. Feeling the atmosphere, he knew the Houses needed the additional encouragement of his support and success. They wanted to believe they fought from more than a renegade spirit. They wanted to know they were justified, by more than battle. Devon also realized Prince John-Mark prepared the way for his own death. The Prince wanted death; Devon could read it in the man's every action. The feeling was more intense than Devon knew in himself when he was resolved to die for the Emperor.

Devon stood only slightly taller than John, not more than three centimeters, but because Devon was more muscled, and because he carried himself with a more regal bearing, he overshadowed the warrior Prince. John led him to the front of the hall. Devon's father, the Duke, walked beside them and Count Acier followed a pace behind.

"Devon," John-Mark whispered at his side, "Devon, you would not believe the cry of anger that rose when the Emperor announced your death. I betrayed these men into the hands of the Empire. I am partly to blame for the state we find ourselves." His fingers dug into Devon's arm. "Devon, my friend, my brother. If Perodus were to die tomorrow, I would not be a welcome man on the Iron Throne. You would be. You are the Fox. These men know you not by feature but by reputation. You are even more well thought of and known than I. They mourned you; the night the Emperor announced your death, Nobility and commoner alike wailed in the Houses of the Landsritters. And Devon, you look like a Prince. Don't say it makes no difference—you are a Prince. As we walk to the place of honor, you can hear the murmurs of approval. They would instate you tonight if your father said the word. When Perodus first banned our Houses, your father, Count Acier, and I decided on this course of action. When we learned of your death, we thought all hope lost, but you are the glue to hold together the cause of our Houses. Without you, they would have to depend only on a despot like my brother…or a manipulator like me."

Devon shook off his hand. "I don't want this, John."

"It isn't what you want or don't want. It is the reality of the moment. After this night, you will be the Crown Prince of the Empire. You must face it. If you do not accept the regency, the rebellion will fail. I can fight for it until death takes me, your father can provide leadership, Count Acier can give us wealth and knowledge, but only you can bring honor and rule to this enclave. Without you, we are manipulators; we fight against the rightful Emperor. With you, we can claim the honor of the House Haupenberg and House Rathenberg. You are the tie. You are our legitimacy."

They reached the end of the table, and John unobtrusively pushed Devon into the end chair, "So look like an Emperor."

Devon composed himself. He didn't like what was going on, but everyone seemed to be expecting it. No wonder his father was so affected. No wonder the mystery of his father's questions.

The hall was absolutely quiet. He could not hear the sound of a cough or the sigh of a breath. John-Mark raised his arms. "Nobles of the Landsritters, I present before you Devon Rathenberg, Count of Gran Stern, Knight of the Red Cross, Chief of Imperial Intelligence, and Crown Prince to the Iron Throne of the Human Empire. Before you, I abdicate my rights to the Throne and place the regency in his hands. Nobles, listen to your Prince: the man of honor, the Fox, is now the honor of the Noblesse."

A murmur of approval rose in the hall. Duke Centri spoke out, "This is Devon Rathenberg, the Emperor's Fox?"

Duke Rathenberg stretched to his full height. "This is my son, child of my lady, Catherine Haupenberg Rathenberg. This is the man to whom I provided the responsibility of my House, to whom the Emperor granted the boon of the County of Gran Stern, and whom you know as the Emperor's Fox. In the name of the House Imperial, I cast my approval on this man and release control of my House fully to him." The Duke pointed at Devon's hand. "Look at his hand. Maricus himself placed his signet on my son. Maricus' endorsement rests on him—and through him, on us."

Duke Centri stood. "In that case, I give my approval." He threw his sword, hilt forward, and it stopped with a hollow scrape on the table before Devon.

Slowly, with deliberation, the lords of each of the other kingdoms rose to their feet. Their swords rushed out of their scabbards and they threw each to land in front of Devon. As a single organism, all the nobles of the Kingdoms rose. Their shout filled the hall from corner to corner: "Prince Devon." They repeated the epitaph, "Prince Devon," over and over. The sound rose. The yells became stronger and stronger. Wilder with enthusiasm.

Devon rose to his feet and stood before them with his head thrown back. His voice, coached by the trials of military command, rose in the hall. He was vaguely aware of an amplifier magnifying his words above the clamor. "Noblesse."

The room quieted a little.

"Warriors."

The sounds grew less.

"Nobles of the Houses of honor."

Except for his voice, the hall became quiet.

"I am not a man of ambition. I seek nothing of yours but your fealty."

In approval, the nobles pounded their hands on the table, walls, and chairs.

Devon raised his fist. The Imperial Signet sparkled in the hall. "I accept your swords into my hands only to replace them in yours. Fight, warriors of the Iron Throne. Fight, honorable nobles of the Human Empire. I yield to you my life and honor, but know warriors, I am proven. I already have given one life for the Empire."

The nobles in the hall had heard the rumors. They knew the Emperor commanded the Fox to die, and they knew he honorably cheated death. In a single voice that rattled the walls and threatened to collapse the roof, the nobles cried out, "The Fox! The Fox! The Prince defeated death."

Twenty-two

Devon Rathenberg, Crown Prince of the Human Empire, stood before the large window in his quarters and watched Acier's continual gale make whirlwinds of the sand. He felt suddenly like a grain in one of those eddies, blown every way by the conditions and Codes of the Nobility, no longer in control of his life.

A knock on the door broke his reverie, and he recognized a familiar tread behind him.

"You performed marvelously, Devon," John-Mark spoke from the doorway. "Your speech was an act of genius."

"John," Devon responded in a whisper, "I never wanted the regency."

"You had no choice in the matter."

Still without turning, Devon replied, "You, Count Acier, my father, all of you dreamed this up long ago."

"Devon, the truth of the matter is you saved the rebellion of the banned Houses."

"Saved it? Saved it for what?" returned Devon bitterly. "Saved it so we can lose the lives of its following as well as its honor?"

Unfazed, John-Mark continued, "When Perodus decided to act against the alliances I made in the name of Neuterra, he revealed me as a villain."

"You know that isn't true."

"Whether it is true or not, the perception of the Kingdoms is that I tried to split the Empire. Perodus revealed me as a man of ambition.

The Houses allied with me were just unlucky; although they are the oldest and some of the most powerful Houses in the Empire, Perodus made no exceptions. He chose to ban all of them. Only a single thread held them to me, the Lady Lyral."

John's voice took on a dangerous hardness. "Her execution cut the thread as easily as it severed her life. After her death, the banned Houses had no reason to grant me any fealty. I had no authority with them, but your father, Acier, and Neuterra drove them to the action I planned. The Houses realized my plan would work, and to regain their honor, I led them in a battle of glory and made them men again. They were revived, they knew victory, but they had no true leader.

"You should have heard them when you were reported dead. The people reject the tyranny of Perodus, they despise my ambition, but you, you are the imminently honorable Devon Rathenberg. Your death brought about a frenzy of anxiety and anger in every House of the Empire. They could understand the death, through treachery, of the stolid Emperor Maricus; they can accept my fall through ambition; they despise Perodus for his insensitivity to honor; but you, Devon, are their altar of honor. They would believe nothing dishonorable about you."

John stepped closer to Devon. "The rumor of the Emperor's command for you to die came to us before we learned of your death. Nobles waited in expectation and prayed the rumor would be false. They feared to know the truth of whether you lived or not." John grabbed Devon by the arm and spun him around. "Devon, you do not realize your effect on the Nobility."

"In that you are right, John. I know I have little effect among the Houses. You are the one who is so capable with the troops. You garner their affection. Through your leadership, you build their strength. I have no capability with people. Why do you think I succeeded so well in intelligence?"

"Because your people trusted you, and you look and act like the commander of an intelligence organization. You look and act like you belong in command. And, Devon, you are a hundred times more effective with the Emperor's intelligence corps, a group a million strong, than I ever was with the Huscarl's twenty thousand. Devon, you look like an Emperor, a Crowned Prince. You act like one—a liability in some cases, but an enormous advantage in this one. Believe me, you are the best man in the Empire to assume this responsibility. And because you are aligned with the banned Houses, you renew their urge to oppose the Emperor. After Perodus dies or is deposed, you give them the hope a legitimate heir will pick up the pieces. Soon the other Houses will tire of Perodus, and they will search for a successor. For the same reasons, they will choose you. You appeal to the loyal Houses in the same way you appeal to the banned kingdoms."

"And what about you, my brother, John-Mark?"

"I lead the Houses in battle. I will provide you with advice and armies. When you are Emperor, I will continue to serve you, and the Empire will prosper. Devon, you will found a new dynasty. A dynasty that has been needed for at least 500 years."

"Did you know I contracted, in alliance, a lady to my House?"

"No." John looked amazed. "I didn't know your father made any overtures."

"He didn't. Through his grant of authority over the House Rathenberg, I contracted myself."

"Who?"

"The Lady Tamar Falkeep Rathenberg."

John whistled. "Is it ratified?"

"By both our Houses."

John's eyes widened again. Then he laughed out loud. "I have not laughed since—since my lady died. Through Lyral, I knew of the Lady Tamar. She will make a magnificent Empress. If I did not know you better, I'd say you made your choice for the throne." He shook his head.

"Now, John, what will we do with the rebellion?"

"The commanders are agreed; your advice to attack the Imperial Fleet at its rendezvous point is our best hope. Tomorrow, the entire fleet goes hunting. This time, a Fox will mark our craft. Some Baron painted a red Fox savant on his ship and now most of the fleet sports the design. You see; they already reject my Huscarls' cross. You belong to them almost like your lady belongs to you. They have fallen in love with you." John-Mark glanced sideways at Devon. "The question now is: what you should do?"

Devon shrugged.

"When I return, we must discuss your options. Or, perhaps, your father already has a solution. You cannot stay here. You must establish yourself. Your independence is a characteristic that will be tainted if you assume an attitude of dependence on Acier. An Emperor is always dependent on his subject's fealty, but he must never appear to be dependent on it."

"Why, when you return? Aren't I going with the fleet?"

"No. We cannot risk that."

"For a long time, I have lived in danger of my life."

"Then this is a good time to stop. Your Lady will thank me for it." John turned to go.

"I have another reason, John. I promised Ian Acier's daughter I would protect her father with my life. I said I would guarantee he did not come to harm. I cannot break that promise. You must either leave Ian with me, or you must let me come with you."

Without turning John asserted, "Ian will stay here. After the planning stages, I will no longer require his expertise; he is a ground commander and an intelligence specialist."

"John," Devon stopped his retreat once again, "one other question. When I am Emperor, will you be able to accept my orders and judgment?"

John-Mark turned. "I...I..." Then he smiled. "Yes, my lord." As he left the room, he bowed.

Devon spent the rest of the day alone, contemplating his new circumstances, based on events not under his control. His separation from the Nobility actually lent a stronger character to his leadership. They attributed his absence to an Emperor's absolute trust in his advisors and his Noble Houses. The nobles endowed him with nerves of steel and imagined him a leader who assumed his suggestions would automatically be adopted. Because of his apparent lack of anxiety concerning the acceptance of his authority, they praised him for not taking advantage of the Houses that just proclaimed their fealty.

Already, Devon's father and John-Mark were surgically planting any rumor they could devise to build on the foundation of the honor of the new Crown Prince. They mulled over the contract with Falkeep and found innumerable bits of gossip they could spread to the advantage of their cause. But they could do little more to build on the Fox's legend than was already being done in pure innocence by the warriors and the Nobility. The men believed any story of honor and prowess attributed to Devon Rathenberg, yet rejected out of hand anything unflattering.

Roger came to see Devon later in the day. He had some important news for the young Rathenberg. "My lord," he began.

"No title, Roger." Devon smiled. "Not in private."

"All right, Devon. I discovered some interesting information. Yedric's forces never made the battle at Acier."

Devon stared intently at the knight. "Then where could they have gone?"

"I don't think they went anywhere. Before I left, my father sent my brother George to clean out Gran Stern. The certainty that Yedric's forces didn't make the rendezvous tells me pressure from Falkeep kept them bottled up in their system."

Devon cut in. "Falkeep doesn't have the forces to defeat Yedric."

"And, that's my greatest fear. My brother is well trained, but he is inexperienced in battle. With the full strength of the Duchy of Falkeep, Yedric's forces still grossly outnumbered us."

"Would your brother attack against overwhelming odds?"

"My father counted on the fact that Yedric's illegal naval forces would be deployed in support of the Emperor."

"And so, because Yedric's Navy never reached the Imperial Fleet, it's possible George Falkeep attacked before they left the system."

"Falkeep could be in great danger."

"Roger, when the fleet is safely away, we must return to Falkeep. John-Mark believes I must assert my independence—very well. My lady and the House Falkeep are my chief responsibilities. I will go to them. Do not let a word of this out. Do you understand, Roger?"

"Yes, my lord."

Devon laughed, "Well, I guess that was deserved."

Devon spent an almost sleepless night. He could not get out of his mind the fear Tamar was dead or a captive of Yedric's forces. He wasted the night in tortuous thoughts that only left him more anxious and bewildered. He had never felt this way about anything before. The concern was nearly debilitating.

The next morning, Devon rose early to oversee the departure of the fleet. He stood on the port tarmac and observed the frantic buzz of late preparations. Every ship was marked with a red fox savant. He shook his head in wonder. Just walking the ramp, he overheard such improbable stories about himself that he almost turned away with embarrassment. The Lady Tamar's name graced the mouth of every warrior. They invoked the name like a prayer. They spoke of her in whispers, that she gave the Fox back his life with a kiss. Devon meant to speak to Roger about some of what he heard, because he never shared those details with his Father or John-Mark. In his hearing, the story of Yedric's death became an epic legend. When the men noticed him, they had the sense to stop talking; they knelt to him and saluted. Devon could not help but return their salutes with an Imperial smile, and that infuriated him because it encouraged them all the more.

By the allotted departure time, Devon was keyed with excitement and anxiety. Excitement because he was starting to believe John's talk about his influence, and anxiety because he felt an immediate need to be in Falkeep's space to protect a certain lady.

To make their final leave-taking, the Dukes of eight royal Houses, his father, and John-Mark approached Devon across the hot permacrete. As the regal group neared Devon and his guard, Devon could read the emotion on each man's face. He could see in his father's eyes a look of unrequited longing. *Always,* thought Devon, *I went away to represent my House. Now, my father must represent me.* John-Mark seemed stern, a figure unfamiliar to Devon. The Dukes were tense, but they immediately went to their knees and presented their sword hilts to him. Their motions were full of expectancy. Their glances filled with mingled hope and anxiety. He knew they wanted him to be their Emperor. To prove to themselves their choice had been wise, they marked his every action with expectation. Devon felt a million eyes on him, waiting with the same degree of hopeful excitement.

Devon stood silent and regal in the dress of a Haupenburg-Rathenberg Prince. His eyes swept the men before him. As though trying to read the soul and loyalty of each man, his glance leveled in turn on each of the nobles.

Then one by one, in the order of precedence, Devon took their sword hilts in his hand. Each nobleman touched to his forehead Devon's hand that held the sword. Then Devon broke with tradition and grasped the blade with his bare palm. He returned the sword to his nobleman—by the blade. The men gasped at the image Devon invoked: he placed explicit trust in the hands of the Noble Houses. Devon accomplished the same exchange for his father and, finally, John-Mark. After the ritual, he lifted them both to their feet and held them in an embrace. His father whispered huskily, "My son, we have so much we need to talk about, but the time is short indeed. We will meet in less hurried times, and we will eat together in full peace."

Devon kissed his cheeks.

In Devon's embrace, John-Mark declared, "My friend, my brother," and he couldn't continue.

With the hand that returned their sword, Devon raised the Dukes one by one, and when all ten men were standing, he dismissed them to their ships.

Devon found himself, alone, in the center of the port, surrounded by hosts of ships. In the next few minutes, most of these would lift to rejoin the rest of the fleet in orbit. When Devon received the ready signal relayed from the last ship, he raised his right palm into the air to show the crisscrossing cuts made by his noblemen's blades. On his palm, the blood stood out dark and dry. As he strained his hand wide, the keen slices opened, and the blood dripped in a thin spiral down his arm. The Imperial Signet rested conspicuously on his finger. His voice and picture were amplified, and broadcast to every ship in the fleet. "The blood of the House Imperial is spilt," he cried. "I send it with you on the swords of warriors. This is my trust. It is my life. I serve you even as you serve the true Empire. Do not return without your swords bloodied. In the name of honor, I send you to finish the Fox's meal you began around Acier. Do not come back to me unsated. I braved the maelstrom to bring you the glory. I spilt my blood to bring you honor. Do not disappoint the House Imperial."

As Devon stood on the open permacrete, the ships of his Navy lifted like bright shimmering stars into the lightening sky. In his mind, possibly reflected from radio receivers around the spaceport, he thought he could hear a thundering roar. "The Fox, the Fox, the Prince defeated death."

The ships were well out of sight before Devon finally returned to the operations building. He later learned that the men turned his long meditation on the permacrete into a story about his prayer that brought final victory to the fleet.

After he entered his suite, Devon sent for Sir Roger and Count Acier. When the burly Count appeared, Devon told him, "Within 24 hours, I want a full complement of your best troops on a ship."

"But, my lord," he stammered, "I…I, should you leave Acier so soon?" he faltered.

"My holdings and my subjects on Falkeep are in danger. I wish to give the House Acier the honor of the combat."

"Thank you, my lord." Ian Acier bowed hesitantly.

"Do we have any attack ships, Count Acier?"

"We have two corvettes for customs duties, but only one of those is FTL equipped."

"What of the ships we salvaged after the battle?"

"Aye, there are a great many of them, but most are not spaceworthy."

"See if you can outfit and man a couple of the better Frigates. I need ships with silent running designs, energy blankers, and standoff drone capabilities. Tell me what your orbital docks can put together in a day to three days. Ian, I need transportation, fire power, and stealth— you work out the details."

"Yes, my lord." He bowed deeply and turned to go.

When the Count left, Devon called Roger in. "Roger, if we are to be of any help to Falkeep, we need a plan. I'm familiar with much of the planet, but you are the expert. Get together with Count Ian's officers and any remaining Imperial trained leaders you can find. From my knowledge of Yedric's forces, I believe, we may be able to counter any force around Falkeep, but to scrutinize the situation, we need better military tacticians than I am."

He and Roger discussed the specifics of Devon's hypotheses concerning the forces of Gran Stern that could be in the Falkeep system. Afterwards, Roger left to impart their conclusions to Ian's military planners. The planning to liberate Falkeep had begun.

Twenty-three

Four vessels plowed through the immensity of null space. In relative close proximity, a black box corvette, two limping electronic warfare frigates, and a converted cargo vessel rode the interspace between Acier and a phase shift convergence with the Falkeep system. Never had so much electronic warfare strength crossed space without a fleet in attendance.

Although he was vehemently opposed to the initial plans, after viewing countless practice exercises, Count Ian Acier came to a grudging and, it could be said, excited acceptance of Devon Rathenberg's designs. At least the Count no longer derided the plan as foolish; he now privately recommended a more conservative timeline so they could acquire less decrepit vessels. The frigates, he pointed out, were barely spaceworthy; their crews, though fielded from some of the best electronic warfare troops in the Empire were still only minimally trained in the shipboard systems. Prince Devon Rathenberg recruited almost 80 percent of the crews from Ian's planetary intelligence forces; all the naval intelligence personnel had departed with the main fleet.

The converted cargo ship, Ian argued, although well armed and manned was never intended for powered military operations. It was a deepspace freighter used as a stationary defense platform during the battle of Acier. Although it was not badly damaged during the engagement, before the confrontation, it was highly modified under the assumption it would never be used for intersystem travel again. Just to operate the weapon systems required the ship's full power rating. All over its surface, missile launchers, plasma cannon, ion field generators, offensive electronic warfare systems, pulse laser cannons, and interdefensive ion cannon bristled from unpressurized hardpoints. The ship looked like a fat porcupine lifting its quills in preparation for a fight. The engines only required a day to reconnect to the reactors, and during this modification, the power systems were channelized so they could be varied between weapons and propulsion. An interesting dilemma for the ship's captain was that the full power of the five fusion reactors could be used to either activate all the weapons systems or power the ship's engines and support systems, not both. In the 24 hours before their departure, the ship was further converted, to house and transport a full brigade of Ian's armored battlesuit forces.

The black box corvette was the only ship of the four in prime condition and fully crewed. The corvette was available because it was too small to be needed in the hunt for the Imperial fleet, and its excellent condition could be attributed to the fact that, due to maintenance problems, it had not participated at all in the battle of Acier. The corvette was their ace in the hole. The design of the ship delicately balanced around a stasis field and ceriplast hull that made it invisible to passive detection.

Other computer-controlled electronics made it almost invisible to active detection systems as well. It could move into the center of the Falkeep system and gather intelligence. It also possessed a unique attack option: the vessel sported four, eight-barrel, gattling-gun slug-throwers. Each of the guns fired heavy, radioactive-tipped 50mm projectiles at 100 rounds per second. The small ship, undetected, could get in close to an unescorted vessel and destroy the target's reactors and drive motors, before it could respond. It was an outstanding attack system. Unfortunately the black box ships were prohibitively expensive for normal combat operations, and their unavoidable small size left them undergunned in any normal ship to ship action.

The final component of the attack group was five attack drones salvaged from the Imperial derelicts still orbiting Acier. These drones were variously equipped with plasma cannon and anti-ship missiles. They were intended for use in a standoff attack capability, and could be controlled, up to two at a time from the frigates or the corvette. The corvette, however, couldn't use a drone without negating its chief defensive protection—electronic invisibility.

Ian Acier reasoned their chief advantage lay in the morale of their troops and the quality of their leadership. The men were at an emotional high from the victory at Acier. The Emperor's ships were decimated, and each of Acier's soldiers felt an inextinguishable pride in their success. They would fight now just to experience that unrequited victory again. But Ian also knew the men would not retain their spirit indefinitely. Although the constant preparation and anticipation of combat buoyed their spirits, Ian could feel it waning in his men. Apathy would destroy them. Their training was good, but their experience with the equipment and in the space environment was low. A single failure might well spell their doom.

Their leadership was unexcelled. Prince Devon Rathenberg headed the battlestaff, and his exploits as the Emperor's Chief of Intelligence were well known. Ian Acier prided himself he had been Emperor Maricus' economic chancellor, a dubious honor he acquired by having the wealthiest holdings and the best planetary armies. Even so, his troops were the finest, his commanders the most qualified. Unfortunately, for this mission, they were qualified primarily in ground operations, and in that, they were unexcelled. Count Acier contemplated this benefit, comparing it to the odds against them and the fact that of their leaders, only the very inexperienced, Sir Roger Falkeep, was trained primarily in space operations. Perversely, he didn't point out this fact to the staff. He didn't, because he believed in their force's ability to succeed. In his heart, he knew they could accomplish the mission Devon Rathenberg set them to. He believed it either because of the strength of the miraculous that seemed to derive from the young Prince or because of the power of the victory at Acier enlivened his spirit.

And yet—and yet, he knew they fought against all odds. Devon pushed forward with a single-minded goal, honor: his honor before Falkeep, the honor of his bride, the honor of the holdings Emperor Maricus granted him, the honor of the Empire, the honor of his brother-in-law, Roger Falkeep. His honor might never be satisfied, but by not acknowledging the possibility of defeat, it could feed on the

Prince's life's blood.

Ian was exultant despite his misgivings, but he would never let the full extent of his fears or his faith be known; he was too good an officer. In any case, Devon, the Fox, knew the odds; he just bet against them.

The ships were dressed out for battle: before they were completely ready to convoy, the men christened and marked each. The frigates, like damaged twins, were named *Achilles* and *Icarus*, the names of two warriors of the past who failed. The ship's crews, in a spate of morbid humor, remarked that though once dead, their ships rose, still wounded, from destruction, and reasoned that they were therefore indestructible. Covering their old Imperial markings, a red fox appeared on their wing strakes and sides.

The professional crew of the black box corvette chose to live with the name *Black Box*, although the other spacers affectionately dubbed them the *Coffin*. A red fox appeared proudly on the small ship's black, retractable shuttle wings.

Ian was glad to see his own troops didn't deal in the black humor of the spacer crews. Some wit christened the converted freighter *Jagerhetzer*, and almost overnight, symbols of fat hedgehogs in various heraldic and other combinations along with the red fox appeared all over the ship. Since the ship never left orbit, how they accomplished this was beyond Ian, but fighting men are tenacious when an idea strikes their fancy.

This rag-tag group blasted toward a hopeful victory. During the entire three-week journey, Ian prayed they might prevail without combat.

Well outside of sensor range, where the yellow sun of the Falkeep system was barely discernible among the rest of the starfield, the group of four ships emerged from null space in a tight battle formation. The frigate *Icarus*, carrying Ian and Devon, appeared first. Then, like silent predators, the three other ships swung in the diamond-sprinkled dark behind and to either side of her. No glimmer of controllable radiation was evident from any of the vessels, and with a sudden acceleration, the black box corvette, *Coffin*, disappeared toward the tangle of invisible planets ahead of them.

Now in the form of a wide and ragged triangle, the *Icarus, Achilles,* and *Jagerhetzer* headed forward at a more moderate pace. Before them, two of their drones ranged nearly a million kilometers ahead and with passive sensors, tested for wisps of energy. They relayed their discoveries through nearly undetectable commlasers. Nothing impeded their small fleet's tense and expectant progress as they descended like an arrow of death toward the system.

At Devon's direction, they planned their phase shift congruence and approach far above the system's ecliptic. Commercial ingress lines lay always just above or below the ecliptic, the plane of planetary orbit. Defensive sensors, outposts, and drones normally crisscrossed the ecliptic with invisible detectors, but the trillions of cubic kilometers of space above and below the system's line of orbit were indefensible and usually unmonitored. A shell of detection normally encircled each planet and radiated as far as a few tens of million kilometers from the system primary, but the resources of any system were far too limited to allow even wartime surveillance of a much larger area.

Generally, ships provided the brunt of armed-system reconnaissance, and they commonly lay close by the objects of their protection. With the incredible speeds generated by high-acceleration maneuvering, intrasystem military vessels were seldom found further from a planet than the detection limit. This kept them no more distant from their planet than perhaps an hour at combat velocities including acceleration. Planetary defenses usually reached as far as one million klicks from low orbit and much less through any appreciable atmosphere. Therefore, during war, the space around a planet became a killing zone.

The ships used in combat were only remarkably different from their commercial sisters by their acceleration potential, weaponry, and accommodations. Through their unrestrained gravity drives, such ships were capable of an unbelievable increase in velocity. And, only through extensive, computer-controlled, internal opposition via gravdampers to the external accelerations could the crew be prevented from turning into protoplasmic goo. These ships could achieve a percent of the velocity of light in an hour. The size of the drives and reactors required to realize acceptable rates of combat maneuvering were enormous; they comprised as much as 60 percent of the volume of an average military ship. This, unfortunately, didn't leave a lot of room for weapons or crew. The crew living space was primitive and crowded. Similar to the cannon on ancient sailing ships, weapons stations shared the cabins of officers and crewmen alike. In this age of sophistication, warfare became a personally experienced trial. But combat in space pitted more than firepower, computers, and magnetically shielded armor. It combined the stamina, morale, and discipline of the crew, together with the tactics, strategy, and leadership of its officers. Success also required a generous application of deception and electronic countermeasures.

With the converted freighter overshadowing them, the two small frigates hovered above the Falkeep system. At the frigate's combat speed, they were still more than a day's travel from the system center. Below them, the system's planets were invisible, although Falkeep's central golden star could now be easily discerned in the viewscreens.

The *Coffin* decelerated suddenly near the ships. It immediately signaled from its formation position and delivered telemetry and orbital data in addition to the passive system scans. Ian and Devon tensely watched the data pour from the spy ship into their planning holo. Inside the multidimensional cube, the *Icarus'* computers combined the black box ship's surveillance with the information it already possessed. In the planning holo, initially the likeness of the system planets formed around their star. The first planet was a gas dwarf, an aborted binary companion. Then the planet Falkeep herself whirled in a moderate orbit and shined with white clouds and wide blue oceans. The primary continents were barely visible. The planet sported a tiny moon. Next, outside the life zone, orbited two smaller, companionless, terra-dense planets. Farther out, brilliant with bands and striations of reds, purples, and browns, a vestigial ring, and various large and small moons, the only gas giant in the system paced in majestic but miniature imitation of the system's star. Finally, twin ice balls shared a far, nearly common orbit. Every millennium they threatened to collide, but that had never happened yet in the memory of man.

As soon as the holographic display revealed all the charted natural bodies, including asteroids, comets, and other small hunks of rock, the *Coffin*'s immediate discoveries emerged. In various symbols and colors appeared the orbital spaceport with its commercial ships, the countless satellites plodding in and around the system, and the enemy's ships in orbit around the planet Falkeep. Devon tensed perceivably as two frigates, four escorts, and a destroyer all wearing the Imperial silver and sporting the black star of Gran Stern blinked into their estimated positions around Falkeep.

"Less than I expected, more than I hoped for," he stated quietly.

"We have a chance." Ian shrugged.

"Perhaps, but where are the other destroyers?" Devon put the question to the council network.

"You mean the ships the escorts support?"

"Yes."

Four escorts sat in different orbits. Together with the frigates, they guarded all the approaches to the planet. The escorts were larger than a frigate, but in comparison were less sleek, less powerfully weaponed, and usually sported a smaller crew. They were designed to duplicate the acceleration of a destroyer, so were slower than any frigate or corvette, but they carried the electronic weapons, supplies, reloads, repair facilities, and additional crewmen that made them indispensable to the destroyer they supported. They were absolutely dependent on that destroyer, and their destroyer was not half as effective without its shadowing escort. So where were the other three destroyers?

The electronic discussion went back and forth. The most logical argument was that the missing Capital ships were somehow hidden in the planet's atmosphere, and that put them at the mercy of the Fox's small fleet. Devon acknowledged the possibility but rejected it as too foolish an action for even the worst of Count Yedric's commanders. In any case, because the assertion could not be proved, Devon would be irresponsible to base their attack on it. The *Black Box* could not look passively through the atmosphere at a safe observation range. A second possibility was that the three destroyers had left the system, but normal tactics would dictate they take their escorts. The council pointed out the defensive positions of the six smaller ships as an explanation why they were left without their big brothers.

"But," Devon remarked, "since their orbits are at common commercial altitudes and not at the high optimum for early enemy detection, they're probably preventing escape more than guarding against infiltration." He drew the hopeful conclusion that perhaps, then, Yedric's forces hadn't yet breached the planetary defenses. Further, the fact no hulks in Falkeep colors orbited the planet was an ominous, but relieving, sight. Ominous because Duke Falkeep would never surrender without a fight, but relieving because Yedric's ships showed excessive marks from plasma and ion attacks. The positions of the ships in orbit showed too much tension and combat planning. Something successfully resisted the attacks of those combat vessels.

"I suggest a second reconnoiter, my lord," proposed Count Acier.

Devon bowed his head in thought. "I don't know if we can support it. The *Black Box* is our best weapon as long as it is not suspected. We gambled to send it once so deeply into the system. Loss or discovery of the ship will cripple us. You must also admit, Ian, our men are a problem; our entire attack group is keyed to combat. I think we either attack soon or give up the effort."

"Your observations are correct, but we know three other destroyers not immediately evident are probably in the system. If they are close to the planet, we cannot hope to succeed against that kind of force!"

"Any force—" Devon smiled—"is capable of being overcome with the proper application of counterforce."

"Bah, you thrust my own teachings back at me."

"Because they are right. I think we should pursue our original attack plan. The situation is as we foresaw—"

"Yes, it meets the criteria," spat Ian, "but we expected a maximum of six small and two Capital ships. We have indications of four Capital ships in the system."

"You suggest caution?"

"Aye."

Devon raised his eyebrows and whispered, "What if I told you, I believe I know where the other ships are, and after less than a quarter of an hour in battle, I can tell you their exact locations?"

"I would say you are telepathic and prophetic," responded Ian satirically.

"I don't care what you think of my psychic capabilities. The immediate question is, whether you will follow and obey my orders," snarled the Prince.

"Guarantees?" spat the Count with ill-concealed anger.

"None! I'll concede that if I am wrong, then we'll withdraw; our execution plan allows for it."

"Very well, my lord, under those conditions, only, I will concede to the basic plan." The Count bowed his large body stiffly to Devon Rathenberg.

Devon nodded to Count Acier. "Sound the call to battle."

In moments, the *Jagerhetzer,* lumbering at full acceleration, disappeared into null space. This was the first step. The large freighter would appear outside the system and work its way inbound directly along the ecliptic. There, debris and asteroids should partially block it from intrasystem detection. Its ingress path would put it on a line exactly between and behind the gas giant and Falkeep. Until it had passed the massive planet, that path should lessen the chance of long-range detection and put the ship in a position to quickly disengage from battle, if necessary.

The *Black Box* moved at combat acceleration from the rendezvous point, inbound toward the system. Its battle position was a juncture with the troopcarrier, *Jagerhetzer,* just insystem of the gas giant's orbit. It would provide escort for the slow freighter until the *Jagerhetzer* reached the position for an orbital attack or planetary assault.

All four ships completed their preparations for battle: every member of the crew put on combat vacsuits, and the crew depressurized the ships. The crewmen expectantly took their battle positions. They tested computers, checked systems, and prepared weapons. The frigates retrieved and readied their drones.

At precisely the same moment, the frigate *Icarus,* under the command of Captain Blackwell, and the frigate *Achilles*, commanded by Sir Roger Falkeep, winked into phase shift. They guided the ships through null space to a point near the planet Falkeep. To use a convergence so close to a gravity well was perilous and required exact computations; the computers had worked on the solution for almost the entire three weeks they spent in transition from Acier to Falkeep. Devon prayed the solution was precise enough.

In less than a minute, the *Icarus,* shuddering in the flux of uncommon gravitational forces, returned to real space. The abrupt transition threw Ian and Devon, strapped to acceleration couches, to the extent of their harnesses. They felt the ship buckle with the strain of spatial reentry, and as the vessel settled into a high orbit around Falkeep, the unusual forces of the phase shift caused the *Icarus'* plasteel hull to vibrate like a high-pitched scream through the thin air in Devon and Ian's vacsuits. Their senses still reeled from the effects of the transition when the battle computer finally rebooted and projected the holographic planning display. In seconds, Ian and Devon both unstrapped and returned to their command stations.

In the display, the *Achilles* appeared on the other side of the planet. It trailed small pieces of debris, but by its sudden acceleration and the deployment of its first drone, Devon could tell the ship was fully operational. Under their own feet, they felt the ejection of their first drone and saw it accelerate quickly ahead of them. With a dizzy whirl that showed the *Icarus'* acceleration compensators were slightly damaged by the shock of convergence, they shot off in direct pursuit of the unmanned vessel.

They caught the first enemy escort completely off guard; a missile from their drone burst the pressure vessel, and in the high atmosphere of the planet, it lit like a sparkler.

"They aren't combat ready. They aren't even depressurized!" yelled Devon as the *Achilles'* drone scored a volley of plasma cannon hits and the second escort crumpled into a ball of plasteel. The ship collapsed, then expanded again in nuclear effervescence and plunged in an uncontrolled decelerating orbit toward the planet.

The other ships scattered and began to accelerate out of the system, but not before a host of signals came screaming through the *Icarus'* electronic sensors. The electronic warfare crew, alerted by Devon's warning, waited for this moment, and Devon received an immediate trace of the signals. The waves of directed electromagnetic radiation pinpointed their targets before their messages could reach the intended recipients.

"The signals are going toward the gas giant and the planet. I think we now know where they hid the destroyers," Devon announced triumphantly. He typed out a personal message, "Send this message immediately to the *Coffin* and relay to the *Jagerhetzer*," Devon ordered the communications officer.

The *Achilles*, streaking from its station on the other side of the planet, turned after one of the escaping frigates. Leaving long tracks of plasma in the wake of both ships, its drone fired repeatedly at the now invisible enemy. While Ian and Devon watched, the enemy frigate began venting. As the plasma fire carved away its armor, its internal atmosphere burned up, and the unprotected crew went with it. Lifeless in their sensors, the ship continued outsystem at combat speed.

By now, the other frigate and the two escorts were only visible in the star-dusted expanse from the heavy vapor trails spiraling in their wake. This indicated they vented the last of their internal atmosphere, suited their crews, and prepared to return to battle.

"They'll be back." Ian frowned and crossed his arms.

In their drone's cameras, partially concealed in the darkness of the planet's terminator, the first destroyer came into sight. Caught unawares, the large ship was set upon by the *Icarus'* tiny drone. Without replying fire, nuclear missiles homed on the Capital ship and filled the space around it with flashing motes of deadly energy. Ian and Devon saw external bulkheads crumple, sometimes two and three at a time as the drone's missile fire achieved penetration after penetration on the larger ship.

"Look at the markings: that's not the same ship the *Coffin* reported!" cried Devon.

"You're right," Ian confirmed.

A burst of signals intercepted, decoded, and transmitted to Devon by the electronic warfare crew warned him, and he relayed the information, "Captain Blackwell, a second destroyer will exit the atmosphere below us. Send a burst signal to the *Achilles* and hold our orbit."

"Below us, m'lord?" piped the captain.

"Hold 'er steady, Captain. Go for the first destroyer," growled

Devon.

A large black hull cleft through the clouds below them. As if its captain were unsure for a moment of the source of the first destroyer's distress, it paused in the lower atmosphere; then, sighting the *Icarus*, it came at them, firing. Under Ian and Devon's feet, two or three blasts rocked the hull. Venting wisps of Falkeep's thin upper atmosphere, the destroyer below them moved in a line that would put it in a defensive position between them and the first destroyer.

At almost the same time, the first destroyer started to vent to space and return the drone's fire. Ian, watching Devon, noticed a wild look come into his eyes.

Devon excitedly keyed his mic. "Blackwell, ram the destroyer with the drone."

"But, m'lord, the drone is still fully active," returned the Captain.

"Ram it, Captain!" yelled Devon.

As the drone approached the venting ship at full acceleration, Ian couldn't help but look askance at Devon.

Staring at the holo and viewscreens together, Devon answered without looking at him, "When we started our attack, the destroyer was sealed and pressurized. The compartments are isolated; that's why the missiles crumpled them in groups. They couldn't depressurize and effectively use their weapons, so they've been searching for us while getting the crew into their combat vacgear. When the second destroyer attacked us..."

An explosion rocked the ship and knocked them to their knees.

As he regained his feet, Devon continued, "The captain decided to fully depressurize. Look! Impatient to return our fire, the destroyer's captain opened the valves all the way. See the increase in external venting? The compartments are no longer isolated, a large enough hole..."

As it penetrated the thick Capital ship, the drone was a gray streak. A huge puff of vapor burped from the 30-meter hole the drone pulled inward as it cleft through the vessel. A bright nuclear flash heralded the drone's destruction and the entire vessel appeared to shudder. Like water out of a bucket, a great gout of shining vapor ran out of the ship, and from one end to the other, the destroyer collapsed like a deflated balloon. Without another attack, its cannon stopped firing, and the ship became electronically silent.

Devon was exultant. "Captain, ram the other destroyer with a drone."

"It's the last one, m'lord," reproved the Captain.

"I don't care if it's the last in human space, ram the ship. Or do you care to fight that destroyer ship-to-ship?"

"If this doesn't work, m'lord, that's exactly what we will have to do."

They felt the drone released from its berth.

"Retreat out of orbit, Captain, and don't fire the drone's weapons," continued Devon tensely.

The Captain sighed.

As they moved quickly away from the silent hulk and the attacking destroyer, the drone rushed unnoticed toward the rising ship.

"Why do they rise so slowly," mumbled Ian.

"Look," cried Devon, "they're venting too. They sat in the upper atmosphere, combat ready, bombing Falkeep, but the outside pressure is the same as the ship's, and that's a substantial amount of pressure for a ship that size to lose. They saw the first destroyer crumple in depressurization so the captain is being more careful, but watch."

As the drone buried itself in the shielded plasteel, a wide hole appeared in the side of the rising destroyer. It glowed red but little vapor escaped the breach. An explosion caused the large ship to vibrate, but the drone was obviously outside and on the other side of the ship before it self-destructed.

"That one's wounded," commented Devon dryly.

"Orders, m'lord?" requested Captain Blackwell in a brisk tone.

"Signal the *Achilles*. They must take the destroyer. We cannot face them without drones. Accelerate after the smaller ships, and report. We will support the *Achilles*' attack."

From the far side of the planet, the *Achilles* manipulated two drones and rained destruction on top of the crippled destroyer. The Capital ship was ready for combat now and few of the missiles had their desired effect. The destroyer's antimissile defensive fire cut the nuclear-tipped streaks launched from the first drone in midflight, while before the destroyer would show any appreciable damage, the other drone's plasma cannon would burn out its own reactors. Even the deep drone scar on the ship's flank appeared to barely affect it as it cast about for the main instigator of its pain.

"Permission to use full electronic countermeasures." Ian exhaled noisily to Devon.

"Granted. Pull out all the stops."

Ian coded the orders to his countermeasures forces on the *Achilles*.

Abruptly, the destroyer's antimissile defenses settled under a blanket of electronic jamming from the *Achilles* and went dead. Now, missile after missile fired from the drone scored the hull of the ship. Suddenly, the destroyer's defenses began to fire again; they were more fitful and less sure, but once more, they easily turned aside the drone's attack. The *Achilles* changed jamming frequencies, and the guns went silent again. The drone's missiles once more made telling blows against the ship and sometimes sent ripples of explosions from one side to the other. Electronic cat-and-mouse continued as the signals and frequencies changed and the computers redirected the destroyer's fire. Still, the *Achilles* held the large ship at bay. The destroyer was unable to seek the author of its attack, and it was damaged slowly but not yet severely by the drones' fire.

Twenty-four

The *Icarus* moved outsystem and perpendicular to the ecliptic. It rose swiftly above the carnage around Falkeep. Its sensors sought the three scattered enemy ships along their computer-projected trajectories. At the same time, from the ship's vantage-point above the system, they could receive nullspace communication signals from the black box corvette and the freighter. Those two ships found the other two destroyers exactly where Devon predicted they would be.

His crew deployed in vacsuits and the ship depressurized, ready for combat, the skipper of the *Black Box* took up an orbital position near the gas giant. The location was perfect because the planet's radiation output masked the electronic emanations of his ship. Only moments after they positioned themselves, an enemy distress signal, followed immediately by a coded burst transmission from Lord Rathenberg, alerted them. And, in response, the skipper sent the *Black Box* into a lower orbit and scanned the gas giant with every means available.

The unlit star was a mass of seething colors and patterns that befuddled most passive detectors. For fear of backlighting themselves, the skipper halted the corvette's approach just outside the orbit of the inmost moon. The *Jagerhetzer* was still invisible behind the bulk of the planet, but the corvette's captain expected its imminent arrival. The skipper thought of warning the big freighter off, but reason caught hold of him. Lord Rathenberg gave specific instructions to the *Jagerhetzer,* while he was directed to use his best judgment. Good judgment was not to disobey his commander's orders.

His visual scanner cried out, "One destroyer—no, *two* destroyers— breaking out of the methane layer. Their refueling scoops are deployed, and they're heading insystem at low acceleration."

The destroyers accelerated much slower than normal, but in the powerful gravitational field and heavy atmosphere of the massive planet that was the best they could do. "As soon as they're clear of the planet, they'll achieve combat acceleration," commented the skipper. *If they do,* he thought, *the* Jagerhetzer *will never catch them.* He suddenly realized the Fox's reason for their positioning. "We must stop those ships," he fiercely whispered.

The two dark destroyers were now visible on the skipper's viewscreens. They plodded out of the grasping atmosphere and grew perceivably in size. Separated by a hundred klicks from side to side and fifty klicks forward and aft, they were positioned in a standard two-ship formation. Just before the huge ships cleared the planet's atmosphere, he ordered, "Pilot, combat acceleration; match the lag ship's maneuver. Astro, attack intercept. Offense, arm weapons."

The bridge crew quickly carried out his orders. His crew was well trained, ready for combat. *Now, we earn our keep.* Through the back of his acceleration couch, he felt four solid jolts as the gunners primed the large guns. With a smile, he imagined the faint smell of ionized oxygen from the heavy radioactive ammunition; it invigorated him.

His small ship deftly matched the trailing destroyer. No one breathed as they approached the giant ship. Every protective shield electronic and magnetic they could employ tasked their reactors. The skipper directed their final approach behind the main propulsion grids. The flux fields of the destroyer's engines concealed the corvette. That should completely hide them.

As the destroyer filled his viewscreen and they tucked up under the right side, the entire crew held its breath. They all stared at him, awaiting his instructions to unleash the power of the corvette against the kilometer-long vessel beside them.

The destroyer was daunting, larger and more massive than he imagined it could be. Without a second's hesitation, a hard grin crept across his features and his dry lips clearly pronounced, "Fire."

The crew took up the call from one side of the ship to the next. The offensive officer repeated it. The gunners cried it out in a fit of frenzied release.

"Fire!" A bone-jarring vibration coursed through the ceriplast hull, and from the bowels of the small dark ship a radioactive spray poured into the destroyer's engines. Where the four streaming, metal fountains touched them, geysers of flame and small explosions rocketed from the gravity grids. The small ship's engines whined up at high power as they compensated for the reaction force of the heavy guns. Through the gravdamper's compensation, the skipper felt the incredible force of the guns pounding almost two hundred thousand rounds a minute into the bowels of the destroyer above them.

The larger ship lurched visibly. As one after another the gravgrids failed, it turned from its insystem course. Its acceleration stopped, and after trying to turn and face the assault it could feel but not detect, the destroyer gave a final shudder and began to wobble out of control.

The *Black Box*'s skipper was exultant. "Now for the reactors!"

The bright lines of gattling gunfire cut upwards ahead of the engines as the *Black Box* matched the large ship's wobble and moved up under it closer to the deeply embedded reactors.

"Skipper," stated the defensive officer, "the other destroyer is turning. It's approaching fast."

"Stop fire," the skipper forced himself to say.

"Stop fire, stop fire," repeated his offensive officer. The guns gave a last burst and then were quiet. In the immediate stillness, the sudden stop of vibration left his body tingling with suppressed exultation.

"Did they see us?"

"No, skipper, but they are approaching with caution. The damaged vessel's communications are confused; they believe they hit a mine."

The Jagerhetzer *will be able to match velocities with this ship. They can take care of it as they come insystem,* thought the skipper. Aloud, he ordered, "All passive. Silent running." At the experienced touch of his crewmen, the unnecessary systems on the ship went dead.

"Maneuver forward of the damaged destroyer."

His ship moved slowly along the bottom of the ship. He directed the pilot to tuck closer into the massive hull. Almost within an arm's length, the conduits and armor of the destroyer passed above them. Under the shadow of the forward section, he halted the ship. From their vantage point, they could see the slowly moving undamaged destroyer. As it moved toward the rear of its companion, the *Black Box*'s skipper commanded, "Pilot, match the ship's maneuver, tuck in behind the grids. Astro, attack intercept. Offense, arm weapons."

With deadly silence, the small craft caught and matched the second destroyer's acceleration. In moments they were in position behind and hidden on the blind side of the undamaged ship.

"Sir," the defensive officer called. Through the man's helmet, the skipper saw the officer's brow covered with sweat. "Sir," rasped defense, "the damaged destroyer may have detected our motion."

"Noted. We are concealed in this position. Fire!"

"Fire!" The guns again sent their crashing projectiles out into the darkness, and they slowly blasted the gravgrids of the second ship into floating garbage.

"Sir, they have detected us, the ship is alerted," cried defense.

"Thank you."

"Enemy communications indicate, they have detected the approach of the *Jagerhetzer*," defense continued.

"I must relay Prince Rathenberg's instructions. Move the *Black Box* to a position above the line of this ship."

In great gouts of plasma energy, the weapons of the second destroyer suddenly started firing. Whether the destroyer's captain recognized the danger from the small ship its companion identified, or whether it attacked the *Jagerhetzer*, now within visible range, was not clear. As the *Black Box* moved above the hull of its target, the bristling shape of the converted freighter, more than twice the size of the destroyers, lumbered into sight.

Dark motes moved briskly around the *Jagerhetzer*, and as the freighter moved closer, the skipper saw the motes were swarms of ship assault troops preparing to attack.

"Commo, relay the Commander's message."

"Sir." The signal went out.

"Detected," yelled offense and defense together.

"Order," cried the skipper.

The *Jagerhetzer* was now close enough to take the brunt of short-range fire, and in consequence, the continual barrage from both destroyers battered its hull. When the assault troops were close enough, their impulse jets drove them toward the wobbling destroyer. As they attacked, bright tracks of ion cannon fire tore them to pieces. Small wisps of vapor, death exaltations of the vacsuits peppered the space between the destroyers and the *Jagerhetzer.*

"Offense, percent damage of this destroyer's maneuver drives?" the skipper snarled.

"Less than forty."

Suddenly, the *Jagerhetzer*'s weapons began to fire and showered the *Black Box*'s concealing destroyer with intense energy.

As he watched the massacre of the *Jagerhetzer*'s assault troops, the skipper made his decision. "Electronic offense, target the first destroyer."

The bridge was immediately silent.

His last order would electronically pinpoint them to the enemy's weapons. His mouth suddenly dry, he repeated, "Target the first destroyer for electronic offense."

"Aye, Aye skipper." The man almost sounded cheerful.

The sudden, unexpected jamming from the *Black Box* silenced both destroyers' weapons. As if on cue, the assault troops swarmed over the wobbling destroyer, and a few attached themselves to the second destroyer.

The skipper waited until the soldiers were all out of sight on the enemy vessels. "Pilot, maneuver into concealment. Discontinue electronic offense."

The crew of the *Black Box* could not tell if the damaged destroyer's computers finally defeated their jamming, or if they just weren't lucky enough. A blast from the wobbling destroyer's rear plasma battery hit the small ship in the outboard port engine. In a gout of plasma energy, nearly a fifth of the ship was vaporized.

Knocked back and above its place of concealment by the plasma's stream's slight mass, and still firing into the destroyer, within the full sight of the three other vessels, the *Black Box* rotated slowly out of control. The destroyer had their range.

"Full jamming," directed the Skipper calmly.

Before the electronics officer could jam the gun batteries again, the full blast of the destroyer's left barrage hit them. The small ship glowed red, then blue. The magnetically shielded ceriplast hull absorbed the energy for a moment and then, with a white hot explosion, the blast converted the entire ship into almost pure energy.

Less than twenty meters from the *Black Box*, the full force of the explosion struck the destroyer. Where the raw energy hit it, the destroyer buckled and shuddered. The blast split open the reactors, and the rear portion of the ship snapped loose and moved slowly outsystem. The remaining portion of the destroyer spun wildly on an axis near center. No energy was available, the destroyer's guns died, and the acceleration compensators failed. Up to five terra gravities threw most of the destroyer's crewmen toward the outer walls of the ship and held them there.

In the *Jagerhetzer* was exultation and anger. The soldiers and crewmen understood the sacrifice of the black box ship. They realized quite well that it gave up its concealment so they could achieve the battle's objective. Ian's newly trained marines attacked the wobbling destroyer with renewed energy, and the unprepared ship's crew immediately folded to their savage attack. In less than an hour the *Jagerhetzer's* crew secured the ship and left a holding force to guard the prisoners while the *Jagerhetzer* continued toward the battle in-system.

Captain Blackwell authorized full active electronic search, but in spite of his precautions, the enemy frigate found them first and not the other way around. The ship ambushed them with bloodlust. At long range they matched the *Icarus'* speed and velocity. They traded iron-fisted blows from plasma cannon and anti-ship missiles. The batteries only quieted when one ship or the other was able to jam its opponent's offensive systems. The *Icarus,* already damaged and with a smaller and less experienced crew, took the brunt of the attack.

Meanwhile, Devon and Ian kept a watch on the battle raging below them between the *Achilles'* drones and the enemy destroyer. One drone was destroyed, and the other was seriously damaged but still in operation. The captain, Roger Falkeep, had just deployed his third and last drone. Unfortunately, the enemy frigate danced between them and the planet. It guarded the battle zone below from interference and the *Icarus* could not succor her twin against its oversized opponent.

"Something's got to break," announced Devon decisively. "Or else this flitting black-starred frigate will blow us out of the sky."

His face pale, the captain addressed Devon. "Do you have a suggestion, m'lord?"

"Not yet." His lips twitched.

"Look below." Ian stared. "There. Now the escorts are rejoining the fight." Beyond the enemy frigate, in high orbit, the two remaining escort ships pressed in toward the *Achilles* and the battle.

"Ram the frigate, Captain," commanded Devon.

"Devon, don't you think you've taken this ramming thing a bit too far?" Ian crossed his arms.

Devon watched the viewscreens more closely. "Don't just sit there, Captain Blackwell. Ram the frigate."

With more fear in his voice than the entire encounter had drawn from him, Captain Blackwell stared at the Prince. "Sir, you risk my ship and my crew..."

"Ram the ship, Captain. There is no risk."

"But..." Lamely, with a voice of tense compliance, the captain ordered, "Pilot, combat acceleration; ram the frigate."

The crew turned aghast at Blackwell. Devon only smiled.

In a blur, the *Icarus* accelerated toward the surprised ship. As the damaged acceleration compensators caught up to the ship's change in acceleration and movement, the bridge crew swayed unsteadily. They approached the other frigate on a collision course and it fired wildly at them. The plasma fire blasted bits of armor from their hull and added to the multitude of blackened striations already on the ship's surface. The frigate grew steadily in their viewscreens, and Devon was suddenly afraid his idea would not pay off. Except for Devon, the entire crew crouched in crash positions. Ian looked up to see the Prince's languid pose and, with chagrin, resumed an easier stance. Just as collision appeared unavoidable, the other frigate suddenly accelerated off at a right angle to their course. They blasted by the collision point and headed straight toward the battle in orbit below.

Captain Blackwell sighed hugely.

"At the escorts, Captain," Devon commanded. Blackwell looked uncomprehending at him. Gesturing toward his viewer, Devon ordered a second time, "At the escorts. Direct your fire toward their aft end. Fire everything. Jammers on. Electronics on. Fire, fire, fire!"

Blasting away with its full firepower, the *Icarus* whizzed between the escorts. As the plasma energy rained around them, the escorts accelerated away to either side.

"Don't let them get away Captain," growled Devon. "Take the escort in lower orbit. Go!"

The *Icarus* cut after the port escort, matched its acceleration, and overtook it. It strafed the ship directly from behind and spewed it with plasma and hot ion blasts. Without warning, the escort began to trail white hot streams of debris, then exploded like a small supernova.

The *Icarus*, in close trail, passed directly through the blast. In seconds, it was covered with burning plasteel and radioactives. Hit by the shockwave, the *Icarus* tumbled. The violence of the motion wrenched bulkheads and sheets of armor from the ship's surface and scattered them in its trail. The engines attempted to realign the ship, but with little affect. When they failed, with a high-pitched whir, the emergency gyros kicked in and stabilized the hull. They reduced the ship's rotation to almost nothing. That was lucky, because in the next instant, superheated plasteel fused the emergency electrical systems into slag, and accordingly they lost the reactor containment. The uncontained hydrogen plasma core burned through the bottom of the smoldering hulk. In a half a second, the ship lost all power. Without acceleration compensation, residual explosions and the random thrust of dying gravgrids crushed the crew against the ship's bulkheads.

Devon was bowled over. He lay stunned and crumpled in a corner until the ship stabilized on its unwinding gyros. As the explosions stopped and the ship's accelerations halted, Devon straightened up in the resulting weightlessness and stared around the decimated bridge. First, he checked his vacsuit: the suit was sound, and he seemed uninjured, although his joints were a little stiff. Floating dollops of flash-frozen blood told him not everyone fared as well as he. He kicked across the cabin and found a breach split the fuselage from floor to ceiling.

Ian lay facedown in the break, half in and half out of the ship. With an inarticulate cry, Devon grabbed for the Count. The ship gave a lurch that threw Ian and most of Devon forward out of the ship. With a grip of iron, Devon grasped the Count's leg and wedged his own legs in the opening. The Count was weightless, but Devon needed all his strength to overcome the inertia of Ian's large body and drag him back into the vessel. Once he pulled the man back inside, he checked the suit: the Count's vital signs were good, but Devon tore off a couple of the emergency patches and used them to stop small leaks in the less armored portions of the suit. The initial internal acceleration from the shock wave had knocked the Count unconscious.

After he tied the Count by a lifeline to the floor, Devon checked the other suited figures on the bridge. The captain was missing, and two of the crewmen were already dead. Except for the ship's pilot, the others were either in shock or unconscious. With the help of the pilot, Devon patched suit leaks, and to insure they wouldn't float away, they attached the weightless crewmen to the bulkheads. After Devon accomplished everything he could for the bridge crew, he tried the bridge's blast door; it was fused shut.

He wandered to the breach in the side of the ship and gazed out through the hole onto the battle far below in the upper reaches of Falkeep's atmosphere. Silhouetted by the planet, the fighting ships were vaguely visible. The *Achilles* did not appear to be holding out too well. The last enemy destroyer, frigate, and escort harried the vessel. Devon could not be sure, but only one of the drones appeared to be active. In the clouds' reflective glow, bright flashes and silent explosions outlined the ships. For a moment the terminator hid the *Achilles* from Devon; in the next instant, plasma fire and bright red missile explosions outlined the ship. When a brilliant nuclear blast lit up the atmosphere on the planet below, Devon thought the *Achilles* was destroyed, but as he watched, the ship reappeared above and behind the planet, and the last escort was not in sight. A second large explosion marked the end of the third and final drone. It tore off a large hunk of the destroyer, but the Capital ship kept firing without pause.

Devon prayed Roger would take the *Achilles* outsystem. He had no hope of success now. In about 48 hours, when their suits ran out of oxygen, he and the remaining crew of the *Icarus* would die. The *Black Box* and the *Jagerhetzer* were likely destroyed. Next, he expected to see the enemy capture or obliterate the *Achilles*. Frigates were difficult to capture; most likely they would annihilate it.

But as Devon watched, the large bristling *Jagerhetzer* moved into his field of view. His heart filled with elation. It tore into the destroyer with all its guns ablaze. The *Jagerhetzer* abruptly stopped firing, and except for intermittent blasts from the few operational weapons on the destroyer, the scene became exceptionally calm.

The *Jagerhetzer!* Devon was surprised. The enemy frigate made a couple of passes over the struggling ships, but by this point, the two were almost touching. Its captain was unwilling to fire on the allied destroyer. The destroyer attempted to disengage. It moved a few hundred meters, then ground to a relative halt, drifting back into its orbital position. Its guns stopped firing. Down below, none of the ships moved or fired. The *Achilles* tumbled slowly, reflecting Falkeep's sun at each unhurried rotation. He couldn't see the enemy frigate. Perhaps it escaped outsystem or hid outside the range of his vision.

Devon decided the battle for Falkeep at last was over, and he hoped he was right in guessing they won it. He looked out through the breach along the ship; all that was left of the once-proud *Icarus* was half an almost-empty hull. Down below, the *Jagerhetzer* seemed to still function properly. He couldn't see the *Coffin*. The ship was too small and well-camouflaged to see anyway, but he wondered if, in the battle, it became a coffin indeed. The *Achilles* was battered to a useless hulk; he wondered if Roger still lived. He and Ian were lucky to be alive.

Devon turned on the emergency beacon, and in the unbroken silence of the ship, his dark musings unanswered, Devon hitched himself to a bulkhead and waited for rescue.

Twenty-five

evon hung weightless and dozed on the *Icarus'* twisted bridge. Outside the ship, a loud clank brought him to full wakefulness. Suddenly, a helmet marked with the gray star of Ian's assault troops poked through the breach in the hull and flashed a light around the interior. Count Acier, now conscious, jarred Devon's arm and pointed. As soon as the trooper noticed the ship was occupied, he quickly pulled his head back. Devon turned off the emergency locator beacon, and a voice crackled over their suit radios, "Identify this ship and yourselves."

Before Devon could key his mic, Ian replied, "This is the *Icarus,* salute your commander, Prince Rathenberg."

For a moment, confused transmissions came over the radios. Then they heard an astonished, "M'lord, I'm coming aboard," and a battle-suited Sergeant Major, carrying a bright lamp, crawled through the breach into the cabin. When they saw the Sergeant Major's uniform markings, Devon and Ian's eyes widened in surprise. The suit was emblazoned as if prepared for dress review. A red fox was precisely painted on the ceriplast armor, and below the fox, a hedgehog, and the gray star of Acier completed the design. A black armband circled the Sergeant Major's left arm.

The Sergeant Major saluted smartly, while Devon and Ian stared at the armband. The Sergeant Major following their gaze, colored slightly. "Well m'lord, we, ah, we didn't expect to find you so healthy." Then he ripped off the armband and smiled broadly. "M'lord, we feared the worst. I am Sergeant Major Godfrey Bernard. Our rescue ship is waiting. Would you step this way?" As an afterthought he added, "Please," but he didn't sound as if he used the word often.

In the blaze of the Sergeant Major's plasmalamp, Devon pointed to the other men on the bridge. "Evacuate these men first. The Count and I will wait until you take care of the wounded."

The Sergeant Major bowed stiffly and barked orders through his radio. He efficiently transferred all the wounded crewmen from the bridge. Under Sergeant Major Bernard's direction, the rescue ship scanned the *Icarus* for survivors. The ship sliced open the remains of the hulk to remove some trapped crewmen. Through the bulkheads, the men on the bridge felt the pulse of the laser cutters.

When Sergeant Major Bernard had removed all the injured crewmen from the frigate, he poked his head back through the breach with an apology, "M'lord, the rescue ship is full. Do you wish me to hold the ship here until I can acquire another vehicle for you?"

"No, Sergeant Major Bernard."

The Sergeant Major seemed pleased Devon remembered his name, and with Devon's next comment, he smiled.

"Don't delay a moment with my men."

The Sergeant Major barked another order and crawled back onto the bridge. Devon, Ian, and the ship's pilot were the only men left aboard. The Sergeant Major shooed the pilot onto the rescue ship and signaled it to launch. It was Devon's turn to smile.

While the Sergeant gave his last set of orders, with his radio off, Ian put his helmet against Devon's. "Is it thrice you cheated death, or do you do this more often?" With deep sarcasm, he snorted, "You garner more respect from my troops than I do myself."

"I seem to affect them most when they think I'm dead," returned Devon.

Ian laughed.

The Sergeant Major turned ruefully toward them. "I pray you are not yourselves injured, m'lords, or my captain may have my ears."

"Have no worries about that, Sergeant Major," crooned Ian, "but what we need the most is information. What was the outcome of the battle?"

"M'lords, was there any doubt? The forces of the Fox, begg'n your pardon, m'lord, overcame the resistance of the enemy in the Falkeep system."

"Well, I'm glad someone was entirely sure on that count," whispered Devon. "I was myself at a bit of a loss."

Ian elbowed Devon. "The Prince related to me the *Jagerhetzer*'s action against the destroyer in Falkeep's orbit. What was the outcome of your encounter near the gas giant?"

The Sergeant Major snapped to attention. In a broad military style, he described the boarding actions against the two destroyers, and the heroic participation of the *Black Box*. Devon was sad the ship was lost, but encouraged; the loss was not in vain. He reminded himself to praise their actions before the command.

The *Achilles* was a battered hulk, but most of the crew survived. The Sergeant Major acknowledged that Sir Roger was wounded, but not seriously. The *Jagerhetzer* lost nearly half its complement, and if the *Coffin* had not provided jamming and a diversion, they would have lost many more.

With chagrin, the Sergeant Major described their search for the *Icarus*; in its last reported location, all they could find was debris. They traced the emergency beacon, but the battle tapes could only identify the mangled and intermingled wreckage as an enemy escort. Only by luck, they didn't shoot first and ask questions later.

Almost the moment the Sergeant Major radioed his find to the *Jagerhetzer,* the captain of the freighter launched his pinnace to retrieve the assault group commander and Count Acier. When the pinnace arrived, Devon, followed by Ian and the Sergeant Major, crossed from the battered hulk to the airlock. After they boarded the small ship, the *Jagerhetzer*'s vice commander greeted the Prince and Count. The crew strained to get a view of Devon, but with a single command, they quickly turned back to their consoles and propelled the pinnace toward the *Jagerhetzer*.

Devon adjusted a viewscreen to look back at the hulk of the *Icarus*. The degree of damage to the frigate astonished him: little of the exterior armor was left, and the reactors and drives were missing entirely. Except where the rescue ship sliced it open, radiation and heat scoring covered the hull, and its shape reminded Devon of a wrung-out washrag. The fact the rescue ship found anyone alive on it amazed him.

The vice commander apologized more than once about the time it took to find the *Icarus*, but Devon waved off the proffered apology. "Your captain's actions were sound, and your troops acted with outstanding efficiency. That is all I require of any man." Later, after Devon noticed the proliferation of black armbands and black crepe-covered shields, he was sorry he'd been so magnanimous.

The exterior of the *Jagerhetzer* was blackened and blasted. All across its surface, vacsuited crewmen toiled on the emergency repair of the ship's systems. Is spite of the damage, the symbol of a fox savant, bright with new paint, decorated the hull. Devon could have appreciated the decoration more if it had not been obviously draped in black until just moments before his arrival. The pinnace entered the large shielded hanger deck and docked directly inside the large ship.

Devon stepped off the pinnace into a full military formation. Devon was impressed: the captain of the *Jagerhetzer* must keep the men well drilled to so quickly organize the honors due a Prince. Around the hangar deck, a thousand faces leaned forward to catch sight of him, and the instant Devon's foot touched the deck, the crew fired an energy volley from the main guns.

Before the last vibration from the guns faded away, the brigade band began to play. The *Jagerhetzer's* captain, Captain Birch, greeted Devon just as the loud strains of "The Prince's March" enveloped them. Devon stood at a weary attention as the band continued with "The March Imperial," "The Acierian Anthem," and "Rathenberg's Call to Arms." The music, played for him, played for the honor of his men, played for his House, awoke a great stirring in his heart. When the last piece sent its trailing echoes across the large assembly area, the men began cheering.

Devon would never dampen their enthusiasm by admitting he was exhausted. He was grateful to be their Prince and to be alive. A lump of pure pride caught in his throat, and for a moment, he found it difficult to focus. The soldier's cheers were loud and stirring. Devon could barely understand the words, but they seemed to cry, "The Fox," and "The Prince of wrath," and "The Fox defeated death." In spite of the loss, in spite of the bloodshed, they still believed in him.

At that moment, Devon felt he was truly their Emperor, and he was more proud of their determination and dedication than of anything he had ever accomplished himself. He brought his arms up in a wide gesture. The men quieted slowly and pressed forward to hear him. Their eyes were rapt with approval, sated with victory, and ignorant of defeat or fear.

Devon spoke, his voice duly expanded through the area mics pointed by the Captain's security and morale crewmen. "My warriors…." His voice was tense with emotion, and the men approved. "Warriors of the true Empire, I mourn every comrade who fell. I feel their death as keenly as though I lost a thousand brothers. You who fight with the Fox are true men. You have accomplished something no other force could. I see, in our colors, not just the four ships that entered this system; I see nine ships that bowed their necks in defeat." The men smiled appreciatively. Devon grinned back. "And I would rather face death than defeat."

A hush caught the men, and they whispered, "The Fox defeated death." Then, when they understood his joke, they began to laugh.

"I will not thank you for your duty. I will rather reward you for your courage, your strength, and determination. I grant you a great victory! A victory that will be remembered as long as the Empire stands."

"The Fox," they cheered. "The Fox."

Devon turned wearily aside. "Captain, I must speak to the commanders immediately. Have you initiated communications with Falkeep?"

"No, my lord, the planet is under a jamming umbrella."

"Very well. Gather my commanders together as soon as possible. Now let's go to a more private place."

While the men still cheered their victory and Devon Rathenberg's success, the Captain led Devon and Ian out of the hanger. The soldiers and crewmen followed them to the corridor, then reluctantly returned to their work. They marveled that they served under such a capable commander, their Prince, who was truly a Prince.

Captain Birch led them up through the levels of the ship to his own cabin. Along the way, the men lined the passageways as much to observe the heir to the Iron Throne, whom they'd heard traveled with them, as to gain a warrior's strength from the sight of the Fox, their commander. They would carry the memory until the day they died, and on their deathbeds, they would tell their children of the campaign in which they followed the Fox.

How tangible the tale was in its creation. How much greater it became with each repetition, and among these warriors, the story grew into a powerful catalyst for morale. It was like a chemical reaction, sometimes slow to start, but unquenchable once the proper ingredients were combined. The force of Devon Rathenberg was encapsulated in the man himself. His power was irresistible. Based on their Imperial society's image of perfection in a noble, he was a leader's leader.

Ian tried unsuccessfully to find fault in the princely stature of the man; the man incorporated faults, the prince did not. When he discovered he loved and desired to follow the man as much as his men, Ian could only shrug. He recalled with disbelief the times he scoffed at his intelligence people's descriptions of the Fox, Devon Rathenberg. Many of the soldiers in his service received their training and experience in the Emperor's intelligence corps. They returned with stories of the young commander who, like John-Mark, was a military prodigy. Except, unlike John-Mark, this man, Sir Devon Rathenberg was universally viewed as a success. He exuded success.

How odd, thought Ian. *I could not see the possibility of such a man before. Devon is the Imperial leader spoken of in the Codes.* As the realization of what this man, Devon Rathenberg, had led them to accomplish in the Falkeep system, he trembled to think no one else could have achieved what the Prince so easily achieved.

As the group plowed through miles of the freighter, they rode elevators and slideways until they finally entered Captain Birch's two small rooms. The forward cabin contained a U-shaped conference table, and around this table, leather-covered chairs—the legacy of the freighter, guessed Ian—provided seating for 17. The rest of the room contained a library of no small quality. The captain's bookdisks were stacked on a shelf that covered one full side of the cabin. Two opposite walls contained the hatch to the main corridor and a door that led to the captain's small sleeping compartment. The wall behind the table contained a large viewscreen and currently displayed the planet Falkeep and one of the captured destroyers.

Devon dropped wearily into the chair at the head of the table. Within seconds, a military steward placed a ration bar and a cup of hot coffee in his hand. He sighed as he took a bite.

"Sit down, Ian," Devon enunciated between mouthfuls.

"Nearly half the brigade lost." Ian shook his head, but he sat down. He fiddled idly with his coffee cup.

"Ian, the cost was high, but it only has to be paid once. Yedric is dead, and in one blow we captured a tremendous amount of the Emperor's naval strength. Neither the Emperor nor Gran Stern will be able to replace the Capital ships we conquered."

"You may be right." Ian shook his head again. "As age overtakes me, I find myself more protective of my people and myself. Although I can readily acknowledge the need of force when politics fail, I am unwilling to be responsible for the risk."

Devon bowed his head in response. "You are less than twenty years older than I, yet I believe I understand; however, I cannot let it affect my decisions."

"That is why you are a Prince." Ian smiled. "You will make a marvelous Emperor."

Devon scowled in reply, but before he could speak, Ian leaned forward. "I think I also need to thank you for saving my life."

"What makes you say that?" Devon made a guarded reply.

"The pilot told me you kept me from being thrown from the ship into space. For that, I am extremely grateful."

"It was no less than any man would have done."

"There you are wrong, my friend. The pilot was quite liberal in his praise."

Devon laughed. "You owe me nothing. Ian. If you must know, I promised your daughter I would not let any harm befall you. If I had lost you, I would have lost my honor."

Ian snorted, then grasped Devon's arm across the table. "I do owe you something. You have my fealty. You know you already earned it."

An embarrassed silence stretched between the two men. The hush was broken when the first of the *Jagerhetzer*'s commanders entered the cabin. Using the prerogative of rank, and thankful because of it, Devon wearily kept his seat as the men entered. Count Ian stood, however, and greeted the men. As the commanders entered, he reintroduced them to Devon. Devon congenially, and with little formality, returned their salutes, and the commanders seemed delighted with his affability.

The *Jagerhetzer*'s captain, the first Acierian light-armored brigade commander, three of the four regimental commanders, and finally, Sir Roger Falkeep entered and stood around the captain's table. Devon didn't have much opportunity to speak to Roger, but he grinned a greeting and made a wry face at the knight's bandaged head.

As soon as the men were in place, Ian sat down beside Devon, though the commanders waited on their feet for Devon to speak. "Please, gentlemen, be seated." Devon smiled graciously at them. "I am glad you could find time from your duties to meet with me."

The commanders glanced from one to another with a grin; who would disregard the orders of Prince Rathenberg, or even lose the opportunity to converse with the Fox. Before he spoke again, Devon directed the steward to serve the men coffee.

"When you so gallantly welcomed me to the ship, I hope I made myself clear to our command. Your men fought with outstanding vigor. They are the best force I have ever seen in combat, and I hope they are ready to fight again for the freedom of our mutual peoples. Communicate my feelings to your men, and let them know my pleasure at their service."

The commanders nodded with murmurs of approval.

"Our next step, gentlemen, is contact with Falkeep and preparations for the relief of Gran Stern. As you know, Gran Stern was the holding of Count Yedric. The Emperor Maricus granted me the county, and I intend, with your permission and guidance, to take the property as a prize for the banned Houses.

"First, we must see to our ships and men. With the approval of Duke Falkeep, the men will be allowed rotational furlough on the planet below. In addition, with the help of my father-in-law, Duke Falkeep, to aid our plans, we will outfit the captured destroyers and ourselves. From you, to prevent Falkeep's displeasure, I require the cooperation of our men and also battle plans to overcome the forces of Gran Stern. I will have the intelligence materials placed at your disposal immediately.

"Sir Roger, are you well enough for duty?" When the knight nodded, Devon continued, "I need you to make contact with the Duke and land with an envoy. I will disembark only after the first of our men have an opportunity to make planetfall.

"Commanders, I am happy with your caution aboard ship: keep the ship under low pressure with the men in their vacsuits, helmets may remain off but must be available. Except for those in pressure bunks or sanitary facilities, I do not want to see a single person, officers included, without a suit. I authorize you to perform whatever drills you require to ensure the men are prepared for attack. I do not exempt my commanders or myself from this policy.

"Captain Birch." Devon turned toward the *Jagerhetzer*'s Captain. "If we are attacked while under pressurization, you will immediately depressurize. You will allow no time for suits-on or for the normal depressurization schedule. I want the ship cleared and ready for battle in five minutes. And I don't believe I need to explain to you why. If we can compute and navigate to a congruence intrasystem, the enemy can also. If you need further elucidation, talk to Count Ian and Sir Roger and review the *Icarus'* and *Achilles'* battle tapes.

"Now I require a report on our operations and resources."

The Brigade commander spoke. "M'lord, we are a little less than half strength. In the initial portion of the battle, our first and third regiments took a beating. I was forewarned by your orders to expect the action, but the *Black Box* was unable to relay your orders before we engaged. I'm afraid I committed the assault too early, before the *Jagerhetzer* could bring its full weaponry to bear. Without the jamming of the *Black Box*, our attack would have been unsuccessful. The second attack in the planet's orbit was more fortunate. I followed your original recommendations exactly, and I find no fault in the execution or the outcome."

"Don't second-guess the results, General." Devon raised his open palm. "I think, perhaps, the outcome is the proof of your tactics. Although I welcome your self-critique, I placed you in a position your

220

troops were barely ready to handle. Under those circumstances, you proved your metal." Devon glanced meaningfully from face to face of the regimental commanders.

"Thank you, m'lord." The General continued, "The morale of the men is excellent. They are settled into the ship's routine, but if we intend to keep an edge on the troops, your furlough order is necessary.

"We salvaged a large amount of our battle-damaged equipment. Most is repairable and being repaired. The second regiment is stationed with the two destroyers near the gas giant. That, by the way, m'lord, is the location of my other regimental commander. They recovered most of their equipment and are affecting repairs to one of the destroyer's engines. They will soon be able to move both ships into orbit around Falkeep."

"What is the condition of the destroyers?"

"Except for the drives, one is fully operational; the *Black Box* completely destroyed the gravgrids. The drive section on the second destroyer is missing and most of the reactors shut down. The ship is partially operational but probably not easily repairable. Of the ships in orbit with us: one is a wreck, but we can use it for salvage; only the pressurized portions of the ship were destroyed. The other has much of its exterior blasted away, but the major systems of the ship operate. We might be able to bring it back to full combat readiness."

"What is the long-term outlook for salvage and repair?"

Captain Birch answered Devon, "A month, maybe two will see the two best destroyers ready for battle. They might be fielded as partially operational in less time, perhaps two weeks. The other two ships should be used for scrap or to augment Falkeep's orbital defenses. Our greatest problem is finding men to crew the ships we can field.

"Of the ships we brought in our assault group: the *Black Box* was lost in the fighting near the gas giant. I understand the actions of the crew were particularly noteworthy and the prime reason for our success. The *Icarus* and the *Achilles* are beyond repair. That leaves the *Jagerhetzer*. We affected combat repairs of most of our damaged systems and weaponry. The ship is nearly fully functional, and, at the moment, our crew manning is sufficient, although not at optimum levels."

"What of supplies?"

"Ample."

"Very good." Devon smiled around the table. "Much better than I hoped or expected. Gentlemen, may I request the presence of the entire officer's mess at dinner tonight."

The brigade's general smiled at the formality. "M'lord, the mess is honored to invite you to dine with it tonight."

Devon nodded. "I will certainly not require formal attire."

The officers laughed gently.

"A very good report, gentlemen. I believe that is all the information I need at present. Sir Roger, would you honor me for a moment more?"

As Devon stood, the commanders rose and bowed. They trooped out of the cabin. Captain Birch turned to Devon. "M'lord, if you have no further need of me?"

"Go ahead, Captain Birch, and thank you for the use of your cabin."

"M'lord." The Captain bowed.

When the Captain left the room, Devon grasped Roger's hand and wrung it in a firm grasp. "It is good to see you again. Roger. When your ship's drive systems failed, I feared the worst. Your ship looked like it turned to slag."

"You feared! m'lord?"

"Just, Devon—the Count will understand."

"Yes, m'...Devon, when your ship torched, I thought you were a crispy critter yourself." They smiled at each other.

"I do have a very important mission for you. I think you know my main concern is your sister—I don't need to say more on that account. You realize the last time I left Falkeep, your father was not pleased with me at all. Before I show my face, I want you to check out the situation. I realize everything should be ironed out by now, but I need to know how things stand. Further, you must see if your father will approve our furlough as well as support us. I don't want to force him, but you understand, as well as I, the role we play in the rebellion of the Houses."

"Devon," Roger sounded slightly breathless, "my father swore to support you and the banned Houses. He is committed to our goals."

"Even so, brother, I would be wrong to not treat my new father with full honor and give him the option to refuse his support. Speak as gently as you can, and let him take the full reigns in your discussions."

"Yes, Devon."

"Go now, you must arrange these things as quickly as possible. To outfit my forces and take over my boon from the Emperor, I need the Duke's full assistance."

Roger bowed and left the cabin.

"So—" Ian drew back his lips in a half grin—"the truth comes out."

"What truth?" replied Devon, matching Ian's smile.

"James Falkeep. I'm sure he did not easily give away his youngest daughter even to you. She has a reputation as the most protected child in his household. What did you do—get the girl in trouble so her father forced you to marry her at gunpoint?" Ian chuckled.

"You don't know the half of it," laughed Devon.

Twenty-six

D evon felt a lurching sensation in his stomach that wasn't caused by the corvette's reentry. Two days ago, Roger had reported from the surface of Falkeep that he'd found minimal damage on the planet. Yedric's forces had kept them under siege for more than a month, but after the first few days of bombardment, the enemy ran out of planetary attack weapons. Then, along with a few abortive raids, the enemy destroyers began a systematic harassment with energy weapons. The ground forces and planetary defenses were too strong for the destroyers to crack, so Count Yedric's attack force had to be content with a random plasma shot that Falkeep's forces usually jammed and some missiles, most of which the planet's defenses easily intercepted. Falkeep kept up a solid sphere of jamming around the planet: on each of their attacks, the big destroyers entered an area where their systems had a remarkable chance of failure. But still, Yedric's forces isolated the Falkeep system for nearly six weeks' standard accounting. That is, until the four-ship attack group led by Devon Rathenberg entered the system.

Roger's father, Duke Falkeep, received him with honor. The Duke was eager to support the small fleet with whatever resources he had available. The first boatload of furloughed troops had landed earlier today. Indeed, they traveled just as Devon was traveling, by way of the Duke's fast courier corvettes.

Devon's apprehension didn't come from his fear the Duke would not support his forces; he feared the Duke himself. The last time he met the Duke of Falkeep, Devon was naked, fleeing the fire of a snub pistol—a snub pistol held in the Duke's hands. Devon was not sure of the welcome he would receive now.

Another wave of foreboding struck Devon, a feeling that principally affected his heart: the Lady Tamar Falkeep Rathenberg. He loved the woman with an emotion stronger than any he'd ever experienced, but she knew him for only a few days before he left Falkeep. Almost ten weeks had passed since he'd last seen her and tasted her love, and he had cold feet about their upcoming reunion. He'd never felt quite this way before. It was disquieting. Roger had told Devon the entire story of what happened after the Duke found Devon in her bed. And because of the circumstances, if Tamar rejected him now Devon would not be surprised.

Although Tamar's love was as tangible to him as ever, Devon could barely remember when he'd last seen her. He was deathly afraid she would not remember and perhaps not care to remember the love they shared. The doubts shook him like nothing had in his past. He could imagine life without anything, but not life without Tamar. His happiness was entirely dependent on her.

The ship set down at last with a gentle bump, and the steward opened the lock. He glanced at Devon, and in the glare of the sunlight, Devon was glad the man could not see the sickly grin he returned. With a shake of his head, Devon resolved himself to the most difficult meeting he'd ever been called to make, yet the thought of the Lady Tamar irresistibly drew him.

Devon stepped onto the sunlit tarmac, and as his eyes adjusted to the brightness, Roger walked up to him with a smile. "Finally, you're here, Devon. Come on." He grasped Devon by the arm and pulled him along to a gravvehicle.

"Well, Roger—" Devon licked his lips as he sat in the car—"you were successful, I see."

"Yes, very. Everyone is waiting to meet you at the terminal."

"Everyone?"

"Yes, everyone. If I didn't know you better, I'd say you were afraid to meet my family."

Devon sighed.

When they reached the terminal, Roger led Devon through a security entrance to the noble's lounge. Roger opened the door and stepped immediately through. Devon hung back a little. As he entered the room, everyone stood up. His heart pounded at a fast march cadence. He couldn't see Tamar, but he recognized Duke Falkeep. The man had aged since Devon had last seen him, yet he stood ramrod stiff, the picture of a noble and Imperial officer. As if unsure which emotion was necessary, the Duke's lips were caught between a frown and the twitch of a smile. At that moment, Devon was more afraid than at any time in his life.

The Duke broke the tension by stepping right up to the Prince. The stern features broke into a great smile, and with an intensity Devon found compelling, Duke Falkeep bowed. "My son, my lord, Prince Rathenberg, let me welcome you again to Falkeep. May I honor you with the fealty of the Duchy of Falkeep, my Prince, as I also welcome you into my home."

Suddenly overburdened, Devon clasped the Duke around the shoulders. "My lord Duke and father, please accept the strength of my House and the strength of my nobles. I offer them freely to you."

The Duke returned Devon's grasp with the same energy. "You gave me back my lands, my son, and I have already accepted your House."

They released their grasp and stepped back appraising each other. Then Devon beheld the Lady Tamar. At first glance, she seemed utterly alone and frightened, as if she were as unsure of him as he felt of her. Her eyes looked at his with longing and fear, fear of what she might find in them, and longing for the man Devon Rathenberg.

The Duke stood back. "Prince Rathenberg, I am sure you would like to greet the Lady Tamar Rathenberg."

Devon glanced swiftly at the Duke, then back to Tamar. She was suddenly her old self. Her chin came up, she threw back her head, her appearance so like the princess she was now indeed. As she stepped up to him, her eyes flashed with a blaze of anger. "My lord." She made a beautiful curtsy.

When she came closer, Devon could see that for all her bearing and ceremony, her eyes were bright with tears. He imagined her feelings. Like his, they propped up the little bit she remembered of him.

When they had parted, their knowledge of one another was trifling, and in time, the immediate remembrance faded. Yet he held her in no less esteem and with no less love than when he'd left. Devon's arms went around Tamar, and with a clasp that at once drove a sigh and a sob from her, he held her tightly for a long moment. Tamar's arms grasped him with an intensity he never forgot, and she hid her face in his neck. When he released her, she looked no less like a princess. The smile he remembered so well danced in her eyes and on her lips. The brightness of tears left her eyes; new warmth replaced them. Tamar stepped back, but she laced her arms through his and remained at his right side. As her father introduced the rest of the family, she stood by him—a little closer than ceremony generally allowed.

The Duke presented an ashen-faced older woman, the wife of the Duke's eldest son, George, and her three young boys. The oldest boy was fifteen, and their mother looked on Devon with awe. Her husband was missing since the seemingly ineffectual attack on Gran Stern, and she was visibly distraught. The sons bowed handsomely.

The Duke's older daughters pleasantly greeted Devon, but they saved their awe for Tamar. They looked at her as if until this moment, they had not really believed who her husband was. Their husbands also greeted the Prince with honor, and Devon was duly impressed the Duke had chosen them for his daughters. Both of them had been stuck on Falkeep since the beginning of Yedric's blockade, and they had wanted to join in the actions of the banned Houses.

Roger just beamed at Devon, and the Duke took on some of that same quality. Devon saw the pride in the man: pride in his daughter and pride in Devon.

After the Duke finished the introductions, they all returned to the Falkeep estate. As they left the spaceport, the sun just started to drop below the horizon, and when they reached the house, it was only a thin, bright line. Although Tamar sat close to Devon and clasped her hand in his throughout the short ride, they said little during the trip.

At the house, they ate a pleasant dinner, and Devon was forced to share stories about Roger and his travels. Devon was certain Roger already narrated all their tales much better than he could. Although Tamar seemed tense with emotion, she barely spoke a word to him and acted as if on the verge of saying something.

Devon narrated the battle for Falkeep and their visit to Neuterra. He self-consciously described the meeting where the banned Houses of the Landsritters declared him the next Crown Prince. Roger irrighteously added the details that Devon conveniently left out.

Throughout the meal, Devon slowly regained the uncomfortable feeling he knew before he saw Tamar. She seemed demure, so unlike the Tamar he remembered. Her eyes sought his, but he could not penetrate her thoughts. Her mind was closed to him and she would not or could not speak her heart to him here. When the dinner finally ended, the ladies and gentlemen separated to parlor and study. Devon felt anxious and impatient the entire hour before the Duke finally bowed to him, nodded to Roger, then went off to bed.

Roger smiled at Devon but was wise enough not to say anything. He called a servant to lead Devon to his room. At Roger's summons, a young girl appeared. She curtsied to them and led Devon through the manor's corridors and stairways to a private suite. As soon as they stood before the door, the girl left. The door to the suite was not locked, and Devon opened the door and stepped in.

As Devon closed the door and walked into the room, Tamar stood. In the dim light of the suite, he saw she wore only a long clinging negligee. The light came from behind her and shown through the thin gown. His breath stopped with the beauty it revealed, and he wondered how he could ever have left her. Tamar was lovelier than he remembered, and his heart swelled with desire for her.

Tamar didn't say a word, but she cocked her head to the side and with a slight smile on her trembling lips, she stepped hesitantly toward him. As she walked, her form pressed through the fabric of the dress; covered by the silky material, her body was revealed as if she stood naked before him.

When she stood right in front of him, he was afraid to touch her, afraid that, at a touch, this moment would pass, that he would wake, and the dream would end. Tamar looked up at him questioningly. He yearned for her so long and this instant seemed unreal. Devon searched her face. Her look was frightened and tinged with anger. The same anger he'd seen at their meeting. Tears filled her eyes; they flashed with fury. He noticed for the first time that a small, discolored mark crossed her right cheek. When she perceived his stare, her hand, of its own accord, crept up to cover the mark. Her eyes widened as if the motion betrayed one of her greatest secrets, and she bowed her head with a sob.

"I know," Devon replied softly.

Thick with suppressed emotion, Tamar forced between clenched teeth, "I wanted to keep our secret from my father, but I couldn't."

"I know, Roger told me. I love you, Tamar. Will you forgive me?"

Tamar was caught between emotions: the tension of siege, the fear for Devon's life, her own love, and the pride that marked the House Falkeep like the mark on her cheek. She wavered a moment in indecision, then, eyes flashing, voice heavy with rage, like lightning, Tamar struck him across the face.

"You left me," she whispered hoarsely. Then, sobbing, she threw herself into his arms, and pressed her lips disparately to his. Her body strained against his, and she cried in a voice of passion and awe, "I love you, Devon. I forgive you."

Twenty-seven

They lay exhausted, and lounged in bed. Beside Tamar's discarded gown, Falkeep's new summer sun spread across the covers. Devon lay half asleep, content and sated. Tamar lay on her stomach draped partially across him, and with great pleasure but little desire, his hand cupped her buttock.

Tamar, nearly awake, possessively traced the scars on Devon's chest. Every now and then she asked him what caused one or the other, but each time he either misunderstood the question or was too asleep to properly answer, so with a grin at the state in which she'd put him, Tamar went on lightly touching him.

A stray thought came to Tamar, and she voiced it with growing wakefulness. "After you left, a message came to Father. It gave your family the County of Gran Stern."

Still half awake, Devon answered her, "I know of it. My father—" Devon yawned—"gave the County to me."

"How do you intend to take it?"

He growled with slight displeasure. "The destroyers can be outfitted shortly to force capitulation."

Tamar kissed him lightly, then provocatively. "I have been thinking; there was little else to do, waiting for the siege to end, waiting for you to return." She kissed him again. "My brother George took a full complement of assault troops to counter the forces we knew were on Gran Stern, yet in the whole time, no assault troops landed here." She nibbled his ear, and noticed his eyes crack slightly open.

"Go on." He shifted slightly.

"Although Yedric stockpiled planetary munitions for years, the destroyers dropped few of them. I think George took the planet or, at least, the Capital and the major military bases. Considering the quality of Falkeep's forces, that would not be hard to do. But the Navy of Gran Stern is much more powerful than Falkeep's. In their plans, Father, Roger, and George figured most of the Navy would be away from the system. That obviously didn't happen. Yedric's Navy never arrived at the Battle of Acier, and a major portion of it appeared in our skies. What does that say to you?"

"I think I understand, but enlighten me."

"Gran Stern is under siege by its own forces. They are using all their assault forces and planetary munitions to bombard their own planet. Sir George Falkeep holds the planet. Yedric's commanders sent part of their Navy here to put pressure on us. They wanted to prevent our reinforcement of the bridgehead on Gran Stern and keep us from sending out our remaining naval forces or requesting support.

"The Navy of Gran Stern had six Capital ships. You took four here. Over Gran Stern their Navy would be unopposed, and two destroyers would have ample capability to effectively wield the munitions and assault troops on Gran Stern. The frigates in Yedric's fleet numbered almost 18. Only two were here. My father sent 20 frigates against Gran Stern. I should think, dependent on my theory, if George captured a large portion of the planet, then Falkeep's Navy handled itself very well. Ten of our ships would be required to provide enough force to take the Capital and the major bases; at a kill ratio of one to one against the other ships, that leaves eight of Gran Stern's frigates operational. Once on the ground, our ships would be useless. They would not be able to takeoff into the fire of the destroyers. Therefore, in the worst case, nine of Gran Stern's frigates and two destroyers are left, the planet is already captured, and the naval forces have been at war with their own planet for nearly eight weeks."

"What do you suggest?"

"You don't need to attack anything, my love. Wait until the frigate that escaped the battle here returns home, give a couple of days for the story of your victory to get around, then take your converted troopship marked well with symbols of the House Rathenberg, House Falkeep, House Acier, and the Fox. We'll travel to the Gran Stern system and enter it as if we owned it. I believe it will fall with little fighting."

Devon's eyes were wide awake. "I think—I think that might work, Tamar. But what did you mean we'll go?"

"You don't think I want to leave you now. We will be going to our County; it is my right and responsibility. Anyway, I thought of the plan." Her eyes flashed.

He appeared equally angry. "I don't want you in any danger. You can't go because your plan might not work, and then what would I do? Let you fight?"

Tamar's mouth opened and closed as if she would speak, her lips trembled. Then she smiled broadly and kissed Devon deeply. Her hands touched him lightly, teasing. He struggled with his anger a moment, but it fled from him as he held her and stroked her with growing desire.

When no one answered her knock, Dulcia opened the door to announce the family's breakfast. Red-faced, she closed the door gently again and went to the kitchen to save some of the meal for her lord and lady to share later.

Flushed with lovemaking, to soothe their growing hunger, Devon and Tamar finally rose. They dressed casually and went down to brunch.

As they sat in the quiet dining room overlooking the remains of an ample meal and sipping hot coffee, Devon asked Tamar, "When do you think we should take this expedition to Gran Stern?"

"I'd say in one week standard." She watched him slyly. "You mean to take me also?"

He frowned for a moment. "No, I simply meant we, as in my complement of forces."

"Oh." She looked disappointed.

"I see I was correct in my estimation of your abilities. You certainly understand politics. The Lady Neuterra may have been right to praise your abilities so liberally."

"You spoke to Duke and Lady Neuterra?" Tamar exclaimed excitedly.

"Yes."

"Well, don't just sit there. Debrief me on the state of the Empire and the banned Houses."

"I would love to, but I don't think this is the best spot. Is our room under any surveillance?"

"No. Do you have a detector?"

"Yes, in my baggage."

"Let's go back to our room." Tamar grasped his hand. Then, catching his grin, she continued, "But no hanky-panky. It's time for serious planning. How you could get along without my help, I just don't know." She rolled her eyes.

In the security of their room, Devon described his travels from the time he left Falkeep. Tamar looked astonished at what he told her and voiced a great deal of alarm over the risks he ran.

"What did you try to do—reduce your chances to nil that you would return to me? You men. My sisters tried to warn me." Tamar ended her diatribe with a laugh.

Devon laughed with her. "You understand much of what I told you cannot go further than the two of us."

"Who could realize that better than I?" she quipped. "Many of the things we share I don't expect you to give to anyone else." And even with her look of assumed innocence, she colored visibly. "Don't laugh at me," she warned. "You are mine now by alliance, and if you want to retain your County..."

"Our County, my love. What next? I'm sure your devious, female, Lady Pembrook's Finishing School mind has involved itself with much more than the situation on Falkeep and Gran Stern."

Tamar looked proud as she accepted his compliment. "I have been making plans..."

"Knowing you from Arient, I'm sure you have."

"Oh, be quiet. I have made plans, and although none are at the point of fruition or even at the point of cognizant coalescence…"

"Don't use those political imagery theory concepts with me." Devon grimaced.

"Ha, you should be happy; at least I understand them. I will provide for you, my lord, and our House a bountiful political agenda."

Before she could launch into another soliloquy of Lady Pembrook's political theology, Devon covered her lips with his and held her until she stopped struggling.

Tamar let herself relax in Devon's gentle grasp. Her eyes said, *The real trick is to figure out how to convince this wonderful, stubborn man to let me go to Gran Stern with him.*

About two days after Devon arrived on the surface, he shared a portion of the Lady Tamar's plans via secure commline with his commanders. Tamar would not let him attribute any of the ideas to her. A problem of seated male egos, she explained, and Devon, understanding the truth in her statement, passed the ideas as his own.

Devon knew that, at some times in human history, women were forced by social pressures to be viewed as politically, emotionally, intellectually, and physically the same as men. Those societies, ideologically based in asexuality, were historically doomed to failure. The Human Empire recognized men and women were inherently different. They shared many features in common, but their emotional and mental makeups were not common. The problem-solving capabilities of a woman were based on different thought patterns and flourished under different circumstances than those of a man. The idea was to encourage those circumstances and capabilities.

Since the dawn of the age of genetics, men and women were taught separately. Their educations were similar but the mode of the education and the training in certain subjects was based on the inherent differences of each sex's propensity and capability for learning. For example, the art of familial manipulation and political image dynamics were taught to women. Men gained a similar but not as specialized course of study in family dynamics and political history.

The increased vigor of human progress and understanding was a byproduct of this type of education, and the Human Empire could never survive without it. What man would trust the political future of his House to anyone other than his wife: the thought was appalling. He would lose all advantage in his day-to-day dealings. What woman would trust anyone other than her husband in the management of planetary resources: the brunt of the political manipulations for her House would be ruined.

The attempts in less-enlightened eras to genetically change the drives and inherent prejudices of the human male and female minds had always ended in sorry failure. You could not have a true woman or man without the mind and desires of a true man or woman. The studies of genetic neuters had brought this truth to a cataclysmic conclusion— the sexes were more capable with their differences and conflicts than a genetically designed neuter human.

Devon read of the problems in the eras of the neuter humans and the times of asexual public dogma. He was certainly glad he had never lived in those periods. Now, at the very least, humans were granted the dignity due their basic sexual worth and were not forced to conform to unattainable roles.

The brunt of this was that Devon could not attribute his House's political plans to the Lady Tamar, even though, socially, everyone understood she was responsible for many of Devon's decisions. The opposite was also true. For her to give credit to Devon for any social operations of their House would cause her and the House to lose face, but everyone understood he would be a driving influence in the management of their Planet and County. In any case, the result was that they worked together. However, the complexities of the social system affected their operations, the operations were the result of the both of them. But, reflected Devon, the women did receive a larger share of the credit for peaceful solutions. He could already hear the Lady Pembrook saying, "Now for example, my dears, here is the Lady Falkeep Rathenberg's Gran Stern solution." The thought was provoking.

Devon let his commanders know enough of Tamar's plan to have them step up the furlough schedule and prepare the ships for departure. Devon explained to them that after some contemplation, he came to the conclusion that the system of Gran Stern might not be so carefully guarded. His men accepted this, and Devon dumped their tentative warplans into Falkeep's computers. Of course, Tamar reviewed his commanders' ideas. She even presented Devon with her estimation of the political, strategic and tactical worth of each of his leaders.

Together, using the commanders' outlines, Devon and Tamar drew up a battle plan. Though they hoped to not need a war plan, the use of parts of his officers' ideas would serve to stroke the officers' egos, and the plan would provide a backup if Gran Stern decided to fight. Devon was impressed that Tamar put together the plan so that the correct officers, in her estimation, were given the exact amount of psychological credit.

"This will build you in these men's opinions," she explained. "When you call on them again, they will perform for you as you cannot imagine."

The final battle plan was adequate as a cover for their actual operations, but Devon did admit it also brilliantly achieved Tamar's stated goals. Devon did not let her know, but by the time the battle group was ready to leave, he was completely in awe of her capabilities.

The week passed in mutual bliss for Devon and Tamar. During that time Devon gained an outstanding understanding with the House Falkeep. The Duke and he were almost alike in their interests in life and completely in agreement in their estimation of the Lady Tamar. The Duke was not easily willing to part with his beloved child, but if he must, Devon was the man he definitely wanted to give her to. In all, Devon began to feel that he had found a home like one he'd never dreamed of before. The days passed too quickly.

When the time came for Devon to depart with his forces for Gran Stern, Duke Falkeep and Tamar came out to see him off. Roger had already returned to the ship. Ian and his command had done their best: most of the men spent at least a day planetside and the ship stood at 80 percent capability. Devon's troops demanded another victory.

At the spaceport, the Duke clasped Devon around his shoulders and held him like a son. Devon could see the man wanted to go himself and would have, if the responsibilities of rule did not keep him on Falkeep. With his emotion already at a fever pitch, Devon held his father-in-law. They both stepped back, their best thoughts about the other renewed.

The Lady Rathenberg curtsied daintily and gave Devon her hand, but Devon was in no mood for formal partings. He swept her into his arms and kissed her deeply. "Don't forget last night, my love. I can't."

Tamar giggled in his ear, but when he released her, she was all formality again. In fact, a slight trembling in the corners of her mouth didn't foreshadow tears in her eyes, and as Devon headed toward his shuttle, he found the detail mildly disconcerting.

The shuttle docked at an internal hanger on the *Jagerhetzer*, and Devon, now arrayed in his vacsuit, stepped out to a reception that included Ian, Captain Birch, Roger Falkeep, and General Locke. They greeted him as though he was gone for years rather than only a portion of a standard week. Devon noticed a large number of off-duty soldiers shared their commanders' interest; they had appeared to catch a glimpse of the Fox.

After the commanders welcomed him, they stood around expectantly. Roger sported a large grin. They all focused their attention on the shuttle. Devon glanced around nervously, and when he turned back, the men centered their attention more firmly on the shuttle's lock.

"Well." Devon shifted his feet impatiently.

"Yes, m'lord?" asked the Captain, still straining toward the lock.

"That can't be all the luggage," remarked Roger, with a glance at the cargo pad.

"Why?" asked Devon suspiciously. "That is all I took down with me."

"Ah." Ian smiled broadly. "The Lady is coming later."

Devon noticed the crowd of crewmen nearly doubled; by then, the hanger floor was nearly surrounded.

"I think there is a mistake," stated Devon cautiously.

"No, certainly no mistake, m'lord," pronounced the *Jagerhetzer*'s captain. "The Lady was supposed to come aboard with you."

"Do you mean the Lady Rathenberg?" spat Devon, ill concealing his anger.

"Yes, the word we got," Roger looked troubled, "was that the Count and Countess of Gran Stern were to go together so the political instability of the system could be more quickly contained once we secured our victory. But if for greater safety you've decided to take the Lady with you on one of Falkeep's ships, then I, for one, can understand."

"Gentlemen—" Devon frowned, dumbfounded—"we need to talk. To the captain's cabin with haste."

Devon and the grumbling group of commanders finally arrived at the captain's conference room. With no formality at all, Devon, livid, questioned them at length. So he could extricate himself from the situation if he lost control of it, Devon asked his questions carefully. After only a few minutes, he realized it was already out of his hands. The Lady Tamar Falkeep Rathenberg was inextricably a part of their plans, and for the good of the ship and to ensure their eventual success at Gran Stern, she must be part of the command. Somehow a rumor had raced through the ship that had become the policy of the command. Even Roger was duped by the unofficial information that swept through the crew.

Devon hoped none of the commanders realized the real reason for his surprise. He explained the whole situation was supposed to be entirely secret, and the lady was preparing herself and would arrive on the next shuttle. Then he sent the shuttle back for the Lady Rathenberg.

When she arrived on board, he didn't meet her but left the duty to Roger and the captain. He heard later almost all the officers and all his commanders were on hand. Among the men, the Lady Tamar Falkeep Rathenberg had become something of a folk hero. Ian attributed it to the force of her association with Devon, but Devon knew the true reason: Lady Pembrook's training—beautiful manipulation of his command. It smacked of the pure efficiency of proper propaganda and political manipulation.

That Tamar—that woman, thought Devon, *well, she may not fully realize the results of her manipulations. Then again, she probably does.* And though still very angry over the way she'd so easily confounded him, he had to admit she would be a pleasant accompaniment to the voyage and when they finally arrived at Gran Stern, a great advantage at the diplomacy table.

Tamar entered his cabin wearing a vacsuit. The helmet dragged unfamiliarly at her waist, and though she held to Roger's arm, she stumbled crossing the blast door seal. Devon looked up only to wave her brother out. Then he turned back to his work. Roger was about to return an angry retort, concerning Devon's impolite conduct, but the lady gave him an imploring look and laid a trembling hand on his wrist. Roger, disturbed, stepped quickly out of the cabin.

After a few moments, Devon looked up from his computer to see the lady still standing where her brother had left her. She was white-faced and he could tell she was frightened. *Rightly so,* he thought angrily.

"I'm glad to see that you know how to, at least, properly present yourself to your justifiably angry lord." Devon glared at her.

"I—are you going to send me back, my lord?"

"You know as well as I do, I can't send you back."

She had the decency to not smile in response to his comment. She looked rather more frightened.

He stood up and paced behind the table. "I'm sure you realize the extent of your manipulation of my crew?"

"No, my lord." She moaned.

"No? When they greeted me, my commanders thought you were aboard my shuttle. If nothing else, the degree of control convicts you. You nearly embarrassed me before my entire crew. I am still not sure if I can properly mend the event in the minds of my commanders."

"But my l-lord—" she stammered. A large teardrop fell off her nose.

"Don't start sniveling with me." He turned from her. "I know you engineered this whole circumstance to disobey my wishes."

"But I didn't," cried Tamar, unable to restrain her tears.

"Come, come, that just can't be true; the whole thing stinks of Lady Pembrook. This entire escapade to Gran Stern may be your idea, but it is fraught with danger. If the expedition ends in combat, I do not want to lose you." He turned around, faced her, and started to sit down again.

Tamar put her hand lightly on his arm. It was wet with tears. The back of her other hand covered her mouth, and she looked Devon in the eyes. Trying unsuccessfully to stifle her emotions, she explained, "I—I didn't. I didn't expect my little effort t-to have the ef-effect it did." More forcefully, she continued, "I admit, I wanted to go with you. I don't want you to send me back. But," she continued brokenly, "I didn't really t-think my plan would have this effect."

He looked fixedly at her, and she dropped her eyes, trembling again. "Please, my lord, believe I would never intentionally do something to harm you." She stifled a sob. "I just tried some of the techniques from school, and they worked."

"I'll say they worked." Devon shook his head. He stepped from behind the table. "Maybe I'm being manipulated myself." He took hold of her arms.

Tamar jerked back angrily, but at the look on Devon's face, she let herself be held at arm's length.

He shook her gently. "Don't let this happen to me again, Lady Tamar."

"Yes," she choked. "My lord, I am so sorry." Her eyes pleaded to his.

He clasped her crushingly to him. "Tamar, I love you."

She gasped at the force of his hold. "Devon, I love you; I would do nothing to hurt you." She started crying again.

"Shush," he breathed, "I believe you." Then he kissed her lightly, a kiss she returned with intensity. He slowly released her and wiped her tears away with his fingertips. "I believe you. And I pray that we both will survive not only this voyage, but this marriage."

Tamar smiled a little.

"Go freshen up." Devon pointed to his borrowed cabin. "I have much to do before we get to Gran Stern. Perhaps now we can coordinate our activities to that end."

Twenty-eight

As the *Jagerhetzer* made the phase shift back into normal space, Tamar stood beside Devon. The ship was depressurized and ready for battle. Through Tamar's visor, Devon could just barely make out the expression of wonder on her face as, at combat acceleration, they entered the Gran Stern system. In her vacsuit, except for the fact she wore the smallest suit on the ship and the crewmen conspired to decorate her combat uniform with even more elegant devices than emblazoned their own, Tamar would have been unrecognizable. On the left breast of her vacsuit, the savant fox was beautifully executed in gold, while below it was painted the symbols of a hedgehog and Falkeep's lion. The designs mysteriously appeared the first ship's watch after leaving Falkeep. Tamar took off her suit to go to bed. When she awoke, it bore the battle symbols.

Devon's own vacsuit was the first the crew decorated. He didn't realize it was marked until just before they entered the outskirts of the Falkeep system and he donned it in preparation for battle. Since the Battle of Falkeep, the crew brought the devices on the suit back to their initial finery, but they left both a burn mark and a gouge that crossed his chest unrepaired. When Devon tried to have the marks removed, he found, through General Locke, the armorers would not touch them.

"The men have developed an unusual superstition concerning you, m'lord," the general explained badly. So Devon left the marks untouched and didn't comment on the fact they seemed to be accentuated with paint.

At full acceleration, the *Jagerhetzer* blazed along the ecliptic into the Gran Stern system. They broadcast their entry with offensive jamming, electronics, and active sensors. The captain immediately turned the system's warning drones and satellites into nuclear flares. With no attempt at concealment, the ship passed the many gas giants and smaller planets that made up the system, and neared the inner planets of the life zone. Around the outer planets, their path of entry was lined with burned-out hulks from the navies of both Gran Stern and Falkeep.

Devon was becoming tense; so far, they had no contact.

Gran Stern was a rich system. Although most of its planets were not colonized or improved, it boasted the greatest number of usable planets in a single County. The system's large golden star placed the three principle inner planets and a large moon squarely within the life zone. The planets' ecosystems were not comfortable, but they were familiar to terra-conditioned humanity. Of the four planets capable of supporting life, only one was terraformed. The rest sported either the sites of temporary operations or an untamed alien landscape.

The richness of the system was its greatest downfall. Historically, by not returning an ample share of their profits to properly develop the system, the Counts of Gran Stern squandered their planets' resources. Dominic Yedric was no exception. He took every credit he could out of the County to build an illegal Navy and a powerful army.

The Yedric family had developed a limited genetic strain of emergency leaders, and therefore, governed by their inbreed attributes, more often than not produced tyrants. In consideration of the urgency that often faced the planet shorted by the Count's diversion of resources to buy and build military forces rather than clothe, house, and feed his people, this was fortunate.

The people of Gran Stern were willing enough; they never knew a less arduous existence, but the climate of the principle and only terraformed planet could not be faced without more monetary investment than the Count was willing to expend.

Unlike most Counties in the Empire, the main planet in the County of Gran Stern was not named for its system: it had its own name. The original survey team christened it Crystal; however, its people called it many different things. During the short spring and summer, they named it the Fiery Green or then again Mistress Persephone, but most of the time they called it the White or Winter, for Crystal was a planet of very long winters and short summers. It orbited near the outreaches of the life zone. Of all the planets of Gran Stern, Crystal possessed the most terra-compatible biomes, but Crystal was a ball of ice and tundra where life was a privilege that could not be taken for granted.

While the week of their travel went by, Tamar studied the system extensively. Devon was certain she already mapped a careful agenda for its improvement.

As they stood side-by-side at the front of the bridge, Devon turned to watch her for a moment: Tamar carefully observed their rapid approach toward the growing yellow sun.

Captain Birch signaled Devon worriedly. "Shouldn't we take a more careful pace, my lord?"

"No, Captain," Devon answered, "continue our ingress directly toward the principle."

"Ship approaching, sir," called the deepspace systems monitor.

With an imploring look toward Devon, Captain Birch ordered, "Put it on the screen."

"Identified," continued the monitor, "Frigate, Echo class."

"That's not one of Falkeep's," breathed Tamar.

"Hold our acceleration." Devon stared at the crono. "What's the time to turnaround?"

"At combat rate, one hour."

"The frigate is marked in the colors of Gran Stern; it is matching our acceleration."

"Turnaround," barked Devon.

"The ship is decelerating with us."

"Wait it out." Devon scowled. "No communications."

In a few minutes, the frigate hailed them. "Unidentified vessel, you are entering sovereign space. Exit immediately, or you will be fired upon."

"Identify us to them," Devon snarled. At almost the same time, Tamar and he stated, "Let them know who is on this ship!"

A long pause stretched between the ships. Then a more official voice answered from the frigate, "Confirm Prince Rathenberg, the Count of Gran Stern, is aboard?"

"Confirm it," directed Devon evenly.

There was another long pause.

"We are closing on the planet Crystal, m'lord."

The communications from the frigate blared, "Will you accept terms, Prince Rathenberg, for the release of Gran Stern?"

Devon looked at Tamar. She shrugged. "It depends on the terms they want," she whispered. "I foresaw their capitulation as unconditional."

Devon keyed his mic to the frequency of the other ship. "I, Prince Devon Rathenberg, Knight of the Red Cross, come to claim my boon. Under the jurisdiction of the Emperor of Human space and the Duke of Falkeep, I come with my Lady to claim my lands and fealty. Who will prevent me in these lawful actions?"

The frigate returned, "Under those conditions, my lord, we will agree to a truce to discuss your requests."

"Perhaps you don't understand," spoke Devon with a little malice, "you have no one of rank to speak for you. My planet is held by Falkeep's forces. I don't need your permission or agreement to require the fealty of my own County."

"Destroyers coming into sight, near the planet," called the monitor.

"Accelerating or orbiting?" Devon half-turned toward the monitor.

"Orbiting, m'lord."

Devon's cheek twitched. His grim face almost threatened to turn into a smile.

Although they picked up some coded broadcasts to and from the destroyers, they received no signals from the frigate. Finally, a weary voice crackled over the speakers, "My lord, Prince Rathenberg, the Navy of Gran Stern is honored to welcome you to your County. May we be permitted to accompany your entrance into orbit?"

"Negative," shot Devon over the comm. "Decouple your power systems."

"Four other frigates in orbit," returned the monitor.

"You're pushing too hard, my lord," whispered Tamar with agitation.

"The ship's decoupled," shouted the short-range monitor.

Devon beamed. Tamar grasped his arm excitedly through his suit.

"Tell them to recouple and flank. Order an honor guard." Devon gazed down at Tamar. He touched his helmet to hers so he would not be overheard. "A risk," he affirmed, "but the proof is in what a man is willing to do, not in what he says he will do." He squeezed her hand. "I'm very proud of you, my Tamar."

Tamar trembled with relief, and just then, she didn't trust herself to speak. She smiled a half smile at Devon he returned in full.

Six frigates, some showing extreme combat damage, limped alongside the *Jagerhetzer.* In response to Devon's command, they formed a guard and accompanied the larger ship into orbit.

"Repressurize, Captain Birch," ordered Devon.

"My lord! We'll be at their mercy," balked the astonished captain.

"On the contrary, Captain, they must appear quite at our mercy. Repressurize and give no impression we arrived depressurized. When they embark, conduct my new naval commanders directly to the conference room. High honors, General Locke, but not to Gran Stern. The circumstances must stink of Imperial formality. Come, my dear." Devon took Tamar's arm.

Captain Birch shook his head with worry as Devon and Tamar left the bridge together.

The brigade's protocol element had turned the Captain's austere conference room onto a reception hall worthy of a Prince of the Realm. The banners and decorative armor strakes of Acierian, Imperial, and Falkeep units already lined the walls. Before they left Falkeep's system, Devon directed Ian in the decoration of the room: "Barbarian with the flavor of the House Imperial." The troops competed to produce the most worthy decorations meeting that description.

Behind the table, using a low podium, protocol raised the captain's chair a few inches. They also repadded it to make it appear larger and more imposing. They mounted the full device of Crown Prince Devon Rathenberg, Count of Gran Stern, Knight of the Red Cross on the wall behind the chair.

After the ship was fully pressurized, Devon and Tamar dressed in their noble finery. He wore the uniform of a Crown Prince of the Empire: satin black with a full drapeau trimmed in gold, and the devices of rank, position, and honors—each pure gold, woven or sewn into the fabric. Tamar wore the formal noble lady's dress, a heavy white and silver gown only donned for the highest of state ceremonies.

The visit Devon expected came more quickly than he predicted. General Locke reported, the Gran Stern naval commanders fell all over themselves to get to him.

When they were allowed entry to the conference room, its decoration struck them dumb. Devon looked at them unsmilingly from his raised seat. Tamar, her hand on the back of the chair, stood behind Devon on his left. In the position and dress of seneschal, Ian stood further to Devon's left. The officers of Gran Stern, all of Captain's rank or higher, appeared very uncomfortable in their soiled battle dress.

General Locke introduced the commanders of the forces of Gran Stern; the first was Admiral Tzilnikov. The unwavering gaze of Ian Acier reminded the Admiral of court etiquette, and with a look of embarrassment, he dropped to one knee. As General Locke presented the other ten men, they each followed their leader's example. Finally the General pronounced, "Now, gentlemen, allow me to present his royal highness the Crown Prince Devon Rathenberg, Count of Gran Stern."

The Admiral nearly had an apoplexy and spoke quite out of turn, "My lord, the Crown Prince?"

No one deigned to answer the impertinent question, and the Admiral continued lamely, "My lord Prince, may I request the honor of fealty under your hand?" He presented his sword to Devon. In chorus, the rest of the officers presented their weapons.

No one spoke. Devon stared silently at the kneeling men. Beads of sweat formed on the Admiral's forehead.

"Don't press them too hard," whispered Tamar at Devon's back.

"The Emperor and I are displeased with the actions of the County of Gran Stern. The result of this displeasure is that Dominic Yedric is dead by my own hand. His family is dispossessed. The County of Gran Stern will be a holding under my jurisdiction. It will prosper under the Codes and by my decree."

The Admiral's hand that held out his sword began to shake. Sweat ran down the sides of his face.

"If you are unwilling to obey my commands, gentlemen, do not offer me your sword. I will be an angel of death to those who lack honor. I will be a murderous taskmaster to those who are less noble than their rank decrees. You choose honor with me now or death, or when you give me your sword, perhaps both. Which do you choose? I offer you the chance to reconsider."

"We are decided." The Admiral's voice was strained.

"You are all decided? You do not choose only for yourselves. I will hold you responsible for your commands and your families. Your fealty is their fealty."

"In honor, we cannot choose otherwise." The Admiral groaned. A whisper coursed through the kneeling men.

One of the Captains went to both knees. "If my lord is for Gran Stern, here is my sword; do with it as you please." The officer tossed his sword to the floor in front of Devon.

"Agreed," the voices of the men rose as they threw their swords. Finally, only the Admiral was left, holding his own weapon.

"Do you choose?" demanded Devon.

With a look of complete resignation, the Admiral copied his men.

At Devon's nod, Ian took up the weapons and brought them to the table. Under the men's gaze, Devon inspected each blade. He held each so it obviously remained within the view of the Lady Tamar. As if they measured the vitality of the man who owned them, they both nodded at each. Finally, when Devon took up the Admiral's blade, Devon scowled and his eyes narrowed. "Admiral Tzilnikov, over Falkeep, to an enemy much smaller than yourself, you lost four destroyers and their escorts. In the system of Gran Stern, you bowed in defeat without a battle. You attempted to give terms to your ruler. You led an attack on your own planet and caused death and destruction to my people and properties."

Devon paused. His eyes flashed. "You are not worthy of your rank or your position." Unexpectedly, Devon leapt across the table and raised the Admiral's sword. The blade slashed through Admiral Tzilnikov's half-bowed neck. As Devon cleanly cut the Admiral's head from his shoulders, Devon cried out, "Your death will barely cover this stain on my Navy's honor."

With a gush of blood and the thump of his severed head, the Admiral soundlessly toppled forward. In horror, the kneeling officers nearly fell backwards. The smell of blood permeated the room. Devon heard the shuffle of feet behind and beside him, but the sound stopped immediately. The officers began to rise, but in the uncomfortable silence, they settled to their previous positions. Devon, splashed with gore, stood with the Admiral's bloodied sword in one hand while his other fist rested on his waist. "Traitors to the crown," he roared, "come in many varieties. Stand, gentlemen, and in return, receive the fealty of your lord."

Without hesitation, the men stood. Devon turned to get their swords. Tamar was wide-eyed and white-faced. He could see her teeth chattering behind her lips. She stared at him as if his actions were a part of him she did not want to understand. He could feel her soundless cry of fear and abhorrence. Ian seemed slightly surprised, but his face displayed approval. As an officer and a noble, Devon had not shirked his duty. Perhaps all of these men deserved the same fate as their Admiral, but now, they would serve him with the unambiguous knowledge of how he distributed punishment and honors, and they would serve him well: honor for success and victory, dishonor and death for failure and defeat.

As Devon handed each man his sword, he lifted him to his feet and touched his cheek to his own. He accepted them as family in Noblesse. They were all nobles, all members of the Houses of Gran Stern. Devon's magnanimous acceptance would spread to their Houses, and their fealty would be already half won. He knew the men recognized his leadership. He tugged at their spirit of honor and manhood. He offered them the honor they lost under the circumstances of the last few months. And they joined with him in honorable victory.

With a salute, he dismissed his new officers to their ships.

As soon as his commanders left, Devon turned to Count Acier and wrinkled his nose at the corpse. "Ian, clean this up." The Lady Tamar rushed from the room into the Captain's small cabin she shared with Devon. Devon immediately followed her.

He found her in the fresher, wretchedly sick. Devon noted that she barely made it to the receptacle and was again amazed at her strength: as sick as she was, she didn't let it show until she could without losing face.

"Devon," she retched, "how could you do that? How could you?"

As Devon knelt and placed his hands on her upper arms, Tamar shrank from his touch. He held her, the contact a slight comfort. After a moment, she sat on the floor and sobbed for breath. He wiped her mouth and gently caressed her cheeks. "Tamar, I had to kill him. I know you don't fully understand, but I could read the men who knelt before me. They were not ready to give me their fealty. Their honor was stained. The solution came to me suddenly; my actions were those any commander would take against a bungling and incapable officer. It was the just penalty for the man's crime against his people and command. You see, just as you decipher the politics of situations and manipulate them, I lead men."

Tamar looked at him, then again, ashen, bent over the receptacle. When she sat down once more, she almost smiled. "Devon," she patted his cheek, "you're right, I don't fully understand, but I do see how the situation worked—politically. I didn't agree with your actions, although Ian did, but I admit they appeared to work. The Lady Pembrook said men were unaccountable in their behavior, and to illustrate what she meant, she described incidents similar to what I saw there in your conference room. Please Devon," Tamar's eyes held his beseechingly, "If you must act this way again, be sure you are fully justified. The greatest danger in men, so Pembrook declared, is they justify their means by their ends. To men, the end is the justification. To women the means is the end." Tamar wiped at the stains on the front of her dress. "Don't destroy what I can accomplish for you by upsetting the balance of the whole."

He replied with as much sincerity as he could put in his words, "Tamar, the reason for war is usually attributed to the failure of politics." He sat beside her. "I know war is a further extension of politics. Just as a government must kill murderers to protect its citizens, the state must protect its people's rights and property by killing other states, or at least rendering them incapable of further action. The actions that maim and kill have a justification if the reason for them out weighs the harm they cause. This is a basic tenant of politics...but enough of this. How are you feeling?"

"Better." She grimaced.

Devon stood up and pulled her with him. "Change your clothes, and ready yourself. We are not finished in either our politics or war making, and we need the formality of our rank and power to over-whelm our adversaries."

Twenty-nine

Initial contact with Baron George Falkeep confirmed Tamar's theory: eight weeks ago, the Army of Falkeep conquered Sternlicht, the Capital of Crystal, and drove the Army of Gran Stern underground. Through superior armament and the Nobility of Crystal's relieved acquiescence, George controlled almost the entire urban area of the planet.

The populace was initially so thankful to be out from under Yedric's militarily enforced yoke, their submissiveness toward Falkeep's forces made intervention unnecessary. Quite disconcertingly, his command actually advised George to provide protection for the beleaguered forces of Gran Stern from the populace.

Balanced on a fine line, the Baron's position of power became ever more precarious with the passage of time. Crystal was actively split between five camps: the Army of Gran Stern, the Nobility, the populace, George's expeditionary force, and the Navy of Gran Stern. Of the five, the Baron had the least difficulty with Gran Stern's Army; it was no longer supported by the people, the Nobility, or the Navy. On cold, stark Crystal, as Gran Stern's Army ran progressively lower in supplies and personnel, the forces of Falkeep were the least of the Army's worries.

George's greatest problem was between the populace and the Nobility. On one hand, the Nobility wanted to hold onto their established power. They were used to a reign of iron, and they slowly reacquired their power by the systematic torture and murder of dissenting subjects. Under Count Yedric, the Army and state police undergirded this tyrannical rule, but Falkeep's occupation made this impossible. The police had silently disbanded; they feared the retribution of the Duke of Falkeep and the people. Opposition on all sides hampered the Army.

Further adding to the problem was the general populace. The people of Gran Stern were not a passive group. The planet provided too harsh an environment for the weak or foolish to long survive. The ultimate control of the people came through the control of food, shelter, and heat. On bleak Crystal, these items were the primary determinants of survival. After Baron George Falkeep's arrival, a popular rebellion built immediately, and large areas of the planet were completely under rebel control. Luckily, the revolutionaries viewed Falkeep as their liberator and, to an extent, bowed to the requests of the occupation force, but this dynamic was quickly changing.

The basic survival commodities were still in the hands of the Nobility, and they held those in a death grip. Rightly so. To release their control on the life of the people would result in their bloody murder. Baron Falkeep, in the interest of noble rule and the control of the populace actually encouraged the actions of the Nobility, and that policy fast eroded the position of Falkeep's occupation force.

The people of Crystal, long-suffering, cruelly used for centuries, decided to use this opportunity to take control of the planet for themselves. Given enough time for resentment and organization to build, a sweeping flood of humanity would soon align itself in open and uncontrolled insurrection. Survival on Crystal was dependent on maintaining modern industrialization for food and energy production. The society could not sustain itself without advanced leadership and knowledge, both unique attributes of the Nobility. Without the populace and the Nobility, human life on Crystal could not continue. The result of the rebellion's success or failure would be the same, the ultimate destruction of a nation and people. Baron Falkeep and his advisors, bound by traditional solutions and values, did not understand the danger. Social forces confounded their every effort at solving the problems, and the other parties, just as ignorantly, rushed headlong into the very confrontation that would spell their doom.

The fifth party, the Navy of Gran Stern, played an equally abhorrent role. In the name of keeping supplies away from Falkeep's forces, they bombed their own people, and with efficiency destroyed the resources of their own planet. All Baron George Falkeep could do was protect his own forces and hope Gran Stern's Navy ran out of planetary assault weapons.

After less than a week of Falkeep's occupation, Admiral Tzilnikov, the naval commander, changed his tactics. His reason took over, and he slackened the bombardment of the planet to only military targets and the outskirts of population centers. This supposedly provided, in his words, "Hopeful encouragement to his beleaguered people." However, the effect of the bombing was the exact opposite. The more armament the Navy dropped, the angrier the people became, and the more they flocked away from their own forces to the support of Baron Falkeep.

Baron George Falkeep was not completely unused to the control of government, that is, government under the direction of competent advisors. He was, however, a man of little ingenuity or flexibility. He provided the proper dignity and appearance for the policies of other men, and in that vein, he was rather set in his ways. If he knew about an alteration in policy, he routinely balked in despair at the change or strategy development. Likewise, he clung illogically to any concept he thought was traditional or conventional. Everyone except the Baron realized the discreet manipulations of his wife controlled his life and career. She was, after all, an accomplished graduate of Lady Pembrook's.

Under Baron Falkeep, the army worked very well. He trusted his commanders' loyalty and competence, and he granted them free reign. They, in turn, gave him full support. As a result, he was reasonably informed and credibly obeyed. The Baron's best quality was that he understood his own lack of professional competence. As long as the guidance appeared traditional and conventional, he listened to and was quick to follow the good advice of his people. In fact, he possessed the unique gift of being able to discern the best policy and course of action when they were presented to him. His ability was not foolproof, but it did not usually steer him wrong and that generated the genuine admiration of his subjects.

George's father, the Duke, sent his propaganda corps, the pride of the army of Falkeep, for just that purpose: to keep George properly advised and well supported by his own forces and the people of Gran Stern. The assignment of them to his battle group honored the Baron, and he realized, in truth Duke Falkeep was willing to part with his famous corps in the hope they would help George prevent an even greater catastrophe than the mobilization of Gran Stern. His father could not have foreseen that the stolid George, so open to competent advice, with that same advice precipitated a disaster.

To put all the blame on Baron Falkeep was not totally fair to him. Whether a man is a figurehead or a true leader of men, the success attributed to him is still a success. Unfortunately, the failure of a leader's people rests just as significantly on his brow. And in the light of the Baron's usual capability to attach himself to the proper course of action, he was an effective, er—figurehead.

Together, Devon and Tamar worked out an agenda very different from the advice George received. First, through the Navy, they made contact with the Army of Gran Stern. By bribes of basic supplies and the force of Devon's authority, he arranged a cease-fire between the Navy, the Army, and Falkeep's expeditionary force. Following that, Devon immediately forced a furlough for all but a skeleton crew on the ships of Gran Stern's Navy. As yet, he didn't allow the men of the *Jagerhetzer* planetside. Tamar, using every wile she'd learned at Lady Pembrook's, inundated the crews of Gran Stern and the *Jagerhetzer* to specifically aimed propaganda. The rumors of their contemplated actions, they hoped, would encourage the people of Gran Stern to their ends. These negotiations and follow-on planning took them nearly a week in orbit. Ian and Roger stayed on board ship to oversee the operations Tamar and Devon formulated. Devon hoped the ultimate goal of their planning would be the result Tamar predicted.

Tamar understood her older brother, George, well. She knew his foibles and his capabilities, and she knew that, when crossed, he was very difficult to influence. At the onset of their communications with the Baron, Devon and Tamar detected a slight problem. They could not pin down the exact reason for their apprehension, but they were alert.

Because of the danger of open combat, Devon did not want to take

Tamar to the surface with him. But she convinced him George Falkeep would not be easy to handle alone. Eventually, her arguments prevailed, and she was allowed to come along.

At Tamar's insistence, both she and Devon attired themselves in clothing of state. Not the same uniforms of Imperial Noblesse they used in the interview with the naval commanders, but simpler clothing representing their new rank as the Count and Countess of Gran Stern. They already designed the attire they would wear in their capacity over the County of Gran Stern. Their pattern was significantly different than the state garments of Yedric's House. They used similar colors, however, white and light blue in concert with the accepted Imperial shades. To these they added the devices of Falkeep and Rathenberg. Devon wore a black, finely cut suit trimmed in the colors of Gran Stern. His devices were silver for his county and gold for his ducal associations. Tamar contented herself with a stunning light blue and silver gown of noble rank—that was not the usual ceremonial garb of a Princess. The ship's military tailors produced all their new clothing.

Tamar and Devon arrived on the surface of Crystal by way of one of their newly acquired naval frigates. They carefully chose the captain and men for this honor from Gran Stern's Navy. The crew expressed intense excitement over carrying the new Count of Gran Stern, Crown Prince of the Empire. The ship sat down gently on Sternlicht's stark spaceport.

In spite of the planet's dreary contrast with Falkeep, Tamar acted much differently than Devon expected. Of course, she knew all she could research about the planet: she had studied it continuously for the last couple of weeks, but a great abyss lay between knowledge and experience. He expected her to be slightly depressed by the planet's appearance and personality; instead, it appeared to invigorate her. When they exited the frigate, to the wonder of the captain and crew, Tamar stood for a moment in the biting wind and glanced over the scene of fitfully blooming tundra. She breathed deeply of the alien wind, and a smile blossomed on her features. She gazed with a rapt expression as if she reached a place she long desired. A bloom of color caressed her cheeks, and with almost a skip, she followed Devon through the buffeting wind to the waiting armored gravvehicle.

George had established his headquarters in the Count's palace in Sternlicht. Although the Baron attempted to liven up the palace by turning up the building's reactor furnaces and putting in as many reminders of Falkeep as he could, an atmosphere alien to the luxury of Falkeep pervaded it. The halls, though warm, seemed drafty. The few graces from Falkeep only accentuated the Spartan and angular decor.

When Devon and Tamar approached the city of Sternlicht and the Count's Palace, instead of the packed buildings of a chilly metropolis, they found the flat, windswept tundra crowded against the palace walls. The city stood on the far side of the palace. As they entered the palace grounds, the sound and temperature of the wind was no different than on the wide open plain beside it. Falkeep's forces delivered them promptly to Baron George Falkeep.

Tamar was right in her estimation of the stubbornness and vanity of her brother George. He greeted them as if he were the Count of Gran Stern. As they entered the palace's hall of justice, an officer of Falkeep announced their entrance. The Lady Tamar, with her hand along her lord's bent arm, walked with quiet dignity. The room was high and bare. It was built of dark stone and furnished with an eye to hard angles and extreme contrast. Baron George Falkeep sat in the Count's throne and conferred with two of his propaganda officers. They were dressed as aides, but both Tamar and Devon recognized the bearing and controlled speech of the men as hallmarks of the Duke's propaganda corps. When they came closer, they saw the Baron expected them. He was dressed in his grandest uniform and carried a Count's baton. The uniform and the baton sported the badge of the County. With a final nod to his aides, he, at least, rose to greet Tamar and Devon. As though he had not expected Devon to bring Tamar into a war zone, he scowled at her but didn't deign to look at the Prince. The Baron's contemptuous manner showed he did not consider the two of them consequential to the planet's future. He obviously didn't realize Devon was the appointed Count of Gran Stern.

Baron Falkeep nodded to Tamar. Then he took her proffered hand and touched it to his lips. "Tamar, I realized Father allied you to this man, but I did not expect him to risk your life by bringing you here."

Tamar opened her mouth to deny the accusation but closed it again and stood quietly.

The Baron eyed his sister in silent appraisal, then turned with a frown to Devon. "You are Devon Rathenberg? I am not particularly pleased to make your acquaintance."

Tamar reflexively clasped Devon's arm, but as he nodded congenially to the Baron, Devon only raised his eyebrow.

The Baron took a step back and slapped the baton against his palm. "Now, what is so important that you take me from my many duties?"

Devon's lips curled into a half smile. "Baron Falkeep, I came to the County of Gran Stern to take up its rule as the Emperor charged me. By the Emperor's proclamation, Tamar and I are the rightful rulers of Gran Stern, and I would appreciate your help to make the transition to civil rule as easy as possible."

"Perhaps, Count Rathenberg, you don't understand the situation on this outpost of Falkeep?" stated George. He turned and, with his baton, waved the two propaganda officers out of the hall.

"No!" whispered Tamar to Devon. "I wanted his officers to moderate our interview. With family alone, we will have greater difficulty."

"I don't think this planet is ready for civil rule." The Baron caressed his baton.

Devon replied, "Even so, we weighed all these problems, and we think we can negotiate a resolution that is acceptable to all parties."

"So you think you can do better than I?"

"No, brother—" George grimaced as Devon said the word—"I think the advice of Count Ian Acier and Countess Tamar Falkeep Rathenberg of Gran Stern are sufficient to justify success."

"So what would you have me do—brother?" the Baron exclaimed.

"I need you to remove your forces from the planet."

"Absurd!"

"I already arranged a cease fire, and as a matter of fact, it has been in effect for nearly four days."

George spoke as if explaining to children, "You don't seem to realize that, each day, I lose more men to the local populace and the Nobility's private armies than to the Army of Gran Stern. People are dying out there." He swept his baton toward the unseen city. "They are ready to destroy themselves and us. God only knows why. No, no! I cannot leave this planet to you, yet. The military situation will not allow it."

"But George—" Tamar stared at the floor—"we think we know why the populace is in rebellion. We think we know how to guide the people back to a more reasonable situation."

"Ha," he spat, "this is war, Tamar. Just because you went to Pembrook's on Arienth doesn't mean you are qualified to solve all the problems of mankind."

"But this is my planet, now. I am its lady. Its welfare is my responsibility. I cannot be its lady unless it exists. You must give me and my lord the chance to rule."

"Your lord," he snorted. "Who left you to face the Duke's anger?"

Tamar's face turned bright red.

George mistook her expression for one of embarrassment. "And that mark on your face—where did it come from? It was the gift of this man, who has not enough honor to claim the right to speak to you."

"Baron Falkeep," Tamar's tone was crisp, "you don't understand. I wear this mark with an honor you don't know. I pray it will not ever fully go away, for by it, I remember the honor of my lord who was willing to die for our Emperor, and who recovered the honor of our House in the very palace of our enemy."

Although the Baron could not have known the events behind Tamar's words, he flinched at her tone. His own face full of anger, George started to speak, but Tamar, not hiding her fury as well as she would have liked, stared him down. "George—" she glowered at him— "Devon Falkeep is my betrothed. He is my legal lord. Our father and the banned Houses of the Empire fully acknowledge our marriage. I love this man, and I am his lady. Isn't that enough for you?"

"I will someday be the Duke of Falkeep, and I do not like him. It disturbs me that you accepted him. He was a coward not to face Father, and he was wrong to take a woman of a rank he could not properly possess in the first place."

Tamar trembled with anger and clenched her fists. "He did not need to take; I gave myself freely to him. Oh you fool," she cried, "can't you see? Without some change in your policies, this planet, *our* planet, will erupt in complete rebellion? We cannot work within the constraints you placed. You will lose one of the Counties of the Kingdom of Falkeep and destroy our people at the same time. George, please, I am begging you. You must let us go through with our plans."

"I cannot." The Baron smirked. "I promised our father and myself I'd do my best to protect our House. How can I do that off this planet? Can you expect me to leave you in the hands of a population that will tear my little sister to shreds? Or that I will trust you to the machinations of this man, Devon Rathenberg?" He walked back to his desk.

Frustrated and thinking, Tamar put her face in her hands. Beside her, Devon glanced at his crono. They all felt a strong vibration through the stone floor. George Falkeep turned around and stared. When a second heavier tremor rolled through the palace, Devon reached out to Tamar to steady her. The Baron stumbled, but when the rumbling passed, he quickly regained his balance.

One of Falkeep's aides rushed into the hall. His lips were white and he spoke with agitation, "The city is under attack."

"Not entirely," stated Devon, "Your troops are safe. But you will find many of the planet's Nobility and your forces without a place to live. You will also discover the Army and Navy of Gran Stern in the process of aiding my people to take the Houses Noblesse. They are also supplying my people with food and shelter."

The Baron's eyes widened, and anger convulsed his features. He took a menacing step toward Devon and stopped.

Tamar stared at Devon. Her eyes appeared as shocked as the Baron's. Frightened, she shook her head in alarm. "Devon, I warned you not to make the attack until after we convinced my brother."

"Another example of his true loyalty," yelled George as he rushed unexpectedly toward Devon. George's baton caught Devon on the side of his face. Devon did not anticipate the attack. He fell heavily and struck his head on the stone floor with a crack.

"Do you think you can take this planet so easily away from me, Count Rathenberg?" the Baron sneered as he pulled out his snub pistol. "I think you cannot. The whole of the Navy of Gran Stern couldn't force my men off this rock. I and they have a certain entitlement to it."

Tamar was dazed; their attack was not to come until after George left. Now Devon was at the mercy of her brother. She stepped toward Devon's prone figure. When she caught sight of George's gun, Tamar screamed, "No!" She fell across Devon and shielded him from the Baron, "No!" The tinge of hysteria in his sister's voice drove the rage from George. He slowly returned the gun to his holster.

Tamar knelt over Devon's still form, "No, no, no," she groaned, "this is not how it was to be." A tear threatened to fall from her eyes, but in her anger, she forced her emotions under control. Thank God, she could see Devon still breathed. As a small pool of bright blood tinged the floor beneath his head, she was suddenly afraid to touch him, afraid that to move him would cause more damage. The blood welled from the side of his face. Gently, Tamar took her handkerchief and held it against the gash on his skull.

Behind her, George commanded, "Arrest the Count Rathenberg. He is a traitor to our House."

Two soldiers stood over Devon and bent to lift him.

"No!" shouted Tamar, resting against him. "Don't move him until he has medical attention."

"Don't be foolish, Tamar." George Falkeep turned to an officer. "Take the Lady to one of the empty suites and place a woman in her charge."

"No!" Tamar was defiant. "I will not leave him. You have injured the rightful Count of Gran Stern, and you will have to answer for it."

"Get up," snarled the Baron.

Devon groaned as he slowly regained consciousness.

"Don't just stand there," barked George. "Place the man under arrest."

The Baron grabbed Tamar's wrist, dragging her to her knees. The soldiers lifted Devon to his feet. George released Tamar's arm. In pain, she cradled her wrist, knelt back on her heels a moment, and choked back tears. Then, with a cry, she stood up abruptly and followed the burdened soldiers. When she passed George Falkeep, she turned her beautiful face, flushed with rage, toward him and spat on him.

"This is my lord and my planet, my people and my House." Tamar's voice trembled. "We are the rebellion you rightly feared." She stepped after her lord with her head held high.

Thirty

Tamar lay back on the bed and cradled Devon's bandaged head. The Baron George Falkeep, her brother, had locked them under guard in this bedroom. *At least,* she thought bitterly, *George sent a doctor. If only Father could see this now.*

The room was as stark as the rest of the palace: harsh with heavy furniture and cold with polished stone. A window of coated ceriplast admitted the last of Gran Stern's afternoon light.

Devon slept. The doctor said Devon had nothing more than a hard crack on the head. He said he found no internal bleeding or other damage and gave Devon a pisiodermic injection of a sedative. But Tamar didn't want Devon to sleep. She wanted to talk to him. Why had he instructed Ian to attack early? The timing was too well planned. Already, she decided, Devon knew George would not relinquish the planet of his own free will. Devon pushed her brother in some way she didn't understand, but it must be an action of a military character—a man's action, like killing the Admiral.

The destruction of the homes and private areas of Gran Stern's Nobility was her idea. The populace, she predicted, would take the Nobility prisoner and raid the nobles' supplies. The people would have what they desired—control of the resources of the planet and enough to eat for a few days. That would defuse the tense situation on the planet. After she studied the character of the people of Crystal, she believed the Nobility would not be harmed.

But Tamar had not slept and had eaten nothing for the last 24 hours. By this time, she didn't care how the people treated Gran Stern's Nobility; they deserved all the retribution and ire of the people. The wait was wearing on her.

With a moan, Devon opened his eyes. His throat convulsed, then he asked weakly, "Where are we?"

Tamar kissed his lips with a new light in her eyes and replied tiredly, "We are still prisoners of my brother in the palace on Crystal."

"Were we successful?"

"Successful in what, my love?"

"We're still here; perhaps my plan didn't work."

"How do you feel, my lord?"

"Like I was hit with a sledge hammer instead of a baton." He smiled weakly. "Your brother has incredible strength."

"That wasn't my brother." She lightly caressed the back of his head. "After George hit you, you cracked your head against the floor."

"Oh. I guess he didn't like my solution."

"That's what I wanted to talk to you about."

Devon cringed visibly.

"Yes, you should act guilty. You could have told me what you planned."

"I didn't want to keep it from you, just from Ian and Roger. They would never have agreed to my instructions."

"Just what did you do? You followed our plans, didn't you?"

"To the letter."

"Well then?"

"I added a little into it. I warned the soldiers of Falkeep of the attack, then when they went on the defense I blew up their quarters and assaulted their ships. The cease-fire didn't apply to the forces of Acier, only to those of Gran Stern and Falkeep. Well, I hope our forces captured George's ships. I tried to reduce the bloodshed as much as possible, but I knew we would have problems with Baron Falkeep." He tried to keep the irony out of his voice.

"Yes." She put her cheek against his forehead. "I didn't realize how intensely he believed his responsibility. So Baron Falkeep should be without ships and his men without shelter. He will have to give in to you."

"Do you have anything to drink?"

"No, my love."

"Have you slept?"

"No. I—I was too worried about you."

"Go to sleep. No. First, how long have we been here?"

"More than a day."

"Go to sleep."

She lay beside him in the dark, and both drifted off to sleep.

As the early morning light poured through the ceriplast panel that served for a window, Tamar woke and walked to the panel. For all its thickness, the view through the ceriplast was undistorted. Their room was located on an upper floor, perhaps 30 meters above the ground. Below her lay a thin piece of cultivated tundra filled with short green grass and red blossoms. Beyond the thin yard stood a high wall, a sentinel to the metropolis beyond. As far as she could look to the left and right, outside the wall, soldiers and military vehicles filled the streets. Many of the soldiers stepped out of the vehicles as if newly aroused from sleep. They stretched and watched the skies with evident fear. They were a ragtag group, not at all like the troops of Falkeep she knew. That they were part of Falkeep's forces was evident in their colors, but they appeared demoralized and leaderless.

I believe Devon's plan worked, she thought as she observed them. *They have no warm barracks, no way off my planet....*

"Tamar?" Devon spoke quietly from the bed.

"Yes, my lord."

"Help me up, please."

A pang of fear touched her. As she moved quickly to his side, Tamar responded a little louder than she wanted, "Devon, what's wrong?"

"All right, just dizzy. Help me up."

With her steady arm, Devon stood a little crookedly. Then with Tamar half in tow, half holding him, he took a couple of stumbling steps to the only chair in the room and sat heavily.

"Devon." Tamar worriedly stroked his hair. "Are you sure you're all right?"

"I'm thirsty, and my head hurts like something's thumping on it. Other than that..." He shrugged.

"Come, lay back on the bed." Tamar tried to lift him to his feet.

"No. Let me rest."

She knelt by the chair and not quite sure what to do, lay her head on his arm.

A loud knock shook Tamar out of a doze. She unfolded herself stiffly from her position beside the chair. Without moving or speaking, Devon stared fixedly at the door. Tamar thought for a moment he was dead until he gave a slight gasp and that quieted her growing fear.

The door sounded again. She looked at Devon, then back at the door. "Who—who is it." Her voice cracked dryly.

"Your brother," came falteringly from outside the door.

"Come in, Baron Falkeep," directed Tamar with renewed anger. As the door opened, she held her head high. "Why did you even give us the courtesy of a knock?"

The Baron wrung his hands as he entered. His face was deeply lined and displayed a lack of sleep. He glanced around the apartment with a jerky gaze, then his eyes rested on Devon. "I would speak with my lord."

"You are perhaps too late, Baron Falkeep," announced Tamar without emotion.

Devon barely moved. His eyes stared through the Baron. On the other side of the door, Tamar noticed two officers. Generals by their rank and age.

The Baron stood directly before Devon and knelt. "My lord," he pleaded, "can you understand me? What's wrong with him, Tamar?"

"The blow, the injury to his head, his disappointment..."

"He has nothing to be disappointed in now." The Baron covered his face. "Tamar, he was right, you were right. I'm sorry. I don't know what to say. I—my men—I don't know what to do. Tamar, please help me."

"First you must get my lord medical treatment," cried Tamar.

"I cannot. I—my forces…we are threatened with death, destruct-tion."

Tamar sagged visibly. "Why did you come to us? We can do nothing for you."

"But you can. Give me back my ships, and I will leave."

"George Falkeep. If I could, I would condemn you to death and hell. Didn't you know who and what you challenged when you challenged, my lord?"

"I didn't know, Tamar. I swear I didn't know he was the Crown Prince."

"Who cares that he is the Crown Prince. George, from the moment you resisted him, you were doomed. He is the Fox." Wearily she proclaimed, "Take us to Ian Acier, and you may have your ships."

The Baron's face took on a crafty look. "You swear, sister."

"If I said it, it is so. Am I not the lady of Devon Rathenberg, Countess of Gran Stern? And I no longer care to be known as your sister, Baron Falkeep! Leave our County and do not return." She faltered. "Now, get a doctor and get Ian Acier." Tamar turned to the door and raised her voice to a scream. "Do you hear me, you honorless traitors? If you want to live, find the Prince a doctor and get the Count Acier."

A shuffling in the hall answered her cry.

The Baron turned to the Prince again. He stood and bowed to Devon. "I have committed a grave error; I ask your pardon."

Devon said nothing. He merely sat and stared.

After a silent moment, the Baron stepped out and closed the door.

"Oh Devon." Tamar fell on her knees before him. He stared in the same direction. His breath came in small gasps. "Oh, my lord," she cried. She grasped his hands, buried her face in them, and wept inconsolably.

After nearly an hour, Tamar sat up in a daze. She felt dizzy herself. Perhaps dizzy from lack of food and water. Devon was no better, yet no worse. Heedless of the time, she lay her head in his lap. A little while longer and strong hands lifted her up. A familiar voice inquired, "What is wrong with the Prince?"

Tamar thickly mumbled something. She was so very tired. She snapped her mind awake and licked her dry lips, "Oh, thank God you're here, Roger. George struck Devon on the face with a baton, and when he fell, he hit the back of his head against the floor." She sobbed uncontrollably. "Help him, Roger." Within her peripheral vision, Ian Acier lifted Devon to his shoulder and they stepped out of the room.

"I promised them their ships," shuddered Tamar.

"Yes," growled Ian. "If I knew they treated you like this, I would have shot them out of the sky." He halted a moment to speak into a communicator. Tamar leaned on Roger's arm and stumbled along. Outside the palace, an armored gravvehicle stopped for them, and she saw Devon finally in a doctor's care. A medic asked her how she was feeling and lifted her eyelids, felt her pulse, but she only shook off the hands and cried, "Not me, take care of my Prince."

Roger spoke gently to her. "Tamar, lie down. The doctor is taking care of Devon. He is all right. Lie down." With Roger's soothing voice in her ear, she allowed herself to be laid on a soft platform and given a pisiodermic injection. Slowly Tamar drifted off to sleep.

Thirty-one

When Tamar awoke, she felt much better: soft sheets and a gentle repulsor field buoyed her in the twilight. She rolled over sleepily and an uncomfortable tug against her wrist surprised her. As she investigated, Tamar found a tube ran from her arm to a liquid-filled bag. She became suddenly disoriented. Except for the tube, she thought she was in her room on Falkeep. Then Tamar recognized a smell. It was a smell she remembered—oh, yes, a hospital. With a rush of understanding, Tamar recalled the events of the last few days, and she remembered Devon. Frightened, she looked frantically around for a call button. When she didn't discover it right away, she yelled for a nurse. Tamar was a little surprised when a woman immediately stepped into her room.

"Yes, my lady?" the nurse curtsied. "Is everything all right?"

"Where is Count Rathenberg?" she asked breathlessly.

The nurse sat gently on Tamar's bedside. She kindly eased Tamar back down on the bed. "I hope you don't mind if I sit, my lady." When Tamar shook her head the woman continued, "My lord is very much better now. He is sleeping comfortably and the doctor says you may see him when he awakes."

"What was wrong with him?" Tamar blurted out.

"The heavy blow to his face caused a slight brain hemorrhage, but Doctor Stiles removed the clot against his brain. The doctor believes our Prince will have no lasting damage. Now, how do you feel?"

Tamar was shocked. She looked beseechingly at the nurse. "You are certain Devon Rathenberg is all right?"

The nurse answered her with more than professional conviction. "The Count of Gran Stern is in the best and most capable hands on his planet, my lady."

Tamar closed her eyes with a sigh of relief. "Now that I know my lord is safe, I feel much better. When may I get up?"

"When you are ready, the doctor will see you, and he will tell you when you are fit enough to get out of bed." The nurse began to get up, but Tamar touched her arm. "Yes, my lady?"

"Where are we?" Tamar asked shyly.

The nurse smiled. "Why, my lady, you are in your own city of Sternlicht, and I, for one, am very glad to see you. We heard so many things about you."

"About me?" asked Tamar.

"Yes, so much about the Fox, and about his lady. It is like the world changed overnight. But I babble too much; let me get the doctor." She curtsied prettily again.

After a few minutes, Doctor Stiles entered Tamar's room. He bowed grandly and dropped to one knee, "My lady, I never had the honor to care for a Princess before, and I am glad my first duty was to the most beautiful Princess in the Empire."

Tamar blushed. "At the moment, I don't feel beautiful, nor much like a Princess."

The Doctor stood and smiled. "Spoken only as the Fox's Lady would. How do you feel, my lady?"

"A little tired, but I'm all right."

"Do you feel well enough to get out of bed?"

"Yes, but how is Count Rathenberg?"

"Oh, the Prince. Didn't the nurse tell you? I gave her specific instructions."

"Yes please, she did, but I wanted to hear it from you," Tamar replied haltingly.

"My lord is healing very well. He will recover completely, but I don't need to tell you, I thought for a time we had lost him."

"Yes," whispered Tamar, with a sigh.

"That makes four times, I think."

Tamar started. "Four times?"

"Yes, the Fox defies death and all that. We heard all about our new lord—and lady." He smiled down at her. "I think you will find most of Crystal has heard. Events are taking place rapidly. As if a guiding hand suddenly moved the right stones to settle an edifice, you and your forces came at just the right time, my lady. I'm afraid without your chance intervention, Gran Stern would be no more."

As Doctor Stiles left, the nurse entered again. She removed Tamar's IV and served her breakfast. Tamar sipped coffee and, for the first time, in a viewer, she read the newspaper of her own city, Sternlicht. With a lightening heart, she discovered by reflection how the plans she and Devon made had bloomed overnight into maturity. The city was stable. Ian Acier guided the city's leadership to locate housing for the people. Heat was abundant. Food was available. Until their owners could return to them, the factories, greenhouses, offices, and businesses opened under a new pay and benefit schedule Count Devon outlined before he became ill. The Count and Countess mapped the economic future according to the example of other planets in the Duchy. The people were rebuilding the city. The Nobility remained at two on the whole planet—Devon and Tamar. The previous Houses of the system had revealed themselves unfit for rule. By decree, they were to provide the basis of a great terraforming experiment on the inner planets. In the paper, Tamar read almost verbatim the dictates Devon helped her write.

She was proud of him, and she hoped the doctor was right, that his mind was not affected by the injury. He thought so clearly concerning political concepts. Even with his primitive political vocabulary and fuzzy male ideas, Devon still could have some great insights.

She prided herself that she didn't laugh at the doctor's comments. While on the ships of the Navy of Gran Stern and the *Jagerhetzer*, through careful manipulation of people and the media, she planted those very stories herself. The power of the not-so-subliminal was incredible.

When she finished the paper, the nurse immediately appeared and asked if she wanted to tour the hospital. Tamar felt almost herself and acquiesced, but she requested more becoming clothing, first—that is, if it were available.

"Of course, my lady." The nurse swung open the closet door. Inside the closet hung almost Tamar's entire wardrobe, plus some new clothing of state.

With an experienced hand, the woman helped Tamar dress. That told Tamar the nurse was more than a simple hospital employee. Tamar picked something simple: a light blue dress with the decorations of Gran Stern in silver. On her left breast, she pinned the savant fox of the House Rathenberg, but she balked over the lion of Falkeep. She bitterly remembered her fear of her own brother. With a comment to herself that she would not need that today, she put the pin away.

The hospital was built in the same efficient and graceless style as the rest of the city of Sternlicht. Tamar hoped that when they rebuilt the portions of the city destroyed in the conflict they could interject some more creative designs.

Interestingly enough, she found the people exactly the opposite of their environment. Though the conditions in the city and hospital appeared dismal and harsh, all the people she met greeted her with a smile. And to her appraisal, the starker the surroundings, the grander the smile. She knew the Imperial archives rated the people high in sensitivity and said they had a great propensity for optimism. But in the flesh, she found that optimism disconcerting. Perhaps a genetic adaptation or a rogue gene spread through the pool. To Tamar's mind, the planet with its people appeared less bleak than when she stood admiring its beauty two, no three, days before.

In the anticipation of seeing Devon, Tamar rushed the tour. When they entered his suite, he still slept, but she kissed his lips and touched his face. Tubes and wires connected him to monitors, and a couple of male nurses and guards stood around him. Tamar was so glad he lived, her eyes filled with tears. When Tamar turned, she noticed her nurse's eyes, as she gazed at the lightly sleeping nobleman, also brimmed with tears. In less than four standard days, Tamar thought, Devon became the true ruler of these people. She tenderly caressed Devon's unbruised cheek as she reluctantly left his side.

Devon woke that afternoon. And the moment Tamar saw him, she knew he was all right. Even in his tired face, his eyes twinkled at the pleasure of seeing her. He could barely speak and Doctor Stiles recommended she visit only five minutes. A recommendation which, though she ill-concealed her disappointment, Tamar honored. The doctor and nurse left them alone.

He looked questioningly at her, and without a word, she understood his question. "Yes—" she clasped her hands together—"the program is working perfectly. I will get a more complete report tonight from Ian, but from what I have seen, we read the people and the planet correctly."

Devon nodded and smiled, then crooked his finger at her. She bent close to his face and he kissed her. While she wasted the rest of the five minutes kissing him, with a grin, he lay back.

Later in the day, without a summons, Ian came to see Tamar. To remain close to Devon, she chose to stay in her room at the hospital. As soon as she acknowledged his knock, Count Acier marched through her door. Tamar was about to rise to her feet, but Ian pushed her gently back into her chair. "My dear lady, princesses just look down their noses at Counts," he quipped.

Tamar tried to look offended but didn't succeed very well.

"I hear Prince Rathenberg is healing marvelously."

"Yes, Ian, the doctor says he will soon fully recover."

"That is good. That is very good. You can't have missed the results of your operations."

She nodded.

"You figured this people and planet to the tee. Roger and I are accomplishing your orders precisely, and in some cases, we discovered the actions you recommended already completed."

"When that happens, you reinforce the behavior, do you not?" Tamar asked quickly.

"Yes, yes, my lady." He smiled. "We are following your dictates to the letter."

"My lord's dictates."

"Oh—yes. I know what you mean, my lady, but don't forget, I'm married to one of those Pembrook prodigies myself. This, uh, manipulation has the stink of a lady's skill." He smiled broadly. "In fact, when I tell my wife, I'm certain this will become one of Pembrook's examples. How about calling it Tamar's something or other?"

"Really, Ian." Tamar wrinkled her nose."

"Yes, Tamar's Reconstruction. Tamar's Triumph sounds too gaudy, don't you think?"

"I think you should keep your tongue to yourself."

"Ha, there, you're equivocating. You know as well as I, a proper lady of Pembrook's never turns down free publicity."

She twisted her face in a grimace.

"Well, I've overstayed my welcome. I'll leave you to your mechanizations."

"Ian can I ever redeem myself in your eyes?" she teased.

"No. Never. I'm having rooms prepared for you and Devon in the palace. They will be ready in about a day." His voice turned serious. "Baron Falkeep and his troops accelerated outsystem today. I thought you might like to know. I sent a message to the Duke for you by way of the force Commander. I'm sure your father may have something to say to the Baron."

When Tamar didn't reply, he continued, "I'm very sorry the way things worked out. If I'd known Devon had given his orders directly to my troops, I would have stopped them."

"Then it is a good thing you didn't know. Since coming here, I have evaluated the people from a more personal standpoint. They may not have lasted another day. As a people, they are much more sensitive and enigmatic than I allowed. The environment, the gene pool—I don't know the reason, but the conditions must be extreme for them to revolt. Devon may have realized that."

"I guess that's the basis of another rumor." Ian laughed.

"Oh, go back to work, Ian Acier," Tamar scolded. She grasped his hand as he left. "Thank you for coming to see me."

"The pleasure was mine. I'll send Roger tomorrow. We are very busy, Tamar."

In two days Tamar moved into the palace. The rooms Ian set up for Devon and her were beautiful. Devon healed slowly. The doctor said his extended convalescence was the result of his physical makeup and lingering wounds from which his system had not fully recovered. The modern rapid-healing treatments, explained the doctor, healed the tissue, but the mind did not recover from its perceived hurt until the total natural healing time elapsed.

Two weeks passed before Devon could share the palace rooms with Tamar, and even then she was careful not to tire him.

As soon as he arrived at the palace, Roger and Ian took Devon in hand. They debriefed the entire operation to him and showed a morbid propensity for detail. Devon's sneak attack came as a surprise to them, of course, but once the battle was in full swing, Captain Birch relayed the information directly to them.

Roger spoke with animation, "We caught George's troops with their shorts down; they never expected an attack from us. General Locke oversaw the assault on the ships himself. He took them with minimal casualties on both sides. The populace responded exactly as you described in your notes. They came to us with their captured nobles and requested that we hold them for the Fox. Everywhere the name of the Fox was on the lips of the people. They watched for you like the coming of a prophet. When they discovered George Falkeep's duplicity we could barely restrain them. And all the time, Gran Stern's Army units joined with us and with the people. They brought their leaders to us—dead. They stated the Fox demonstrated the proper way for a man to regain his honor."

Tamar wailed at this when she realized the exact wording of one of her rumors had triggered the slaughter.

"Baron Falkeep told us where to find you," Roger continued, "and in the interests of peace with Falkeep, we accepted his information in return for the ships, but he didn't tell us you were hurt. Father will have something to say about that.

"The most unusual thing, though, was the throng of Gran Stern's soldiers and civilians, who crowded the hospital grounds as a vigil for you both. They all sought for just a glimpse of the Prince and Princess, the lord and lady of Gran Stern—the Fox and his lady. The interest of the people in you two personally was a pleasant surprise, and as they mingle with the soldiers from the *Jagerhetzer* and your Navy, don't be astonished if your reputation grows."

Devon and Tamar just shook their heads. They had read their people well.

Roger and Ian did not want to leave Devon and Tamar, but both had to return to their respective responsibilities. They said they would remain on Gran Stern until the government stabilized, but using that basis, they should have left the week prior. As it was, they remained with Devon and Tamar for another two weeks after Devon moved from the hospital.

When they stood in the lock of their shuttle and waved at Devon and Tamar out on the permacrete, they knew the County of Gran Stern remained in incredibly strong hands. Devon leaned temporarily on a cane, and Tamar stood protectively near him. As Roger and Ian departed Gran Stern, they carried with them letters and news that would proliferate the legend of the Fox, Crown Prince of the Empire.

Well before the fourth month since the coming of the Fox—as the people termed it—the society of Gran Stern was stable.

Devon recovered completely from his injuries, but his people and Tamar still treated him as if he were a fragile invalid. To the active nobleman, this was a desperate problem.

Tamar was pregnant, and this, in itself, caused Devon a second and more significant problem. The Noble Accords, the Codes of the Empire required Tamar and Devon to register their marriage on the planet Arienth. If they did not accomplish this before the birth of their child, the child would not be considered legitimate and could not inherit anything from Devon. In fact, until their marriage was registered by them, in person, on Arienth, the Codes prevented their marriage from being considered legal and binding.

"We can only hope, like the other banned Houses, we can

eventually force a concession from the Emperor," stated Devon.

"I am working on the problem," Tamar returned with a smile.

And they still had another problem: except for Devon, Tamar, and the few military commanders Devon pardoned, the Nobility of Gran Stern was nonexistent. The people of Gran Stern would have been content with this except that their pride was enveloped by the Imperial tradition that placed each man under an oath of individual fealty. Tamar and Devon sent the previous Nobility off to colonize and terraform of one of Gran Stern's underdeveloped planets, so they needed to supplement the supply of Nobility on the planet Crystal. Tamar's best solution was an invitation to the Houses of the Duchy of Falkeep for a social event during which Devon and she could pick the Nobility they would ask to receive their boon.

Devon preferred a dinner or business conference. Tamar suggested a ball.

"But why a ball?" asked Devon.

"The answer is simple," stated Tamar as she smoothed her growing abdomen, "A ball is a ceremony of peace, and I like them."

"All right, all right. I'll agree," Devon grumbled.

"Good." She turned abruptly toward him. "But no duels."

Thirty-two

"Well, Rathenberg," growled the Emperor.

"It is the change, your majesty."

"So that is that. I accept my brother, John-Mark, or..."

Perodus smiled. "Then—there are two Count Rathenbergs."

Frederic Rathenberg nodded at the often-quipped joke.

"I will not have John-Mark, nor will the majority of the Landsritters. You know as well as I and the rest of the Empire that he and your cousin, Duke Rathenberg, led the massacre of the Imperial fleet. He is the reason for my lack of power now, and he is the reason for the revolt of the banned Houses. He will not be my successor!"

"In that case, your majesty, there is a solution," sighed Count Frederic Rathenberg.

"You are correct, Rathenberg. You bring me news that my lady is past the age of bearing children. I have nothing but daughters. Unless I totally disregard the Codes..."

The Count's eyes widened in horror.

"No, of course I won't abdicate the Codes: the entire Landsritters would be on top of my head," snarled Perodus. "You spoke with the Lady Pembrook?"

"Yes, your majesty."

"Very well, show me the invitation again." Perodus read the finely decorated card. "That woman, Tamar. She has her fingers in everything. Every note I get from each House banned, neutral, or loyal stinks of her manipulation. And so—there is another reason." The Emperor bowed his head in thought. "You will go to Devon Rathenberg's ball for me."

"Your majesty?"

"Yes, it will be viewed as a slight weakness, but it can't be helped. Either I have a legitimate Crown Prince, or I am in violation of the Codes, and I lose the Empire. I will lose the Empire to this man, Devon Rathenberg, anyway. Haven't you read the reports? Haven't you seen how that young witch of his casts her spell over each of our loyal following in turn? You'd think Gran Stern, instead of Arienth, were the center of the universe."

"Your majesty, the situation is not as bad as you portray it."

"No, it is as bad as Pembrook portrays it. The Lady Tamar's Reconstruction has become the most talked about coupe around the tea tables, and Pembrook herself told me that she is teaching it as a source example in political dynamics. The Lady Tamar is not content with that success—by sheer force of will, her opinion seems to hold sway in every House in the Empire. I saw her at work, in the flesh; she is a demoness in the guise of a Princess.

"Listen well, Count Rathenberg number two: you will represent me at the Lady and Lord Rathenberg's ball, you and your lady. There you will stay. I will guarantee you as a hostage, and you will invite them to Arienth to register their marriage and birth their child."

"That could take up to two months, your majesty," protested Count Rathenberg.

"If I have my way, it may be as long as three. I will acknowledge Devon Rathenberg as the Crown Prince. His lady will be an Imperial Princess. And with that single stroke we will get the Landsritters off our backs."

"But, your majesty, what of Duke Falkeep? Gran Stern falls properly under his authority, and he is banned. In addition, the family Rathenberg on Gran Stern is not on the greatest terms with Falkeep."

"Hah," snapped the Emperor, "I happen to know Duke Falkeep sent a personal apology for the Baron's actions to his daughter and son-in-law. I feel Baron Falkeep will have little to say in any matter in the Duchy of Falkeep."

The Count nodded.

"Send a courier to Duke Falkeep. Tell him my plans and request his agreement. Tell him I offer a concession: his House is no longer banned."

"He will not accept without a concession to the other banned Houses."

"He will not accept at all, but if you time it right, Devon Rathenberg and his lady will be here, and we will lose no honor. In fact, if you explain the situation properly to the Duke, I'm sure he will hold onto the letter until the Rathenbergs are once more on Gran Stern."

"Your majesty." The Count colored. "Your intentions?"

"They are entirely honorable, Rathenberg. I have no other recourse. I must adhere to the Codes; in this at least, I must appease the Landsritters. I can have no other children; therefore, I must have Devon Rathenberg as my acknowledged Crown Prince. As you know, every other House in the Empire already accepts him as such.

"Now, do as I say. We must gather the little strength available to us to counter the banned Houses. This small concession will pull the neutrals back toward us and grant a more solid footing to the loyal Houses. If we intend to spring my trap against John-Mark and the banned Houses, we must have their trust. Do you understand, Rathenberg?"

Count Rathenberg bowed reluctantly.

Tamar Rathenberg had her way.

The Emperor himself was forced into the now-famed Nieva's Concession. After the destruction the Imperial Fleet, the Emperor accepted all the banned houses back with honor and banished Prince John-Mark to the County of Gran Stern.

Tamar's snare was sprung. While the seneschal, Count Frederic Rathenberg visited the Duchy of Falkeep, the Count and Countess Rathenberg of Gran Stern visited the Imperial Capital. The Emperor gladly accepted Prince Devon Rathenberg as his regent, the marriage of

Devon and Tamar was ratified, and their first child, Mark-Devon Rathenberg, was born.

Of course, the whole affair was popularly called Tamar's Triumph—much to both the Emperor Perodus' and Tamar Rathenberg's chagrin.

You won't want to miss…

The End of Honor

BOOK ONE

An intragalactic war
threatens to tear apart
the Human Galactic Empire…

The death-knell of the Human Galactic Empire has sounded—it is the crash of an axe against the virgin white marble of the Hall of Accords. It is the bitten-off cry of the Lady Lyral Neuterra, whose head lies sundered from her smooth shoulders. It is the death of the Emperor at the hand of his own son. It is the whirlwind of a thousand ships sent to enforce the new Emperor's will. And only Prince John-Mark, the Emperor's youngest son, can bring the Empire back from the edge— back to peace and honor.

Prince John-Mark had intended to wed the Lady Lyral—now he can only mourn her. Revenge is his great desire, but he cannot be revenged without tearing apart the civilization and people he loves….

For more information about L.D. Alford and *The End of Honor:*
www.LDAlford.com
www.TheEndofHonor.com

A Season of Honor

BOOK THREE

Baron Shawn du Locke must choose between
honor and desire…with the fragile peace of the
Human Galactic Empire hanging in the balance.

Shorn of his lands, regency, title, father, lady, and name, the only thing
left to the Baron Shawn du Locke is his honor. Nothing in the past has
shaken it and nothing would cause him to compromise it—until he
meets the Lady Elina Acier.

Elina Acier is the last hope of the Noble Houses of the Human
Galactic Empire. To protect the planet Acier from the Emperor, she
must marry a Duke's son.

Before Shawn meets Elina, he vows to convey her to the Imperial
Capital to marry Duke Nior's son. But Elina is a startling lookalike for
her cousin, Shawn's long-dead love, the Lady Lyral Neuterra. Shawn
once loved Lyral enough to grant her his House and fight a war in her
name. Now he is honor-bound to deliver Elina, Lyral's "twin," to marry
another man.

Shawn must safely deliver Elina to the Imperial Capital before the
Emperor discovers and kills Elina, and before her presence drives him
insane…or he falls in love.

For more information about L.D. Alford and *A Season of Honor:*
www.LDAlford.com
www.ASeasonofHonor.com

Also by L.D. Alford

CENTURION

A longing heart.
An unlikely friendship.
Love…and the bitterest of betrayals.

The son of a Galilean concubine—a Jewess—and a Roman ambassador: Abenadar suffered disapproving stares in the village of Natzeret, but so did the boy Yeshua, son of Yosef and Miryam. Perhaps it wasn't unusual the two became fast friends.

As Abenadar rises through the ranks of the Roman Legion to assume the rank of Centurion, he finds love with Ruth, a woman he rescues from the streets of Jerusalem. She believes the prophet Jesus is the One—the Messiah—everyone has been waiting for. Abenadar is dubious. He's seen too many messiahs…and they all died on Roman crosses. But what if Jesus is telling the truth? As advisor to Procurator Pontius Pilate and a Roman, Abenadar has a duty to uphold….but it may cause him to lose everything.

Hauntingly compelling, Centurion *will transform every life it touches.*

For more information:
www.LDAlford.com
www.CenturionNovel.com

Aegypt

L. D. Alford

*An unspeakable evil
and an unbelievable power
is about to be released into the world...*

Lieutenant Paul Bolang, stationed at Fort Saint in Tunisia in the 1920s, discovers a hieroglyph. Suspecting that the fort might have been built beside an ancient Egyptian foundation, he summons an archaeological party. When a tomb is discovered and opened, death strikes immediately...and reveals a grisly secret.

Lt. Bolang soon uncovers two other tombs: the tombs of the Goddess of Light and the Goddess of Darkness. As the first tomb is opened, a being escapes into the desert...and is pursued by Bolang. What will the next tomb hold? Will opening it unleash a great evil and suffering on mankind, as many believe? Or is all that simply a myth?

A fascinating tale of technology, cultures, and ancient magic

For more information about L.D. Alford and *Aegypt:*
www.LDAlford.com
www.AegyptNovel.com

About the Author

"The finest escape in literature is an escape into a real and inviting culture," asserts novelist **L.D. ALFORD.** He enjoys exploring with originality and intimacy those cultures and societies we think we already know. He builds compelling tales that make ancient and future worlds real to his readers. His stories uniquely explore the connections between events close and familiar and those that are possible—all woven together with threads of reality and fascinating technology that bring the future alive.

L.D. Alford is familiar with both technology and cultures. He is an experimental test pilot with over 6000 hours in more than 60 different kinds of aircraft. He also served in worldwide military operations as a member of three different operational combat squadrons. L.D. earned a B.S. in Chemistry from Pacific Lutheran University, an M.S. in Mechanical Engineering from Boston University, and is a Ph.D. candidate in Aerospace Engineering at the University of Dayton. He is a graduate of Air War College, Air Command and Staff College, and the US Air Force Test Pilot School. He is widely traveled and has spent long periods in Europe and Central America. He is a featured writer for **www.WingsoverKansas.com** and the author of the acclaimed novels *Centurion, Aegypt,* and *The Second Mission,* as well as Book One, *The End of Honor,* and Book Three, *A Season of Honor,* in The Chronicles of the Dragon and the Fox series. He has also written and published over 40 technical articles.

L.D. Alford is currently working on the sequels to *Aegypt: The Goddess of Light, The Goddess of Darkness, The Shadows of Darkness,* and *The Shadows of Light.*

For more information: **www.LDAlford.com   www.AFoxsHonor.com www.oaktara.com**

Printed in the United States
206779BV00002B/322-369/P

9 781602 901070